Alice Ackerman

To Barbara,
My Weston Sister

Y Harris

YVONNE HARRIS

ALICE
ACKERMAN
THE CHILCOTIN SAGA

DRAGON
HILL

The Publisher: Dragon Hill Publishing Ltd.

Library and Archives Canada Cataloguing in Publication
Title: Alice Ackerman : the Chilcotin saga / Yvonne Harris.
Names: Harris, Yvonne, 1935– author.
Identifiers: Canadiana (print) 20220265402 | Canadiana (ebook) 20220265445 |
ISBN 9781896124841 (softcover) | ISBN 9781896124858 (PDF)
Classification: LCC PS8565.A6524 A79 2023 | DDC C813/.54—dc23

Project Director: Marina Michaelides
Project Editor: Ashley Bilodeau
Maps: Yvonne Harris and Gregory Brown
Cover Image: Gregory Brown
Proofing: William Giroux
Design: Ryschell Dragunov

Front cover image credits: Yvonne Harris. GettyImages: dnsphotography,
    Georgethefourth, redfishweb.
Back cover image credits: GettyImages: Xurzon.

Produced with the assistance of the Government of Alberta. Alberta Government

Printed in China
PC:38-1

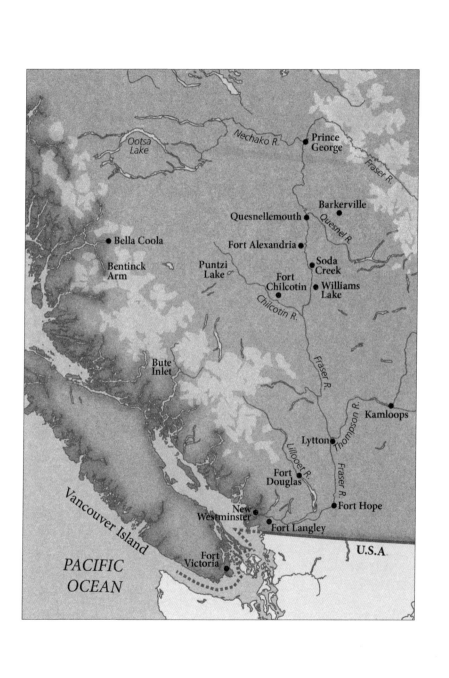

Acknowledgements

I received assistance from many people in the preparation of this book. The main research was assisted by the wonderful archivists at the BC Archives. They helped me despite the 2020–22 pandemic, showing me how to access the archives remotely. Thank you to the staff of the Coquitlam and Port Moody libraries who searched for books through interlibrary loans. Towards the end of my research, I visited the Quesnel Museum. The manager went out of her way to assist me in my search for the sites along the Fraser River that played in the Chilcotin War. I want to thank Elizabeth Hunter for her time and patience.

I visited the Tŝilhqot'in Government and was graciously welcomed by Randy Radney. Our trip to the Tŝilhqot'in lands was most revealing, especially our stay at Puntzi Lake, the site of conflict between the First Nations and the colonizers.

My study of Victoria was facilitated by Sharon Chow and Bo Martin, who took the time to show me all the buildings from the 19th century, and the staff at the Victoria Library who guided my research of the city. I read the thesis by E. Hewlett and relied on the work of Tom Swanky, BC historian, to clear up the inconsistencies written about the Tŝilhqot'in. I am grateful to our daughter Emily Kirkham for assisting me with the final edits and for Faye Boer of Folklore Publishing for her patience and editing expertise.

I completed the research in the western United States as part of my book *Redemption* and once again wish to acknowledge the staff at the wonderful museums across several states. We visited Georgia and California to gather background for that 19th-century novel and drove most of the Oregon Trail visiting museums across all the states.

Dramatis Personae

Historical Figures in British Territory

Alexis: Tŝilhqot'in chief

Brewster: Bute Inlet Road crew boss 1862–64, employed by Waddington

Cox: led the Colonial militia

Governor James Douglas: Hudson's Bay Factor, first governor of British Columbia in 1858; governor of the Colony of Vancouver Island 1851–64; born in Guyana, part Creole

Dr. John Sebastian Helmcken: Hudson's Bay Company employee; physician in Fort Victoria from 1850

Robert Homfray: mid-twenties engineer; surveyed the Bute Inlet Road for Waddington with canoeists Balthazar, Bouchier, Coté, McNeil and two Songhees

Captain Howard: captained the supply boat to Bute Inlet and took down the Tŝilhqot'in names

Lhats'as?in: Tŝilhqot'in war chief; led the Chilcotin War of 1864

Peter Lester and Miffin Gibbs: Successful Black shopkeepers, Victoria, 1860s

John McLain, Angus McLeod and Jim Taylor: assisted Poole in spreading smallpox

Donald McLean: led one group of militia; was the founding colonist of the Hat Creek Ranch in the Chilcotin

Olahl: fictional name for Lhats'as?in's 12-year-old daughter. Her name was not recorded in written history

Francis Poole: trader; believed to have spread smallpox deliberately among the Indigenous Peoples in 1862

Governor Frederick Seymour: Governor of British Columbia 1864–66 and Governor of the united colonies of Vancouver Island and British Columbia 1866–69

Toowaewoot: Lhats'as?in's young wife

Alfred Waddington: English; promoted the Bute Inlet Road; immigrated to the British Colonies

Warriors: Talhpitt, Chessus, Chedekki, Telloot, Tnananski and his son, Cheloot, Peille, Lhats'as?in's son and ?Ahan, along with Lhats'as?in. They were the Tŝilhqot'in warriors put on trial for murder by the British Colonial Government. Spelling of their names differs in various documents.

Historical Figures in the United States

Abolitionists: Frederic Douglass, Charlotte Brown, Ellen Mary Pleasant

Brown, John: A radical abolitionist in the 19th century

Civil War figures: Lincoln, Generals Lee, Grant and Sherman, and Major Burnside

Freeman: An explorer and military man in the mid-19th century. He led the massacre of the Yana people.

Foster: Captain of the *Clotilda*, the last slave ship to America

Meaner: Owned the last slave ship that sailed from Africa to America, the *Clotilda*.

Fictional Characters

(Minor characters are not listed)

Alice Ackerman: originally from Springfield Illinois; Gold Rush roadhouse owner in Victoria and Quesnel

David Ackerman: Alice's distant relative; soldier/sharpshooter/ guide; in 1867, solicitor in British Columbia

Mary Ackerman: a Songhees orphan; Alice's adopted daughter

Mr. Colby: lawyer; Black anti-slave advocate in Macon, Georgia, after the Civil War

Jamieson: southerner Plantation owner; held Blossom illegally

Lucy: Tŝilhqot'in warrior

Colonel McClennan and Ernie Richmond: Ku Klux Klan members

Millie and Callie May: women kidnapped by Jamieson after the Civil War

Charity Cooper: former slave from Virginia; hatmaker/entrepreneur in San Francisco

Jem Cooper: Charity's husband; former slave; Union soldier in the Civil War

Nate and Polly Cooper: Charity and Jem's children

Blossom Cooper: Charity and Jem's baby daughter; kidnapped following the Civil War

Charlotte Dupré: beautiful young woman; migrated with her father to Victoria, BC; married to Homfray

Shooleetsa: a cultural Tŝilhqot'in; worked at the Silver Spoon in Quesnel

Tahoma: worker in Alice's roadhouse

Matike: a Musquem historian; Walter's nephew

KKK Victims: Aloysius Walker, Virgil Etheridge, Lewis Rufus

Walter: sawmill owner; married a Musquem wife; travelled the Oregon Trail with Alice and David

Author's Note

Although based on the historical events of the 19th century in Canada and the U.S., this a work of fiction. Many characters, businesses, places and events are depicted as recorded in history, both oral and written. Other characters are the product of the author's imagination and purely fictional. The author has taken literary license to depict some historical events so they fit more with the fictional characters and the story.

Prologue

This novel is a sequel to *Redemption*, published by Dragon Hill Publishing in 2016. The novels are inspired by my ancestors, the Ackerman family, that immigrated to New Amsterdam (New York) in 1661. My father, Robert Ackerman Russell, is descended from the original family. He was a man of many careers—a surveyor, a farmer, a sharpshooter in the United States Marine Corps and a graduate of University of California, Berkeley. He did not discriminate; he believed Black peoples' rights were being abused. He was the inspiration for the character of David Ackerman, and my grandmother, Almina Ackerman, the inspiration for Alice Ackerman. She raised eleven children after the death of her husband. She was a competent woman, capable of making everything from scratch. She made soap, canned fruit and vegetables, carded wool, wove blankets and cured most ills. She kept her boys in starched collars and the girls in beautiful hand-sewn dresses.

The novel takes place between 1861 and 1868, and is based on the historical events of the gold rush, colonization and slavery. It documents the mistreatment of Indigenous Peoples in Canada's northwest and the rise of the Jim Crow era at end of the American Civil War (also known as the War Between the States). It highlights the abuse of People of Colour across these two countries during the formative years of our two countries. The concepts are still topical especially in light of the dark days we have experienced lately.

Today, the world is witnessing intensifying discrimination and racial slurs against Asians and First Nations, and an increase of voter suppression in the U.S. It is past time we confront the ugly legacy of how the land was taken from Indigenous Peoples and their children were sent to residential schools.

It is one hundred and fifty-seven years since slavery ended in the U.S., yet in the 2020s, Blacks are having their voting rights taken away. For years they have suffered discrimination in housing, and many do not have the economic security of home ownership.

In my research, I found some hope for the future. During the 1860s Gold Rush in British Columbia, Mrs. Hance, a homesteader in the Chilcotin region of central British Columbia, fed the poor and tended to the sick, especially the Indigenous People. In the United States, a wealth of information exists about abolitionists who risked their lives for Black people. Although these are troubling days, if we look back at the past, we might find our way to a more just and equal society in Canada and the United States.

PART I

CHAPTER ONE

Victoria, Fall 1861

Waddington's Road

Miners and citizens walked to the hall through the rain-drenched streets of Victoria to hear about the road Alfred Waddington planned to build at Bute Inlet. They crowded into the hall, many smelling like wet dogs. There was a buzz in the room, not only because the people were eager to hear about the Bute Inlet Road but because they were hoping for news of the Civil War in the United States. The Confederates had fired on Fort Sumpter, and Lincoln had declared war on the rebels. Many of the miners were Americans, both Confederates and Union supporters.

The British Colonialists could not fathom slavery—slavery had been illegal in the British Colonies for decades—so they sided with the Union. Maybe it was money that drove the south to separate from the union. Without slaves to pick their cotton, southerners might actually have to do the physical, backbreaking work themselves. But here in the British Colony the people came to listen to the road builder who would promise riches to everyone.

It was 1861, and gold had been discovered in 1858 on the Fraser River in British Territory. Thousands of miners arrived on Vancouver Island seeking transport to the goldfields. Thousands crowded into Victoria, a small town on Vancouver Island that grew to thousands that spring. Thousands more found their way across the U.S./Canada border, avoiding the fee imposed by Governor Douglas of the Hudson's Bay Company. If a faster and cheaper route could be built, the miners would take it, and Waddington claimed to have the route.

It was a noisy crowd. Waddington stood at the podium, waiting for the room to quiet down. He was not a handsome man, with his lidded eyes and mop of hair that looked like a toupee. He was in his mid-sixties and dressed in a rumpled, fine-wool suit, at odds with his genteel upbringing. Despite his disheveled appearance, he had the air of an aristocrat. It was rumoured that his family held several cotton mills in France.

When he spoke, Waddington was captivating—well, captivating to most of the audience. David and Alice, who stood near the back, were not so enthralled. The other three hundred in the hall listened intently, some lapping up every word Waddington had to say while others were skeptical.

David leaned his lanky frame against the wall and turned to Alice. "He can't mean that he intends to build a road through Tŝilhqot'in country? The tribe will send him packing. They don't want our pots and pans; they don't even want our muskets. Though if Waddington encroaches on their territory, that may change. They'll take up arms."

David had seen too many tribes in the U.S. devastated by settlers, their villages plundered and people massacred. He hoped the British would be different, treat the Natives fairly. Not repeat the holocaust that occurred in eastern Canada and throughout the U.S.

Alice, considering David's words, watched Waddington at the podium. The entrepreneur was trying too hard to impress the audience, as if he had something to prove or didn't wholly believe his own spiel. There was uncertainty behind the braggadocio's façade. Alice never talked about herself. In fact, she spoke very little and certainly would not exaggerate her abilities.

"Is it true that his family is rich?" Alice asked.

"That is what people say," David replied. "It makes me wonder what he is doing in British Territory."

David sighed. "I'm skeptical. Likely his spiel will lead to a lot of investors suffering financial ruin. I don't think 'Old Waddy' really discovered a route to the goldfields. It's something thousands of miners are looking for, so they will believe it because they want to."

Waddington's voice boomed out across the hall. "I'm going to build you a great road," he said in a self-assured manner. "Yes, a great road. It will get you and your supplies to the goldfields in half the time and half the money you are paying now. Just a short boat trip across the Georgia Strait. Yes, a very short trip, then across the mountains onto flat prairie to Fort Alexandria."

He paused and wiped his forehead with a sweaty hand. "And the fine Mr. Tiedeman ascertained the route to the Fraser River. He crossed two hills, then a grassy plain with plenty of feed for your horses, a country much like your English parks all the way to Alexandria on the Fraser River and the gold-rich bars. Much cheaper than the Bentinck Arm or Douglas's route through the Harrison Lakes. Much cheaper, I tell you. Much cheaper." He paused again to take a large handkerchief from his vest pocket and sponge his brow before he continued. "And Mr. Downie, the finest man you will meet, has explored Bute Inlet and reported the route doable."

David leaned over, whispering to Alice. "Downie told me he saw nothing to justify any man spending money or time going there. I don't know how much longer I can listen to Waddington's bull."

Waddington carried on. "I'm willing to take on one or two investors, but you must commit soon!"

"The Tŝilhqot'in won't like this," David whispered to Alice. "They just want to be left alone."

"You're right about that. When I had the roadhouse in Lytton, we rarely saw them."

"I hear that Homfray, the young engineer, has been contracted to survey the road," David said. "Waddington likely filled his ears with this sales pitch. Robert Homfray is too much of a greenhorn to see through him."

"Do you mind if we go?" Alice asked quietly.

"No, I think we've heard everything the two of us want to hear and more."

They left the fetid room and walked out into the cool evening. The rain had stopped. They enjoyed the fresh air, the tall cedar trees glistening with raindrops and the promise of spring after a winter of freezing rain. The air was refreshing and warmer than it had been. Alice removed her bonnet and smoothed the strands of dark hair that had come loose from her bun.

"When do you go back to the Fraser River goldfields?" Alice asked.

David looped her arm around his as they strolled along the banks of James Bay.

"I have another day. I have supplies to buy, and I must visit the governor." David paused before he added, "Just a social visit since my orders now come from Colonel Moody in New Westminster, another aristocrat from London who knows little about the people who lived here for centuries. He'll serve his time in the colonies lining his pockets."

A wash of moonlight fell on Alice's fine features.

"You are beautiful, dear Alice. You know that I've loved you since our days on the Oregon Trail and believe that eventually you will heal from your terrible loss."

Alice leaned her head against his shoulder as a gentle breeze wafted inland from the sea. "The journey across the continent was so long ago. I should have left my sorrow behind by now."

CHAPTER TWO

Victoria, Late Fall 1861

Homfray

Homfray was a gentle man. He was slender, tall and not the type you would expect to see in a frontier town or travelling in the wilderness. He had the appearance of a learned gentleman, more accustomed to the parlour than the wilds of the Colony of British Columbia. Yet here he was in a fragile canoe with six men paddling across the Georgia Strait on a cold, wet October morning.

It all began when Waddington first approached him.

"Robert Homfray, me boy!" Waddington placed his mitt-like hands on Robert's shoulders. "So, you are an engineer? Just the man for the job. And you like adventure, I am told!" He talked fast and spittle gathered in the corners of his mouth, becoming thicker with every word.

"Yes, Sir, I do."

"This is going to be the greatest road. A fast route to the goldfields, and you are going to be in at the beginning. How does that sound, me boy?"

Homfray didn't like being called "boy," but Waddington seldom referred to anyone on the crew by name. Even Balthazar, an experienced frontiersman, was called "boy."

"It is good to know, Mr. Waddington," Homfray began. "I hear there is already a trail from Bentinck Arm, and isn't Governor Douglas building a road through Harrison Lakes to the Fraser River? Won't that be the major route, Sir?"

"Well, now listen to me, young man." Waddington smiled as he expounded his dream. "The route I propose is much shorter.

The Bentinck route is farther north, and Douglas's route crosses several lakes before getting to the goldfields. My route is superior in every aspect. *Veritas omnia vincit*, my boy, *veritas omnia vincit*."

"I studied Latin, Sir. I believe that means, 'Truth conquers all.'"

"Investors must know the truth about my route to the goldfields, and you are the key, m' boy. Just a quick trip by water to Bute Inlet. Do you know where that is?"

Robert cupped his chin, thinking. "I believe Captain Vancouver sailed into Desolation Sound which leads to Bute Inlet. It is north of Vancouver Island and east. A steamer would make it in a day. By canoe, maybe two days or more."

Before Robert could continue, Waddington interjected enthusiastically. "Then after landing at the head of Bute Inlet, you will see beautiful land there, flat and excellent for a townsite. You make your way up the slow-moving Homathko River, take a quick trip over the hills, and you're in the Chilcotin plateau."

"Well, I don't know." Robert was uneasy. "Isn't it too late in the year to be going through the Cascades? It is already November. The snow…"

"No, not too late," Waddington assured. "Plenty of time to make the journey. Especially for a young, healthy fellow like you!"

"Look," Waddington continued, "I have rounded up a crew for you. Balthazar, he is the greatest canoeist; then McNeil, he knows the Chilcotin area. Balthazar, Coté and Bouchier are Frenchmen. Frontiersmen. Good men. I am also sending two Indians. They speak a bit of the Queen's tongue and will also be able to converse with the Indians." He paused, sizing up the young engineer. "What do you think? A terrific adventure, Homfray! You'll be back before Christmas."

"I suppose that will be adequate," Robert said hesitantly. "And the remuneration, Sir?"

"Well, I hadn't thought of that."

"I need to be paid, Sir," Homfray insisted, though he did not like pressing Mr. Waddington.

"How does two dollars a day sound? Fine for a young man just starting his career! That's American dollars. How does that sit with you?"

Robert thought the wage of an engineer should be five dollars a day but said nothing. It was difficult for Homfray to be persistent with the entrepreneur. Then he thought of the Chilcotin, a land as cold as Siberia, protected by rugged mountains. He would be risking his life and reputation for two dollars a day.

It was a breezy autumn day when most of the town gathered at the dock in James Bay in Victoria. Friends of the frontiersmen threw quips at their fellow canoeists. Families of the two Songhees brought dried salmon and bannock for their kinsmen, sharing their anxiety about this journey led by white men. Many were onlookers, curious about the trip, and investors hoping the explorers would determine that a road could be built, the road that could earn them a fortune.

There was only one person Homfray desperately wanted to see on the docks. He searched among the throng, trying to see her billowing skirt and colourful hat topped with flowers.

Ah, there she is. Come to see me off. His heart lightened at the sight of Miss Charlotte Dupré, standing apart from the crowd and looking down on him from the rocky bank. She was dressed in a fitted bodice of blue satin with bell-shaped pagoda sleeves and a floor-skimming skirt of purple velvet over wide crinolines. He thought, *She is the most beautiful woman in the British Colonies, no, in the Americas.*

Charlotte walked slowly down to the dock. "Robert," she said with a sweet smile. "You are undertaking a perilous journey. I shall pray for you every day until your return."

Homfray was speechless. His deepest wish was that she would consent to be his wife. She would make him the happiest man in the world. *So much depends on this journey,* he thought. If he should fail, her father would lose his substantial investment. Homfray would be disgraced, and he might lose the one he cherished most in this world.

She took his hand and held it, her gloved fingers so light and sensuous. Although he was a fit man, for a moment he felt faint at being so close to his love.

"We shall miss you, dear Robert."

Homfray laced his fingers with hers. "Did you bring me the miniature I requested?"

"Oh, yes." She dug in her small, beaded reticule and passed him a tiny painting mounted in a pewter frame.

"Please discover a safe pass," Miss Dupré urged. "My father and I are counting on you. He invested all our savings into Mr. Waddington's road. You don't want my father sent to debtors' prison, do you?"

She said this in a whimsical tone, but Homfray swallowed the words as if heavy stones fell into his stomach. His mission had become a burden, not an adventure.

The crew, anxious to leave, were already seated in the canoe, paddles at the ready. Balthazar sat in the stern, wondering when his lovesick boss would let them be on their way. There was only so much daylight, and they had a long journey ahead.

Homfray bid a final farewell to Charlotte, taking her hand in his and kissing her fingertips. He stepped off the rocks at the landing, glancing at her one last time before climbing into the canoe. Coté sat in the bow with Homfray and pushed the canoe off with his paddle, the frontiersmen waving to the crowd and giving a whoop.

The three Frenchman and the two Songhees, Pete and his son, Kauvsiya, or Little Pete, as the others called him, paddled with energy. Lefty, sweat pouring down his tired face, couldn't keep pace with the others.

"Pick it up, Lefty," Balthazar yelled. "You're slowing us down, girly. You paddle like a duck hit on the head. It's catch, stroke, release. Keep time, you dolt. Paddlin' in time is everything in a canoe."

Lefty tried to sink his paddle in unison with the others but still couldn't keep up even when the ocean was calm. Perspiration poured across his brow while he tried to follow the paddle strokes of the others. The Songhees paddled effortlessly, as if they were born with canoe paddles in their hands.

The canoe left the Fort and warehouses behind and headed out to sea. They were making their way along the east coast of Vancouver Island when the ocean blew up into two-metre waves that poured over the gunwales of the canoe. The paddlers followed the strokes of the bowman, powering up the wave and slowing the light craft down in the trough. Lefty missed the catch, hitting the wave at the wrong time and causing the canoe to tip to one side. Water soaked the men.

"You'll send us all to be eaten by the fish," Balthazar yelled. "Place that bloody paddle on your lap, or I'll scatter your little gonads like bloody marbles over the effing waves."

For the next two hours, they fought the waves then turned north so the following waves could push them along. Hours passed. The rain poured down, making the journey even more miserable. Pete and his son wore cedar hats and capes that shed the water. They didn't seem bothered by the downpour.

"Hey Balthazar. Methinks we should git them outfits that Pete and Little Pete wear," Bouchier yelled over the sound of the driving rain. "Good for this bloody weather!"

"What would our friends say if we went Native?" Balthazar scoffed. "I'd rather feel the rain in my face."

The light faded, and night would soon be upon them. Homfray could make out the tower of the Bastion at Nanaimo. His chest filled with relief.

"We've made it!" Lefty shouted.

"Not yet," Balthazar said. "The worse is to come. The tides here are vicious. It will take all our strength to make it through."

The waves boiled up, and the ocean current pushed the flimsy craft to and fro. Lefty shrieked every time a wave threatened to capsize the boat.

"If one of you grabs the gunwales, I'll carve you up and throw you overboard," Balthazar yelled, while they piloted the small craft over the swirling tides.

"The canoe is leaking!" Bouchier called out. "We'll never make it."

"Two girlies in the canoe," Balthazar grumped. "Just my luck."

"Stay calm," Homfray urged. "It won't be long 'til we get through this."

At last, they could see the village of Nanaimo. A few log cabins surrounded the fort. Several Hudson's Bay men walked down to the beach to meet them.

"Dis is where Victoria mines its coal, right?" Bouchier said, his voice still shaky.

"Coal Ty'hee," Pete, the Songhees Native, spoke a few words of English. "*Che-wich-i-kcan.*"

"What is he saying?" Lefty grumbled.

"He's right," Balthazar said. "The Hudson's Bay Company traded with the Indians, and they called their chief Coal Ty'hee, and Nanaimo they called Che...well, my tongue can't spit it out."

They approached the shore and the bastion of the fort with its guns mounted, guns that had never been used against approaching ships or the peaceable tribe of Nanaimo. Low clouds obscured the landing, and a gloom settled over the village.

Balthazar climbed out of the boat, his legs cramped from the hours of sitting. The men were stiff from the long hours of paddling. "The commander of the Hudson's Bay Fort will give us a bed to sleep in so we can get out of this bloody rain," he said while he tied up the canoe and hoisted his pack.

The crew stumbled into the fort, cold, wet and cranky. They were met by Donald MacAskill, the Scotsman who managed the fort. "I kin have the cook make you a meal, but it won't be fancy."

MacAskill had a cropped silver moustache and muttonchop whiskers framed his round face. Balthazar could smell his sour breath and thought he, too, would take to drink if he had to be posted at this remote fort.

MacAskill sat with them as they ate their supper of potatoes and bits of moose meat swimming in grease. "The trip up from Victoria must have been hell, with the wind blowin' and the rain pissin' down. 'Tis near on one hundred and eighty miles so my guess is that you camped on the way."

"I had to kick a few asses to get dem paddling right. Ya, we camped one night. Soaked right through. Tomorrow will be better as long as de men pull their weight."

"Yes," Homfray said, joining the conversation. "We'll overnight, mend the boat and cross the Georgia Strait early tomorrow. Mornings are usually calm, isn't that right, Balthazar?"

"We won't make it across the strait with calm water. Winds usually come up in the afternoon. When it gets rough," he glared at the men, "I want you to pull yourselves together. No screaming. Just paddle." He eyed Lefty, Balthazar's burly six feet and muscular arms no doubt intimidating the greenhorn. "Now I give you a lesson, so you don't send us to the bottom of the ocean."

Balthazar woke the men before daybreak. They had slept in bunks at the Hudson's Bay Fort and took a hasty breakfast of hard tack and cheese. "Dis coffee is strong enough to float a witch."

"At least worms aren't crawling out of the hard tack like it were when we paddled across from Montreal to de west," said Coté. "Remember that bloody trip, Balthazar?"

"Dis ain't over yet."

It was a foggy morning. The sun had not burned off the damp mist when they launched the repaired canoe, paddling into a calm sea, the frontiersmen singing in French and paddling to the rhythm. Bouchier sang with a deep lilting voice, leading the others.

That is the reason he was brought along, to sing while the others paddled, Homfray thought. He had wondered about Bouchier because he was not the bravest of men. Now he knew. Homfray remembered reading that a voyageur would be hired for his voice alone rather than his ability in the canoe.

The men were rested, and this morning they synchronized their paddles to the rhythm of the song, hitting the water at the same time. At midday, the wind came up, at first just a light breeze, then a roaring wind that spawned towering waves.

The seas threatened to overturn their canoe as the ocean grew violent, carrying the birchbark canoe up a wave and then down, each time almost burying the bow. The men had to dig their paddles in to keep the canoe from being pushed off course. Lefty paddled better now that he had a lesson and a healthy fear of Balthazar's temper.

They were all wet and hungry, but they couldn't stop paddling for even a minute for fear the canoe would tip. The boat pitched in the open sea; the wind was so strong the men could feel the icy blast through their wet clothes. The huge swells rose before them, breaking over the bow and covering Coté and Homfray in freezing water. It took all of Balthazar's strength to keep the boat heading north.

Untold miles faced the crew.

"How long in this death trap?" Bouchier yelled. "What about the easy paddle across Georgia Strait like that scum Waddington said? I should have stayed with the Hudson's Bay. At least de bosses looked after de men. Dey told us the bloody truth about the dangers."

"I never thought I would hear you say a good word about de Bay," Balthazar yelled. "You hated dem."

"Now I hate Waddington."

The crossing took longer than Homfray had calculated. They crashed through ten hours of turbulent seas before the storm died down, and the driving rain turned to a spatter.

Not a "quick trip by water" as Waddington had extolled. Eventually, they finally saw the faint outline of the mainland with the scattered islands of Desolation Sound. The rain drizzled down, dampening their spirits and soaking them and the gear. Strong currents caught the canoe near Savary Island. Once they fought through the waves, the water calmed, and they made camp on a sandy beach.

"Dis is a beautiful place," Balthazar said eying the sand that stretched for miles on a quiet bay of water. "In summer this would be a pleasant spot, no? I would bring my woman and our six enfants here. They could play in the water while my wife and I would...vell … you know what we would do."

Coté laughed and turned his head to Balthazar. "Your young wife and six enfants are in Montreal, no? Vat you do when you're months away? Are you always faithful, or vould you take another to dis sandy beach?"

"Dat's none of your business, Coté. Now I want you to paddle out of dis paradise and onto the next stretch. De crossing is over; it vill be easy paddling, so pick up de pace. Ve need to find a camp before nightfall."

"That was a bugger of a crossing," Coté said. "I've paddled across the continent from the St. Lawrence River in the east to the Pacific Ocean, and this one takes the cake. That man Waddington wouldn't be sending us to our deaths, would he?"

"He's a good man," Homfray replied. "Maybe he exaggerates a little, but he means no harm."

"Then why is Waddington sending us with winter bearing down on us? The ocean is hellish in winter," complained Coté.

"It should be an easy trip up the Homathko River and a quick trip across the pass to the Chilcotin plains, or at least that is how the Old Man described it."

"Waddington is full of merde! You just want to coat yourself in glory, Robert," Balthazar scowled. "There are better ways of climbing up the ladder than taking six men to their deaths."

"No one will die. We have to be successful. I gave my word." Homfray thought of Miss Dupré, who had captured his heart, and the weight of his promise to her. That night in his tent he whispered her name over and over. His love for the beautiful Charlotte had overtaken him. His every thought, his every action. Everything was for her.

She is the reason I must succeed. If the expedition is successful, it will win her heart. I must finish the task. If I don't, she will see me as a failure. If the road isn't built, her father will lose his investment, and I will lose Charlotte. He did not share these thoughts with his companions.

Homfray was beginning to size up his crew. He had been with the Victoria Royal Engineers when Waddington recruited him for the trip. He felt he had little in common with the French Canadians; the Songhees spoke a fractured English; then there was left-footed McNeil—Lefty, they'd nicknamed him. At least he conversed in the Queen's English, but he irritated Homfray. Lefty was the clumsiest of men without the slightest trace of experience in the woods—falling over logs when they made camp, tripping as he put his feet in the canoe. Homfray wondered why Waddington had chosen Lefty for this trip.

The Frenchmen huddled together in camp, grumbling. At times Homfray could hear them mocking him and making remarks about his poorly equipped journey. He understood enough French to make out Bouchier's sarcastic jibe, "He is all set to make himself a hero and will care little if we die on this trip."

The words stung Homfray. *If that is what the men think of me, I'll prove them otherwise. I must succeed; no one will die.*

The drizzle continued through the gloomy night.

The next day they paddled across wind-whipped channels between islands shrouded in mist. Ragged fingers of rock reached out from the islands of Desolation Sound.

"I can see why Captain Vancouver named this bloody place Desolation Sound," Coté griped as he brushed the rain drops from his face.

The rain and mist hung over the sea, and the gloom encompassed them. They camped on one of the islands, pitching their tents in the drizzle and building a smoky fire. Night was upon them early at this time of year, so the men took to their sleeping blankets, shivering and wet.

The next morning dawned bright with a November sun burning off the mist. The tide was out, and part of the ocean floor was exposed and carpeted with oysters.

"Breakfast," Coté smiled as he carried a bucket full of oysters back to camp. Bouchier shucked them, dipped them in flour and fried them in lard. This feast brought a little relief to the paddlers.

If only we could turn back now, Balthazar thought. He was certain it was too late to attempt a mountain crossing. Besides, he was a river man, not a mountain climber.

When they left camp, the ocean was as smooth as glass, the water a deep jade. "Dis is better," Balthazar said. "Now we make it fast to Bute Inlet as long as you laggers do your part and keep your paddles in the water."

"I want to place me feet on terra firma and leave this death trap," Bouchier announced. It had been more than a week in a still-leaking canoe.

But before they could make shore, they spotted four canoes lashed together and several Natives paddling hard. The boat came straight at them, the Natives raising their muskets when they were within range.

"Sacrebleu!" Balthazar yelled. "I thought the Indians were peaceful."

"I wish I'd never come on this trip," Lefty grumbled. "What next?"

As Homfray stood in the canoe offering gifts as a sign of peace, his heart raced.

The four canoes, containing at least two dozen Natives was now within a few metres. The leader saw the gifts and motioned to the others to lower their muskets. They came alongside and accepted the gifts from Homfray. The presents allayed their fears.

The tall Native spoke to them. Pete could understand a little of their language.

"He say Indians coming. They murderers," Pete said. "Hate King Chautsh. Mesahchie."

Lefty, who had recovered from his fright, was now belligerent. "What the hell is he saying? Can't they speak English?"

"He is speaking Chinook," Balthazar explained, "which every white man who treats with the Indians should know." He was tired of Lefty. "Pete says a raiding party will try to capture us, and that they are wicked, 'Mesahchie,' and that they hate King George's Englishmen, 'King Chautsh.'"

The next day Pete's prediction came true. They spotted a canoe with twenty armed Natives. The men looked fearsome, naked above the waist with bright red paint on their faces and torsos.

"Lower the sail and paddle for all your worth," Balthazar commanded as he turned the canoe. They allowed the wind to push them across the inlet, but it was bearing them directly toward the unknown canoe.

"They may be friendlies," Homfray suggested. "Waddington told me he had met the Indians at Bute Inlet and given them presents."

"Until we know their intentions, best not let dem catch us."

But the warriors' canoe was far faster with their twenty paddlers. Within moments, they were within shooting distance. By the time they were a few feet from the canoe, it was clear they were intent on harm or even murder.

The warriors came alongside and boarded Homfray's canoe, quickly overpowering the six paddlers. The leader pointed to the far side of the inlet and, using sign language, ordered them to make haste to the shore.

When they reached the gravel beach, the warriors pushed and hit Homfray and his men with paddles, making them kneel.

"Do you understand these savages?" Homfray asked Pete.

"Yes, some. They say they kill us. They not sure they kill us now, maybe tonight. I worry I never see my wife again."

"Take heart, my men. All is not lost." Homfray tried to reassure his crew. Bouchier and Lefty cried. Coté, Balthazar and the two Songhees remained stoic. The warriors tied their hands and feet and left them kneeling awkwardly on the gravel beach. Two of their captors guarded them; the others slunk back into a cave in the mountain.

"They say they return," Pete translated. "They tell us, don't move. They bring many warriors."

All the men were cold and feared for their lives. As the dusk fell on the beach, the Frenchman chanted the rosary. "Hail Mary, full of grace. The Lord is with thee. Blessed art thou among women and blessed is the fruit of thy womb, Jesus."

Homfray was Anglican. He had few prayers to soothe him. He came to the realization that they may be facing death. The thought of Charlotte, his dear love, grieving over his death, gave him comfort.

As he knelt on the beach, he played over the memory of their meeting at the ball in Victoria. The early evening sunlight beamed through the high windows, catching her hair in a dazzling white light and surrounding the girl as if she were an apparition. He was bewitched. He had never been in love before, and the feeling overwhelmed him. But it did not make him tongue tied; instead, he felt released from convention.

Homfray approached her. "I am dazzled, no, bedazzled." He was so taken with her that he showed no restraint, struck by her beauty and poise. This was the woman he had waited for all his adult life.

Several weeks prior, she had been introduced to Homfray by her father, an elderly gentlemen who was one of the investors in the road.

"Charlotte, this is Robert Homfray, the educated young man who will survey our road."

Homfray held Charlotte's hand, not relinquishing it. He whispered to her. "You have taken hold of me, my heart and my soul. You have bewitched me."

Charlotte laughed gracefully, pulling back on her hand when he held it too long.

It was the beginning of their courtship. By autumn, when Homfray was preparing to leave on the trip to Bute Inlet, he pleaded with her. "I cannot leave you with so little encouragement. Please say that you favour me over your other suitors."

She laughed. "Of course, I favour you."

The memory sustained him through the fading afternoon light as they waited to discover their fate. Would it be death by knives or muskets, or would they suffer torture? Homfray hoped it would be quick and painless.

His men grew quiet as the hours passed; the Frenchmen continued chanting the rosary in soft voices. Homfray and the two Songhees were quiet, waiting to see if they would live.

Hours passed before the leader returned with his band of warriors, chanting and threatening Homfray and his men. They closed in, poking their spears lightly into the seven helpless men.

Homfray bowed his head. *Surely this is not the end*, he thought. To die in a remote region of British Territory, never to see his beloved Charlotte again. He was brave 'til this point. His fear was that in death he would lose her forever.

Across the inlet they heard a war whoop. "Not more bloodthirsty Indians!" Bouchier cried out. "Dey are going to have a party. Dey all want to watch us die!"

All eyes focused on the fast-approaching canoe where a tall man stood in the bow calling out. Their captors stopped tormenting the prisoners, fright replacing their amusement, then they scurried away into the bushes.

"What is he saying?" Homfray asked Pete.

"You no worry," the older man smiled broadly, showing missing front teeth. "He is the Klahoose chief we gave presents to. Rescue, not harm."

They were saved, delivered from their captors! The rescuer was Yay K Wum. He told them in halting English that the murderous bands patrolled the Inlet and robbed unarmed strangers. He was their savior.

They quickly got into their canoe and paddled away from the dreadful beach where they thought their lives would end. They landed across the inlet at the chief's encampment, *Pixphneek*, the winter village built on stilts along the hillside. It was the prettiest village Homfray had ever seen. Houses sat on the hillside in tiers with pathways winding up between the sturdy plank dwellings.

Homfray had no idea the Natives could build such beautiful, large houses. Before coming to the British Territories, he thought all Indigenous peoples were nomads, living in tents. But then he was discovering that he had many misconceptions about his adopted country.

The village looked down on the entrance to Bute Inlet. A calm ocean, the gentle swells rising and falling. Across the bay from the village, steep cliffs rose up from the sea, casting shadows on the water. The rain had dissipated, replaced by a sunset that sent rosy hues across the mountain peaks.

Homfray had never seen anything so beautiful. Strange for a young man from England, who was accustomed to the bustling, crowded streets of London, to come to this remote valley with its snow topped mountains and unspoiled rivers.

Yay K Wum's canoe landed on the beach beneath the terraced longhouses. Many of the Klahoose's skinny boats lined the ocean. The chief led them up a rocky path to the biggest house. It was a roomy log structure, longer than it was wide. Women were cooking and weaving; children were dashing around.

Everyone stopped what they were doing to watch the strange men. The small children hid behind their mothers' skirts. The older children bravely stepped forward to get a closer look at the men. Yay K Wum spoke to one of the women, who nodded and placed meat on the cooking fire. The delicious aroma of grilling meat made Homfray's mouth water. The seven men sat on the plank floor surrounded by the curious villagers.

The chief's wife offered them sheep, beaver and bear meat. The meat was tender and delicious, except for the bear meat that had a strong flavor. After the meal, Homfray's men were exhausted from their traumatic experience, so the chief took them to another lodge farther up the hill. It had sleeping platforms set back along the cedar walls.

After their harrowing day, all but Homfray were soon asleep. Homfray lay awake wondering if Yay K Wum could lead them to the trail over the mountains. Then, as the early night fell around him, he thought of his dear love. He imagined her touch, so light, so sensual. He fell asleep dreaming of Charlotte.

In the morning, Homfray offered Yay K Wum tea and presents, and eventually approached him to ask about guiding them through the mountains. The Klahoose chief spoke Chinook, and together with Pete's help and sign language, they understood each other.

"Would you take us to the trail that leads over the pass?" Homfray asked.

"You no go. Much snow. Winter is there." He drew signs on the sand to indicate many moons before the pass would be clear.

"But we must go," Homfray replied with the first niggle of worry. What would Charlotte think if he came back a failure?

"You go, and you die."

Homfray's crew listened, the Songhees shaking their heads, Bouchier looking frightened.

"Yes, there is a trail," Yay K Wum explained in Salish, "but there is snow in the pass, and no one goes to the Tŝilhqot'in land in the winter." Pete translated for the crew speaking partly in Chinook and broken English. Once they understood the significance of the chief's warnings, some couldn't contain their anger at Homfray for the folly of the trip. Others were accepting.

"You still going, boss?" Balthazar asked.

"Yes, I must. I have no choice. Waddington is counting on us."

With more persuasion and more gifts, the chief agreed to lead them to the beginning of the trail. But first they had to navigate the swirling water that separated Bute Inlet from the river. Timing was everything. High slack tide only lasted minutes.

They launched their canoe with Chief Yay K Wum leading the way. Balthazar encouraged his men to stay close to the Klahoose boat, fearing they would be caught in the receding tide if they were too slow. They almost cleared the sand bar when the ocean began to boil, catching the light craft and spinning them in the turbulence.

Lefty cried out, suddenly paralyzed with fear.

"You dumbass!" Balthazar yelled at Lefty. "You gon' send us all to Davy Jones's Locker! Come on, men. Fight with all your strength!"

Sweat poured down Balthazar's face, and his powerful arms strained with the effort as they faced towering waves. "Pull you laggards! Together, now!"

The crew realized the danger of capsizing the boat and strained to breech the oncoming wall of water. Gradually, they made headway.

The Tŝilhqot'in watched, amused by the crew's struggle. Yay K Wum heard the French Canadian's booming voice. They saw the canoe spin in the dangerous entry to the Homathko River and thought that ,with the exception of Balthazar and Coté, they were ill-equipped to tackle the mountain pass in the winter.

Exhausted and tense, Homfray and his men breathed a sigh of relief on seeing the smooth Homathko River. They had a reprieve. The river was wide and deep, with majestic mountains rising in the distance. They beached on a flat strip of land near some fishing huts that banked the river. Men in their spoon boats were out on the water fishing, their wives busy gutting the fish, the children running on the beach and watching the strangers coast by in the quiet water. This was where Waddington had planned his townsite.

Soon they were paddling again, trying to keep up with the faster spoon boat of the Klahoose chief. It was a pleasant evening, made all the more enjoyable by the adrenaline rush from their narrow escape from the swirling water and the bloodthirsty Natives.

As they wound up the river, the valley narrowed, and the mountains closed in until they were paddling up swift water and struggling against the current. It was necessary to tie a rope to the canoe and push and pull it up the rapids. They camped on the banks of the Homathko, and the river bouncing over the rocks soothed the men to sleep.

Homfray remained awake pondering the expedition. He must succeed. Many people counted on him. Charlotte would be proud of him. Lying in his tent, Coté and Bouchier snoring nearby, he thought again about the ball. Seeing Charlotte for the first time was like a bolt of lightning. He couldn't take his eyes off her.

"We will dance the night away," Homfray had told her. "I beg every dance with you—the quadrille, the round, the cotillion and the waltz."

"But it would be improper," she said. "I must dance with others."

"Tonight, I must have more dances than is proper."

"If I am seized by the wrist, what can I do but submit," she said with a coquettish smile. She enjoyed this flirtation. But for Homfray, it was anything but a casual romance.

"I offer you devotion of a lifetime."

"I beg you say no more, Sir." She left him to join her father but turned back to Homfray. "Young ladies do not decide their fate. My father has plans for me. I know it to be so."

I will approach her father upon my return, Homfray thought. *She is everything to me—the sun, the stars, the moon.*

With these pleasant memories, Homfray drifted off to sleep with the roar of the rapids and dreams of his love, calming his mind and sending him peacefully to slumber.

CHAPTER THREE

Homathko River, December 1861

Meeting the Tŝilhqot'in

The next morning, the crew had to abandon the boat as the river now cascaded over rocks, rendering canoeing impossible.

"If only we had the Klahoose spoon boats, we could handle the swift water and could travel farther upriver," Homfray said, as he reluctantly unloaded the canoe. The next day they would continue their journey on foot, packing their gear on their backs.

As Homfray feared, the chief would go no farther.

"You not make it. Snow too deep." The chief tried once more to convince Homfray about the dangers ahead, but to no avail. He turned back with his companions. The light maneuverable spoon boats shot down the rapids, disappearing around the cliffs. Homfray imagined what the chief would be saying: "Stupid King George men."

The crew left their tents behind because they could not carry the heavy canvas. All they took was one piece of canvas to hang over themselves as they slept. For two days they struggled on beside the frigid waters, making camp on the riverbank each night. Thankfully, the rain held off, but dark, ominous clouds began to gather in the western sky.

Homfray worried that if it snowed, his men might refuse to go farther and being exposed to the elements as winter approached would cause a mutiny. He couldn't sleep, kept awake by thoughts about the problems his expedition would face.

Homfray's crew consisted of three experienced Hudson's Bay men. They had crossed the continent in worse conditions. Pete and Kauvsiya, the Songhees men, were silent, uncomplaining and stoic.

Then there was Lefty. Homfray thought he might become a problem. Lefty held them back, trodding clumsily over the narrow, rocky trail, his clothes catching on branches, falling when he climbed over logs or slippery rocks.

They continued up the valley. The Homathko River whirled, boiled and roared over huge boulders. Towering rocks rose thousands of feet high. At one point, they had to veer away from the river because their passage was blocked by a landslide.

Homfray worried they would not find the pass once they no longer followed the river. The next day they saw patches of snow along the riverbank.

If only we could fall in with some Indians who know the path, he thought.

"Surely we are not in snow already," Lefty grumbled. "We haven't even reached the pass."

"Dis is one hell of a trip." Balthazar was pleased at the adversity they faced. "Worse than crossing the Rockies back in 1850 when we first came out west."

"Shoot the crows," Coté said. "I don't want to go into ten feet of snow. At least with The Bay, we had tents to shelter us and whisky each day."

"Why you not bring us our whisky, Homfray?" Balthazar asked. "A little dram would keep the crew walking during the day and would take the chill off at night."

"Waddington wouldn't allow it," Homfray replied.

"The Bay knows it best to give the men something to look forward to; den we don't mind the slog through icy waters," Coté added.

"I see footprints." Balthazar was in the lead. "Dey better be friendlies. I don't want to have muskets lowered at me. Dis time I kill de bloody Indians first."

Balthazar hesitated before carrying up the trail. "I don't like dis. We used to be friends with the tribes. We traded. Both The Bay and the Indians got something. Dey got blankets and muskets; we got furs. Well, dey got less than their furs were worth, but dey weren't war-like. Dey was partners of a sort."

"We never built roads in their territory either," Coté added. "We respected their territory. Understood it was their land."

"I don't think Waddington had dealt with Indians before he arrived in British Territory." Balthazar kept his eyes on the snowy trail, following the footsteps that became more numerous as they walked toward the pass.

"He was some kind of big wig in England. Den he owned steel and cotton mills in France." Balthazar talked to keep his mind off his disquiet.

"Didn't Waddington just arrive in Victoria, and now he buying up tracts of land like they were pancakes. He don't know nothin' about the Indians here or the country," Coté said with contempt.

Homfray listened to the voyageurs, wondering whether Waddington was the right man to bank his career on.

The men walked into the deepening snow, seeing more footprints as they reached the top of the pass. As they turned a corner on the trail, a tall man, his body decorated in green with vermillion rings around his eyes watched them approach. He looked suspiciously at the ragtag group. A woman stood behind him, cringing in fear.

"Holy Mother of God. Sacrebleu!" Balthazar had his musket out; he was ready to fight this time.

The powerful, muscled Tŝilhqot'in waved his bow and arrow and danced up and down.

Bouchier was almost in tears. Lefty held back.

"Put your firearm down Balthazar. Let me talk to him." Homfray offered a gift of beads as he walked slowly toward the fierce-looking warrior. Homfray closed and opened his mouth, signing that he and his men wanted to eat and laid his head on his shoulders, indicating they wanted to sleep.

The Tŝilhqot'in chief appeared to understand. He lowered his bow and stepped forward to take the gift.

The imposing Native used sign language to indicate to Homfray to open his mouth. His fang necklaces rested on Homfray's chest as the Tŝilhqot'in pried open Homfray's mouth.

"What's he doing?"

"He don't know if you human or not," Lefty said.

"No. Medicine Man seeing if you got disease," Pete said. "They scared of pox. He not hurt you."

After examining all the men, the Tŝilhqot'in turned up the trail, motioning the group to follow. Within minutes, they approached an opening in the cliff wall.

"They're bloody trog...whatever the murderers are called," Lefty struggled to remember. "I will not go down there. They will kill us. They'll eat us!"

"You mean troglodytes," Homfray said, "and I don't think they'll harm us."

"Coming face to face with death on this journey should have made you strong," Balthazar said. "Instead, you are just a little kitten, crying for its mother. Come on. We must go in. Homfray, you lead us. You be as skinny as a whippet; dey don't want to eat you."

They crawled on their hands and knees into the cave, Lefty and Bouchier shaking with fright, while the others moved quickly, seeing this as an adventure. The cave was warm though fetid. Several families sat around the fire. The men and women stared at the white men as if the strange creatures had dropped from sky. The children hid in blankets on the sleeping platforms, dark eyes peering out, afraid yet curious. A beautiful girl watched them boldly from the back of the cave.

An old woman bent over the low fire, cooking. She took a bowl, spat in it and wiped it with her hair. Homfray's stomach lurched. She opened a cedar box and fished out foul-smelling meat.

"You must eat everything she give us," Coté told them. "She is offering us der choice food. Do not insult her, or they might do us harm." The meat was fermented and slimy. He passed the bowl to Bouchier.

"Here. You complained about hunger," Coté laughed. "You be the first. Bouchier grabbed a finger of the grayish mush, gagged and spit it out in his hand without letting the old woman see.

"I can't eat it. It makes me sick." Bouchier's face turned green.

"Now smile to show you like it."

Coté passed the bowl to the others. "You can slip da food to the dogs as long as the old hag don't see. Take care like a thief with jewels to hide."

"Hey boss, can you spare us and the old lady a little hard tack," Bouchier asked. "I'm near down to my last energy, and this shit is too much for me to stomach."

Homfray passed the hard tack to his men and gave the old woman a piece. She bit into the hard tack and spit it out. Then he made signs to show they enjoyed their meal and, putting his head down on his hands, he signed that they wanted to sleep. Despite the foul-smelling air, for the first time in days, they were warm.

If only I could have coffee, Homfray thought, *I would charge across the pass.*

They left their subterranean house after a restful night of sleep. Homfray, using sign language and with Pete's help, asked the chief about the trail through the mountain pass. The Tŝilhqot'in protested, saying in sign language and Chinook, that the route was blocked with snow.

It took some time for Homfray to come to grips with reality and admit that he may have failed in his task. He had given his word to Waddington that he would make it through the pass.

I have to think of the men that I might lead to their death. Then he thought of his dear love. *But I can't bear to lose her!*

Homfray was fraught with indecision. If he aborted the trip, Waddington may not pay him, and Charlotte would likely reject him. Yet if he continued through the mountains without provisions and with winter upon them, they might perish from hunger and cold. Reluctantly, he gathered the crew.

"We must go back. There is no other choice. The pass is deep in snow, and our supplies will last only five days. We'll never make it through the pass let alone to Fort Alexandria. It has been madness."

"You made da right decision," Coté said. "We cannot go on. It was an ill-conceived plan from the start. You are the leader! You should have known it was too late and told that lying cheat to send us in the spring."

"Waddington may refuse to pay us," Lefty grumbled.

"I'll smash his head in if he refuses to pay," Balthazar said, picking up his gear and hoisting it up onto his wide back.

They turned back toward the ocean; the men were relieved that they would not have to risk walking into deeper and deeper snow. Homfray thought of his loved one and felt the crushing weight of his failure. What will she think of me? What will Waddington think?

They roped up and began the descent to the wild river, walking along the bank, at times on a trail high above the raging current, at times walking in the frigid water on ice-glazed rocks. They struggled along for two days before reaching the buried canoe and their gear. They would have coffee again and a tent to keep the rain off. They would no longer be wading in their soggy, cold, nearly worn-out boots. But they still had ninety miles in miserable weather to get to Bute Inlet.

With Balthazar in the stern and Coté in the bow, they shot down the river, bouncing over rocks and trying to miss sweepers. Lefty screamed every time the bottom of the canoe scraped over boulders. The others focused all their energy and skill on paddling, wishing for the calm waters in the valley below and praying that their fragile craft would not be split in two by the rocks.

But it was not to be. The crew raced around a sharp bend in the river directly into the path of a logjam. They scrambled out just before the canoe impaled itself on a sharp branch, and water poured through a hole that threatened to sink the canoe and all their gear. Homfray edged his way along the slippery logs, and the men formed a line to take the gear safely to shore. Moments after Homfray rescued the last items, the canoe broke apart and disappeared beneath the logjam. The dispirited crew watched as the pieces were thrown up on the far side of the logjam and churned up in the rapids.

Homfray's foot slipped on the log, was immediately thrown into the freezing water and then swept under the logjam by the force of the torrent. But just as his feet gave way, he managed to grasp the edge of a large boulder with one hand and saved himself from the fury of the rapids. He didn't know how long he could hold on. He could feel his legs growing weak. He was focused on maintaining his hold when Balthazar waded into the river, trying to reach Homfray, his big hand outstretched. But there were limits to the big Frenchman's strength. Homfray and Balthazar knew the water could sweep them both away.

Balthazar turned to shore, yelling at the others to find the rope. The men anchored the rope on shore. Balthazar tied one end around his waist to keep from being swept away. He walked cautiously into the freezing rapids, but his feet went out from under him. The rope held, and he regained his purchase before staggering toward Homfray. He reached his fallen comrade just before Homfray's numb fingers lost their grip on the boulder. Balthazar swung Homfray over his broad shoulder and, with the men pulling the rope, brought them both to shore.

Homfray and Balthazar lay on their backs, gasping and shivering, trying to recover their breath.

"I think I earned my pay, eh, Boss?" Balthazar grinned through his chattering teeth.

"I wish Old Waddy would have allowed me to bring whisky. You certainly earned your dram today." Homfray got up on shaky legs. "We'll make camp here. Balthazar and I need to dry out and find our legs."

"Speak for yourself, Boss. I've been through worse, crossing the Rockies. But if you need your rest, rest it will be."

The morning mist hung in the valley as the men packed up their gear. At least the rain had abated. Unfortunately, with the loss of their canoe, they were on foot, wearing ragged clothing and cold, wet, worn boots. Would they ever make it to Bute Inlet? Without their canoe, how would they get back to Victoria? Homfray tried to shore up the men's spirits, but everyone knew how desperate their situation was.

They trudged through thick undergrowth alongside the roaring river, each night pitching their tents on rocky ground. They were surrounded by steep cliffs and had only a narrow shelf on which to make camp. Each night it took Coté an hour to coax a fire from the sodden branches.

"Sacrebleu!" Coté shouted. "*Ce bois de merde ne brulera.*"

"What is the Frenchy saying?" Lefty asked.

"He say da wood is wet," Bouchier replied.

"Dis isn't a Presbyterian rain; dis a bloody Baptist flood," Coté grumbled. "I'm tired from blowing to make it burn. Lefty, could you find witch's broom without stumblin' over your feet or gittin' yourself lost?"

"What is that?"

"Witches' broom. *Tu ne sais rien?* Do you know nothing Lefty? It is the dry twigs and small woody stems that grow on tree trunks.

Now ya know. Come. I'll search with ya," Bouchier offered. "I want my supper before morning."

Soon smoke curled up and before long Coté had a blazing fire going. The river roared by, spitting up spray as it bounced down the canyon.

A week later they reached the section of the Homathko River that was so calm it didn't seem like a river at all. They chopped down a towering cedar tree and spent ten precious days hollowing it out under the guidance of Pete, the older Songhee. All seven men climbed in, not too worried as they stayed close enough to shore so they could make it to land if they tipped.

After two days of paddling on the lazy river, they arrived at Bute Inlet.

"I'll take the log across to the village," Balthazar offered. "Maybe, Coté, you come help me keep dis clumsy canoe from dumping us when the winds are bad. I give some presents and ask the chief to take us to Victoria. Is that good boss man?"

Homfray agreed and stayed behind with the other men as Balthazar and Coté paddled the awkward boat into the calm water and mist.

Lefty and Bouchier were constantly fearful that the fierce group that had captured them at the beginning would find and kill them. He believed his fears were realized when a war whoop sounded across the inlet. The canoes were too far away to make out its occupants. Lefty was certain this was the end and ran to hide in the bushes. The canoes came closer, and Bouchier saw Balthazar in the bow standing behind the Klahoose chief who had saved them earlier.

"You scared the shit outta me," Bouchier raged. "Why did you tell the chief to yell?"

"Just yanking your chain," Balthazar said with a grin. "You scare too easily Bouchier. We need to harden you some."

The Klahoose chief took them to his hilltop village again. The ragged, exhausted crew felt relief at last. Most of the men were asleep in the longhouse as soon as their heads hit the bearskin rugs. Pete stayed awake, conversing with Chief Yay K Wum while the women baked salmon.

The chief's wife signed that the feast was ready. Homfray was anxious to speak to Yay K Wum and plead with him to take them to Victoria. He would offer all they had: axes, pots, tents. They had to get home; winter was upon them. The weather might turn any day, and he longed to see Charlotte.

"Wait 'til we've eaten," Coté told him. "It would be impolite to make your request while they feed us." The Frenchman had years of travelling from Montréal to the coast of the continent, engaging with many different tribes on the way.

The salmon was delicious and plentiful. The seaweed dipped in eulachon grease made a crispy snack. It was the first nourishing food the crew had had in days.

Once the meal was over, Pete spoke, "Chief, he tell me this part of the river, it called *Xwemalhkwa*. You maybe no say that. It means swift water because of the tidal flows."

"Swift. No, I say treacherous," Balthazar said, remembering the effort it took him to keep the canoe from throwing them into the waves. *I'll never get in a canoe again with the likes of Lefty*, Balthazar thought. *Greenhorns like him don't know nothing about rapids or waves. Men who will overturn a boat even in calm water and den, tell you he didn't do it. Stupid!*

It was late December when Yay K Wum's men paddled Homfray's crew into James Bay. They landed the big ocean-going canoe at the wharf. Stone storehouses bordered the top of the bank. Yay K's men were reluctant to disembark, afraid of the crowd that awaited them. Waddington and a group of men walked down the steep bank to meet them. One was Amor de Cosmos, dressed fashionably in a deep blue suit with a velvet vest. He was Waddington's man and fellow investor.

"My God!" he said, stroking his glossy, neat beard. "What happened to you? You look like you've been at Bull Run, taking a beating from Lee's army."

Their clothes were tattered, their boots dog-eared. Not the easy trip Waddington had extolled.

Before Homfray could say a word, Waddington cornered Homfray. "I don't know what befell you," he whispered, "but I want you to say it was an easy trip, and there is a trail along the pass."

"It was not easy," Homfray replied. "We were almost killed by a war-like group of savages. We nearly perished in snow that was ten feet deep. It was dangerous; our lives were at risk."

"Enough," Waddington said emphatically. "You are in my employ. You will say it is a passable route."

Rife with conflict, Homfray paused. "I don't fancy lying, Sir."

"It isn't lying." Waddington put on a sugary smile. "You are saying what your employer needs you to say. It is an alternative truth."

"I should do what is right."

"Tell the people it is a good trail and will make a fine road." Waddington's smile disappeared, replaced by a harsh look. Homfray felt weak. "Tell them, or I'll make sure you don't work in the Colony again."

Homfray thought of the beautiful Charlotte. He struggled, knowing that if he was blacklisted, he would be destitute. Charlotte would not marry a man without a position, without means to support her.

He nodded to Waddington. "If you say so, Mr. Waddington."

Homfray felt sick to his stomach, knowing that his decision would haunt him.

Why didn't I have the courage to tell him the real condition of the valley? Why can't I speak the truth? I do this for Charlotte; everything I do is for her love.

CHAPTER FOUR

Victoria, December 1861

Charlotte

Homfray had to see Charlotte. He scanned the crowd at the docks hoping she would be there. His heart sank. Surely, she would hear that he and his men had arrived. Word of arrivals at the dock spread quickly throughout the city.

People came to meet the paddlers, loved ones they feared had died. Others came to see the strange tribe that had rescued them.

Why did she not come? Did she not share his feelings?

Homfray had waited so long to see Charlotte. He dreamt of this moment and now, while he was occupied getting the Klahoose paddlers settled, he kept looking for his beloved, anticipating the long-awaited reunion.

The Klahoose boatmen were afraid of the cows and horses, which they had not seen before, and they clung to Homfray, fearful of the animals and fearful that the Songhee's tribe would take their lives. They followed Homfray to his lodgings and pitched their tents in the yard. After a few days, they settled down and soon enjoyed their adventure and the many gifts showered on them for risking their lives to bring the explorers safely back to Victoria.

Homfray couldn't wait to see Charlotte, though he worried about why she hadn't come to the docks to greet him. Surely she would come to the meeting tomorrow. He would have to clean himself up. Shave. Buy a new suit. He looked at his ravished, sinewy body. *I am so thin, bags under my eyes, wrinkles where my muscles were. The trip has taken my youth.*

Next morning, Homfray read the advertisement in the *British Colonist* over breakfast at Alice's Eatery. What is Waddington talking about?

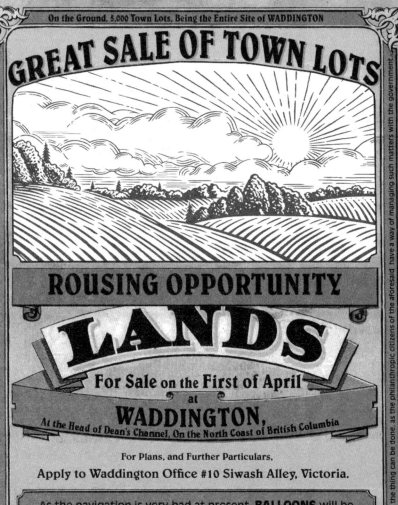

On the Ground, 5,000 Town Lots, Being the Entire Site of WADDINGTON

GREAT SALE OF TOWN LOTS

ROUSING OPPORTUNITY

LANDS

For Sale on the First of April
at
WADDINGTON,

At the Head of Dean's Channel, On the North Coast of British Columbia

For Plans, and Further Particulars,
Apply to Waddington Office #10 Siwash Alley, Victoria.

As the navigation is very bad at present, **BALLOONS** will be provided to convey intended purchasers to the place of sale, **FREE** of charge.

A few citizens of Victoria, having been moved by philanthropic desire to build up a town at that point, are prepared to offer Extraordinary Inducements! And, in order that said point may be the **Seaport of British Columbia**, steps will be taken to fill up the present dangerous entrance to Fraser River and Burrard Inlet.

P.S. Should parties making purchases at the above sale desire to have half the purchase money refunded, the thing can be done, as the philanthropic citizens of the aforesaid have a way of managing such matters with the government.

COMMERCIAL ADVERTISER PRINTING HOUSE.

Homfray shook his head in disbelief. *What have I got myself into? A town at the head of the inlet? A road through that impossible terrain? A seaport? What is he thinking? Has Waddington not heard a word I said?*

Homfray's stomach heaved. He would have vomited over the linen tablecloth if he'd had any food in his stomach. *Should I tell people exactly what we faced? The truth about Waddington's dream, the steep mountain pass, the raging river with no way to cross except hundreds of bridges. Snow covering the pass from October, 'til late spring. Impossible!*

"You look as pale as a ghost," Alice said as she brought in a plate of crisp bacon, eggs and a stack of pancakes. "After your months of near starvation, you should be anticipating my fine food like a hungry horse."

"Oh, hello Alice. I was just reading about Waddington's plans in the paper."

"That blaggard! I don't believe he will ever build a road. David told me the Tŝilhqot'in won't let them and that the pass is impossible to navigate."

"Yes, yes," he mumbled, perplexed. "Where is David? I'd like a word with him."

"He'll be off soon. He's stationed in New Westminster for the winter. If you don't catch him today, you likely won't see him till spring."

"Maybe he'll be at the meeting tonight." Homfray pushed his food aside. He had an ache in his stomach and a pounding headache.

He was overwhelmed with misgivings. His secret would turn him into a small man, but if he told the truth, he would lose Charlotte. If he lied about road, it surely would come back to haunt him. Homfray struggled. His conscience demanded he tell everyone the conditions he and his crew faced. His infatuation with the beautiful Charlotte blocked the way. He was certain,

though the conflict and misgivings soured his stomach. He would
have to lie at the meeting.

The townspeople crammed themselves into the hall. They rel-
ished the entertainment Waddington offered, since there was not
much to do on a cold December night in Victoria. Miners were back
from the goldfields, their work halted for the winter. It was a boisterous group, a mix of the upper class from Victoria and gold seekers
from around the world.

Waddington stood at the speaker's pulpit with Homfray and
Amor de Cosmos, Waddington's flamboyant co-investor, the man
who had changed his name from Smith to de Cosmos, Smith being
too plain for a man who had great plans. He needed a name that fit
the man he hoped to be. The fiery de Cosmos was impeccably
attired in a frock coat and beaver hat. He was trying to reinvent his
personality along with the name change. Having been a journalist,
photographer and now a politician, he was infamous for his public
harassment of the Black community.

Waddington, though born rich, did not concern himself with
his attire. Instead, he wanted to convey confidence through his
speech, despite having niggling doubts about the project. Was the
pass really as hazardous as Homfray had reported? he wondered.

Among the crowd of locals and entrepreneurs were many
Black residents who had recently travelled to Victoria from the
U.S. They were owners of a shoe store, a general store and barber
shops, but they were businessmen, not road investors. They mixed
with the crowd, accepted by most of the British but not by some
Americans. Alice and David overheard Cat Hawkins, an American
miner, harassing a couple of Black men. Wellington Moss, a sturdy,
well-attired man owned the Pioneer Shaving Salon, and Miffin

Gibbs, a stately man, dressed modestly in a fine wool suit and black tie, was a merchant with a thriving business in dry goods with his partner, Peter Lester.

"Bloody niggers. If'n we was back in Georgia, we would string you up to the nearest tree. Why y'all coming north?" Cat, a southerner who had come north for the gold rush and brought his love for whisky and the southern hatred of Blacks with him.

David couldn't abide him harassing the men, solid citizens who contributed to the city. He turned to the drunk with an icy stare, his fists tight. He wanted to punch the miner in the face. Instead, he thought he should educate this rude bumpkin.

"They're escaping the new laws in California. Laws that take away their right to vote, that kick their children out of the school they attended. The Blacks are welcome in British Territory."

David was intimidating when he was angry, and it was clear to the miner that one didn't want to pick a fight with the tall, hardened soldier. Cat moved away, searching for companions that shared his views. On the stage, he could see Amor de Cosmos. *There's a man with influence, a smooth politician, who would put those Black mongrels in their place,* Cat thought.

"We don't take offence," Miffin Gibbs explained to David. "In the U.S., violence threatened us, not words. Let's listen to what Waddington has to say."

David held his temper and turned his attention to the stage.

Most citizens in the city were united behind Waddington. There was an almost mob mentality about the Waddington project. Not everyone was behind it, but to speak against it, to seed some doubt, was considered disloyal to Waddington who would bring wealth and progress to Victoria.

Waddington and his investors viewed the road and the new town at Bute Inlet as a golden opportunity. Residents of Victoria feared that the City of New Westminster, the Royal City as it was called because Queen Victoria chose its name, was gaining importance and would overtake Victoria soon. There was even some talk of making New Westminster the capital of both Vancouver Island and British Columbia. They couldn't let that happen, and Waddington had the answer. The promoter was determined that his plans for a town at Bute Inlet would eclipse New Westminster and give Victoria a boost.

People fed on his dream. The pass from Bute Inlet would replace the Fraser River as the route to the goldfields, and the boom period would never end.

On the stage, Waddington spoke quietly to his investors and employees. "We have to show a united front. Be positive, confident. Can't have Mozart and Chopin playing different tunes on the piano, can we?" He put his arm on Homfray's shoulder. "Stay by my side, me boy. People want to hear from someone who has seen the road firsthand." Waddington beamed at his audience, playing to their greed. He oozed confidence like warm honey; Homfray looked like a starved and beaten dog.

Balthazar watched from a dark corner of the hall, his collar pulled up so the shadows hid his face. Homfray glanced his way, but he couldn't look Balthazar in the eye. Homfray had to lie in front of his companion about the journey that almost took their lives. Balthazar knows there will never be a road through the pass to Tŝilhqot'in country.

Homfray slumped, stuck his hands in his pockets and looked at his shoes. Many of the best things are done because of love and loyalty; many of the worst things as well. Homfray was a loyal man, but he was also a man in love.

Waddington puffed out his chest and held his hands up to silence the audience. "I know you are all here to get the news about the road. Well, I can tell you good folks there is not just a trail but an easy route through the mountains. It will be the greatest road ever built in the Colony of British Columbia or, for that matter, the greatest road west of the Rockies in both the British Territory and the United States of America!"

There was a sense of relief among the audience, pleased to hear that the route had not only been explored but was found to be a good route.

"I will ask Robert Homfray, the leader of the expedition, to tell you in his own words. He has a degree in engineering, and he's the smartest of young men. Yes, the smartest. Homfray…" Waddington gestured at Homfray to step up to the podium. "Tell the fine folks what you saw."

As Homfray moved forward, Waddington whispered in his ear, "Are you willing, not to lie but play down the seriousness of our situation? Make it clear that you won a victory, even to ordinary newspaper-reading butchers."

Just then, Homfray saw his beloved, Charlotte, enter the hall on her father's arm. She looked even more beautiful than he remembered. She wore a green velvet bodice and skirt with a fur throw over her shoulders. Her blonde hair spilled out from a matching velvet hat.

Homfray knew her father was one of the investors. He felt a stab of worry as he took the podium.

"Yes, uh, as Mr. Waddington says the road can be built. Of course, winter came upon us, so, our exploration was not completed."

Waddington was not pleased with Homfray's tepid endorsement and quickly added, "Yes, the road can be built, the young man says. And built it will be! Construction will start in the spring, and by the following year, it will be making us all rich." The spectators cheered, whistled and clapped.

He paused and scanned the crowd. "You can still invest. There is room for more men with a vision who will put their money into this venture. Men who see the Bute Inlet as the cheapest and fastest way to get to the goldfields. Not a trip of miles upstream on the Fraser River, through a dangerous canyon, with unfriendly Indians to deal with. That is Douglas's latest proposal." Waddington scoffed and continued. "Do you know how long it takes to reach the goldfields by way of the Fraser? Three hundred miles and weeks on a treacherous river." He took out a handkerchief and wiped his brow.

"Men die in the swift water. In the steep canyon called Hell's Gate. Yes, Hell's Gate. Why would anyone take that long and hazardous journey? Our route is just a quick journey across Georgia Strait, through the beautiful islands of Desolation Sound, up Bute Inlet and to the Chilcotin plains and the goldfields on the Fraser. Ten days at most. Ten easy days.

"We will have developments springing up in Victoria—theatres, stores, industry. This will be the Mecca of the West Coast. Forget about the swampy land around the Fraser River. This will be the centre. Bet your life on it!"

Alice and David listened to the exaggerated speech, not believing his hype.

"Waddington would say anything to his investors," David whispered to Alice. "He lies so often he doesn't even realize he is lying. He says the Tŝilhqot'in are friendly. How does he know? He has never been in their territory. He only visited the coast and met the Homathko, never ventured into Tŝilhqot'in land."

"We met only one Tŝilhqot'in family," Alice replied. "They keep to themselves. When I had the roadhouse at Lytton, the Forks as they called it then, I spoke to someone from the tribe. She told me the people didn't want white men's heavy pots and noisy muskets. A woven basket suited them better when they moved their camp to the fishing grounds, and arrows and spears kill silently."

"I think they have muskets now, but not for hunting, for protecting their people from us. Waddington thinks he can just drive his damn road through their country, and they will welcome him with open arms. I don't think so."

While Waddington waved his arms and enthusiastically hyped his project, Charlotte moved toward them, her father in tow.

"Hello, Alice. Greetings, David." Charlotte approached the couple with an engaging smile on her lips. She could not resist trying to capture the attention of every good-looking man, and David, while twenty years her senior, was very attractive.

"Miss Charlotte, Mr. Dupré," Alice greeted them, returning Charlotte's smile with her own. "Please come for tea with us tonight."

"It would be our pleasure," Charlotte answered.

"Robert Homfray will be joining us once he is released by Waddington," Alice said. "We understand you are his friend."

"Yes, he is a friend," Charlotte paused, "but only a friend."

Alice's brow furrowed with concern, knowing Homfray hoped Charlotte would become his wife.

"Father, did you ask Homfray to exchange his wage for an investment in the road?"

"Yes, darling, I did, but the young man vacillates. If he is not willing, then what are we to think?"

"Let's talk with Robert at the roadhouse," Alice suggested.

They walked through the festive streets of Victoria to Alice's Eatery. It was a week before Christmas, and the townscape was magical. It was a cool, crisp evening. No snow yet, and the incessant rain had stopped at last. The streets, usually muddy and rutted, were hardened by frost.

Alice unlocked the door to the roadhouse. She had decorated the room with bows of cedar and garlands. She lit the astral lamp and a row of candles. While David entertained Mr. Dupré and Charlotte, Alice made tea and arranged treats on a silver platter.

She was carrying the tray to her guests when Robert entered the restaurant.

"Charlotte." Homfray's voice cracked; he felt weak at the sight of her beauty.

"Come sit down Robert," Alice said. "We are celebrating your safe return."

"Oh, yes. Thank you, Alice."

Before sitting, Robert took Charlotte's hand in his. "I have missed you so much, Charlotte. You have no idea what it was like to be away so long."

"Hello, Mr. Homfray," Charlotte said coolly. "I hear you had to be brought back to Victoria by the Indians."

"You must tell us more," Mr. Dupré said, as Robert took a seat at the table. "What happened out there?"

"I have not much more to say. We lost our boat to a logjam, and the Klahoose Indians ferried us home."

"How was the pass in winter?" David inquired. "I've been through there in summer, and I can't imagine it was easy trip with deep snow on the pass and ice forming on the river."

"It's a fair route," Homfray answered, his voice barely a murmur.

"The road will go through, won't it?" Charlotte pressed. "Father, you are banking our fortune on its success, are you not?" She touched David lightly on his arm. "I hope you men have also invested in the road as it will make us all rich."

"Am I an investor?" David repeated. "I think not. I am familiar with the country and the Tŝilhqot'in. I'm certain they don't want a road through their territory."

Charlotte turned to Homfray. "You must invest, dear Robert." Charlotte smiled. "You have seen the country; you know the road can be built. It will give the others confidence in the endeavour."

Homfray had the appearance of a deer caught in the lamplight. "I am…weighing my options. I would have to give up my salary to buy shares, and I will be without funds to pay my landlord." He looked uncomfortable, knowing he must please Charlotte, yet for someone as frugal as he was, it was difficult to try to do both. He rose from the table and reached for his coat and hat.

"Why are you leaving so soon? You should stay awhile," Alice insisted. "Have some of my fresh cinnamon buns, Robert. I made them especially for you."

"I must go, Alice. My sincere apologies. I'm not myself these days and not suitable for society."

Alice nodded. "If you must depart, we'll bid you goodnight. Look after yourself, dear Robert."

"Come Father, we will accompany Homfray to his lodging." She took Homfray's arm. "The wind is something fierce, and I must get back to our hotel before my hair is blown about and I look disheveled."

Homfray thrilled at her touch. He admired her willfulness as well as her beauty. The fact that she controlled her father didn't bother him.

Alice waited until they were alone before turning to David. "I am not sure she will be good for Robert," Alice said as she cleared the plates away. "She is so self-centred. Did you notice how she talks to her father and deceives Robert?"

David carried the teapot to the table. "A little manipulator, I think. You're not like her in the least Alice."

"I was quite the opposite. I allowed people to take over my life; I married Saxby because my brother-in-law forced me. I didn't stick up for myself." A gloom descended on Alice.

"You are a changed woman. You bought the roadhouse and managed the workers." David laughed. "Soon you will become bossy."

Alice smiled, her good spirits back. "Never."

CHAPTER FIVE

Victoria, Spring 1862

The Wedding

The news of Charlotte and Robert's upcoming wedding came as a surprise to Alice and David. It had been only two months since Homfray's return from Bute Inlet. Alice was certain Charlotte didn't love Homfray, but Charlotte likely felt he would soon be wealthy and successful. He was an engineer and Waddington's confidant. But Alice wondered at the haste. Why so soon?

Of course, Robert was beside himself with joy. He couldn't believe his fortune, marrying a woman so beautiful, the vision that had filled his dreams during the hardships of the Bute Inlet trip and gave him courage in the face of death. She would soon be his wife.

Homfray asked David to be his best man. David wondered if all was well with the couple. There seemed to be so little physical affection between them. Whenever Robert reached for her hand, she pulled away.

Charlotte insisted on tails for the groom and the best man, all ordered from San Francisco. David was aware of Homfray's financial problems, and with the expenses of the extravagant wedding, Robert had to borrow money to pay his landlord each month.

A constant drizzle fell on Victoria every winter from November to February, but the event was a bright spot in the gloomy weather. The wedding ceremony was grand, despite Homfray's financial straits. Christ Church Cathedral was decorated with pink bows and candles. Victorians came in carriages, buggies, on horseback or walking.

Governor Douglas with his part-Cree wife, Amelia, and their five daughters and one son, sat in the front row. The imposing Judge Begbie, and of course Alfred Waddington and Amor de Cosmos, were in attendance. It was the event of the year, a celebration to see the end of the dreary winter.

Charlotte was dressed in a creamy white, billowing tulle gown with lavish lace trimmings and bows. It was a gown fit for a princess. Most brides in Victoria wore gowns more on the plain side with high necklines. Charlotte's dress signified self-importance, not modesty, though she did wear a traditional white tulle veil over her long, blonde hair. The bodice was cut low, and the veil was trimmed with orange blossoms.

"She is gorgeous," Alice whispered. Alice wondered to herself about the cost of a dress like that, shipped up the coast from San Francisco. She would never spend that much on a dress. Alice sewed her dresses, preferring plain to fancy, and she believed that David admired her simple, almost Puritan mode of dress.

Charlotte walked up the aisle on her father's arm. His eyes shone with tears; he doted on Charlotte and lived for her. She was all he had since his wife had passed away so suddenly of smallpox.

Charlotte drank in the admiring looks of the wedding guests, smiling coquettishly as she walked slowly up the aisle. As father and daughter approached the altar, Alice could hear Charlotte whisper to her father, "Kiss me on both cheeks when you leave me at the altar." She did not smile at her father or Homfray as she took her place at the altar; she smoothed her gown and looked serene and composed.

Homfray looked edgy. The expensive tails were too big for his undernourished frame. David stood beside him, occasionally offering encouragement to Homfray. David appeared robust beside the emaciated bridegroom.

The reception was held at the Maplebank House in Esquimalt, even though guests had to travel three miles over a muddy road to get there from the church. The two-storey house was grand with a balcony on all four all sides. David and Alice arrived in a brougham pulled by one horse. A hundred guests gathered in the grand ballroom, and a four-piece orchestra played.

Charlotte danced with several men while her new husband sat bewildered and out of place. Her cheeks grew rosy as she drank more and more wine always smiling at her partner and the guests.

Alice and David left early, not wishing to travel late at night.

"What did you think?" David asked her, as the horse pulled the carriage slowly up the dark road to the centre of Victoria. The rain had stopped, leaving a fresh smell in the Victoria's streets.

"I really don't know what to think, though I wish them well. Homfray deserves happiness. I only hope that Charlotte is the right woman for him."

CHAPTER SIX

Victoria, Spring 1862

Songhees Village

Across James Bay, smoke rose above the Songhees village. At first, Alice thought it could be from cooking fires. She stepped outside to watch from her restaurant door and saw flames leap up among the many houses and shacks built on the rocky peninsula.

"Tahoma, come quickly!" Alice called for her employee. "It looks like your village is on fire!" Alice knew Tahoma's aunt and her two young children lived in the village. The father was a Hudson's Bay man, and Alice knew he was away. She had a sick feeling in her stomach. So many little children and babies! So many mothers, grandparents, aunts and uncles.

Alice and Tahoma rushed out the door and dashed to the boat moored at the waterfront. Tahoma rowed them across the bay in minutes only to find homes entirely engulfed in flames, women wailing and children screaming.

Tahoma found his aunt and children sobbing outside their burning house.

"We've lost everything but our lives." Esther, normally a calm, unruffled and respected woman of the Salish tribe, was panic-stricken. "There was no time to save anything. My man wouldn't let me leave even though I knew we were ordered to go. This is our land for God's sake. They come and take it all, burn us out because some of our people have disease—their disease. The English brought the sickness. We never had this before," she wailed, kneeling and pounding her fists on the rocky ground.

Officers stood back from the burning village, torch in hand. Tahoma could hardly contain his anger as he approached the man. "What have you done?" he demanded. "This is inhumane!"

"We gave you fair warning," the constable said. "The fault lies with you Indians for not leaving when ordered. Chief Freezy saved his people by relocating to Discovery Island. Why didn't you go with him? You Indians are stupid, risking the lives of your family, and for what?"

Tahoma tried to contain his temper. "Who ordered you to burn down the village?" He felt like smashing the constable's face.

"The Committee of Nuisances, that's who. They have power by law to burn, order evacuation, you name it." The officer softened his tone when he saw Alice. "You know, Miss, the Indians should all have been vaccinated because the vaccine has been available for fifty years. Now there are thousands of Indians dying. They have no resistance. They get infected with smallpox and die the next day."

"What you are doing is wrong." Alice was distraught, almost beside herself with grief. "The Songhees need a hospital, not to have their homes burned, their food supplies destroyed. Victoria is becoming heartless in its treatment of Natives."

"The police were told to rid Humboldt Street of the houses of ill repute, and we did. The same week, we were ordered to destroy another village close to Victoria. We put it to the torch and ordered the Indians to move to Ogden Point. Most died at Ogden Point. More than one hundred. Only twelve escaped the disease. Do you think I like my position, Miss? But we must do what we are ordered to do."

"A good Christian would not follow such orders," Alice said. "This is Songhees land, their home."

"Victorians will miss the convenience of the Songhees," the Constable said. "Now they will only have the Chinese to clean their houses, do their laundry. No more salmon, cheap meat or hand-crafted moccasins."

"It is dreadful when the citizens of Victoria think only of the inconvenience to them that the smallpox epidemic causes," Alice remarked.

He scoffed at that. "These are my orders, Miss. They say burn the village, and I burn. What else can I do? The women should have taken their children before we set fire."

"Don't you know that Indian women married to white men could not leave Victoria," Tahoma told him. "The women would not leave their children, and the men will not let their children leave with their wives. Now they are homeless. Without clothing, pots or food! That is unchristian, just plain wrong!"

Tahoma was baptized and had worked first for the Hudson's Bay Company. He was well respected among his people as well as the English-speaking community. He surveyed the devastated village. What could he do? There were many families left without homes. He couldn't ask Alice to take them all, but perhaps his aunt and her children.

"Alice, will you give a room to Esther and the children, at least until her husband returns and can rebuild."

"Of course, I will."

"Thank you, Alice," Esther said with tears in her eyes, "But I ask you, please take this one with us. She is all alone. Her mother and father died in the fire. Her two brothers and two little sisters taken as well. Mary has nowhere to go. She is a good girl. A Christian from a devout family."

"Yes," Alice agreed. "I'm sure I can find room."

Tahoma thought of the daughter Alice had lost, the girl who died of starvation in the Sierra Mountains, a girl who would have been about the same age as Mary. He wondered if the orphaned girl

ALICE ACKERMAN: THE CHILCOTIN SAGA

would bring back painful memories that Alice tried hard to leave behind.

Tahoma and Alice led the family and Mary to his canoe and paddled across James Bay. Night had fallen, and the moon's reflection shone across the water. It was eerily calm and quiet, as if the souls of the Songhees were departing this Earth and creating a spell of gloom.

Alice smiled sympathetically at Mary. "I'm so sorry about your family."

The girl was slight with black eyes and bones as thin as a gull's. She was clean and neat, with her long, black hair plaited.

"Father Mouchet told me I have the three angels to look after me: Hope, Faith and Charity." Mary spoke in perfect English. "He promised me the angels would also look after my loved ones in Heaven, so I needn't be so sad. My mother and father's work on Earth is done, and they needed a rest. My little brothers and sisters will help in the Lord's work." She had a peaceful face, as if blessed.

Alice couldn't help her tears from falling. *Could the Native people take more tragedy? First the disease, then the death of their loved ones and destruction of their homes. It was their land for God's sake!*

Tahoma paddled to the wharf near the fort, and the grieving group clambered up the rocky bank. Alice and Tahoma led the family to her establishment and asked the staff to get rooms ready for them.

"What is our mistress thinking?" Molly scowled as she carried sheets upstairs. "The filthy Indians should leave Victoria. They should know better than to impose on good citizens."

"Where is your Christian spirit?" Kate replied. "You are Irish and have for years been persecuted by the English. Don't turn your back on the poor now that you have a position and a few pretty dresses."

Both women were young, chubby and happy to be in the Colonies.

After they settled into their temporary lodgings at the Eatery, Esther worked for Alice, cooking in the restaurant while her two children and Mary attended the mission school in Victoria. Alice felt at ease with her guests. Mary was exceedingly independent for one so young. She helped dress the two younger children for school. She said her prayers each night and grace before dinner. She was sweetness itself, not pushing her pious ideas on others but following the words of Jesus in everything she did.

Mary helped bring harmony to Alice's life. Gradually, Alice was able to feel love for the child, and Mary loved the kind, sad woman who had given her a home.

While there was peace in Alice's home, it was just the opposite in Charlotte and Robert's. He couldn't make a decision without his wife's approval. Now there was a child, born early. So early that it left questions as to who had fathered the child. Not something Homfray questioned; he would not have dared. Besides, from the moment Annette was born, Homfray was devoted to her. She was a beautiful baby, whom Homfray adored much as he'd once cherished Charlotte.

He often took Annette for walks in her carriage, partly to remove himself from the unhappy household. Charlotte's temper was always close to the surface, snapping at Homfray and criticizing him for the slightest mistake.

Charlotte also targeted her father. He was in his early sixties, but worry had aged him. His once fine woollen suit sagged, and his shirts were no longer laundered and starched. Mr. Dupré had spent his savings on the investments in the Bute Road. He had nothing to offer Charlotte. She offered no respect, no sweet smiles, no hugs. He felt abandoned.

Bute Inlet Road construction would begin in the spring. Mr. Dupré, along with hundreds of investors, counted on it opening and showing a profit.

Homfray's modest salary afforded a rented house on Yates Street, a two-storey frame house that was cramped and cold with mould in the basement. The bare floorboards were scuffed by previous renters, and the roof leaked. Demands for housing increased, and costs skyrocketed as thousands of prospectors poured into Victoria. Many houses were hurriedly thrown up.

Homfray was employed to survey lots for the town. He had a fair wage but never enough to meet their obligations. The only joy he had was his daughter, Annette.

Alice met him one Sunday afternoon during her walk around James Bay. Ships sat in the calm water, gently rocked by the swells. Seagulls wheeled overhead as Homfray pushed Annette in her carriage.

"Robert, I haven't seen you since Annette was born. How are you?"

"Fine," he replied without conviction.

"The baby must be two months old now," she said, changing the subject and looking at the healthy child. "And how is sweet Annette. She is a beautiful baby."

Robert beamed and looked at the child, his face almost rapturous when he smiled at his daughter.

"She is sweetness itself I can't imagine living without her."

"Why do you say that? Of course, you won't have to be without her." He had a tormented expression when he looked at Alice.

"I must get home; Charlotte took an afternoon nap and will be waking soon. She doesn't like it when I walk too long. I bid you good day, Alice." He paused. "You and David have been true friends."

There was a sadness in his demeanour that Alice recognized. She had spent years mourning her daughter and saw in Robert's expression the same deep sorrow that had afflicted her for years.

What could be troubling him so much? He had been so taken with Charlotte before they married. Now when he spoke of Charlotte, he was miserable. Many things about the young woman bothered Alice. What sort of mother slept on a Sunday instead of walking with her husband and child? But then Alice had always thought that Charlotte loved the social life more than child-rearing.

CHAPTER SEVEN

Victoria, Spring 1862

Smallpox

The saloon was dark, smelled like wet dog and was crowded with miners waiting for passage across Georgia Strait. Most were heading for the Fraser River, but Jim Taylor and his partner Angus McLeod had recently returned from Bentinck Arm. They were packers for Alex MacDonald, and there was a trail from Bentinck Arm to Fort Alexandria. It was a rival to the Bute Inlet Road but was farther up the coast and one that would take miners longer to reach the goldfields.

"Never seen anything like it," Angus crowed. "Them Injuns just dyin' like flies. From Ogden Point to Nancootlem, they are dying by the hundreds. We could smell the dead a mile off. Smallpox is a gift from heaven, don't ya think? Well, the Injun, he gets them pocks one day, and the next day he's dead. Rid the country of them varmints." McLeod was a recently arrived miner from the goldfields of California.

"Ya, we do them in real good, don't you figure?" Jim was his partner on the Bentinck Arm trail. He had been drinking whisky since early afternoon. It was almost closing time, and his tongue had loosened. "Ya, we done 'em in real good."

Angus didn't like what Jim was saying. "You shut your trap."

"Why should I? They ain't gonna prove nothing."

Miners from the U.S., Hawaii and Britain sat in the dank saloon, bored and eager to listen to a story. "Tell us what you mean, Jim."

"I said to close your beer hole, Jim," Angus insisted.

"I gotta tell them. It's a good joke on them savages." Jim spat a wad in the spittoon and wiped his mouth on his dirty sleeve. "You know what we gone and done?" He paused to gulp his beer. "We took the blankets off the rotting dead and sold them to the healthy savages in the next village. Nancootlem it was. They thought we gave them a bargain instead we gave 'em smallpox." He laughed, gagging on his drink. Jim stumbled from his chair and weaved to the door, still cackling. "My boss man, Poole, he done come up with the idea. 'Smallpox would clear the country of Injuns,' he said. Well, we cleared it. Now there is not one dirty Injun left in that there village."

"Don't repeat this story," Angus spoke low to the miners. "He is so tanked up, he don't know what he's sayin."

"Is it true like he said that all the people in Nancootlem are sick?" Walter asked. He had listened to Jim Taylor's story with a sick feeling his stomach.

Walter was sitting with his nephew, Matike. Walter was a friend of Alice and David from their days on the Oregon Trail. He had married into the Musquem tribe and had a successful sawmill business. He had also packed for Angus. Baptiste overheard him.

"We saw one old man, all pock-marked," Baptiste said. "He was sitting by a fire yelling at the whites, 'Cultus white man,' he shouted. 'Cultus white man bring smallpox. Kill all my people.' He was crazy with hatred; *cultus* means 'evil.' Would have killed Angus and his men if he could stand and hold a musket."

Walter turned to Matike and whispered, "There's going to be trouble. They purposely infected a Tŝilhqot'in village."

Matike shrugged. "They will reap what they sow."

"Most of the rabble rousers in this dump don't care. All they want is to get to the goldfields. If the Natives die, they think it will clear the land for them," Walter said. "I think I'll do my drinking somewhere else in the future so I don't have to listen to them spewing their hatred for Indians. Before the gold rush, the Musquem people were respected. Gave the whites salmon, saved miners and explorers from starving! Now the miners take the salmon for themselves, so much salmon that there is little left for the Musquem."

"They say because of Darwin's theory of natural selection that they have rights. That they are superior, and if the Indians die out that proves the theory." Matike was a historian for the Musquem, well read and political. "The newcomers use that as an excuse to kill off the Indians. The tribes have been here forever; the miners just two years."

"Ten thousand died from smallpox this year alone. Maybe more. I'm surprised the Indians don't go to war to save their lives and the salmon," Walter said as they walked out of the saloon and into the fresh, cool air.

"There has never been an Indian war in the British Colonies, not a real war."

"Wait until Waddington tries to build a road through Tŝilhqot'in country; then we'll see," Walter mused. "Tŝilhqot'in warriors don't have much patience; it might be the flame that starts a war."

"Let's go to the Eatery. It's Alice's place, and can she ever cook! I was with David and Alice on the Oregon Trail in '46," Walter said. "Alice made delicious stews and pies, while my first wife spent the days sleeping. But that is far in the past." Walter shook his head and changed the subject. "David should be back from the Fraser River goldfields. I want to have a confab with him and a cup of that good Nicaraguan coffee that Alice makes."

"Better than the chicory we have on the Fraser River gold diggings."

"You mean that watery, tasteless, brown slop they try to tell us is coffee?" Walter smiled and looked at his nephew. He could see the resemblance to his wife, Matike's aunt. Matike was a tall, muscular young man, so beautiful that he turned heads of the young women, both white and Native.

The two walked along James Bay, enjoying the fresh breeze off the water. Ships floated in the bay, lit by the evening sunset.

They saw Robert Homfray ahead of them, stumbling along the street, barely able to walk. As he approached Alice's Eatery, he stumbled and groaned, as if in terrible pain. Walter caught him just as he reached the door to the roadhouse.

"Hold on, man. I've got you." Matike held the door for them while Walter supported the sick man, easing him onto the chair beside the hearth.

"Git that drunk outa here." This came from an unkempt miner shovelling down his meal of beans and pork chops. The other patrons looked on, some with disgust, others, who recognized Homfray, with concern.

"This is my restaurant. Hold your tongue," Alice said bending down to check Homfray's hot forehead. Homfray gagged and his stomach heaved. "Quick, Mary, fetch me a basin." As soon as Mary put the basin on the floor, he spewed the contents of his supper, retching and holding his aching stomach, obviously in pain.

"That's good, Robert," Alice said holding his head over the basin. "Get it all out." She wiped his face with a cool cloth. Robert sat back in the comfort of the chair, breathing heavily and holding his stomach. His face was pale, and he was shaking.

"What can I do to help?" David asked. He had stood back watching, along with several patrons in the eatery.

"Will you come with me to inform Charlotte?" Alice put on a light shawl and turned hurriedly to Walter.

"Walter would you please take Robert to the hospital, then meet us at Charlotte's? My horse and carriage are in the stable at the back."

David and Alice ran through the dimly lit streets. David held her hand lest she slip or catch her feet on the rough boards of the wooden sidewalk. They slowed as they approached Homfray's house, caught their breath and knocked. Charlotte met them at the door, an engaging smile on her face.

"Oh, hello. What brings you here?"

"We have some bad news, Charlotte. It's Homfray."

She looked flustered. "Is he…alive?"

"Yes. He is still alive," Alice said, still breathless from running, "But very sick, maybe cholera, smallpox or something that has upset his stomach. Walter and Matike took him to the hospital and will be here shortly."

Charlotte continued to look dumbfounded. "Would you like some tea?" She said, moving to the parlour. "We could sit, and you can tell me everything you know." She smiled sweetly.

"No, thank you, Charlotte," David said, somewhat bewildered. "Walter took him to the hospital, and we thought you would go immediately to your husband. Walter said he would meet us here with our carriage to take you to the hospital."

Alice glanced out the window, noticing flies on the sill and the torn curtains. "I believe he just drove up."

"Oh, yes, but…there's the baby."

"Could you ask your father to watch over her?" Alice asked, puzzled by Charlotte's response but reminded herself that everyone reacts to tragedy differently.

"Yes, of course," Charlotte said. "I must tidy myself a little first. Put on another dress. Talk to Father."

David shook his head, disbelieving. Both David and Alice could not understand her lack of empathy. They waited for Charlotte for some time, taking in the cluttered room and worn furniture.

"What's taking her so long?" David asked.

"Her father may have been sleeping. He is elderly and not well. I'm confident he'll be here shortly."

"Women can be unpredictable, can't they? Would you change your dress and tidy your hair if I was clinging to life?" he said, smiling at Alice.

"Well, it would depend on whether you have been treating me properly," she gave a little laugh. Joking was not common for her.

At last Charlotte appeared, looking well-groomed and dressed in a mauve silk gown, with a wide skirt, supported by crinolines. She had put on pounds since the birth of her child. She tried to keep an hourglass figure with the help of a tight corset.

"We hope Robert will recover," Mr. Dupré said, standing at Charlotte's side. "What happened to him? Charlotte didn't say."

Alice realised that Charlotte had not even asked.

"Robert appears to have eaten something that has made him very ill," Alice replied. "Did he eat anything rancid, Charlotte?"

"Well, that there might be an answer to the mystery." She paused thinking carefully about her words. "Robert likes to take Annette for walks every Sunday." She spoke with a pleasant demeanour. "I woke from my nap before Robert's return and decided to gather some wild mushrooms. They would be tasty with a stew of beef and carrots. As soon as I tasted the stew, I knew right away that something didn't taste quite right. Isn't that the truth, Father?" Mr. Dupré nodded, and Charlotte continued. "I threw the stew and those deadly mushrooms out, but not before Robert had eaten his first bowl. I...I saved his life, I did."

She is a bald-faced liar, David thought.

With Charlotte finally ready to go to the hospital, they all crowded into the carriage for the trip. Charlotte chatted amicably the whole time.

Homfray was still with the doctor when they arrived, so David and Alice left Charlotte at the hospital. The sun had set by the time Walter returned the carriage to Alice's roadhouse.

"Will you come with me to hear Waddington talk about his Bute Inlet Road?" David said. "I want to see who is supporting his lies this time."

"Not me," Alice replied. "I've heard enough from that braggart."

"We'll come with you," Walter replied. "We were on our way to ask you to go when we came upon Homfray. Yes, of course, we want to hear what the old windbag is spouting tonight."

The men walked through the streets of Victoria to the hall where Waddington was to speak. "Do you know that Homfray will be in hospital for the week?" Walter asked. "He's very sick from the death cap mushrooms, but according to Dr. Helmcken, he will survive."

"Would your wife ever mistake death cap mushrooms for edible ones?" David asked Walter.

"No, never. She could write the book on mushrooms."

CHAPTER EIGHT
Victoria, Late Autumn 1862

Mary

The theatre was crowded with more than three hundred investors, local politicians and the curious. They had waited an hour for Waddington to speak. On the wall of the big room were the maps showing Bute Inlet, the Fraser River and Bentinck Arm.

"So, he has Jim McNeil, or Lefty, telling lies this time. Why do these men perjure themselves?" David asked.

"Money, power and lack of moral compass, but mostly money," Walter whispered.

"Well, here is the man of the hour at last." David was not happy to listen to Waddington's spin once again.

The developer came to the stage to loud applause. The old man clapped as he came forward. Waddington waited as the audience applauded. He clapped all the time as if praising himself, then raised his hands to quiet the crowd. His voice boomed across the theatre.

"I was ridiculed and laughed at when I first brought this marvellous project to the people of Victoria. One of the newspapers even wrote fake stories about my road and about me, if you can imagine." He grinned. "How dare they! How dare they!"

The audience chanted, "How dare they," mesmerized by his lofty rhetoric.

"I have proven the route. Yes, proven that the road will be built. Mr. McNeil walked the route last year. A fine gentleman. Let's give him a hand."

The audience was with him and would believe anything he said. Waddington was so admired. They believed he would make them rich.

"Do you want to take Governor Douglas's route along the dangerous Fraser Canyon or take Douglas's route through Harrison Lakes and unload and reload your pack mules fourteen times?"

"No!" they replied.

"Fourteen times, can you fathom? Or do you want to take Bute Inlet and unload once before reaching Fraser River goldfields?"

"Bute Inlet!" they chanted.

"Do you want to pay sixteen cents a pound on Douglas's route?"

"No!"

"Or pay eight cents a pound on Bute Inlet Road?"

"Bute Inlet!"

"Would you prefer a route of only two hundred miles, over two small hills and then through a grassy plain on the Bute Inlet Road?"

"The Bute Inlet Road! The Bute Inlet Road!" they yelled, fired up by the thought of getting to goldfields so quickly, and so cheaply, and excited by Waddington's speech.

The applause was deafening. Waddington clapped along then raised his hands once again to bring silence.

"Thank you, good people of Victoria. Thank you." The applause continued. Waddington waited for the noise in the theatre to quiet down.

"I know many of you fine people want to invest in this road. Tonight, and only tonight, I will let four hundred shares go at one hundred dollars each. To show my commitment, I have invested five thousand dollars myself. Yes, five thousand." The audience erupted in cheers.

"I want each and every one of you to prosper. Yes, I want to make you rich. You can make your investments at Captain Nagle's office or McDonald's Bank. Don't delay. I don't want you to be disappointed. This is the surest investment you will make for your family and your heirs."

David walked out of the theatre, shaking his head. Walter joined him.

"They believe him. Can't they see through his lies?" David said.

"Waddington is a scoundrel of the first order. He will bilk people of thousands and get the hornets aroused."

"You mean the Tŝilhqot'in warriors."

Victoria, Spring 1863

Alice was cleaning the restaurant, singing as she went about her work. Esther had left with her two children to live at Ogden Point. Only Mary had stayed. The girl turned nine that spring, but she was troubled, and Alice could not place why. Alice paused in her work, thinking she had to find out. Little Mary had become quiet, not sharing her thoughts anymore.

Alice put her dust rag and broom away. Cleaning could wait. It was a beautiful clear day with blue skies, and the bright noon sun poured in through the windows. Alice decided to meet Mary at her school. It would be a pleasant walk along James Bay to the Catholic girls' school with the sun flashing its light across the ocean and the fresh smell of spring.

The girls were lined up at the door ready to be dismissed. Mary was the only Native child because most of the Songhees families had left Victoria after the fire.

Once the girls were free of the Catholic sisters, they ran into the sunshine. Mary walked over to join them.

"You can't walk with us, you dirty Indian."

"Forgot to wear your moccasins? Trying to look like us, are you?"

Several girls looked on, not interfering but uncomfortable with the unkind words.

Alice was listening and could not stand the hateful words. "You should be ashamed of yourselves. That is not the Christian way."

The tall girl scoffed. "The Indians should move away. They don't belong in Victoria or in our school. They'll give us smallpox."

"Come, Mary. Let's take you somewhere else. It seems Victoria is no place for your people anymore."

That evening, Alice spoke to David about moving. "I've decided that Mary and I are going to move to the Fraser River goldfields. It is part of your district. We'll see more of you, and Mary will be happier. What do you think?"

"You are your own woman, my dear. Of course, I want you close by. Besides, all the action is happening around Quesnellemouth. You should do well with your roadhouse." He lit his cigarette and stubbed out the match on his fine leather boot. "There's been a recent gold strike by Billy Barker, a day's ride from Quesnellemouth. All the miners will pass through and want to order your delicious flapjacks." He smiled, thinking how Alice had loved to cook for her friends on the Oregon Trail.

CHAPTER NINE

Bute Inlet, Spring 1863

Brewster

The *Enterprise* sailed into Bute Inlet after a smooth crossing of Georgia Strait. There were ninety men on board—choppers, bridge builders, a cook and a ton of supplies. All the men were in the employ of Alfred Pendrell Waddington. Governor Seymour of the new Colony of British Columbia had granted Waddington a lease to build his road, and Waddington had grand plans. There would be a townsite on the flat land, a road stretching miles into the Chilcotin plateau all the way to Fort Alexandria and to the new goldfields.

Waddington disembarked first and surveyed the land that would become his townsite. He strutted about, proud as a peacock.

"A beautiful piece of land, isn't it, Brewster?" His road crew manager joined him as the supplies were unloaded.

"We'll have to tear down the Indian shacks first." Brewster was a toughened man with a hard face. He had come from working in the goldfields of California where his job was to manage the men and get the job done.

"Indeed," Waddington agreed. "We can't stop progress now, can we?"

"No, Mr. Waddington, we cannot. I'll have the place cleared today. The Indians can pitch their miserable houses anywhere."

But their homes weren't miserable houses at all; they were huge and solid, built along the river from the towering cedar trees that framed the valley.

"Have the men start on the storehouse. The road will follow the river." Mr. Waddington pointed up the slow-moving Homathko

River, where mountains soared in the distance. "I can't understand how my man, Homfray, encountered so many difficulties. It is a marvellous flat trail for miles. This will be the greatest project since the building of the Great Wall of China. You must finish the road this year, Brewster, so we can start packing supplies across to the goldfields next spring as soon as the snow melts."

"I'll try my best, if the savages don't give us no problems."

"They won't. I parlayed with them last year. Gave them gifts. They are the friendliest tribes, willing to do anything." Waddington looked at his future townsite, his workman busy unloading supplies. Then he saw the Indigenous men waiting for any small task they could carry out for the price of a little food. "They are gathered around like vultures waiting for a feast. The tribes might be sorely disappointed when they see we've brought mules to do the packing, but that is how we do business, Brewster. Get the most for our inves-tors' money, don't you agree?"

"For me, I'd rather not hire a single savage." Brewster was a newcomer to the colony and had not dealt with the Indigenous Peoples before. He had already developed a strong prejudice. "Lazy bastards, all of them."

"You must treat with the tribes fairly, now. Don't allow the men to fraternize with the women and never abuse them. Pay them promptly when they work for you—guns and blankets, not food."

"You have a way with the Injuns, boss. I don't have the time of day for them. We will use the mules and won't need them for nothin'."

"What about the Tŝilhqot'in?" It was Russell who spoke up. He was younger, a tall, strong man who had worked for the Hudson's Bay Company. "Will they have any objections when we reach the pass and cross into their land? You only met with the Homathko last year. You have not met the Tŝilhqot'in. You can't foresee what their reaction will be."

"I can handle dem varmints," Brewster wiped the sweat from his face. There was not even a breeze as the sun beat down on the valley, trapping the air. "In any case, I'm told the Tŝilhqot'in tribe doesn't come down from the plateau until the salmon run in the autumn. By that time, we'll have the road built."

The people of the Homathko and the Nuxalk tribes gathered while the supplies were unloaded, waiting patiently, some smoking and others standing about talking. When the mules were led off, an angry murmur rose from the crowd.

"Old Ty'hee lie to us! Promised work. He bring his beasts instead." The chief of the Homathko tribe spoke to the tribes gathered at the site. "We welcomed many ships in the past; we met Waddington last year. He promised food for our labour."

Several Homathko members spoke, their anger building as they recounted the white man's dishonesty.

"The white man always lies."

"I go tell him he lies. I speak King George's tongue."

"It won't do any good," the Klahoose chief said, joining the group. "Leave it. Do you really think the proud Tŝilhqot'in will let the British bring their axes and mules across *their* land?"

"Not without paying to cross their land."

"The Old Ty'hee will take the ship back to Victoria," the Klahoose chief added. "Leave us with the man with the angry face. Watch out for him. He's trouble."

The Klahoose chief could speak a little English. This was Yay K Wum, the same chief who had rescued Homfray from near death and saved the seven men by getting his men to paddle them to Victoria.

The Klahoose chief angrily confronted Brewster. "Old Ty'hee said he give us work. We all willing, good workers. We work for food." The chief paused sizing up Brewster. "You people sent us the smallpox," he said, becoming frustrated with the white man.

He wondered why Brewster treated them with such disdain when the Klahoose had been the one to save the starving crew, took them to his village, fed them salmon and even clothed them. "The salmon don't come yet. Our people are hungry. We work for food."

Brewster was impatient. "You vamoose now. We have work to do. Your packers aren't needed."

"Old Ty'hee lie," the chief grumbled. "White man's word changes like the wind."

It was Brewster's job to deal with the tribes, but he had no experience. Brewster planned to make the laws for his camp without any meddling from the governor.

The tribe's houses were built along the Homathko River for twenty kilometres, exactly where the road was going.

"These houses must go. Clear them off," he ordered his men. Brewster's task was to build a large storehouse and a cabin on the flat land, and to drive a road through to Fort Alexandria on the Fraser River. The crew dismantled the huge dwellings, not caring if the women and children were still inside. A few women managed to drag their heavy cedar boxes out before the crew brought the roof down on them. The boxes held their main food supply until the salmon came in the autumn. Others carried rolls of dried berries. People screamed and wailed as the crew set fire to their homes.

Russell had been at the Fraser River blockade in 1858 when the American militia burned the villages. He didn't like it then, and he didn't like it now.

"How would you feel if strangers arrived in your town and pulled down your house?" Russell yelled at the crew members that were ripping the sides off a fishing shack. The men looked at him as if he was crazy.

"The boss orders us to take down the houses. We take dem down, or we lose our pay."

Disturbed by the destruction of the homes of the Natives, Russell approached Brewster.

"Can't you understand the Indians have rights? Douglas issued a proclamation protecting Indian houses, fishing huts and gardens. Don't you see the hatred in their eyes?" He was so angry he was hesitant to speak to Brewster lest he lose control of his temper and smash the man.

"Why should we give a damn?" Brewster scoffed. "They're just savages. Douglas ain't here; Waddington doesn't give a damn; and neither do I. Burn the houses, men. Don't listen to this pussy."

Russell turned away, mumbling, "You will reap what you sow."

The people were angry; the women were crying, their children clinging to them. The elders huddled together, wondering what to do.

That night the crew members sat around a fire, eating steaks and biscuits. The hungry, homeless people sat in small groups, grumbling. Did the white men not remember the many times we fed them, guided them? Is this how they repay our friendship? We are the people who rescued that stupid King George man. The one who tried to cross the pass when snows were up to his ass. Not only are they mean; they are stupid.

Two small children crept up to the fire, smelling the roasting meat. They had to have food. Their mother had kept a supply of smoked salmon and rolls of dried berries in the huts, but most was lost in the flames. The four-year-old took his smaller brother's hand and approached the men. Their eyes were on the food, pleading with the men. Russell passed a chunk of meat to the children. Brewster saw this.

"Don't feed them brats." Before Russell could object, Brewster grabbed the meat from the boys and tossed it to the dogs.

"Skedaddle, you little varmints. No food for your lazy folks either." He swatted their backsides as they ran from him, wailing.

"Why did you do that, Brewster? It's just not right," Russell said. "First you destroy their homes and their food supply, and now you deny a scrap for the children. You are disgusting."

"And you had best shut your beer hole, or I'll send you back on the next ship without pay. Then your wife and children will starve. We have a road to build, and the Injuns will be paid in blankets and guns. Absolutely no food. Those are my orders. I won't have some Brit with an upper-class attitude countering me. So put that in your pipe and smoke it!"

"Did Waddington give you those orders? I heard Waddington tell the Indians they could work for food."

"That is not what Waddington told me. He says one thing to the Injuns and another to me. Now he is on the ship to Victoria. I'm in charge, and I give the orders. There is only enough food for the crew. No food for the Injuns. We don't want 'em hanging around and begging."

The tribes spoke among themselves reminding each other of the times they helped the white men, fed them, saved them.

The Homathko chief spoke, "We have always been friendly to the whites. My ancestors met King George's man, Vancouver, when he visited these waters. My grandmother told me. We remember."

An old man spoke up in a reedy voice. He spoke slowly. "I was told by my grandparents of the Spanish who came to our shores in big ships. Many, many winters and summers ago. Too long for anyone to remember." Tiring easily, he waited, sipped his tea and continued.

"The grandparents told us about the Spanish captain. He wanted to take a small ship up the Homathko. He tried to sail the dangerous tidal narrows. There is only a short time with slack waters. Of course, they did not heed the Homathko People. The ship spun 'round and 'round in the rapids," he laughed thinking about the incident. "They almost breeched on the rocky cliffs. That is the same with most whites. They are stupid; they think we know nothing. No respect."

The Klahoose chief spoke up, telling them of the young, skinny man who tried to wade through the snow. "We saved his skin when the plundering murderers were going to kill them, then he wanted us to guide him across the pass. He wouldn't listen to us when we said that no one crosses when the snow covers the pass. Dumb as a prairie chicken. And the whites think they are superior."

By autumn, the rough road covered twenty kilometres up to the first crossing of the Homathko. It was late August, and the Tŝilhqot'in started to arrive. They were waiting for the salmon run. The Tŝilhqot'in were taken aback at the destruction of the lodges. They had relatives among the Homathko, family who would normally offer the tribe food and shelter.

Homeless and hungry they talked in small groups, watching the road crew.

"Old Ty'hee said there would be work, and we would be fed," the Klahoose chief grumbled to the others. The Tŝilhqot'in, the Homathko and Nuxalk tribes were all there. "I should have let Old Ty'hee's men die. Why did I send my men across to Victoria to risk their lives in the middle of winter? Is this fair? They are greedy men. Men who don't respect us. Is this how they thank us? Next time we let them die; they are fools."

There was a warehouse filled with food in plain sight. It was a large log structure built on the very land where their houses had been. The hungry people eyed the warehouse, thinking if only their children could eat a little bannock, they would survive 'til the salmon came. There had been less game harvested because small-pox had devastated their people. Many hunters had died of the dis-ease. Soon the women were giving in to offers of food in exchange for sex. Their children had to live. Some of the road crew took the younger girls by force, even the girls who had not had their first bleeding.

A group of children played on the beach, building houses and making a trail in the sand. They were hungry, always hungry. They were waiting for the salmon to come up the river, thousands of them. They remembered how the men would spear and net the fish, and the women would gut them and dry them slowly over smoldering the fires. The dried salmon was just like candy to the children. They tried not to think of food.

Olahl was eleven, the oldest of the children playing. Soon she would be too old to be with the youngsters. But she loved playing. As daughter of the Tŝilhqot'in chief, she was special.

She saw twelve men, all unkempt, roughly dressed, some with beards, none had kind eyes like the white man she had seen last winter. Olahl had met Homfray two years ago when her uncle gave the seven hungry explorers a place to sleep and food to eat. She remembered he was a gentle man. She had thought all King George's men were good like him.

One of the men offered biscuits to the children. They were hungry and tired from their long trek over the pass. Olahl felt a niggle of worry and held back even though the sight of the biscuits made her mouth water.

Then the men turned to watch her.

"Beautiful squaw," said one of the men. "And young."

He had small, beady eyes and a large belly held in at his waist by a wide belt. He walked up to her leering, smelling like rotten salmon.

"I daughter of Lhats'as?in." She made signs to show that she was hungry and wanted to eat.

The men all laughed. "The pretty little squaw thinks we are going to give her food." They guffawed in chorus. She only understood the word squaw but did not mistake their intentions.

"Smelly Breath" looked at her. She was afraid but also desperately hungry. She put her hand to her mouth again to show them she needed food. Smelly Breath moved close to her and reached to touch her breast. Now Olahl was terrified. She kicked him and turned to run, but the man caught her. She screamed and struggled but was powerless in his grip. She hated his smell. She hated his fat belly.

The other men chuckled and followed as their mate dragged Olahl to the dock and onto the boat.

Her parents searched for Olahl all night and through the morning of the following day. They were frantic with worry, as was Olaha's brother. They could not find her. It was if she had vanished into thin air. Then they thought of the river. It had been unusually hot yesterday. The smaller children had been playing near the water. Olahl couldn't swim.

Tears streamed down Olahl's mother's face. She thought this was surely her daughter's fate. She stopped two boys playing on the shore, little ones maybe three and four. "My daughter, pretty with long braids. She is lost. Did you she her?"

The boys didn't speak Tŝilhqot'in and looked puzzled, even a little scared by the fierce-looking, distraught woman. "Tell me! Olahl. Did you see her?"

Then they understood. They pointed to the boat at the end of the wharf before running off to find their parents.

Olahl's family found her unconscious, bleeding body in the boat. Lhats'as?in's anger burned as he untied the ropes binding her frail body.

"I'll kill them all, Olahl. This must be revenged. They will die for this. I'll kill them all."

Olahl's mother carried her bruised body up the trail to the Tŝilhqot'in encampment. There, she washed her gently, lamenting over her injuries. "Poor baby. My poor little girl."

She carefully applied healing oil to Olahl's sores and wrapped her wrists and ankles in soft rabbit skins. Olahl didn't speak. She was numb and in pain. Her mother nursed her for a week. She told the other women in camp that Olahl would never have a child. The women muttered their hatred for the men who did this to a child. Soon Lhats'as?in knew the extent of Olahl's injuries.

Olahl was ashamed to talk about the rape, of the horrible men who took her over and over. She only confided in Peille, her big brother. With him, she poured out her rage and humiliation. She told him that she felt like sinking a knife into her chest, but first she wanted her father to sink a knife into every one of the stinking, horrible men who had violated her.

"I can't live after this. I am ruined." Peille took her in his arms as she sobbed.

Her father couldn't bear the thought of his child being raped by these wicked white men. He flew into a rage. Her shame had to be avenged. He could not walk away from it. "This is war!" he shouted to the sky.

Olahl did not recover. She lay on the mat in their tent. Her sores and cuts healed somewhat, but she would never fully recover from the brutal attack. She was wounded for life.

It was late in the year when the crew boarded the ship and left Bute Inlet.

"Don't say a word about the little squaw," Brewster ordered his men. "Waddington doesn't take offence when we have one of their women, but if he found out about the girl, he would take away all your pay."

"We won't say a word, Boss. We ain't stupid."

"Not sure about that." Brewster smirked to himself.

The men huddled together as the ferry took them over the quiet sea of the Georgia Strait.

A recent recruit from the goldfields spoke up. "Why didn't Waddington give them Injuns food? They was starving. I don't care for Injuns that much, but the little ones with their bloated bellies beggin' for scraps and that Brewster grabbing the food from their mouths and tossing it to the dogs. That just ain't right."

"We won't even tell anyone about the women who gave their bodies so they could feed their children and themselves. Me wife would kick me out if she knew."

"If only Old Waddy had given the tribes food instead of muskets. Was the project so ill-funded that they couldn't spare a few sacks of flour?"

Once the crew left, Lhats'as?in climbed up to his encampment to visit his broken, injured daughter. He stayed by Olahl's side, cursing the men who had done this, hating himself for not being able to protect her.

"I'll kill them all! Mutilate them. Cut their testicles off, their filthy heads off their ugly bodies. I promise you Olahl. I promise."

CHAPTER TEN

Bute Inlet, Spring 1864

Lhats'as?in

Frederick Whymper walked up the Homathko Valley entranced by the spectacular scenery. It was sublime. The artist had been hired by Waddington to sketch the views so Waddington could use the paintings to advertise the road. As he walked the route, Whymper took notes: the purple cliffs rose, pine clad and abrupt, whilst below the Homathko River made its way to the sea. Whymper took little notice of the starving, homeless people. Instead, he walked and climbed, oblivious to their suffering.

Snow still covered the pass when the road crew returned. Brewster was still in charge.

"What the hell is this?" Brewster yelled as the men opened the warehouse. "We left sacks of flour, sugar, grain. Those damn savages stole it! I'll have their heads for this," Brewster fumed. He realized they would have to send another ship from Bute Inlet to Victoria and back to replenish their supplies. "Rice and beans. That is what we have to eat until Old Waddy can send us more flour. Them Injuns won't get away with this."

Brewster did not see any of the tribes for a week. Then, a group of Tŝilhqot'in arrived at the Inlet looking for work.

Brewster approached Lhats'as?in, yelling at the chief and pointing his finger. "I know you sneaky bastards broke into our warehouse. I should have you all whipped! But if you admit to your thievery, I will let you work off the cost."

Lhats'as?in understood what Brewster was saying but refused to answer the crew boss in English. Brewster was the man responsible for his daughter's rape. Lhats'as?in tried to control his fury and turned his back on Brewster.

"Don't walk away from me when I'm talkin' to you." Brewster grabbed at the chief's shirt. Lhats'as?in slapped his hand away.

I could kill him with one swat, Lhats'as?in thought. *They might hang me, but it would be worth it.*

The chief towered over Brewster. The crew boss was in his forties, ruddy and hardened from his years of working outdoors, but he was no match for the sinewy chief.

"Hey, I told you to come here," Brewster commanded.

"You in our country." Lhats'as?in spoke in English. "You owe us bread,"

This enraged Brewster.

"What do you mean your country? I'll show you Injuns who's in charge here and whose country it is." He took out a pencil and his notebook. "Ask each of them bloody varmints their handles," Brewster commanded the blond-haired sea captain.

"I don't understand them. They speak gibberish."

"You." Brewster pointed at the interpreter. "Squinteye. Help him." The interpreter went to each Tŝilhqot'in and blond-hair wrote down the names as best as he could.

"Why you take our names?" someone grumbled in faltering English.

"He's doing as he is told, taking down your names because you would not tell us who stole the flour," Brewster answered.

"We don't like. Don't put names in your book. You steal them."

Brewster ignored their objections. Who did they think they were to tell him he can't write their names? And what did they mean when they said he was stealing their names? The only stealing here was them Injuns stealing his flour.

"Someone stole our flour, and I'm going to find the thief. If I have to put you all in chains, I will! Savages all of you. Just a bunch of savages."

Brewster fumed and then made a threat that the Tŝilhqot'in heard and would not forget. "All the Tŝilhqot'in are going to die if you don't tell me who stole the flour. If I don't find the bloody thieves, we shall send sickness into the country that will kill you all."

The Tŝilhqot'in looked frightened. They huddled in a group and grumbled. An elder recalled how another white man had threatened them with disease two years earlier. He had said that smallpox was coming, and that winter, their village was devastated by the disease. Was this happening again? They knew they could not risk taking this as an idle threat. The white man's disease would kill them all!

Lhats'as?in along with the other Tŝilhqot'in left the Inlet to talk about the threat.

"Those bastards. They take my daughter. They threaten us with disease. Take down our names. Enough. Enough!" He paced back and forth, anger building in his chest. "We should rid ourselves of the whites. Letting them steal our land, take our spring where we drink and water our horses. They take our fish, defile our women." His anger was palpable.

Several of his people agreed. Others advised caution. They wanted work and felt they should wait to see if there were jobs and if they would get food. The Tŝilhqot'in had little to eat. Hunger filled many Tŝilhqot'in with anger; others were tired and submissive. The men begged for work because it was the only way their wives and children would have enough to eat.

Lhats'as?in led his group to the job site. A tall man with piercing blue eyes, he was accustomed to being feared. Brewster stood facing the chief, his arms crossed on his chest, showing disdain, not fear.

"We will hire you, but there will be no wages until the flour you stole is paid off." At first the Tŝilhqot'in chief did not understand. The Tŝilhqot'in knew nothing about the missing flour.

Lhats'as?in refused the work, instead leaving with his followers. He gathered them together, all the time burning with indignation and hatred.

"White men took my daughter. For that I must kill him." He pounded his fist into his hand. "Are you with me? He has offended all of you. He said we stole his flour when we didn't; threatened all of us with the killing disease; took our names down. I have had enough of these whites. They violated my daughter, a girl who has not had her first bleeding. Who do they think they are? It is an act of war!"

The men surrounding him saw the injustice in the actions of the road crew.

"We have to make a stand before our land is overrun by the whites." Lhats'as?in boiled with anger. The war chief had not faced an enemy since the Tŝilhqot'in fought the Carrier invaders. "Stop seeing yourself as individuals but as a body of warriors. Channel your anger."

Lhats'as?in had the men behind him.

"War is a scourge, but there is a time we must fight to save our people," an elder said. He was wizened, wore an embroidered deer skin vest and European cotton pants and a cotton shirt that hung over his thin frame. "They use dynamite to blast the sacred mountain. That is not right. The gold is making them crazier than ever. They will do anything for their greed." He spoke quietly but with passion. "The gold in our rivers is our gold! Isn't this the land our people have lived in for more moons than the whites can count?"

"Those King George men won't pay us for work; they won't share their food though we fed them when they were starving; saved them when they lost their canoe." A warrior spoke up. "Who are these people?"

Lhats'as?in's followers, whipped up by the flame of injustice joined in a chorus of protest. "The poor salmon run means fewer fish in our weirs and traps, fewer for our pronged spears. We won't survive the winter if this continues."

"Our wives sell themselves for scraps of food for the children. It makes my heart sick."

"One of the crew gave a scrap to my little son. I saw that boss man grab the scrap and throw it to the dogs. King George's men are evil."

A younger warrior spoke up. "It's Queen Victoria now, not King George."

"Will she protect us from these filthy men who invade our country?"

"I don't think so. All English are the same. Poison us, kill us, starve us, they only want our land."

CHAPTER ELEVEN

Victoria, May 1864

Massacre

t was spring when the news reached Victoria. *The Colonist* reported the story.

HORRIBLE MASSACRE

The steamer *Emily Harris* arrived from Nanaimo this morning. She brings three men as passengers who are the sole survivors of Waddington's party of seventeen workmen, the remaining fourteen having been massacred by Chilcotin Indians who had been hired to pack for them.

"My God! David!" A worried look crossed Alice's fine features. "Don't tell me the British Territory will be embroiled in an Indian war. I thought the Indians were peaceable in the Colony."

David read the article out loud, shaking his head. "Waddington developed a relationship with the tribes, but sent that foul-mouthed, Indian hater Brewster and his men to build his road. I knew there would be trouble when it became clear he intended to build right through the heart of Indian Territory."

"Remember when we went to hear Waddington speak two years ago? All those people in the theatre listening to him babble on 'til our ears ached." Alice took David's arm and walked with him in the warm spring day.

"Sure do. We listened to the old windbag give his spiel. 'I'll build the finest road to the goldfields. Just a short trip across Georgia Strait and a quick trip over the pass.' A quick trip, he said. I walked the pass myself; it is hazardous. Mountains like the Sierras." David held his fist in a tight knot. "A road would cost thousands because you would have to blast the mountain away. Waddy can't distinguish fact from fiction."

David paused as he helped Alice over the ruts in the streets of Victoria. "He lied about everything, even when he didn't need to lie. A fraud. That's what Waddington is. He thinks he is the greatest, the smartest. The best scientist, best negotiator, best builder. He is nothing but a bald-faced liar."

"But the murders?" she said perplexed. "Why, when you said the Tŝilhqot'in liked Waddington?"

"Waddington's a snake charmer; he makes promises to everyone but never intends to keep them. Then, Brewster stirred the hornets' nest, refusing food to the workers and not controlling his men. And your friend, the handsome Homfray, he is as much to blame. He said nothing but a pack of lies."

"I can't believe he would perjure himself so. He's such a gentle, kind man."

"He was sweet on you," David smiled at Alice. "At least until he met the dazzling Miss Dupré."

"The poor man. He loved her so. Now all is lost for him."

"He was in love with love, a quixotic adventurer, caught up in his passion for a flighty woman and a romantic idea of adventure. Even if Charlotte still loved him, she was not right for him. She is a taker not a giver. The world revolves around the beautiful Charlotte Dupré."

"And Robert was relieved of his position with the Bute Inlet Road. His wife disdains him, and her father lost all his money on

Waddington's road. Now Charlotte will have to live on the modest income Homfray makes, and they still have debts to pay."

"A person can taint his life forever by one mistake," David agreed. A light breeze played on the ocean as they walked along Wharf Street, bordering James Bay. David watched a Songhees family in a canoe, paddling across the bay to the streets of the gold-rush city that was strained to the limit with thousands of newcomers.

"I feel sorry for him even though I know he misled investors," Alice said. "He did it for love, not greed or power."

"Homfray painted himself into a corner. He must live with his crime."

Alice thought back on her own disastrous mistake. She'd married a man she didn't love to keep her fortune away from her brother-in-law. Her foolish decision led to the death of her little daughter.

"That shadow is crossing your face again, my dear friend." David gave her hand a comforting squeeze. "Please let it go, for my sake."

"I'm much better. I promise." Alice realized her depressions affected David, yet he remained by her side. She looked up at him, wondering what he was thinking. Did he miss his family out east, the luxuries of a grand house, his sisters? How many of them? She couldn't remember.

.

CHAPTER TWELVE

Bute Inlet, Spring 1864

Inspector Brew

Inspector Charles Brew, who was called to survey the site of the killings, travelled by boat to Bute Inlet. Brew had immigrated from Ireland in 1859 where he was with the Irish Constabulary. He had a military bearing, and he was broad shouldered and fit in his middle age.

This was the first uprising he'd had to deal with, yet he described each of the fourteen deaths in meticulous detail in his journal. He was a man dedicated to his job, more of a bureaucrat than a field soldier.

But this was different. Native people killing. It didn't make any sense to him. But he had seen the hatred the Irish had for the dominant English and wondered if Tŝilhqot'in felt equally oppressed. Despite his misgivings, he carried out his task thoroughly, writing in his notebook in neat script.

> The place where Openshaw's head lay, there was a large pool of blood.
>
> Brewster was viscously mutilated, his heart cut out. Such savagery!
>
> Plunder was certainly one of the objectives; there can be little doubt, however, that the main object in my view was to put a stop to a road through Tŝilhqot'in Territory. If sound discretion had been exercised toward them, I believe this outrage would not have been perpetrated.

As Brew struggled up the pass, he found minimal progress on the road. The public had been led to believe that the road was near completion.

No just idea of the country can be formed from Waddington's flattering description of it, Brew wrote in his letter to Governor Seymour.

Brew's other task was to meet with the people involved in the road. On his return to Victoria, he asked that Waddington be interviewed at the police station. Waddington was evasive.

"What could you possibly want to ask me? I'm busy. Much to do these days to get that road built. Can't stop progress, can we?" Like most British gentry, he disdained the Irish.

"Well, Sir," Brew began. "There was more white blood shed in one day than there has ever been shed in the Colony. We must get to the cause of the tragedy."

This conversation was held a week before Waddington came to the station. Accompanying him was Alfred Penn, his lawyer.

"What is this all about, Brew?" Penn asked before taking his pipe out and lighting it. Waddington sat beside him, irritated by the young Irishman. Penn was a slight, middle-aged man, impeccably dressed in a topcoat and an embroidered vest. He sat beside the rumpled Waddington and across from the uniformed and muscular Brew. Although it was clear to Brew that Penn was present to intimidate him, he was unruffled. He looked at his papers and began the questioning.

Brew stroked his thick, black beard. "Ken ye please explain for the record how ye thought it possible to build a road through the pass?" He thought these men were not listening to his words, but he continued anyway. "I walked up your road, if you ken call it that. It took me several hours, over the flat part and then scrambling up the ravine. It was near impossible to make my way up the canyon to where Brewster was killed."

Brew's Irish brogue became more pronounced as he remembered the horrors of the scene and the rough country he had walked.

"There it was, a frightening ravine ahead. There is no discernable path, just hundreds of hairpin turns and the need for hundreds of bridges. You say the road to the goldfields was to be finished this year. I do not ken how that could be done. So please explain to me what is going on, for the people of Victoria want an explanation." Brew's face was red with frustration. He thought of the men killed, the investors who would lose their life savings and the Natives who would be hunted down.

"I left everything up to Brewster," Waddington replied in a calm voice, his thumbs hooked into his suspenders. "We promised to get the road built. I had confidence in my man that he took the best action."

"The best action," Brew repeated. "Really, Sir? I was told Brewster refused to give the people food, instead giving the starving Tŝilhqot'in muskets. Was that your order?"

Penn spoke up, his lips curled, his tone condescending. "My client has no responsibility for the trail boss's actions. You're overstepping your position, Brew." He wore a superior attitude. After all Penn was an Englishman and an Oxford graduate, and Brew *just* an Irish constable.

Brew felt his blood rise. So often in his life he had seen the English treat his people in this condescending manner. He held his tongue and continued his interrogation, turning back to Waddington.

"You are responsible for your workers' actions. Would it not have been more humane to feed the people rather than arm them? Do ye not think ye are responsible for this violence?"

"I had nothing to do with the uprising, Mr. Brew. You can't blame me. The Indians are violent. How was I to know they would murder my men?" He got up from his seat, brushing his coat off as if he was brushing off all responsibility. "It has nothing to do with me. Nothing at all."

"You delude yourself, Mr. Waddington, and you make a hobby of lying to yourself and to the good citizens of this city. Many will lose their fortunes because of your schemes. This time your lies have serious consequences." Brew felt relieved to speak so forthrightly.

Penn rose and put his top hat on. "You don't need to listen to this jumped-up policeman, Waddington. I'll speak to the governor about him and see that Brew is reprimanded for these accusations."

Brew saw the men out. He was not the least worried about Governor Douglas, who had told him that the Tŝilhqot'in uprising should be placed on the head of the road builder who incited violence with his actions and those of his men. However, there was little Douglas could do about the war with the Tŝilhqot'in as his tenure was ending. He had been replaced and recalled to London.

Brew had other support, too. Robson, the editor of the *British Columbian Newspaper* wrote:

Depend on it. For every acre of land we obtain by improper means we will have to pay for dearly in the end, and every wrong committed upon these poor people will be visited on our heads.

But his was only one opinion. Robson had never supported the Bute Inlet Road. The citizens of Victoria were divided, with the majority siding with Waddington and appalled by the atrocities committed by the Tŝilhqot'in.

Brew felt confident public opinion would turn against Waddington, and the once-charismatic entrepreneur would be censured. On his shoulders would be the deaths of the road crew, the loss to investors and the financial costs of the war. Most Victorians knew that Bute Inlet, with its tortuous canyons, steep cliffs and treacherous rapids, was impossible terrain on which to build a road.

No, Brew thought, *I will not waiver.* He knew Douglas supported him, and he suspected the new governor, Fredrick Seymour, would as well, though he didn't expect to meet him anytime soon. Brew was stationed in Victoria, and the governor of the newly formed Colony of British Columbia would be stationed in New Westminster.

~

New Westminster

Frederick Seymour, having only recently arrived from the British Honduras, slumped in his chair when he received the dispatch from Victoria. He had expected his posting to be uneventful. There had only been one isolated incident in the Colony, unlike in the United States where there were outright massacres and open warfare.

"Some bloody pencil-pusher from Victoria sent the dispatch with a civilian as if he was informing me of the menu for a dinner rather than of war with the Indians!" Seymour rose from the comfort of his armchair. "An uprising in my colony. Not in the Colony of Vancouver Island where Douglas's replacement would have to deal with the savages, but on the mainland of British Columbia where I must deal with them." But what was he to do? He was just weeks into his job.

Seymour had been accustomed to the diplomatic life of British Honduras when he was abruptly removed from his post.

The Colonial Office thought I was too old to deal with the Mayans and the landowners and sent me to this wilderness. I'll show those arrogant Londoners at the Colonial Office. I'll show them how to deal with insurrection.

He must move cautiously. He would first ask Douglas for advice, but he had to go to Victoria immediately as Douglas was leaving soon. He needed a fast boat to cross the Georgia Strait to Vancouver Island.

Douglas was preparing for his departure for England when Seymour knocked on his door.

"Seymour, what are you doing here? I thought you would be going to Tŝilhqot'in country to tend to the crisis."

Douglas was also surprised that he had been pulled from his post. He'd had years of dealing fairly with the Natives. Now that blaggard, Waddington, and his damned road had spoiled his last days in Victoria.

Douglas waved Seymour into his cluttered library. He continued sorting papers as he waited for Seymour to speak. Seymour watched Douglas but said nothing.

"Speak up, Seymour. You've travelled across the strait to see me. What can I do for you?"

"I'm seeking your advice on the killings. I don't want to start a bloodbath, just bring the guilty to justice."

"That is the right way, good man." Douglas put his work aside and gave his attention to his visitor.

Douglas thought for a minute, cupping his chin. "Well Seymour, I suggest you get a message to Cox, the mining commissioner. Order him to form a posse of at least thirty men from the Fraser River digs and dispatch them to Fort Alexandria. Do you know where that is?"

"Yes, a crossing of the Fraser River north of the falls."

"Right. There is something else." Douglas continued. "You should go north with the Royal Engineers by way of Bentinck Arm. That's your fastest route until a proper road is built to the goldfields. Most important, you have to order the men not to shoot unless their lives are threatened. There are many vigilantes from the States who want to slaughter every Indian they see. You don't need any frontier justice. British justice is needed—British law.

"We've had uprisings in British Honduras. The Mayans and the settlers are killing each other. I tried to find men who could handle a musket without blowing their heads off, good men who would keep their cool under fire. I could have stopped the bloodshed. The London office thought differently.

"Whenever there is a problem, the Colonial Office thinks it will be solved by changing the governor. Well, I think I've had enough of the colonies. Time to settle down and spend my time with Shakespeare, maybe even read that new book by Darwin. It is quite sensational. Are you familiar with it?"

"I read only the classics. No time for a scientist who wants to contradict the Bible," Seymour said, pulling on his black frock coat. "My wife wouldn't have it in the house. He writes that we are descended from monkeys." Seymour scoffed at the idea. "I have more serious matters to deal with, and you will want to finish your packing. So, I shall leave you. If you are returning by way of Cape Horn, have a safe journey."

"My wife wants to wait until they lay the rails through to Sacramento. My thought is that it will take too long to complete the rail to the west coast. I suppose we could take a coach overland and see America. That might please Amelia and the girls."

After bidding goodbye to the weary Douglas, Seymour thanked him for his advice and left for New Westminster to gather his militia, before heading up the coast by steamer.

CHAPTER THIRTEEN

Soda Creek, Summer 1864

McLean

onald McLean, second in command of the militia, reporting to Commissioner Cox, gathered at Soda Creek with a rabble of twenty-three men. They were a group of miners from several countries and a few settlers and traders.

"We're gonna fight them savages." One of the miners had had too much to drink and was all fired up. "Kill every last one and rid this place of dem."

"It's not so easy to kill a man when you ain't had no practice. You gotta calm the rabbit in your chest." McLean looked the man up and down. He was a young man. Ginger, they called him; likely hadn't shot anything but coons back in Alabama.

"I been known to kill a man or two," Ginger bragged.

"So has lightning," McLean said sarcastically, wondering if these recruits would be fit for an Indian war in British Territory. McLean, a Scotsman, had been in North America for decades as a fur trader then owned a ranch and a roadhouse in the Cariboo region. He was in his fifties, sinewy and tough from his years on the frontier of New Caledonia.

"Well, we best git busy and wipe out all them marauding Injuns. If this were in the States, the entire tribe would be slaughtered, and I'd be on my way home to Carolina." This time it was Bo speaking, a man in his thirties with an angry scar on his face.

"We are not in the States. We are in British Territory," McLean answered, stroking his handlebar moustache. "Instructions from Governor Seymour are to bring in the Tŝilhqot'in to face British

Justice and to avoid unnecessary deaths. Not my way, but I gotta follow the rules, unless they're not watchin' me." He chuckled.

"That don't sound like you." Ginger piped up. "You never shrank from a fight. I heerd a story about you chasing a murderer up near Quesnellemouth. You thought the chief was harbouring a savage. When the murderer was nowhere to be found, you told the chief, 'Then for today, you will be him.' Then you put a musket ball in the chief, then killed his son-in-law, wounded his daughter-in-law. But the worse, you killed a baby. Killed a baby! Ain't that right?" he grinned. "Even I wouldn't do that, and I like killin' Injuns."

"There are plenty of stories about you, McLean," Bo said. "My guess is that the Injuns hate you good and plenty, even though I know you have a Tŝilhqot'in wife."

"Is it true that you wear a chainmail vest?" Ginger grinned.

McLean scowled. "Why don't you two padlock your mouths? Just because we are sitting on our asses for days waiting for that bloody Cox and his men to show up doesn't mean I want to listen to your prattle." McLean walked off to his tent and his bourbon.

The men sat on logs or on the dirt, eating their supper of beans and biscuits and grumbling. "That McLean is just like the Yankee General Grant, drinking because he is bored waiting for action." This was one of the Americans, nicknamed Yankee Jack, though he came from South Carolina. Despite his name, his sympathies definitely lay with the rebels of the war between the States.

"Me thinks," Yankee Jack said, wiping crumbs on his sleeve, "that we best git home to the States before all the fighting is over. I want to whip these here Injuns first and then go south to kill off them Yankees. Why they fighting for the niggers anyway?"

Six-toed Pete was an American miner who had been working the creeks for three years with very little to show for it. He was about to return to his home in Tennessee. "I think I gotta join Lee's army.

Now there's a man of action. He's beating them Yankees with half the troops. I've had enough of that cocksucker Cox; he's slower than a constipated donkey. I need myself some action. If I can't kill Injuns, maybe I'll kill those nigger-loving Yankees."

"Well, I tell you, we killed Injuns before we even came to the Fraser River," Six-toed Pete continued. "Back in fifty-nine we were travelling from the States into British Territory, and we came upon twenty savages fishin' at Okanagan Lake. Our group was armed, and they wasn't armed. Just arrows. They sees us coming. They jumped in the lake, and when they came up for air, we picked 'em off. We sat there all morning shooting them just like fish in a barrel." He chuckled at the thought. "We passed the morning so pleasantly. Them duckin' and divin' and us pickin' them off. The Injuns didn't have a chance. I saw what the Indians was made of that day. Cowards."

"They are bloodthirsty when they have the numbers, just like them Tŝilhqot'in, cutting men down in their tents, hacking them, taking their hearts like they did to that Brewster." Yankee Jack used a biscuit to wipe the last of his beans from his bowl.

"Yah," Six-toed Pete added. "And you have to watch them sneaky bastards. They can hide under a wolfskin so you barely know they're there until one just jumps you and cuts your throat. They can disappear in their shadows without a sound. Just you wait and see."

"If we ever get some action. I'm sick of sittin' here chewing the fat in the heat. We want to hunt Injuns, not sit on our thumbs waiting for that useless Cox to arrive with his men. If there's blood to be seen, I'll be right in the middle."

Baptiste, a voyageur from eastern Canada and, was the translator for the group. His mother was Cree, his father French Canadian and his grandmother English. He listened intently to the miners and was sickened by what he heard.

Six-toed Pete saw that Baptiste had his ears cocked. "Keep your fucking Indian nose out of where it don't belong."

Baptiste kicked the earth with his moccasin clad foot and spat as he walked away speaking in Cree to the guide.

"Dey're Boston men who slaughtered Indians in the States," Baptiste said to the guide. "Wiped out an entire village in Oregon. A peaceful village, people who did them no harm. Now dey're in British Territory to do the same."

"I wish Governor Douglas was still in charge," the guide replied in his language. "This mob will kill all our people if someone doesn't rein them in. Maybe Seymour will talk some sense into them."

"I don't think Douglas would be a hell of a lot better even though his wife is Cree. The citizens of Victoria want blood for blood."

"Wasn't it Brewster's men that took that girl, just a young thing, Lhats'as?in's daughter. I don't blame the chief one bit. I would cut out Brewster's heart, too, and slaughter all his men if they did that to my daughter."

CHAPTER FOURTEEN

Fraser River, Spring 1864

Cox

Cox led a militia of fifty men, many of them Americans, many with experience killing Indians. He'd recruited the fighters from the Fraser River gold digs and was marching them north along the river. All the militia could talk about was slaughtering the enemy, yet Cox's orders were not to kill. He and his men were to persuade the perpetrators to give themselves up. No western vengeance. The British rule of law was to be followed.

While most men came west to seek gold, Cox was different. He had been a banker in England before coming to the British Colony and holding down several government jobs. Still in his forties, he became the Gold Commissioner for the Fraser River. He liked his job and carried it out on his own terms. When there was a dispute, he had the rivals foot race each other and gave the disputed territory to the winner. He used unorthodox ways.

Cox took his time getting to Fort Alexandria. He didn't want to start a war by killing and risking the lives of his men or murdering innocent Tŝilhqot'in. He would wait for Lhats'as?in to surrender. He respected the tribes; he'd learned from them, their admirable qualities and their weaknesses. He was the Queen's man and would do his job. With little digression, he would follow the rules.

The last leg of the journey was by paddlewheeler from Soda Creek. His men boarded the *Enterprise*, relieved to be off their feet and on the water. The steamer churned upstream, past banks of spruce and dense underbrush. As evening fell, the sun lit the river, turning the surface of the river to gold. Men slept on the deck or played cards. Cox gazed at the river, contemplating the task ahead.

The light grew dim just as the steamer approached a bend in the river where there were shallows. In the fading light, the captain failed to see the gravel bar and beached the paddlewheeler so far into the gravel that the men could not get it floating again. Cox couldn't wait for another steamer to come, so the men piled out. They made camp, still miles from Fort Alexandria.

Finally, they arrived at Alexandria, and the two makeshift regiments met up.

"It's about time," McLean, who had been waiting for the crew, barked. "What took you so long?"

"Our steamer grounded on a gravel bar. We made ourselves some rafts and had to pole up the Fraser River. My men need food and rest."

"We gotta march to Puntzi and meet Seymour, and we leave today. We've been waiting for too long already." McLean was exasperated.

"I'm in charge here if you recall. We'll camp here for tonight." Cox directed his men to settle in and pitched his tent.

McLean scowled. "Seymour made a big mistake. My guess is you did some bootlicking to land the command."

"I did no such thing, McLean. As Gold Commissioner, I am in the employ of the Colonial Government. You just own a roadhouse. And it is well known that the tribes would like to have your head."

"I have been in the country for decades," McLean countered. "I know those sneaky bastards."

"Yes, and they know you. Are you still hanging on to bitterness of having Fort Chilcotin closed down?" Cox was younger than McLean, sure of himself as was McLean. Both had contempt for the other.

"I'd already have those murdering thieves if I wasn't told to wait for you." McLean scowled. "Waiting for you was like watching an ant crawl across the Chilcotin plains."

Cox heard McLean's complaints but wouldn't budge until his men rested for the night. The next day they got underway, travelling to Puntzi Lake, now a combined force of eighty, some on horses, some on foot. Soon they would be joined by Governor Seymour and Inspector Brew.

Cox and McLean led their troops over the rolling hills and dunes of Chilcotin country. As they started down the slope into the Chilcotin River, a Tŝilhqot'in scout galloped toward them shouting, "Dey're here! Dey mean trouble." Immediately, McLean and his son started after them on horseback.

"Wait! Don't chase them," Cox yelled. "you'll get yourself killed."

"Sit there if you like," McLean retorted, waving his rifle. "I intend to kill those bastards." Twenty men mounted their horses and dashed off, heading straight into the waiting Tŝilhqot'in.

The men were unprepared for fighting. Anxious for action, the undisciplined mob rushed at the Tŝilhqot'in, muskets firing. It was complete chaos. The first gunfire wounded Six-toed Pete in the leg and sent the militia into a rout.

"It ain't so easy to shoot a man," Six-toed Pete complained as he nursed his wound. "Especially if they is shootin' at you."

"We are supposed to be an army," growled Cox. "You listen to me, or it won't be the Injuns that get wiped out. It will be you! Get your heads straight!"

McLean scowled at the militia. "The Tŝilhqot'in will be back," he warned. "They don't wait 'til you're ready. They sneak up and surprise you in your tents."

"Why are they fightin' us anyway?" It was the miner from Colorado. "I thought there weren't no Indian wars in the Queen's Territory."

"They are fighting for their country," answered Cox. "Just like you Americans did in 1776."

"Dat's no ways near the same. We were fighting for our freedom from King George. I don't know what is wrong with youse people, staying under the yoke of kings and queens."

"The Tŝilhqot'in lived here for centuries before whites came. We are invaders to them," Cox continued. "They believe whites gave them smallpox on purpose to rid the country of Indians. Then a road was blasted through their land. If that wasn't enough to get them riled, the road crew raped the chief's daughter, only a child. Would you not kill the men who defiled your child?"

"Youse are an Injun lover," the miner scowled, spitting on the dusty trail. "Not fit to command us."

Cox, who'd had enough of this prattle, ignored the miner and nudged his horse into a canter.

McLean felt remorse and anger at the ill-advised rout. He rode back to camp, grumbling to himself. He had to rid himself of that useless Cox and be free to train the men and lead them.

The militia would follow a man like me, he thought. *Someone who knows who the enemy is and fights rather than turns tail.*

New Westminster

"Captain Ackerman, I'm sending you to meet up with Governor Seymour," Colonel Moody said to David. "You know the territory. You'll be a great help in capturing the murderers. Brew and Seymour are travelling by steamer to Alexandria by way of Bentinck Arm. They are both new to the country and could use your knowledge of the land. You would make less trouble than that renegade Mclean and be more decisive than Cox. I want you to make haste up the Fraser River and meet them at Puntzi Lake."

"I'm sorry, Sir. I can't be part of an Indian hunt, their capture and execution," David said.

"They will be brought to justice, Mr. Ackerman, not slaughtered. Where is your loyalty?" He was a spit and polish soldier, recently arrived from England.

"They are defending their land. We are the oppressors, or at least Waddington is, crossing their land without permission or compensation."

"I don't believe this. I give you an order, and you refuse?" The colonel was red in the face. "You have some cock-a-billy story that Indians have rights after what they did. I'll have you in chains, Ackerman."

"Sir, my contract was up a month ago. I stayed on to assist at the Fraser River goldfields. I have no further obligations to the Colony of British Columbia."

"So, there we have it. You're just leaving at a time when we need all our men, especially a good rifleman like you. I am disappointed."

"I am returning to the States to fight in the war. I have word that my father has been wounded. He was a surgeon with the Union. He asks that I do my duty and take his place, not as a surgeon but in the cavalry. As well, I must return to look after my mother and sisters in New York."

"You're going to fight the rebels." The colonel paused. "That does make a difference. I support the Union as should all citizens in a democracy. They need men who can shoot. From what I hear, you're a wizard in the saddle, and with the Henry repeating rifle you can shoot a flea off a dog's ass." He chuckled, thinking of how David's skills would be needed more against Lee's army than a small band of Natives.

"Yes, Colonel. The Union Army has lost thousands in the three years of fighting, and it isn't over yet. At least I will be fighting for a cause I believe in."

"Going to war to keep your country together, are you?"

CHAPTER FIFTEEN

Bentinck Trail, Spring 1864

Governor Seymour

The third party made its way from Victoria by boat up Burke Channel. As Governor Seymour and Inspector Chartres Brew disembarked at Bella Coola with the contingent of seventy-five Royal Engineers, they were met with a thunderous gun salute by white settlers and Hudson's Bay employees. The Nuxálk, the local tribe, was alarmed by the intrusion as the small party of whites on shore cheered.

The contingent wound its way by horse and pack train up through the pass in the mountains across the plains heading to the meeting place at Puntzi Lake.

Chartres Brew led his troops in military fashion, wearing his uniform but with no side arms. He hoped to bring the Tŝilhqot'in to justice without further bloodshed. The Irishman came from a country often torn by strife, his people under the rule of English kings and queens. Now he would have to fight Natives defending their country from outsiders. But Chartres couldn't let his misgivings get in the way of success. He was a soldier; he would follow orders.

The move to the Colony had been positive for his family. His wife embraced Victorian culture, content not to have the condescending, upper-class English look at them with contempt because they were Irish.

Brew was a handsome man, with a thick head of black hair and full beard. Seymour was quite the opposite in appearance. He had a receding hairline and deep wrinkles, likely from his years in the posting of sunny British Honduras. His wife had thought it was the end of the world to be posted to this remote colony with wild savages and the endless winter rain. Seymour wanted to make the most of his tenure because it would be his last posting. If he could bring the murdering Tŝilhqot'in to justice without needless casualties, it would cap his career.

Seymour thought Governor Douglas was relieved of the post because he meddled too much in politics, favouring the Bute Inlet Road project, wasting money on the Harrison Lake route and then pouring funds into a road up the Fraser River. Now Seymour would have to quell the uprising and complete the road to the goldfields. With the murder of fourteen white men, he was certain the Bute Inlet Road was doomed.

The troops reached Nancootlem exhausted and without food. There were long days ahead before they would reach Puntzi Lake, and they had been on starvation rations for days. The militia and their leaders had hoped the Nancootlem Natives would offer them smoked salmon and berries, but when they arrived, not a single living person remained.

"Where is everyone?" Seymour was counting on being resupplied at the village. Instead, it was deserted and reeked of death. Life in the British Honduras had been insulated. Fredrick Seymour had been accustomed to fine living and luxuries afforded the governor, and he had never suffered for lack of food.

"All dead, Sir," Brew replied. "Smallpox. It is a terrible epidemic, just terrible."

"Why weren't they vaccinated? The vaccine has been available for decades." Seymour was astounded at how backward this country was.

"Sometimes I think the white community didn't care whether they lived or died." As he said this, Brew thought of his own people in Ireland under the heels of British royals and snubbed by the gentry. The Native Peoples were like the Irish, ruled by the Brits in their own country. He knew how it rankled.

117

The men and horses grew uneasy with the stench of death enveloping them. "They best move us out," one soldier grumbled, "before I chuck up what little food I've had to eat."

Without help from the Natives, Seymour, Brew and their men had to scrape the bottom of the food barrels for scraps or try to find berries and the odd rabbit to survive on. Starving and demoralized, they continued on to the meeting point at Puntzi Lake. They were marching toward Puntzi when a rider approached from the east with a letter.

Brew scowled as he read the note. "What is Cox thinking?" he growled in his thick Irish accent, his "r"s rolling. "He says we are not needed! Well, I'll tell him that the governor and I will be at Puntzi Lake to take over command whether he likes it or not."

"They want to have the glory of capturing the Tŝilhqot'in," Seymour said. "I gave a strict command to Commissioner Cox and McLean that they were not to take any lives unless fired upon. We will find the murderers and bring them to justice, British justice."

The governor wiped his brow, took his hat off and wiped his balding head. "Why is it so bloody hot in this country? I can barely endure it. Honduras was in the tropics, but at least we had civilized houses to live in, not tents pitched in a dust bowl."

"It will fry you in the summer, freeze your butt in December," a Hudson's Bay Company man said wryly. "Welcome to the Colony, your Excellency."

They were ten miles east of Anahim Lake when the vanguard came upon the horror of an ambushed pack train.

"Sir, you gotta see dis." It was the Métis guide. "The Tŝilhqot'in must have hated dem pretty bad to do dis."

"Dear God! This is Alex MacDonald's pack train!" Seymour said looking at the field of horror—bodies partially eaten by wolves and covered with flies. He held a handkerchief against his mouth to lessen the stench.

Seymour's face had turned grey before he spoke again. "Waddington wanted me to rush here to protect the pack train. I did not heed his words." Seymour shook his head. He dismounted and counted the dead. "Four slaughtered. Did anyone survive the attack?"

"Alex usually travelled with eight or nine men," the Métis guide said. "Dis here is Alex MacDonald. He was Manning's partner," he said, standing beside the rotting corpses.

"Who is Manning?" Seymour was confused and frustrated by a country he didn't understand.

"Manning owns the trading post at Puntzi Lake. Dat is another story." The Métis guide kicked the sandy earth with his boot. *Don't dis governor know nothin',* he thought.

"Dey also killed MacDougall and his Tŝilhqot'in wife, Klymdetsa. It's not like dem to murder their own. My guess is that they hated her for warning them of the attack." The whiskered Métis guide shook his head. "The other one, I don't know him. Five got away. The Tŝilhqot'in stole the horses and the pack train goods."

"We are fighting evil," Seymour said, inspecting the grizzly scene of bodies decomposing in the summer's heat. "Why would they attack a pack train? Don't the Tŝilhqot'in need to trade at Manning's post?" Seymour threw out the question, expecting Brew to answer. Instead, the Nuxalk guide responded speaking in broken English.

"The packers stay at spring. They Manning men. Manning build his rancheria on Tŝilhqot'in land."

Seymour shook his head, thinking, *What have I got myself into? This is worse than Honduras.*

They buried the victims, digging graves in the loamy soil of the plains. One horse lay wounded and in pain. Brew went up to the horse, spoke quietly to him, found a rifle and shot him in the head.

"You didn't deserve this, fellow. Did you?" Brew said before walking away from the grisly scene. As soon as the men finished burying the four victims, they continued on to Puntzi Lake.

When they finally arrived at Puntzi Lake, they were met by Cox. He waited until the men dismounted and spoke to Brew and Governor Seymour. "There has been another murder."

"Yes, we know," Brew replied. "My men dug four graves for Manning's pack train. That makes eighteen victims."

"Make that twenty," Cox said. "Manning was killed, and I believe his Tŝilhqot'in wife, likely by the same Tŝilhqot'in that ambushed the pack train."

Seymour grimaced at the horror of Manning's mutilated body. "Why are they filled with such hatred?"

"I can tell you, Sir." This was Baptiste, the Métis guide, who showed no deference toward Seymour. He burned with indignation as he spoke.

"The spring beside the buildings was a regular stopping place for the Tŝilhqot'in for as long as people remember. Then that bloody Manning and his partners talked your government into giving them this beautiful piece of land. Not just a little site for the roadhouse, but acres and acres around the lake, cutting off access to the spring we use during winter when the lake is frozen. The most beautiful site in the Cariboo. Now you know why the Tŝilhqot'in are so angry."

But Baptiste wasn't finished. "That is not all. Manning came from America and landed in the colonies just a few years ago. He took a Tŝilhqot'in woman and gave her an English name, Nancy, even though he already had a wife and children in California. You English think you are so moral and superior, flaunting your Christian values in our faces. You give away their land, take their women."

Cox intervened. "That is quite enough, Baptiste. This is Governor Seymour you are addressing. Show some respect."

"Your man has a point," Brew said to Cox. "The settlers, road builders and miners want the Tŝilhqot'in land and we, that is, the whites, are encroaching and taking everything, even their homes, which according to Douglas's proclamation is not permitted. Gold has a way of making men abandon their moral upbringing. We set aside land for the tribes, and they grab it away. A golf course built on their village at Nanaimo, homes torn down for Waddington's townsite, a village burned to the ground in Victoria. We must treat them fairly to avoid the war the Americans fought against the Indians."

Seymour sighed, thinking of the task ahead of him. "I think my job might not be very easy in the Colony," he said. "My wife was looking forward to a few years of peace before retiring to London."

McLean had listened to Baptiste's rant. He had his own views and certainly didn't share the opinion that the Natives were justified in killing. "Pleased to meet your Excellency and you, Chartres. McLean's the name." He spoke with a disdainful attitude, having been in the Territory for decades. He knew the enemy and didn't need a newly appointed official telling him how to deal with the Indians.

"Cox and me'll bring them murdering savages in. With all due respect, we don't need no governor nor policeman. I've lived among these savages for years. I know their thievin' ways. They're almost too good for killin' but kill them we shall."

"You will kill no one," Seymour barked. "Cox, didn't you inform McLean of my orders?"

"Yes, Sir, I did. But McLean here is a bit of a hothead. He won't listen to me."

"I am in charge here, and I will not sanction unnecessary violence." Seymour wondered again what he had got himself into.

"Cox, I want you to see the men are fed. They've had nothing but berries for days."

That night, the men of the two groups set up camp together. Governor Seymour and Brew to their roomy tents. McLean, gloomy with the prospect of being ordered around by these newcomers to the Colony thought, *I know the Injuns and their sneaky ways better than an aristocrat from Honduras?*

Brew's Royal Engineers were settled early. McLean's contingents from the gold diggings, a mix of miners and settlers from around the world, were up late complaining and drinking long into the night.

"My guess some of Douglas rubbed off on Seymour, 'cause he is every bit as stubborn," a miner said, waving his jug of whiskey. "Don't want to harm the savages, even though they slaughtered our people in cold blood, cutting Brewster's heart and taking the man's head off."

"Yeh, looks like there won't be any fighting. If McLean was leading us, we wouldn't be sitting on our thumbs like Cox. That man is useless as a fork in a sugar bowl."

"At least we didn't nearly starve like Brew's men," one of the soldiers said. "They couldn't even find berries the last few days. Plumb ran out of victuals, they did."

"Seymour expected our men to live off flies and didn't bring enough provisions to feed a group of seventy-five, just like someone from the upper class. No sense. And he don't know nothin' about huntin' Injuns."

The next morning, Brew woke the militia at first light; his men were up and ready for the march to Fort Alexandria where they would get provisions for the hunt. The men under McLean woke with hangovers and in a foul temper.

CHAPTER SIXTEEN

Quesnellemouth, Spring 1864

Alice

Alice moved to Quesnellemouth, along with Mary, and purchased the Silver Spoon. It was one of several businesses located along the Fraser River at mouth of the Quesnel River. The land was covered in thick underbrush and heavily treed with Douglas fir and birch. The miners had moved to the creeks, hills and mountains east of the town. Quesnellemouth was the nearest supply point for the miners and a stopover for travellers on their way to and from their claims.

David entered Alice's roadhouse, reticent about sharing his news.

"Alice, I must tell you something. Let's sit down." He took her arm and led her to a chair.

Alice felt a shiver go up her back. Her hands were icy despite the warm day.

"I'm not going to fight the colonists' war against the tribes. If I remain in my position with the Colony, I'll be sent to capture the Tŝilhqot'in. I don't want to contribute to this dirty war."

"It won't be like Oregon and Colorado, where they massacred the tribes. There is justice in the British Colonies," Alice protested, already fearing that David would leave her.

"If there were true justice, they would know the people had a right to defend their land. That the usurpers were in the wrong for crossing tribal lands without compensation. Besides, there will be hotheads, who kill indiscriminately. I can't be part of it."

Her voice was shaky. "What will you do?"

"My sister wrote begging me to return. My family needs me. My father is wounded, and his life hangs in the balance. He has been mending and patching the wounded for four years. You understand that my duty lies with my father, sisters and mother, don't you?"

"What are you saying? You are not going to fight in the war between the south and the north?" She had seen the pictures in the newspaper—soldiers, thousands of young men, dead on the battlefield.

"My sister sent a letter to say father has not long to live. She wrote in the letter that he wants me to join the Union Army. I will be fighting something I believe in, the end of slavery."

Tears pooled in her eyes. He may never come back. She could lose him forever.

"Alice, you are stronger now. You don't need me by your side constantly."

She wanted to cry and beg him not to go, not to risk his life. She sat numbed by the revelation.

"I will write every week. I give you my word. I'll come back to you. Maybe by that time you will have left your past unhappiness behind you. Maybe we can marry and live our lives together. You must realize I have always loved you. I am just waiting for you to commit yourself to me. This break will give you time to make up your mind."

"Please stay. I'm so afraid you'll never come back. Thousands are being killed on both sides."

"The war will end soon, but I must go within the week because I fear my father has not long to live." David held her hand. "Please give me your photograph, and I will give you mine."

David cupped her cheek gently with his hand. "You have my promise that I will return."

But even as he made this promise, David thought of the picture he had seen of the aftermath at Gettysburg. Dead and rotting corpses on the field, both Union and Confederate. Death didn't discriminate between the warring parties.

Alice sat, her head bowed, not meeting his eyes. *This was all my fault*, she thought in anguish. *If only I had accepted his proposal, he wouldn't be leaving. I might never see him again. What have I done?*

David left that week, riding his Arabian horse, Lightening, south along the bumpy, newly constructed Cariboo Road. Alice couldn't hold back her tears when they parted. She felt lost. She had tried to bury her grief so she could give herself to the man she loved. Now she might never see him again. He was going so far away, miles across the continent, to fight in a bloody war.

After David's departure, she kept busy in the roadhouse. Customers flooded into her dining room, miners on their way to the diggings at Williams Creek and men joining up to fight the Tŝilhqot'in. Little Mary was exposed to the cruel remarks from the men about the massacre.

"Them bloody Injuns. They not only killed fourteen white men but dismembered the road crew. They're filthy savages, they are," bellowed the loud-spoken miner with a ragged beard.

"Don't pay them any mind," Alice told Mary, as the young girl carried empty plates into the kitchen at the end of the day. "They are ignorant. We will feed them, give them a cot and look after their horses if they have any, but we won't be bothered by their prattle. Come here, Mary, and give me a hug."

Mary nuzzled up to Alice, resting her head on Alice's chest. This comforted Alice and Mary. The child was like her own now. Alice couldn't imagine life without her.

"Maybe we will have a letter from David," Alice said, smoothing Mary's dark hair. "That would cheer us up."

"I asked my angels to look after him. He is fighting to free the Negroes, isn't he? He is in much danger, but the angels said they would keep him safe."

Alice was near tears. "Thank you, dear Mary." She kissed the top of Mary's head. *She is so much like my dear Amelia,* she thought. *Mary has come into my life to save me from grief over Amelia's death on the Oregon Trail.*

By this time, David had joined the Army of the Potomac under General Grant. Alice scoured the newspapers for any news about the war to the south. *The Colonist* newspaper wrote that Grant was nicknamed "the Butcher" because of the thousands that had died under his command. Grant, however, was the first general under Lincoln to stand his ground; he didn't back away from a fight with the Confederate General Lee. The Union generals who preceded him were cautious, almost afraid to engage the Confederates.

The Butcher! That is what General Grant is called! She only hoped her dear love did not become fodder for a general seeking fame, one who cares nothing for the lives of his men.

She could only pray and wait for his letters. The news, what little there was, only added to her worries. Surely the war in the States had to end soon. It was in its fourth year, and so many young men had died! At least Stonewall Jackson was dead, dying at the hands of his countrymen at Rappahannock. Friendly fire, the papers said. Stonewall, a tough Confederate soldier, hated Negroes, thought they were subhuman.

"I don't mourn his death," Alice told Mary as they worked in the kitchen. Alice was making biscuits, and Mary stirring the porridge. "It is people like him who encouraged thousands of soldiers to give their lives."

"I hope we never have a war here. Jesus said, 'Thou shall not kill,' so why are soldiers killing each other?" The nine-year-old girl was guided by her religious beliefs and her natural tendency to be kind.

Alice wondered if she should talk to Mary about the war with the Tŝilhqot'in People, but she decided she would spare her the grim story for now. So many of Mary's people were dying from smallpox and hunger, and now war. It would overburden the child. But there was so much chatter in the roadhouse that she couldn't miss hearing the ugly words.

Alice continued reading the news of the war in the States. *The Colonist* had a story in each issue. She summarized the newspapers for Mary. "Lincoln is a good man and thought the war was for a just cause. He's the president, you know." Mary listened to every word. "He is a fine leader, though it took him sometime to declare that the purpose of the war was to end slavery. There were many politicians who wanted to keep the Union but cared less for the slavery issue.

"Lincoln also had a story for every event in the war." Alice turned the page of the newspaper. "These are the words he wrote instructing his generals:

When you find General Lee, do not take the risk of being entangled upon the river, like an ox who jumped over half the fence and is liable to be torn by dogs, front and back without having a fair chance to kick one way or the other.'"

Mary gave a little chuckle.

Thank God for this sweet child, Alice thought. *I would be mad with worry if she were not with me.*

CHAPTER SEVENTEEN

Fort Alexandria, Spring 1864

McLean

"**B**rew rules with an iron rod," one of McLean's recruits said to his boss one evening. "Up at six; to bed at nine. I've had enough of British discipline and enough of this godforsaken country."

"I'm sick of the men who lead us," a disgruntled McLean said. "It beats the hell out of me why they brought 'em all the way from England to do a job I cudda finished by now."

The next morning Brew split the soldiers up. Cox and McLean to go west, back to Puntzi Lake. Brew would go south with his Royal Engineers to hunt the Tŝilhqot'in. Governor Seymour took his entourage to the relative comfort of the gold towns to the east. He'd had enough of sleeping in tents, with only scraps of food in a day and riding hours each day through the heat.

McLean and Cox rode to Puntzi Lake with their rabble of eighty men. They were on the trail four days, their militia cutting a swath through the grassy rolling hills and then raising dust in the dried marshes and sandy dunes of the Chilcotin plains.

McLean mulled over his dissatisfaction with the leadership. *If only I could rid myself and my men of that fool Cox. And Brew, that Irish policeman with a stick up his ass, a newcomer who doesn't know bugger all about this country or the savages.*

At last, he could see the lake shining in the distance. The sun was setting, sending shafts of golden light over the water.

"I think I sees them varmints," McLean whispered to Baldy, his second in command. "I'm gonna try to ditch that lazy Cox and kill us some Injuns."

McLean and ten of his men galloped off but were quickly followed by Cox.

"What are you up to?" A breathless Cox with Six-toed Pete in tow caught up to McLean. "Remember, Seymour doesn't want us to engage the enemy. We're ordered to induce them to surrender."

"We have them, Cox. It'll be easy to surround their camp."

"Naw," Cox ordered. "We'll just show the enemy our forces. We out number them. No need to face them in battle."

"You are a lily-livered, useless piece of…of…" Mclean fumed. "I could have killed Lhats'as?in, his warriors, the squaws and all the little savages in one fell swoop."

Six-toed Pete scoffed. "The hen is the smartest animal in creation because she never cackles until the egg is laid," he remarked with a grin. "McLean cackles all the time."

The Tŝilhqot'in had disappeared, packing up their tents and moving on. The encampment inhabitants were either dead of smallpox or had left to fight with Lhats'as?in. The elders, wives and children followed the warriors.

Once again, Cox forced Mclean to stand down. *Why did Seymour make that cocksucker head of the militia? He don't have my experience. He never fought the savages,* Cox thought.

Cox rested at Puntzi Lake, drinking his brandy and not moving. Days passed in the heat of August with the flies swarming around the camp. McLean's frustration grew to a boiling point.

Disgruntled and bitter, McLean quietly left the camp in the dark. He wasn't going to sit around waiting for those savages to show their faces. He would go with his son and a few trusted men to hunt the enemy at Eagle Lake. The moon had just risen over the blue hills as they rode quietly out of the Puntzi Lake camp.

I don't give a cotton-picking dang whether Cox tails us. I'll have them savages before Cox is even mounted, Mclean groused to himself.

It took them two days to ride to Eagle Lake, and it was dusk when they rode down the hills to the lake.

"I see 'em boss!" Mclean's guide yelled.

Before McLean could stop them, the undisciplined men, anxious for a fight, dashed off only to be met by fire. One of the men took a musket ball in the leg.

"You men can't even handle a musket without blowing your head off," McLean lectured, once his men had retreated to safety.

"Very queer when a gun is being fired; a man is all fired up until he hears a shot or sees a man wounded. I'll bet my bottom dollar that a few of you wet your trousers." McLean wasn't finished yet. "One bullet and you were all done in. This wasn't your Gettysburg. More like Cold Harbour, where the Union was outfaced by Lee who had one-half the troops." McLean, strode in front of his men, angry that their foolish actions had cost him a chance to surprise Lhats'as?in.

"Next time, I want you to stay down low and be ready...very quiet. When the firing starts, you have the full permission of Her Majesty the Queen to yell and shout and shit yourselves." McLean stared at his men, shaking his head. "Now carry Ginger to my tent, and we'll patch him up. Tomorrow, I'll go alone to capture that bloody Lhats'as?in. Youse miners can't be trusted."

McLean stood near Eagle Lake with Jack, his Shuswap guide. McLean told his son, to be the lookout and left him behind as he moved forward with Jack to where he had heard the enemy.

"Come. We hunt the savages. Do you think it matters to the wives and children of the murdered which Injuns we kill? They just want 'em killed," he growled, ignoring the fact that his guide was Native.

The old frontiersman followed a path near the lake that he thought the Tŝilhqot'in had had taken. The guide was nervous. "Hey boss, I think they are very close. We should skedaddle back to safety."

"You good for nothin' slacker. Can't I find anyone with the balls for a fight and the skills to not get shot in the back?" McLean moved down the trail.

"Don't go, McLean," Jack urged. "They come and kill you. I'm sure of it."

"I don't hear a sound. There ain't nobody here." He was bending down. "But I see fresh signs on the trail."

"The enemy ain't dumb. They want you to follow their trail." Jack had a bad feeling about this. "When you don't hear anything, that's when the Tŝilhqot'in will strike."

The Tŝilhqot'in hate McLean for the murder of their chief at Fort Alexandria, the guide thought. *McLean hates the Tŝilhqot'in because of his humiliation at Fort Chilcotin. Killing McLean would be a great coup.*

Jack tugged on his coat, whispering, "Dey near."

"Shut your trap." McLean leaned his gun on a pine tree and wiped his brow. "It's goin' to be as hot as frying grease today."

"We turn back now," Jack cautioned. "You think your chain mail will help you. It won't."

"Hold your tongue, or I'll cut it out." McLean turned, confused about the location of the enemy. A musket ball struck McLean in the back.

When the news reached Cox at Puntzi Lake, he was furious. "I told that stubborn mule not to confront the enemy. Now looka what he done. Got himself killed. I promised Seymour that no one would be killed unnecessarily."

The men broke off from Cox, sharing their views of McLean's death. "McLean was not good at waiting," said a militia man.

"I don't blame him. He was sick to death of sittin' around."

"Damn shame to lose a good frontiersman like McLean."

"Curiosity killed the cat, or at least it done in McLean," snorted another militia.

"McLean had backbone; I'll tell you. Backbone."

"He wasn't no coward like that Cox with his ass in a chair waiting for his morning fart."

McLean's men grumbled among themselves, wanting revenge for their dead leader.

Cox paid little attention to what the men thought of him. He ignored their jibes and retired to his tent with his brandy to think. He didn't notice McLean's followers slink quietly out of camp.

"Now that McLean is out of the picture, and Seymour is enjoying a hot bath in the gold mining towns to the east," he spoke aloud to himself, "I have full control. First, I'll take the troops to Eagle Lake to bury McLean. Next, I'll ask that if he brings in the murderers, no harm will come to the Tŝilhqot'in warriors. Alexis is a reasonable chief from Anahim. His people don't want this war."

Cox was sure Alexis would find the Tŝilhqot'in warriors. The chief wanted one thing…to end the war.

"Then," Cox continued his musings, "all we have to do is wait." And waiting was something Cox was good at.

Alexis was relieved when a messenger arrived from Cox, asking him to find Lhats'as?in and take him and the warriors to Governor Seymour.

There was a gift of tobacco for Lhats'as?in and Alexis, and a promise the militia would not harm the Tŝilhqot'in. They just wanted to negotiate peace. Alexis was aware that the warriors were tired of being hunted and that their wives and children were close to starving. He knew they would come. All he had to do was find them. But that would take time.

CHAPTER EIGHTEEN

Chilcotin Territory, Fall 1864

Lucy

The Tŝilhqot'in warriors were camped near a lake surrounded by steep rocky cliffs. They missed their families, and they were hungry. They wanted to hunt moose and deer and net the salmon that would come up the Fraser River in the autumn. Their wives wanted to smoke salmon to store for the winter and pick berries, not follow the warriors in a hopeless battle.

But Lhats'as?in was still fired up. He couldn't dismiss the fact that his people were being killed by smallpox, their land taken from them and his young daughter despoiled, violated and so seriously injured she would never bear children or walk again. How could he give up? They killed the famous Samandlin—his chain vest did not protect him. They could still win the war over the usurpers.

"When will we return home? My wife is having our baby any day," said a young warrior. "She needs me. My four children need their father."

"We should all go home," said another warrior. "Nights are getting cold now, and winter will soon be upon us. I need to hunt and take my family to our winter home before the snow flies."

"What is the matter with you?" It was Lucy, the only woman warrior in the camp. "Are you men, or are you rabbits?"

Lucy was different. One arm had been paralyzed since birth, yet she rode her horse like a trick rider. She could mount while her horse galloped, drop down one side of her horse to avoid gunfire and shoot with one arm, seldom missing her target.

"You warriors must support Lhats'as?in. We will win. We *must* win." The diminutive, muscular woman held sway over the young warriors.

"We killed Samandlin," the warrior chief said, in an effort to stir up his men. "That is a great victory."

"You mean McLean, don't you?"

"Yes, of course," Lhats'as?in said. "We called him Samandlin. That made him angry; he didn't want an Indian name. Now, we must go to war."

The Tŝilhqot'in warriors nodded. Inspired by Lhats'as?in and shamed by Lucy, the men picked up their muskets and readied their horses.

"We'll go along the top of the hill and surprise the Brits," Lhats'as?in said, mounting his horse. "I think it is McLean's rabble that are stirring for a fight. Cox and his men have become lazy, sitting at Puntzi Lake. That man is the Gold Commissioner. All he does is wait. Like most government officials, he's used to waiting, not fighting."

Lhats'as?in's army numbered twenty warriors; some were youngsters like Lhats'as?in's son Peille; others were in their late forties, seasoned and excellent shots. They left their horses and moved quietly up the hill, keeping out of sight, sneaking through the pine trees. Lhats'as?in looked through his sights, hoping to determine the readiness of the Brits.

As he watched from the hilltop, Lhats'as?in sensed a motion behind him. "Damn it! It's that traitor, scouting for the enemy. I'm sick of the Nuxalk, joining Seymour's army, giving in to the Brits."

Lhats'as?in swung his scope behind him. He watched with trepidation as forty militia men stormed up the hill, surrounding them on both flanks. The militia had the Tŝilhqot'in warriors cornered. This unsettled Lhats'as?in. He had not expected action from the Brits.

"Lhats'as?in. You must order the men to jump!" Lucy yelled. "It is our only chance. They'll wipe us out, kill us all."

Lhats'as?in looked at the sheer drop down to the lake. Impossible. He, Lucy and Peille and a few other warriors would make it but not the older men; some of them could not swim. Was he prepared to send his men to their deaths?

Peille was at his side. "We have to jump, Father. We can help those who don't swim."

This was all the encouragement that the chief needed. Lhats'as?in jumped; his contingent followed, splashing down a hundred feet to the cold, deep waters of the lake.

"Well, I'll be dammed," Six-toed Pete said with a chuckle. He wanted some action and had joined McLean's men. "I never figured them Indians had it in 'em." He and his troop watched as the Tŝilhqot'in made it to the far side of the lake, the younger men helping those that couldn't swim. Lucy, with her one good arm, powered through the water, leading the way to safety.

McLean's militia returned to camp to ready themselves for the march back to Puntzi Lake. It was a dispirited crew.

"We must lick our wounds," Six-toed Pete grumbled. "They're too wily. We ain't never going to catch those bastards."

"A handful of savages outfoxed us," a militia man said as he mounted his horse for the ride back to Puntzi Lake. "Now we have to take our orders from Cox. He don't want to fight. He's a coward, afraid of his own shadow."

Cox decided to ignore the militia's disobedience.

"My guess is that McLean's followers had to get it out of their system." Six-toed Pete was his audience. "Now they will settle down and follow me. I've sent Chief Alexis to offer peace to the Tŝilhqot'in. They'll come in. No one can run forever. They know we'll dog their heels 'til the day they die."

"You ain't goin' to negotiate peace after what they did to us?" Six-toed Pete objected. "The colonials will have your head."

"No, but that is what Lhats'as?in will be told. Time to be as scheming and deceitful as the enemy."

Alice and Mary sat on the porch of the roadhouse in Quesnel-lemouth. It was the end of a busy, blistering hot day. They served meals to the new recruits joining Seymour's forces. It was hot and windy in the town. The recruits were boisterous and loud-mouthed. Most of them were Americans who had come to the Colony to work in the goldfields.

At last, a letter from David arrived. Alice trembled as she slit the envelope open with a kitchen knife.

"Oh, Mary, I am afraid to learn of the battles he has endured. There have been so many soldiers injured and killed in that horrible war."

"Don't worry, Alice." Mary hugged her. "My three angels, Charity, Faith and Hope, have kept him safe. I pray for his safety every night."

"You are a comfort, dear child." Alice kissed her on the cheek and opened the letter.

"He is safe and not injured, though he was in a terrible battle. He mentions the battle of Cold Harbour. I read about it in the newspaper. Another Confederate victory. When will his side have a win? If only all wars would end."

CHAPTER NINETEEN

Puntzi Lake, August 1864

Chief Alexis

66 **Y**ou're wasting your time, Brew," Cox said. "Chasing Lhats'as?in over a country where he knows every trail, every copse of trees is pointless."

Brew had returned from his search and joined Governor Seymour and Cox at Puntzi Lake.

"Instead of being eaten by bugs and wearing your horses out in this immense country," Cox continued. "I will persuade the murderers to surrender, and we can wait for them by the lake."

Seymour was not pleased. He'd taken a tour of the new gold diggings at Williams Creek and received an earful from the miners. Their angry comments still echoed: "Why haven't your men killed that scoundrel? You should wipe out all those savages. Dey slaughtered fourteen men! Men who were just doin' their jobs."

"I have to agree with Cox, Sir," Brew said. "The men are tired, and we're nearly out of provisions. If the Tŝilhqot'in don't want to be found, we cannot find the bastards."

Seymour was furious. "You men are going to finish this and not go back with your tail between your legs," Seymour yelled, his face growing red. "I thought you had more spine, Brew. I didn't come all this way by boat and miles by horse to this godforsaken country to have the Indians get away. We're going to bring in the perpetrators. They will face justice, or I will have your jobs."

"But Sir…" Cox started to say.

"Do as I say. There is no shutting my eyes to the fact that this is war. We can use rifles as well as the Tŝilhqot'in. I might be compelled to follow in the footsteps of the Governor of Colorado and invite every white man to shoot every Indian he meets. Such a proc-lamation would not be badly received in Victoria or in the gold-fields. But no, we must bring them in without resorting to a massacre. That is what our Queen would want."

Cox listened and nodded his head. He would do things his way. If Seymour would get out of his way, he would wait, not wear out his men and horses.

It was nearing the end of summer, and the sun lit the canvas tops of the tents as it rose. Brew's men were already washed and fed when visitors approached the Puntzi encampment. It was Chief Alexis and a small contingent of his followers. They looked around the encampment, watching the soldiers who had been busy polish-ing boots or grooming their horses.

Alexis turned to the men sitting around the fire. He was search-ing for the great chief, the governor, but he didn't know what Sey-mour looked like.

Alexis was middle-aged and dressed in traditional clothing. He was not a warrior; he hoped to bring peace to the land. There had been enough fighting. He was the chief who would end the war and save the Tŝilhqot'in from starvation.

The Brits will give them food once the warriors surrender. They are my people, Alexis said to himself. He was from the long line of chiefs born to lead.

Then there was Nancy, the beautiful young Tŝilhqot'in woman from Alexis's family. Now she was nothing but the whore of that white man, Manning, who had fenced off the freshwater springs. No wonder the Tŝilhqot'in hated Manning.

Alexis moved cautiously toward the firepit where an older man dressed in a grey three-quarter topcoat and a wide-brimmed hat sat with several others. Some were soldiers and wore uniforms;

others were from the mining camps. He recognized Cox, the Gold Commissioner.

Alexis didn't want to talk to Cox or the soldiers. He had come to talk to the big chief. He looked around at those gathered at the firepit. *Not the broad-shouldered man with the beard. He is the Chief of Police. Maybe the pale, skinny man is the governor,* he thought.

He glanced about the encampment from Brew's disciplined soldiers to the ragtag crew under Cox. *There may be almost one hundred Brits hunting for Lhats'as?in, but these King George men are no match for the Tŝilhqot'in. Lhats'as?in is too clever; he knows the country and will sneak up on them when they least expect it. But now they're hungry. They cannot fight forever.*

I think that the little man with the wrinkles is the big chief; he needs me to bring the warriors in and end this useless war.

Seymour rose to greet Alexis, and Cox introduced them. "Chief, this is Governor Seymour. Alexis is from the Anahim country to the west. He knows Lhats'as?in well."

The two talked about the war between the Tŝilhqot'in and the Colony, agreeing that it was taking too many lives and that the end result will be disastrous for the Natives.

"Chief Alexis, can you please help us end the fighting?"

"Yes, your Excellency," Alexis said to the great chief, Seymour. "Lhats'as?in will listen to me."

CHAPTER TWENTY

Puntzi Lake, August 1864

Treachery

Afterter Alexis left in search of the warriors, Seymour sent Brew west to Anahim country and ordered Cox south to Fort Chilcotin.

"But Sir, I won't find the Tŝilhqot'in. They always know where we are, but they are elusive as..."

Seymour cut him off. "We can't have you sitting at Puntzi twiddling your thumbs. Your men are bored and restless. They need to keep moving or you'll have an insurrection on your hands. Go to the fort and send your men scouting each day. You leave at once, or I'll hear about it." Seymour glared at Cox. "I'm at the end of my patience with you. You'll return to Puntzi in two weeks to meet up with Alexis."

It was a day's ride to Fort Chilcotin, so Cox took his time getting there and setting up camp. Seymour was right, Cox's men were relieved to be on horseback and moving,

The governor rode to Fort Alexandria and then south to New Westminster. He had given his orders. Now it was time to leave this bug-infested wilderness. At least he would soon be in his own bed and his comfortable chair.

After a week at the fort, Six-toed Pete galloped into the encampment. "Hey Boss, I see'd one of dem warriors. He'll be here any minute." He was out of breath as he dismounted.

Within minutes a Tŝilhqot'in rider approached the encampment. Cox rose to greet the scout; he was not surprised to see the Tŝilhqot'in. As he told Seymour, the warriors always knew where their adversaries were. The scout, who spoke broken English, brought him a message from Lhats'as?in, one that raised Cox's ire. Lhats'as?in wanted Cox to stop his hunt, or the Tŝilhqot'in would wipe them all out. Cox knew that he had the numbers on his side. He would not bend to the renegades.

Cox had his own message for Lhats'as?in: "You are welcome to come in. I know that the wolf is at your door. If Lhats'as?in comes in, we will give his people food. If they don't turn themselves in, we will kill every man, woman and child." Cox gave the scout a gift of tobacco to take to Lhats'as?in. It was both the feather and the club.

After the two weeks, Cox and his contingent returned to Puntzi Lake where he would await Alexis; he was good at waiting.

It was weeks before Alexis found the Tsilhqot'in camp. He told Lhats'as?in that surrender would not mean death. It would mean an end to the war. Lhats'as?in was suspicious. Could he trust the Queen's men? Alexis said that no harm would come to them. Cox had sent a gift of tobacco, a peace offering.

"Our warriors have had enough," said Telloot, Lhats'as?in's second in command. "We are all hungry and tired. Our wives and children have little to eat. The Queen's men will never give up. Lhats'as?in, please go and meet the governor. At least hear what he's offering."

Lhats'as?in pondered for two days, not believing he could trust any whites. They were all liars. Then he thought of his young wife and their newborn. He thought of the old people near starvation because their men were fighting, not hunting. He thought of the salmon that did not come back in numbers this year. He remembered the words of Alexis: "Cox promised to hand you over to the Big Chief, and no harm would come to you or your men." Surely the Queen's man would keep his word.

Cox was awakened early on August fifteenth at Puntzi Lake.

"They're coming!"

"What are you saying?"

"The murdering savages, that's who," Six-toed Pete said. "Methinks it's about time. This bloody country is getting me down."

Lhats'as?in and seven men arrived with Alexis. Wives, children and elders followed the warriors into camp. They all looked hungry, tired and dusty.

Cox straightened his coat and stood erect to greet the illusive Tŝilhqot'in.

"Welcome!"

"Well, look at what the cat dragged in," Six-toed Pete said. "Dat's the leader, Lhats'as?in. Does this ever take the biscuit!"

"Shut your trap," Cox snapped. "I don't want to scare them off. I have to play this carefully."

Lhats'as?in led his people into his enemy's camp. The warrior chief of the Tŝilhqot'in was a tall man, proud, with startling blue eyes and wearing traditional clothing. He approached the militia looking around, studying the faces.

"Where is Big Chief?" He meant Governor Seymour.

Cox moved forward bringing his translator with him. "He's coming soon."

Baptiste translated as best he could, using a combination of Chinook and the few Tŝilhqot'in words he knew. He knew Cox was lying. Seymour had already left for New Westminster. *There's another sneaky colonial, talking with a forked tongue,* he thought.

"Come, sit with us and smoke tobacco." Cox smiled and gestured toward a firepit.

Lhats'as?in and his warriors moved to the benches around the fire. Their wives and the children sat on the ground some distance away. It was mid-morning in August and already hot. The children were hungry and tired from the long walk.

Cox passed each of the warriors a pipe and lit his own pipe, sitting back and thinking how to take the Tŝilhqot'in into custody. He restrained a chuckle, wondering how Captain Brew would react to the surrender, if that is what this was.

"I want to speak to the Great Chief English," Lhats'as?in spoke in broken English. His son, Peille, sat next to him with Telloot and Talhpitt close by. All were tense, not trusting the Brits who had cheated them, lied to them and broke promises.

Armed soldiers stood around the group, making Lhats'as?in uneasy, but this did not alarm him because they were smoking together, which to the Tsilhqotin was an offering of friendship or peace.

"He asks for Governor Seymour," Alexis said in English.

"Not here now. He will come," Cox did not say that Seymour had left for New Westminster. "I am in charge here. You can surrender to me."

Baptiste translated. "Surrender!" Enraged, Lhats'as?in rose to his feet. "I am not surrendering. I came to make peace. I want to talk to Great Chief English!"

"Yes. Yes, you shall." Cox tried to diffuse the situation. "Sit Chief Lhats'as?in. We'll talk until Governor Seymour comes. Now tell us what you want. Speak your language. Baptiste will translate."

"We will kill no more. You will kill no more. Stop sending the sickness that kills all our people. Stop the road through our land." Lhats'as?in spoke slowly so Baptiste could translate. "I come to make peace and save our wives and children. I bring seven warriors fighting a war, and I am one."

Baptiste translated: "I brought seven murderers, and I am one myself. We wish to give ourselves to you to save our wives and children."

Cox wondered if anyone would call themselves murderers. Despite this, the significance of the words was not lost on Cox. He stood, letting Lhats'as?in's words sink in. Puffing up his chest, he said in an officious tone, "In the name of Queen Victoria, I am placing you under arrest. You are my prisoners."

When Baptiste translated, Lhats'as?in threw his pipe to the ground.

"What is this? Where is Great Chief English?" He spoke in English. "I parlay with Great Chief, not you. We not prisoners. You smoke with us in peace!"

Lhats'as?in was livid. "You said no harm come to us, that you would hand us over to Big Chief. You lie!"

"King George's men are great liars," Telloot grumbled.

"Mr. Cox must speak with two tongues," Alexis said. "I did not bring Lhats'as?in and his men in to surrender. You said no harm would come to them! Lhats'as?in is right. You are a liar."

Cox's soldiers surrounded the Tŝilhqot'in, taking their guns and knives. Cox didn't give a damn what the warriors thought of him. To the Tŝilhqot'in, this was the worst betrayal. Smoking together and then taking them prisoner.

CHAPTER TWENTY-ONE

New York, Late Spring 1864

David

D avid knew he'd done the right thing by joining the Union Army. The south fought to save its lifestyle, but that included owning slaves. How could anyone own another human! It was a medieval practice that must end.

When David returned to his family in New York to see his wounded father, his heart was in his throat. He had left his father many years earlier after a bitter argument. Now, he had come to try and mend the rift.

The Ackermans lived in a three-storey brownstone. As David walked to the front door, he looked down the street and saw the Stars and Stripes flying from every house, all supporting Lincoln and sending their sons into battle and often to their deaths.

This would be a difficult reunion for David and his father, who had begged David to read law or follow in his footsteps and study medicine. But David wanted adventure; he'd dreamed of crossing the continent to the Pacific Ocean. He never argued with his father but left when he was eighteen without saying goodbye. David realized his dream of travelling west as a wagon-train guide, an occupation his father disagreed with.

He lifted the brass door knocker on the heavy, ornate oak door and let it fall. What should he say to his dying father? He had feelings of remorse for leaving his family suddenly and regret that his father enlisted and was now badly wounded. He should have been the one to fight in the war, not his aging father.

He heard the footfalls on the tiled corridor before the door was opened by a servant. "Yes. Can I help you?" She wore a green uniform and looked to be in her forties with brown hair swept back neatly in a bun.

"I'm David. David Ackerman."

"Ah, you are the son he talks about. Come in, come in." She had an Irish or Scottish accent and a warm, pleasant voice. "I'm Shawna, by the way. Your father has been waiting for ye. Let me take your coat and portmanteau, and I shall take ye to him."

"And my mother and sisters?"

"You'll see them anon. Mr. Ackerman asked to see ye first. Come this way, Sir."

She led him up the stairs to a bedroom where the curtains were drawn. It was dim, and David could barely make out his father's form under the covers. The robust man he remembered was frail.

"Father. It's David."

"What's that?" he said in a weak voice.

"David, your son."

Tears came to his rheumy eyes. "At last." He caught his breath. "David, the family needs you." He coughed, struggling to speak. "I'm dying. Your mother can't manage Elizabeth. I worry about them." His voice grew weaker. "Your other sisters are married and have their own troubles and responsibilities."

"Father don't talk. You must rest."

"That is all I've done is rest. I must have your word. I know that you will go and fight. You must survive this war and stay to help the family. Please promise me."

David thought about Alice who waited for him and Mary who counted on him. He could not answer immediately. He struggled, knowing that he couldn't let down his dying father. "I will. I promise. Now please rest."

His father gave a sigh of relief and seemed to collapse into the pillows.

David walked quietly from the room, agonizing over his promises to Alice and to his father. Shawna met him in the great hall. David looked at the walls covered with the paintings of his ancestors and a war photo of his father, dressed in his colonel's uniform with its gold buttons on a frock coat. He looked so vigorous.

"He is poorly, isn't he? Your father would nae die 'til he saw ye. He waited 'cause he had to talk to ye first. Shall I take you to your dear mother?"

"Yes, please, Shawna, and my little sister."

"She's a bonny wain, not wee anymore. She'll be home anon once her meetin' is over."

"What meeting?"

"Abolitionist. Elizabeth is their leader, a very young one at that. She is so innocent and sweet, yet so serious at her age." Shawna opened the door to a bright, sunny room with a view of the gardens. "You'll find your mother in here. I'll bring the tea, and you two kin have yourselves a fine chinwag."

Shawna disappeared down the hall, and David stepped into the room. His mother sat with her needlework.

"David, it's so good to see you at last." She placed her embroidery on the end table and stood up to greet her son. David embraced his mother, noting the wrinkles around her eyes. She was still a beautiful woman, dressed in a light grey silk gown that met the floor. "Come sit down across from me and tell me all about yourself. What are your plans?"

"I've joined the Union forces as Father wishes. He ordered me not to get myself killed, and I told him I won't." David smiled at this, knowing how disastrous the war has been. "After the war, I gave my word I would look after the family."

They were just finishing their tea when Elizabeth burst into the room. "Oh David! I thought you would never come home." She threw herself at him, tears of joy streaming down her alabaster cheeks.

David held his little sister 'til she composed herself. "I hear that you are nothing but trouble, Lizzie, marching and yelling in the streets." He smiled and kissed her on both cheeks before sitting beside her on the sofa.

"I had to help my fellow abolitionists repeal the Fugitive Act. When I was too young to protest, and you were heaven only knows where, a runaway reached New York, and, rather than being granted freedom, he was captured by the police and put in chains by his slaver." She took a breath and continued in a serious voice. "He died before he reached Georgia." Tears pooled in her eyes. "That is when I vowed to help former slaves now that Lincoln has passed the Emancipation Bill. Humans are still enslaved. We must defeat the south and free those poor people. I won't rest until they are all free."

"Lizzie, you are a firebrand, and I love you dearly. But you must promise me to be safe. Please don't do anything to get yourself arrested because it would break our dear parents' hearts."

"I'll try. Several of Lincoln's party are so stupid; they want to appease the Confederates and allow the south to hold slaves and negotiate the end to the war. I thought we were fighting for people's freedom!"

She paused, realizing her passion was inappropriate at the moment. She had not seen David since she was a toddler. She wondered if he shared her views.

"You're going to fight aren't you, David. We must win, not negotiate a peace that keeps people enslaved. I can't stand it. I just can't."

"Elizabeth, please have your tea," her mother said. "You get so worked up over slavery that I worry about you."

David took Elizabeth's hand. "I will not get myself killed if you promise you won't get arrested."

"I'll find shelter for the runaways, see they are fed and help teach the little ones. I'll protect the former slaves from being captured illegally, shackled and taken south to be whipped, lynched and sold off without their babes. Slavers are so evil. It has to stop. I wish that women could join the Union Army and fight for the cause."

"You are doing useful work in New York, Elizabeth. Keep it up, and we'll all be together after the Confederates are beaten and the war ends."

Within the week, David was heading south to join Ulysses S. Grant's Army of the Potomac. His first taste of war was at Cold Harbour. He survived the battle, but many Union soldiers died. Once again, a victory for the south.

CHAPTER TWENTY-TWO

Quesnellemouth, Fall 1864

Mary

Alice ran into the roadhouse. Little Mary was busy setting the tables. "You have a letter from David," she sang. She could tell because of Alice's smile.

"Yes! Come and sit with me," she said with a wink. "I will read it to you, or at least most of it,"

Dearest Alice,

I have a break from fighting and am well. The Army of the Potomac under General Grant is making progress. Lincoln was so frustrated with his former generals. He called them no-good generals that would not stand and fight.

We expect to be in a battle against Lee. He is clever, never wants to engage. Bobby Lee, they call him. It would be a shame if the Union were dissolved and that slavery should continue. All those lives lost for nothing. There are twenty-one million people in the north, only nine in the south, of which four million are negroes. We should prevail.

At the beginning, when the Confederates attacked Fort Sumter and the war began, recruits feared the war would be over in six months and they would not see any action. The war is now in its fourth year. Whole towns signed up. Now Lincoln is calling for additional recruits and paying them fourteen dollars a day. As an officer, I earn more, and the negroes are only paid seven. Which is unfair, especially because the Blacks are often in the vanguard and the loss of life and injury is so great.

The south is enlisting too, and my guess, paying them half that. They're just boys. It would break my heart to have to fire on them.

Write me about the hunt for the Tsilhqot'in. I hope the Brits don't start a war with the Indians. They know there are seventy thousand of them and only six thousand colonists. I can only hope that reason will prevail.

Now, I must tell you of camp life. We are fed well and there are luxuries such as velvet camp stools for the officers. The only reason I am an officer is because of my sharpshooting.

Our unit is off to Petersburg. General Grant hopes to take Richmond and choke supplies to the enemy. This will end this terrible war, so I can come back to you.

I miss you, Alice. Your picture is on my pillow every night. My love to you and to little Mary. She must be a comfort to you.

Your beloved,

David

The Battle of Petersburg

David rode a stallion from his family's stable, crossing Virginia with the cavalry, supporting the troops at Petersburg. An army of thousands marched behind. It was a hot day and getting warmer as they travelled south.

The Union forces needed a victory. Lincoln needed a victory. Opposition to the war had grown, and there was a movement to end the war and negotiate a peace with the South. David thought about the idea of negotiating with the South as he rode across the fields in the June heat. All those boys who died for nothing. It would be a tragedy if the South could keep slaves. David couldn't abide the idea.

By late June, Grant's army controlled the eastern side of Petersburg, a critical location for both armies. Several trains intersected here, provisioning the South with supplies for the army. Petersburg was twenty-four miles south of Richmond, the capital of the Confederate resistance. Lincoln had to capture Petersburg to cut off supplies going to Richmond; General Lee of the Confederates had to defend Petersburg with everything he had. It was a stalemate. The men were anxious for battle, but neither side seemed ready to risk an offensive.

A caravan travelled with the Union Army carrying supplies for the army of sixty thousand. David's regiment was camped on the outskirts of Petersburg. The smaller Confederate army was well protected by earthworks that circled the city. David wondered how they would ever breech the barrier even with their greater numbers. For more than a month there was little action. David used the time to write letters to his family and Alice.

Part of the Union line was held by General Burnside. He led a troop of former miners and a division of mostly Black foot soldiers. The men approached the general with the plan to tunnel under the ground to the Confederates position and fill the tunnel with explosives, breaching the enemy's line and giving the Union forces the advantage.

David's cavalry was held back, having been ordered to wait until the infantry stormed through the breech. The infantry of mostly Black soldiers was at the forefront.

The tunnel exploded, blowing a gap in the Confederate defences. Then everything deteriorated. The infantry poured into the bottom of the crater and tried to scale the sides of the hole. Most died there, pinned down by the enemy.

The Rebel soldiers differentiated between whites and Blacks. When the Blacks surrendered, most of them were executed; when the whites surrendered, they were sent to the Anderson prisoner-of-war camp.

Instead of ending the siege with the explosion, both sides settled in for eight months of trench warfare. No one could claim victory. General Burnside was relieved of command for his role in the debacle.

CHAPTER TWENTY-THREE

Quesnellemouth, Fall 1864

Tricked

Alice searched for every scrap of news on the war. Instead, she found reports of the Tŝilhqot'in capture. *The British Colonist* wrote:

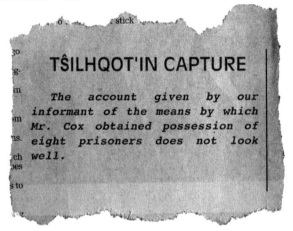

stick

TŜILHQOT'IN CAPTURE

The account given by our informant of the means by which Mr. Cox obtained possession of eight prisoners does not look well.

"I didn't think Lhats'as?in would willingly surrender," she told Mary. "There must have been some trickery. Cox lied. I am sure."

A week later Alice read an account of the Petersburg Battle given to her by an American miner who received regular dispatches. His son was with the Confederates, and each of Lee's victories was an event to celebrate.

"We sure as hell gave the Union a licking at Petersburg," he chortled. "Did you read how the stupid Union built a tunnel and filled it with explosives. The explosions made a big crater that the Union soldiers ran into but couldn't get out. Our men picked them off like shooting fish in a barrel."

While the American laughed, Alice felt weak with fear. *David was there?* She sat down, her face in her hands.

"Are you all right, Missus? I fear the news of war upsets you. Women are such gentle creatures. It is better if you stick to making your good pies, Miss Alice."

Puntzi Lake

Cox led the Tŝilhqot'in to a log enclosure at Puntzi Lake hastily built by his militia.

"We are not going in there," Lhats'as?in railed. "We've been tricked!" He struggled as two militia men pushed and shoved him.

"Clap him in irons," Cox said calmly. "That's the only way we'll get the murderer to submit."

They finally succeeded in locking Lhats'as?in in the makeshift jail. Lhats'as?in pounded his fists on the log walls.

"I have failed my people. I've been tricked. Queen Victoria is unjust! We were always told she is a good queen. Her people lied to us. Tricked us. I would never have brought my people in if I had known."

He hit the log walls until his fists bled. Finally sobbing, he gave up and was resigned to his fate. All was lost. He fought a war and tried to negotiate a peace. He was not a criminal. He was defending his people and their land.

The militia treated the Tŝilhqot'in warriors like scum. Conditions were unbearable; the enclosure was much too small for eight men. They were fed cold beans for supper and thin porridge for breakfast. Lhats'as?in refused to eat.

Reinforcements arrived to take the prisoners to Quesnellemouth. Cox marched his prisoners east to the Fraser River, where they crossed at Fort Alexandria. The families of the prisoners followed, including Lhats'as?in's young wife, Toowaewoot, and their new baby and toddler.

Brew and his men returned to Puntzi without engaging the Tŝilhqot'in. That was frustrating enough. Then he heard the news.

"You're telling me that Cox took Lhats'as?in prisoner? That sloth who doesn't have the sense that God gave a fish." Brew was not only astonished; he was bitter. He had well trained forces, the Royal Engineers. He was the chief lawman of the territory. He should have brought the murderers to justice, not that lowly official posted to the remote goldfields. He would not live this down for his remaining time in the colonies.

Brew stormed around the Puntzi camp looking for Cox. "I want to tell that undisciplined, lazy excuse for a soldier exactly what I think of him, why my men laugh at him. I don't care if he had captured Napoleon single-handed. He must have tricked the murderers to surrender."

"Gone! You mean that good-for-nothing excuse for a soldier is taking the prisoners to justice, that worm who refused to confront the enemy!" Brew's voice became louder with each word. He noticed the puzzled looks on the faces of his men and paused, then said in a bitter voice. "At least I don't have to see the self-satisfied smirk on his face."

With that, Brew ordered his men to mount up and continue to Fort Alexandria. The hunt was over. Brew would return to Victoria and the Royal Engineers to New Westminster.

The sky was dark and brooding as the storm clouds moved in from the west. A few spits fell on the men before the heavens opened up, drenching the contingent. The dusty, dry earth soaked up the rain as it fell in a deluge. They were soaked to the skin by the time they reached Fort Alexandria. It was a dispirited crew that took the newly built Cariboo Road south to New Westminster. They had searched for the Tŝilhqot'in for months and never saw action, never brought any of the murderers to justice.

The rain subsided as the Royal Engineers travelled south, skirting the dangerous canyon on the rough road. The men trembled with each step as many of them dismounted and led their horses along the edge of the sheer drop. They could not look down. The water boiled and seethed with a deafening roar of the rapids that spawned five-foot waves as it passed through the narrow opening between cliffs above the Fraser River.

Weeks later, Brew reached New Westminster and paid a visit to Governor Seymour.

"You've heard word that the Tŝilhqot'in have been apprehended, Sir?"

"Yes. I received a telegram. It looks like our man Cox captured them. I always thought he was the right man for the job."

Hearing this was like rubbing salt into sore wounds. Brew could feel his anger rise in his throat. Although it was humiliating, he held his tongue.

Seymour sized up Brew, realizing that Brew, the lead lawman in the Colony, had been outperformed by Cox, a lowly government official.

"I want you to testify at the trial, Brew," he said. "Your observations of the dead and mutilated men on the road crew will be invaluable. There was no use shutting my eyes to the fact that this was a war, merciless on their side, in which we were engaged with the Tŝilhqot'in nation. The Tŝilhqot'in are not murderers."

This is what the Governor thinks? Brew couldn't believe his ears. At trial, Brew knew Judge Begbie would decide differently. *The people of Victoria will not allow sentiment for the Tŝilhqot'in cloud their need for revenge.*

CHAPTER TWENTY-FOUR

Cariboo Road, Fall 1864

Lhats'as?in

Cox marched the eight captors north to Quesnellemouth, guarding the prisoners closely. Some of the Tŝilhqot'in were angry, others despondent. All felt tricked.

They reached the boomtown on the Fraser River late in the day. The warriors were tired, dusty and hot. Lhats'as?in stood straight and proud, always certain that he was right to defend his people, the land of his ancestors.

What else could I do? he thought. *Let the white people overrun our land? Let filthy men defile my young daughter? I am their leader. I had to fight. My only regret was that I believed the word of that snake, Cox.*

Locals, miners, entrepreneurs and Natives gathered to watch the prisoners. Some jeered. Natives looked on sadly. They watched the prisoners pass and felt their misery as the Tŝilhqot'in were led to yet another hastily built enclosure. Would this be the end of their people? Since the fur trade ended and gold was discovered, the Native Peoples no longer had a place in the Colony.

The confluence of the Quesnel and Fraser Rivers held a special place in the lives of the Peoples that had made it their home for centuries. They buried their dead by the river, traded with other tribes and fished for the abundant salmon every autumn. It had been hard, but it was a good life. Now they feared the future dominated by whites who had no respect for their People.

Lhats'as?in fumed. He did not speak but brooded angrily.

It was war, not murder, he thought. *I was completely in the dark about what would happen when we entered Cox's camp. Cox smoked with us. He lied and lied. He promised us we would have the honour of an interview with*

Governor Seymour. He tricked us! What should I have expected from the Queen's men? Colonists who sent smallpox to our People, trespassed on our land offering nothing, dynamiting our sacred mountain to build their hateful road. And the rape of my young daughter! At least I killed the men who assaulted her.

Lhats'as?in didn't eat; he couldn't sleep in the rancid enclosure. His son would give his life for his own lack of judgement. Lhats'as?in wished he were dead. The days before the trial were torture.

Judge Begbie arrived in Quesnellemouth two months later to hold the trial. He was an arrogant man, tall and distinguished looking with his fine woollen suit, a cravat at his neck and a trimmed moustache. He even spoke a little of the Salish language. That did not make him a friend to the Natives. He was known as the "Hanging Judge" and would likely hang all Natives if he could.

Begbie could not be trusted to rule justly against anyone of colour, especially Natives. He considered Natives, Blacks and Chinese to be inferior races. He ruled against them in almost every case. Once they were tricked into surrender, their fate was sealed.

Lhats'as?in knew this. His men knew this. They would die, and no trial would save them. It was already decided before Begbie left Victoria. It was all a farce. The white residents expected blood for blood, and Begbie would deliver.

Alice was upset by the capture of the Tŝilhqot'in and sick with worry for David. In her nightmares, David rushed into the crater and was butchered by the enemy. In others, she saw the young Tŝilhqot'in hanged by the neck. She would wake in a sweat, not sure for a moment if her dream was real. Mary tried to comfort her.

If only a letter would come from David telling her he had survived.

Please, God, she prayed. *Let him be safe.*

CHAPTER TWENTY-FIVE

Quesnellemouth, October 1864

Judge Begbie

Quesnellemouth was already a boomtown as a result of the gold strikes at Williams Creek. Buildings, two and three storeys high, lined the main road. Fraser's General Merchandise and BC Express Seed Store stood on the main street, convenient for the packers who often travelled from the coast over the Cariboo Road with twenty or more mules.

As Alice walked on the path along the Fraser River to the courthouse, black rain clouds moved across the sky and the wind whipped up the water into whitecaps. She pulled up the hood of her coat and shivered from the sudden dip in temperature.

Alice slipped into a seat in the courtroom. She did not want death for the warriors. She wanted them sent home to their families. Like David, she believed they were only defending their land.

The Tŝilhqot'in warriors sat at the front of the courtroom. She could see Lhats'as?in. He had an imposing presence, dressed in embroidered, fringed deerskins. Alice knew him to be in his thirties, but he appeared younger. He sat on the prisoners' bench, his moccasin-clad feet planted on the floor, defiant yet regal. He eyed the crowd with fierce eyes.

He is indeed a leader, a great warrior, Alice thought. *I don't believe he surrendered.*

Beside Lhats'as?in she could see seven others. Alice knew one of the men, Talhpitt. He spoke English and occasionally came to the roadhouse for her pies. She did not know the other men—Chessus, Chedekki, Telloot, Tnananski and his son, Cheloot. Then there was

Peille, just a young boy of barely sixteen. He'd followed his father to war. She couldn't bear the thought of him going to the gallows.

Judge Begbie sat at the front, wearing his robes. He was applying British law to the Tŝilhqot'in who had little concept of British law. The jury of white men sat on benches at the side. It was impossible to find anyone for jury duty who was unbiased. What if the English found themselves governed by a foreign country, like Saudi Arabia or China and had to submit to their horrible form of justice? Hands cut off for stealing bread. Beheaded for speaking against a harsh regime.

Alice was among the few white people in the courtroom who had serious misgivings about the fairness of the trial. Walter was present, and she knew he sympathized with the Tŝilhqot'in. But most of the miners wanted the warriors hanged and, if they had their way, would have strung them up to the first sturdy tree they came across.

She asked Mary to stay in the roadhouse and see to any customers. The child knew the trial was on. No one could miss hearing about it, especially in the roadhouse where opinions were vehement. On this morning, Mary couldn't avoid the loud talk of the two miners sitting at a table having breakfast.

"Them savages will get what's coming to dem. Murdering and butchering fourteen innocent men, men just doing their jobs buildin' a road into dis godforsaken country. What's wrong wid dat?" groused a former Hudson's Bay Company man.

"We gotta rid this country of them varmints," the other miner said. "Kill 'em all just like the U.S. army done in Colorado." He was one of the thousands of Americans who had come to the Colony seeking gold.

"Begbie is a Brit," said the Bay man. "D'you think he'll be soft on dem Indians?"

"If'n he lets any of them murdering savages off, there'll be a riot. We want an eye for an eye, blood for blood."

The Bay man grunted in agreement and slurped up the last of his coffee. "Better git your butt off dat seat. We gotta go, or we ain't gonna git a seat in the courtroom."

No one would want dinner today. Everyone wanted to see the trial. If they couldn't get in, despite the cold day, they would stand outside.

William Cox was the first to testify. Knowing he would be the main witness for the prosecution, Cox took care with his grooming, wearing a pressed but well-worn suit of black wool with a black necktie and a rumpled linen shirt. It was the same suit he wore as Gold Commissioner; he bought the same suit every year at the Bay to last him for twelve months.

When Cox took the stand, the prosecutor asked him to describe the capture. With a satisfied look as he began his testimony.

"Lhats'as?in rode into our camp, and in his own words, said, 'I have brought seven murderers, and I am one.' There was no inducement whatsoever. They came willingly." Cox retained his Irish brogue.

Begbie listened with disdain to this rough, sometimes unorthodox Irishman.

Alice wondered why the great warrior had come in willingly if he knew they would be hanged. And what man would call himself a murderer? She didn't believe Cox. He was a devious type, who would colour events to make the Tŝilhqot'in warriors look guilty.

Cox continued with his testimony. "I promised I would not hurt them. That I would hand them over to the Big Chief."

Then Alice understood and so did Begbie, but he would not do anything that would enrage the fine citizens of Victoria. Begbie was a loyal Colonialist. Although he knew the Tsilhqot'in had been tricked, he would lose his position if he didn't rule against them.

The Tŝilhqot'in believed they would not be harmed and didn't understand that they would be brought to trial in a British court to face the death penalty. Only one or two Tŝilhqot'in could speak English, and the others relied on the interpreter, Baptiste. Likely they thought the Big Chief was Governor Seymour, not Brew, the Chief of Police. The trial was turning into a farce!

It was time for the Tŝilhqot'in to testify. Talhpitt was the first defence witness. He spoke in his language.

"A white man took down all our names in a book last spring and told us we should all die of smallpox. That is main reason we went to war, our fear of white man's sickness, sickness that kills our people."

Chedekki was the next to testify. "When the whites would be eating, they would give a bit of food to the children, and the boss man, Brewster, would take it away and throw the food to the dogs. The children were hungry, some starving. We were starving."

Telloot stood and spoke in his language. "They built their road on our land. They didn't pay us. They must pay when they cross our land. That is why we went to war. We are not murderers. We are warriors. We smoked the pipe with Cox. He tricked us."

Judge Begbie pondered over the testimony, questioning whether or not there was deceit, whether the Tŝilhqot'in were tricked. He had an uneasy feeling about the capture. The judge realized the Tŝilhqot'in had been deceived; they had smoked the pipe with Cox. They had been told by Alexis that if they came in, they would not be harmed. He also realized he had to find them guilty or the colonists would be furious. Begbie disdained the Natives but believed firmly in British law. This left him conflicted.

The trial went on for hours. Most of the time was spent on testimony from Inspector Brew, who described the brutal murders of the trail crew. The spectators did not want to hear from the accused; they wanted to hear descriptions of the murdered men and women. Men like MacDonald, who was killed on the Bentinck Arm trail.

Women like MacDougall's Tŝilhqot'in wife, Klymdetsa, who tried to save the white packers by warning them of an imminent attack. She was considered a traitor by the warriors and was killed alongside her husband.

They listened in horror to the descriptions of how the trail crew was attacked in their tents and of the horrific mutilation of Brewster, the trail boss.

Testimony ended, and Begbie had to give his judgement. Begbie could not find enough evidence to convict Tnananski and his son and let them return home. Chedekki, another prisoner, was transferred to New Westminster to stand trial. The other five would be sentenced in Quesnellemouth.

The next morning dawned bright and sunny. The storm had moved east over the mountains, covering the peaks with snow.

This is beautiful country, Begbie thought as he looked out upon the town and surrounding area. The Fraser River flowed past the town. Leaves were turning yellow and gold, and it seemed like a fairyland to Begbie. As he walked from his rooms to the jail, geese rose up from a backwater and took flight. They are going south for the winter; I must leave the north, too, before the ice freezes the river, and it's too cold to travel. Finish this business. More than twenty citizens are dead, and I don't how many Tŝilhqot'in. The people are calling for retribution.

Begbie entered the roughly made cell. He gasped at the fetid smell. The shackled prisoners sat on the ground. Some moaned; others were silent, as if their fate had already been decided, and they wished to get it over with. Lhats'as?in stood up as Begbie and Baptiste approached.

"The Great Chief will decide if you live or die," Begbie said. "My letter will go out to him today. But before I send my advice to

Governor Seymour, I wanted to talk to you," said Begbie. He wasn't wearing his robes but still looked imposing in his black wool jacket, velvet waist coat and white linen cravat.

"We made war, not murder," Lhats'as?in said in English.

"Yes, but you killed twenty whites and must pay for it."

"Tŝilhqot'in died, too. That is war."

"What I need to know is whether or not you were induced to surrender."

This was translated, and Lhats'as?in looked puzzled.

"Would you have come in if you knew you would be jailed and face death?"

He understood the translation. "No. Never!" His answer emphatic.

"Why did you surrender?"

"Surrender? No!" Lhats'as?in's voice boomed, his resentment and sense of betrayal raw.

Begbie questioned him for an hour before finally asking Lhats'as?in, "Your people were starving; your wife and little babes had no food; the salmon run was small. With winter approaching, would you have come in to save them from hunger?"

Lhats'as?in didn't answer immediately. He looked out to where Toowaewoot stood with their two young ones. It was a difficult question. But he knew the British would give his people food, would save his wife, his small babe, his toddler. Lhats'as?in knew it was a trick question.

He spoke in his language. "We are starving because you destroyed our food supplies, killed our hunters with your disease. You wanted us to starve so we would surrender."

"But would you have come in because your people were starving?" Begbie pressed him.

Lhats'as?in paused, not wanting to answer and hesitant to lie. He answered truthfully. "I could not let my people die of hunger."

Begbie had the answer he was looking for. They had smoked with Cox. Surely that meant they were safe, that no harm would come to them. One thing about these Indians is that they don't tell lies. They don't sugarcoat the truth like Cox in that courtroom.

Begbie left the warrior, believing he and his men had been tricked, and that Cox knew the Colony would demand revenge.

With the trial over, everyone waited for the sentence from Governor Seymour. The telegraph had not yet reached Quesnellemouth, so letters took weeks to arrive from New Westminster by horse and rider over the Cariboo Road.

Alice felt only sadness. *Yes,* she thought, resigned. *The colonists will have the death of the Tŝilhqot'in warriors. They wanted revenge.*

Alice wrote David every week, catching the post going to New Westminster. She described the trial in detail, knowing that David wanted to know the fate of the warriors. Thank God he was fighting for a cause he believed in, to wipe the country clean of slavery, to give the Blacks some hope for their future.

Would the Natives ever be treated fairly in their own country? In a way, they were like the Blacks, looked down upon, disrespected. She wished the world would see people with a different skin colour as brothers and sisters, not treated as sub-humans.

She worried how her letters would get to Petersburg, thousands of miles away. She waited anxiously for news of David, praying that he was alive. Mary also prayed, saying that her three angels were watching over him. That gave only cold comfort to Alice. David's last letter was dated July 15, 1864, before the fiasco of the crater at Petersburg. Alice was so worried about David, she barely ate and slept fitfully.

"You must eat more," Mary urged. "You are getting so thin, and there are dark circles around your eyes. Please, Alice." The child was only ten but wise beyond her years.

"If only there was a letter from David, I promise I will eat a big meal of caribou stew. You're a sweet girl, and I love you, Mary."

"I love you too, Alice."

Alice put her arms around Mary, as tears pooled in Alice's eyes.

"Can I be your mom, Mary?"

"You are my mom."

CHAPTER TWENTY-SIX

Quesnellemouth, October 1864

The Silver Spoon

"Did you hear that Governor Seymour condemned the savages to death?" It was the miner who breakfasted at the roadhouse every morning. There was a buzz at the roadhouse as the news of the sentencing circulated.

"Chedekki will stand trial in New Westminster along with Ahan and Lutas, once those two have been captured. There are witnesses in the Queen's city who can testify to their guilt. Five will be hung right here. Lhats'as?in, Peille, Chessus, Talhpitt and Telloot," said Fredrickson, a government official.

"We need to rid the damn country of Indians," Billy, one of the Americans, chimed in. He sat in the Silver Spoon with Fredrickson and six miners waiting for their dinner. They were travelling from Barkerville on their way to New Westminster.

"What we really need is women," said another miner, "I heard that the Anglican Church is asking London to send women to the goldfields. Make this hellhole civilized."

"Better not be too civilized. I like my freedom, don't want a whole raft of rules."

"Miss Alice is a fine lookin' woman." One miner lowered his voice. "But she don't give nobody the time of day."

"She runs to meet the packers whenever the mail comes. I think she misses her friend, David."

"Good sharpshooter. We coulda used him against them renegades."

"He's off fightin' fer the niggers. Can't figure why."

"It's 'cause you folks from the South think it is just fine to enslave folks," Fredrickson replied. "The Brits outlawed slavery in 1833. It's about time the States joined the civilized countries."

"Youse Brits like to rule over all the dark-skinned folks in the world, but youse tried and failed to rule us Americans."

"Enough. The past is the past," the whiskered old timer growled, picking up the newspaper and spreading it on the table. "Listen. It says here that 'Lincoln had to fire another general' cause of the fiasco at Petersburg. Did you hear about that?"

He continued, reading from the *Colonist*. "The Union soldiers ran into the crater and were massacred. The north had five hundred casualties that day, and Lee took fifteen hundred prisoners. They gave the order to shoot the Blacks but capture the whites."

Alice overheard this exchange, and she had to steady herself.

"Mary, look after the customers. I have to sit down."

"You are as pale as a ghost. Is it David?"

"Yes. I think David may have been taken prisoner. That's why his letters stopped. I would have heard from the army if he was a casualty." She staggered to the kitchen, shaken. "I read about the Confederate prison. At Anderson Prison, men are starved and beaten. They don't survive."

When she finally got far enough away from her customers, she burst into tears.

CHAPTER TWENTY-SEVEN

Quesnellemouth, October 1864

Toowaewoot

Reverend Brown shook hands with four of the Tŝilhqot'in, bidding them farewell. He found Lhats'as?in sitting on the ground, shackled and looking morose.

We could have won the war, Lhats'as?in thought. *There are sixty thousand of us and just seven thousand whites. All the tribes should have fought. They will regret their cowardice.*

"Here," the Reverend offered. "Take a mouthful of liquor. That will help you get through this. Your men have had a drink."

Lhats'as?in pushed the bottle away. "No! Don't want white man justice or his liquor. You all liars."

The October wind blew cold. A skiff of snow covered the ground. Lhats'as?in's family stood expressionless at the back of the crowd. His young wife, Toowaewoot, with a blanket around her, held their baby. The two-year-old clung to her skirt, crying from the cold and wanting to be picked up. He couldn't understand why his father was in chains and why his mother was sad.

Alice understood the pain the young mother felt. What if David were about to be executed by the Confederates? She couldn't bear it.

Alice judged it would be an hour before the prisoners were led out to the scaffold. The cold would be too much for the toddler. Her heart went out to the family, not just the young mother but the families and friends of all the prisoners, standing in the bitter wind along the river. The condemned waited for the hangman, some clearly angry, others resigned to their fate.

This is our land! Not the Brits, they must be thinking. *Why execute us for protecting our land, our salmon, our women?*

Alice walked back to the roadhouse. She wept for David, who likely faced death in that horrible prison camp, and she wept for the Tŝilhqot'in people who didn't deserve their fate.

"Mary," Alice called. "Wrap up a dozen biscuits and make a jug of tea. Lots of sugar. Come with me. The roadhouse will look after itself for a few minutes."

They gave a mug of hot tea to Toowaewoot, knowing that the young mother would refuse food. She handed a warm biscuit to the toddler. He was frightened of Alice but took the food from Mary and crammed it into his mouth, butter and crumbs clinging to his cheeks. He licked his fingers, then pushed the crumbs and butter into his mouth. He smiled shyly at Mary.

After offering the others tea, Alice stood with the families, trying to show them that some whites were on their side. She was shunned by the gawkers.

A party-like atmosphere prevailed for the crowd of at least two hundred gathered in the streets as if a circus was coming to Quesnellemouth to entertain them. Miners came from the gold diggings; shopkeepers closed their businesses. A newlywed couple attended, giggling in happiness. McLean's son was anxious to see the men who killed his father swing by their necks, the longer the better as far as he was concerned.

"There they are!" yelled one of the onlookers. The prisoners, in chains, walked up the twelve steps of the scaffold. The crowd became silent.

Reverend Brown spoke to each of the condemned men. When he reached Lhats'as?in he said, "You don't want to die unshriven do you, son? Confess your sins, and God will take you in his arms."

Lhats'as?in didn't understand.

Reverend Brown explained, "If you don't confess, you won't enter heaven."

Lhats'as?in turned away, ignoring the Reverend's warning. He looked longingly at his family standing near the back of the crowd.

"Have courage!" Talhpitt yelled to the other Tsilhqot'in warriors in the crowd. "Put down your muskets and fight no more."

Alice saw Lhats'as?in react. He scowled. It was obvious he did not harbour the same sentiments as Talhpitt. He had done nothing wrong; he was defending his land, his people, and the foreigners were going to exact their revenge on the enemy they had conquered through trickery.

The hangman placed hoods and nooses on the prisoners and gave the signal. The drops fell. The crowd cheered and clapped.

Toowaewoot sobbed. The Tŝilhqot'in people turned away; they couldn't watch. They wailed, their voices tormented; others felt only hatred for the English, the invaders who had stolen their land. There was no justice for the Tŝilhqot'in in this world under British rule.

Alice, saddened and disheartened by the event, returned to Mary and the roadhouse. Customers wanted a dinner after waiting in the cold for so long. They talked loudly about the hangings. Alice couldn't bear their good spirits. Her thoughts were with the young mother, mourning her loved one, and on David, far away in the U.S.

Mary ran breathlessly into the roadhouse. She had gone to meet the packtrain.

"There is a letter for you, but I don't recognize the handwriting."

A cold shiver ran up Alice's back. She opened the letter slowly, fearing the news.

ATIONAL

Potomac, July 30, 1864

Mrs. Ackerman,

    I take the sad task of informing you that your husband, one of my Co. is missing in action and believed dead. He fought so bravely at the battle of the Crater at Petersburg. The Confederates killed the Negroes indiscriminately and likely killed your dear man. His body was not found.

    I but speak the feelings of his whole Company when I say they deeply feel the loss of so Courageous and Kind a Soldier ever redy to lend a helping hand to those who were in need. Prompt in all his dutyes, he was esteemed by his officers and Each and Every one sends their wishes that somehow he survived and was taken prisoner. We don't know for sure.

                    Our prayers are with you.
           Sergt. Bellows of the IX Corps

Alice held the letter for some time. Tears fell down her cheeks. "How can I live without you? Please, please don't be gone. Stay alive, my love."

Winter came to Quesnellemouth, bringing bitter cold. Snow covered the hills to the east, and the river ice formed. The burgeoning community had seen buildings go up each week—churches and houses. A feeling of optimism prevailed. Would Williams Creek lead to more gold strikes? The last pack train of the season arrived with as many as one hundred mules, each mule carrying five hundred pounds of supplies. They arrived at Fraser's General Merchandise led by Castelene, the tough Frenchman. Locals said that he slept in the open in rain, sleet and snow.

Alice felt desolate. She wore black and cried every night. Little Mary did everything she could think of to comfort her, but Alice ate sparingly, cups of tea and a little soup. Her sleep was interrupted by visions of soldiers running into the crater and being slaughtered.

The roadhouse remained busy until the cold and snow drove the miners from the diggings south to New Westminster or Victoria.

Mary went to school each morning. "Don't be sad, Mom. David is not dead. My angels are looking after him. They are better angels. They won't let him die."

Alice smiled softly, kissed Mary and held her tight.

One afternoon, Mary came home from school, the frost almost closing her eyelids. She looked pleadingly at Alice.

"Would you mind if this dog lived with us?" The puppy was a cross between a German Shepherd and a wolf. It crawled under the table and lay quiet, as if acceptance depended on good behaviour.

Alice was too depressed to think. "You want a dog? Why?"

"The men were going to shoot her. She stole food from their tent. Please, Mom." Mary's voice cracked. "I'll take care of her."

"I don't know, Mary. A dog in a roadhouse? The customers won't like it."

Mary stifled her cry. She turned and took the dog out.

Alice, seeing Mary so upset, went after her. The little girl had never cried since Alice had taken her in two years ago. Now the child sobbed uncontrollably, as if she was weeping for her lost family as well as the dog.

Alice caught up to her, bent down and held the girl in her arms. "Of course, you may keep the puppy, Mary. I am sorry I made you cry. I am so wrapped up in my own misery that I'm not thinking straight."

Mary's tears froze on her cheeks.

"Come inside where it is warm. And bring that ball of fur with you. What will you call the puppy?"

"Tasha." She wiped her tears and bent to nuzzle the soft furry pup. "Thank you, Mother. Thank you."

Later, Alice confided in Walter, a regular, as he was eating biscuits and moose stew in the roadhouse. "I wish this frightful business was over. Haven't the colonists exacted enough revenge from these poor people?"

Walter remained slim and fit, despite the good food his Musquem wife cooked. Salmon—baked, smoked, boiled in a soup—with bannock, and best of all, salmon dried in the sun until it tasted like candy. His wife also sewed the beautiful, beaded vest and moccasins he wore.

"It will get worse for the Indians before it gets better," Walter replied sadly. "My dear wife was refused service in Victoria. She is a moral woman, dressed in fine clothes, has money, but they treat her like...well...like shit. It makes my blood boil."

Walter paused as he mopped up the gravy with his biscuit. "Did you hear that Chedekki escaped from the carriage on the way to New Westminster?"

"Thank God. One less soul to pray for. I guess Judge Crease will see ?Ahan hanged. He and Lutas have been hunted since the beginning of the war. It was so unfair because they surrendered and offered a tribute as was their custom. They couldn't understand why their gesture of goodwill was ignored. The Colony had to get its pound of flesh.

"?Ahan was sent to the gallows in New Westminster. Judge Crease convicted Lutas, but Governor Seymour pardoned him. He said he considered the horror of smallpox felt by the Indians."

"Well, bless my soul!" Walter said, smiling. "A colonial official with a bit of heart."

"I am relieved to hear of Lutas's release from hangman's noose. The death of the Tŝilhqot'in warriors has been on my mind, along with the news that David is missing in action." Alice placed a hand on her worried forehead. "Mary says I must not fret, that David is being watched by her angels."

"Her angels best watch over Chedekki as a well. If he is caught, the renegades will string him up."

"I've heard he is in Tŝilhqot'in territory, being sheltered by his people," Alice replied.

"There's news from the creeks that Billy Barker has found gold," she continued. "Miners are pouring in, and I've had more customers than I could handle, that is, until the real cold came down on us."

"How do you know all this, Alice?" Walter asked, wiping his mouth with a napkin. "Do you have your own telegraph?"

"Their people talk to me. They trust me." Alice gave him a tiny smile, a smile that she had repressed since the news of David's capture.

CHAPTER TWENTY-EIGHT

Quesnellemouth, Spring 1865

Alice

A lice often walked along the Fraser River, enjoying the return of the sun and the fresh scents of spring. *Where is David,* she wondered. *Is he alive, injured? Surely the war will end soon, so that I can learn of his fate.*

And finally, a letter, but not from David; she would know his fine script anywhere. Alice couldn't open the letter; she feared its contents. He was dead. She was sure of it. The letter burned in her hand. She headed back to the roadhouse, her stomach knotting in pain.

She walked slowly under a clear blue sky, the cool, spring wind buffeting her long cotton skirt. Frost still coated the branches of the poplars. *How can so beautiful a day be the day I learn that you are still missing, captured or dead,* she thought.

It was mid-afternoon, and the roadhouse was quiet. Mary was not in school and would be home. *Thank God for Mary,* Alice thought. *What would I do without that child's love? Without her, I could not live if David is dead.*

He knew I would need someone, didn't he? David told me Mary would be a comfort. With thousands and thousands of soldiers dead in that dreadful war, David knew he might be a killed. He didn't want me to be alone.

"You have a letter!" Mary met her at the door and noticed the tears. "Why are you weeping? Alice, you must open the letter. David could be in hospital or captured."

Alice thrust the letter at Mary with trembling hands. "Read it to me. I can't bear it."

177

PETERSBURG FIELD HOSPITAL

October 19, 1865

Mrs. Alice Ackerman,

I am writing to you from the field hospital at Petersburg as you are listed as the wife of David Ackerman of the 5th New York Cavalry. He suffered terrible treatment at Anderson prison, but he escaped with three other poor souls. They reached Sherman's army at Milledgeville, the lost army they called it because no one knew where Sherman was from January to March.

That man, Wirz, who ran the prison, will be charged with war crimes. Sherman will see to it. Wirz put the prisoners on rations that no man could survive on. The two men who escaped with David had been there a year and were only skeletons. The prisoners' condition sickened the commanders and soldiers who welcomed them back to the Union lines.

The prison had no fresh water. When David tried to reach over the fence for a drink, a guard shot him. The ball ripped through David's arm, and because of the filthy conditions, his wound became gangrenous. If he hadn't escaped, he would have died. Unfortunately, his arm had to be amputated here in the field hospital.

Tears poured down Alice's face. "He's alive, Mary! He's alive!"

"Shall I keep reading?"

"Yes, of course," Alice said, tears of joy streaming down her face.

I'm writing you as David will not. He told me he is not a whole man; that you must let him go. He asked me to tell you he was going back to his mother and sister in New York. His father passed away, and they need him.

"But I care not if you have lost an arm, dear soul. I want you home with me."

"Shall I continue?" Mary said quietly. She was a good reader, pronouncing every word clearly with a slight French accent she learned from Sister Angeline who taught her.

"Yes, I must hear more."

I don't believe you should give up on him, and I urge you to write to him. I am enclosing an envelope addressed to the Army Square Hospital in Washington. He will be transferred there.

The war will end soon. Atlanta fell in July last year, and now Sherman and Grant have old Bobby Lee surrounded.

Why did the Confederate soldiers fight to retain slavery? Most were not slave owners; they were poor wretches. I beg your patience as I digress. David and I talked often; he has strong views as well, as you likely know.

I implore you to write to David. Many of the amputees give up on life. Please give him a reason to live.

Your faithful servant,
Sergeant Altwater
Surgeon, Field Hospital

"I will write to David. He must know that I love him and want him to return to me." Alice ran to her office and sat down at her rolltop desk.

Dearest David,

I cannot and will not give you up. I would love you if you were so wounded that only your dear heart remained. Don't you understand? It has taken me so long to learn to love again after the death of my daughter. Now I am healed and want with all my heart to hold you and love you forever. It matters not that you have lost an arm.

Please come back to me.

Alice

She mailed the letter addressed to the hospital in Washington. All she could do now was wait.

Lee surrendered, and the war will be over soon. The news was passed from miner to miner. Most miners were from the United States, and many had brothers or cousins fighting in the war. And again they were lamenting about the war and their hardships while having a meal at Alice's roadhouse.

"We couldn't beat those bloody Yankees. They had too many guns and three times as many men," griped the Confederate sympathizer that had taunted Alice about the Union deaths at the Crater.

"The South will never forget. Never. And givin' the Negroes freedom, like they was one of us? You might as well give the Injuns land and rights. It's downright criminal."

"At least there's an end to the fighting. Isn't five years long enough? At least now we can go home to a united country," a ragged miner said.

"Some country. I'll never go north and live with those Yankees."

"Didja hear that there's been a big strike on the creeks, and a town is growing up around it? Or, several towns, but Barkerville is the biggest."

"At least the road to the goldfields is built. They ain't goin' through Lillooet no more. They finished the road up the canyon."

"We won't have to pay two hundred and fifty for a sack of flour that should cost only a few bucks."

"The road will help you, Miss Alice. You'll get your grub cheaper and faster. That right?"

"Everyone was waiting for the bridge over the Fraser River except the Natives," Alice said.

It will put them out of work. There won't be any packing once they have mules and horses pulling huge freight wagons. But she didn't share these thoughts with the unsympathetic miners.

No letter came for Alice for months though she had written to David every week. She was despondent, and she couldn't sleep or cried herself to sleep. Nights were the worst.

Finally, she received a package from the hospital.

Alice walked back to the roadhouse from the post, afraid to open the bundle. It was more bad news, she was certain.

It was May; the trees were in leaf, and a fresh smell lingered in the air. Alice should have been happy. Mary saw her come into the dining room, clutching the package to her breast.

"Is that from David?" Mary had grown to be a graceful girl with beautiful dark eyes. She was dressed in a clean gingham frock and white apron. "Can I help you open it?"

Alice handed the package to Mary without a word; she felt so weak.

"Sit yourself down, Mother. You look so pale; don't you worry yourself so."

The parcel revealed a stack of letters—Alice's letters—all unopened. Alice gasped, and her eyes filled with tears.

"He must be dead," she cried.

"Wait." Mary reached over and held Alice's hand to comfort her. "There's a note."

December 20, 1865

War Hospital, Washington

Mrs. Ackerman,

David has returned to his family in New York and told me you should not write again and that you must let him go. I am sorry to say that he did not read your letters. He does not want to be a burden to you.

I am the surgeon who amputated David's arm and looked after him while he recovered. Despite what he has said to me, I urge you to write to David.

He still loves you. I am sure. He spoke your name over and over when he was delirious with pain.

Please do not give up. I have seen many amputees. They want to end their lives because they cannot face living with one arm or no legs. They become isolated and take to drink. Rarely are they able to come to terms easily with their new life. It will take David time. With love he may be able to find ways to deal with it.

He was a sharpshooter and an excellent rider. He is accustomed to helping others. Now he cannot even cut his own meat, and his skill with the gun is gone. You must understand what he is going through. He believes all is lost.

Do not let him go.

Your servant,

Captain Altwater

Surgeon, War Hospital

Alice was silent, taking in the surgeon's message.

"He's alive?" Mary asked.

"Yes. He's alive, but he does not love me or want me."

"You don't know that. He loved you very much. He loved both of us. I could see that even when I was a child. I do not believe you have lost his love."

Mary was now of an age that she read Jane Austen's novels, and she saw love overcome all obstacles.

"Oh, Mary," Alice said between sobs. "That is not the way the world is. It is a cruel world where the ones you love are sometimes lost forever."

"I love you, and you love me, I will never leave you."

Alice held the young girl and cried. At first, she wept for the child she had lost in the snows of the Sierra Mountains and then for David. At last, her sobs subsided, and she let Mary go.

"You are so right, dear Mary; we have each other."

Alice went on with her work with Mary at her side. The flow of miners into Barkerville became a flood. The town built up seemingly overnight, with many miners passing through Quesnellemouth.

"We must expand, Mary. There are twenty more customers than I can look after."

Alice asked Walter to build a second storey with bunks, a larger kitchen and a dining room that would feed thirty. A local farmer partnered with Alice, supplying meat and vegetables for the dining room as well as feed for the horses. Alice hired a Tŝilhqot'in man to look after the stable and four more women to help with the cooking and housekeeping.

Shooleetsa, a young Tŝilhqot'in, did more than cook and clean. Her mother had taught her everything a woman should know to live off the land. Shooleetsa was often out gathering fiddleheads and roots to serve at the eatery. She could tan squirrel hides for moccasins and make sturdy baskets from birchbark, all to sell in the roadhouse.

Shooleetsa watched Alice and wondered what was making Alice so sad. Shooleetsa also suffered from the death of her young husband, killed in the war between the Tŝilhqot'in and the Brits. She realized that work kept Alice from dissolving into tears and misery. She understood.

Alice was so busy during the day and into the evening that she did not have time to think about David. Only when she tried to sleep did she regret rejecting David's offer of marriage. How many times did she refuse him? Now he no longer wanted her. How cruel life is…how unfair!

The dining room was particularly busy in the spring of 1866 as the miners surged into Barkerville in search of gold, most travelling the new Cariboo Road through the Fraser Canyon. Alice listened to the chatter as she served plates of pork chops and baked beans. With the road and the telegraph completed, news reached Quesnellemouth within days.

"Alice," Mary said as she helped clear the dining room. "May I speak to you? I have a proposal."

"Yes, of course. What is it, Mary?"

"You know that now the Cariboo Road is finished, you can travel to the Queen's City in days, not weeks; that the war in the United States has ended; and the stagecoach across America takes only a month."

"Yes, I've heard. The railroads should be completed next year, and then it will take only days to cross the continent."

"I think you should go to New York now, before the snow closes the route. You should go and find David."

"He cares naught for me."

"He needs you. I am sure. He thinks he will be a burden. The surgeon wrote that you must not give up."

PART II

CHAPTER TWENTY-NINE

The United States, Spring 1866

Mary

In less than a week, Alice and Mary were prepared for their journey. The hardest thing for Mary was leaving Tasha, now almost full grown and shadowing Mary's every step.

"You be a good dog for Shooleetsa," Alice said, petting Tasha. "No chewing her moccasins or stealing meat pies from the kitchen." Alice had hired Shooleetsa, to run the roadhouse while they were gone.

Mary kissed her dog on his furry head and hugged her. Tasha sensed that she would be parted from Mary and raced around the girl's legs as they packed for their trip. When Mary pulled the door closed, she could hear Tasha's whimper until they reached the stagecoach.

Alice and Mary boarded a coach pulled by six horses. They travelled along the Cariboo Road, stopping at roadhouses along the way. When they reached New Westminster, they took a boat to Victoria and then a ship to San Francisco. From there, the overland stagecoach would take them across the several states to the head of the railroad.

Mary was a cheerful companion, never complaining about the crowded stagecoach as they bumped along, stopping only to change horses every twenty miles.

Alice, as usual, stoically endured the difficult stages. She had endured far more of an ordeal when, as a young woman, she had crossed the Sierra Mountains in winter, watching her dear daughter, Amelia, falter and die in the snow. Their wagon train was caught in the snows of the Sierra Mountains and finally reached

ALICE ACKERMAN: THE CHILCOTIN SAGA

Sacramento, California in February. The loss of Amelia was devastating. Alice grieved for many years. She feared the pain would return if she crossed on the same route. Fortunately, they were to take the central route from Sacramento to the plains.

When the stagecoach stopped at Sutter's Fort in Sacramento, a Black woman boarded, dressed impeccably in a practical dark green travelling ensemble. Her boots were well-crafted, and she wore leather gloves and an embroidered cloak. Alice smiled at her and shifted over to make room.

Mary had never seen a Black person before. She knew it was not polite to stare but couldn't keep her eyes off the beautiful woman.

"I'm Mrs. Cooper," she said in a southern accent. "But call me Charity."

Alice introduced Mary and herself and settled in for the next stage. Alice was intrigued by Charity, wondering what a rich Black woman had been doing at Sutter's Fort. Alice had stayed at Sutter's Fort when she first came west.

"Why let the darky in?" a moustachioed man grumbled as he stepped into the coach. "Now that the war is over, those people think they can share our coaches."

"She is welcome," Alice said with a kind glance at the elegant Black woman. "Thank God Lincoln ended slavery, and the Negroes are now treated with some decency."

"John Wilkes Booth did us all a favour when he shot Lincoln," the moustachioed man retorted, "We'll see now if the niggers are treated like us. We'll see."

Alice did not respond and thought of the sad news that had been carried to the Cariboo, along with news of the end of that bloody war. Alice had learned that Lincoln had been killed just days after the Confederates surrendered.

"I cried for a week after I heard," Charity said to Alice. Charity wanted to show the vulgar man to see she was not afraid to speak up. "It was such a tragedy. Did you know that thousands of our people stood outside the White House weeping for Father Abe?"

"Yes, it was so heartbreaking. After everything he did for his country," Alice said before changing the subject. "Tell me, why were you staying at Sutter's place?" She didn't want to give the moustachioed man a chance to spout hatred about Lincoln and upset her companion.

"I own a haberdashery in San Francisco. The hats sell well in the city, but I also brought baskets of hats to sell at Sutter's Fort. The business provided the funds to pay passage for my husband and two of our three children. They were freed after the war whilst my babe is yet to be found." Charity paused, thinking back on the separation from her little baby, only six months old when the slave owner sold her. The pain of this loss felt like a blade cutting her into her heart.

"I am going east to search for her. She might have been rescued by abolitionists or may still be in the hands of the slaver who bought her."

"I can't imagine what it is like to have a child sold off like she was a goat."

Charity glared straight at the moustachioed man. "Thanks to Lincoln, it won't happen anymore."

Alice didn't want Charity to raise the ire of their travelling companion, so once again, she changed the subject.

"How did you manage to earn the money to start your business?"

"Yes, tell us," the man said with a sneer. "I'll bet my bottom dollar you did it on y'alls back."

Alice placed her hand gently on Charity's. "Don't respond to him."

Charity held back. "At first it was hard, after I was freed. It was in San Francisco. I had to work late into the night, almost as hard as I had worked on the plantation. Gradually, the ladies noticed my wares. I made beautiful hats. Expensive hats. The wealthiest ladies bought them. My husband was hired as a crew leader, and he makes a good wage, too. Now, we have enough money to search for Blossom. She was sold off when she was a babe to a lady wanting a child to cuddle and then for the master to use as he saw fit."

"That is terrible." Alice thought of the icy mountains where her young daughter died of exposure and starvation. "How you must have suffered."

"The master didn't care. He sold mothers from their children. I was sold to a family moving to California. They needed a wet nurse for their child. I cried every time I nursed that white baby."

Charity lowered her head, tears in her eyes. "That was two years ago." Her voice choked. "Now I must find Blossom."

Mary took this all in, thinking of the loss of her family. *At least the people of our tribe were not sold off like horses or chickens,* she thought.

"The family freed me when their child was weaned. They were good to me. They also helped me start my business." She wiped the tears from her cheek. "I learned to love that white baby. It helped heal me to hold her. But I did not forget my child; I thought of her every day. How Blossom would be walking…saying her first words. When she becomes attractive to the slaver, she will become a target for him. I must rescue her soon."

"You'll find her. I'm certain." Alice held Charity's hand. "Life is filled with tragedy. We must have hope, and we must pray for happiness." Alice thought of her journey across the continent and her hope to find David, to tell him of her deep feeling for him. To bring him back with her.

They were crossing the Sierras, a more southern route than Alice's party had taken twenty years before. Snow glistened on the peaks, stark white against the blue California sky. Soon they would be in the Humboldt Valley and then Fort Bridges. The journey went faster now that there was a rough road instead of just a trail. While they were in the mountains, it was difficult to fall asleep with the stagecoach bumping and heaving them from side to side. Alice finally fell asleep when the stagecoach reached the eastern flank of the Sierras.

In the morning, Alice asked Charity to tell her about her children and husband. Charity did love to talk. Alice could see why she was a successful businesswoman. Her diction was perfect, her manner refined. Apparently, unlike so many of her people, she had learned to read and write. The moustachioed man was uncouth, yet he thought himself superior. He sat across from them scowling, chewing tobacco and spitting on the floor of the carriage.

"Jem fled to the Union Army to fight for Lincoln and our freedom. He's a fine man." She paused and looked out the window to see the land flatten out as they sped over the dusty valley. "He joined the Fifth Maine Infantry, the Union Army's coloured division. He was sent to the Battle of the Wilderness."

"At the end of the war, he brought our two children west on the Wells Fargo Stage. They joined me in San Francisco. Our Polly is eleven; she's minding the shop while I'm away. Nate is seven. He's in school."

"The Wilderness was a dreadful battle," Alice said. "I heard of it way up north in the British Colony."

"Yes, it was. Wounded soldiers burned to death. They were screaming, and Jem could do nothing but listen and hoped they would die fast and be quit of their torture."

"Your husband survived?"

"He's been lucky all through the battles. Even at Petersburg when so many were killed or wounded in the crater."

"He was there?"

"Yes, and that is when the Grey Coats called out, 'Kill the niggers! Take the white soldiers prisoner!' My Jem escaped because he had a good captain."

Alice was silent as she took this in. Her face was white.

"What is it, Alice? Did you lose someone in that battle?"

"Yes. Not killed. Taken prisoner at the Battle of the Crater and incarcerated in Andersonville, in the deep South. The Confederates marched them hundreds of miles."

"I'm so sorry," Charity said, putting her arm around Alice. "Jem heard the men in the prison were starved, beaten and shot for getting a drink of foul water. Was it your husband?"

"No, my betrothed. He lost his arm. Amputated in the hospital after he escaped."

"Jem's captain, he was a white boy. Jem was captured and escaped Andersonville with four others. They tunneled out. It's a frightening story."

"David never told me how he escaped," Alice said. "I think I shall never know because David has rejected my love."

"Jerome was the captain. He went through a tunnel they dug. He knew the dogs and the chasers would be waiting for him. He stayed in the tunnel 'til midnight. Then he took his prison clothes off because the dogs would follow the scent of decay and hid naked in the tunnel."

Mary and Alice listened with rapt attention as Charity continued and moustache man snored in his sleep.

"He killed a guard and took the guard's rifle and uniform. Then he sent a signal to his men, and they crawled out through the tunnel." Charity paused to look out the window. They were passing a distinctive mountain at the edge of Humboldt Valley. "We have Captain Jerome to thank for my husband's life."

"What did they do then?" Alice asked. "Surely the guards would have captured such a large group?"

"The captain pretended he was a Confederate, taking the prisoners to cut trees for the stockade. It worked. They went by night and made their way to the Union lines. It was just in time.

One of the men had an injury to one his legs. It became swollen and red. All the men suffered from scurvy, their mouths filled with ulcers, some with their teeth falling out."

Her voice changed as she spoke with vitriol. "Wirz, that terrible man who ran the prison, gave the men so little to eat— a few spoons of cornmeal, no vegetables or fruit. He wanted them to die."

"My intended escaped as well. He was shot in the arm by a guard when he tried to drink some water."

"He crossed the deadline."

"What's that?"

"There was an area next to the stockade called the deadline. Men who stepped across the line were shot, often killed, sometimes wounded. If they had wounds, they would likely have died in that filthy place."

"I don't know very much, only information the surgeon passed on to me."

"There was almost no food, no shelter," Charity added. "Just makeshift shacks made from their coats. The place was rank with vermin, a place you wouldn't even keep animals. The prisoners were beaten to the bone."

"David's wound was gangrenous by the time he reached safety," Alice explained. "The surgeon told me he had to amputate David's arm, and I think that must have been impossible for a man like David to accept. He was a sharpshooter and a fine horseman. Now he needs help to cut his meat. He must hate it. He is a very independent man."

"Yes, it was a terrible war. They say five hundred thousand Americans died. Then someone murdered Father Lincoln, just days after the surrender? Terrible, terrible." Tears pooled in her eyes once again at the loss of their saviour.

Alice had no idea the death of the president had such an effect on the Black people. She cared naught for the governor of the British

Colonies. He was born in England, just an appointed hack who did London's bidding.

"I'm sorry you lost Lincoln. He gave your family freedom." Alice noticed moustached man still slept, his mouth open, reeking of stale liquor.

"He gave all of us our freedom. But without Lincoln, they will try and take it away. President Johnson, that lying, cheating, evil man is already revoking our freedoms, taking away the land General Grant gave us. Congress is trying to impeach Johnson because of his lies." Charity dabbed her eyes and looked out the window, watching the light fade over the bleak landscape.

The stagecoach went north, crossing a small mountain range during the night, and then the road followed the Snake River. The passengers were tossed from one side to another. Mary slept with her head on Alice's lap. It was a comfort to have the girl's soft body next to her. Alice bent to kiss Mary's cheek and gently pushed her dark hair back from her face. The child smelled like lavender even after weeks of travelling.

Charity was quiet. Alice welcomed the silence. Alice thought Charity might be thinking about a country without Lincoln to guide it. Perhaps she was thinking of her daughter in the hands of a slaver.

The passengers slept until they reached Salt Lake City, the home of the Mormons. They were relieved to have a hot meal after so many days in the coach. The next stop would be Fort Bridges. Alice dreaded Fort Bridges because it was from that town that Saxby, her former husband, had rashly taken the route over the Sierra Mountains, and half the members of their wagon train perished of starvation or exposure. His choice was the reason her young daughter, Amelia, died in the bitter cold and snow.

The memory from twenty years ago pained Alice's heart. She had recovered somewhat from Amelia's death. It had been many years, and the pain came less often. But now she wanted to be

David's wife. *How ironic,* she thought, *that when I am finally strong enough, when I had put the loss behind me, and David no longer loves me.* This was a new pain. Pain that set in her heart. She had to find him just to know for certain that he no longer cared that she should give up hoping.

The stagecoach took them along the Snake River, high above the winding waters and boiling rapids. The road was wide enough for one coach with no room for another coach to pass. Mary was on the side of the coach that overlooked the canyon.

"Jesus, Mother and Joseph!" Mary clutched the seat. "What if the coach slipped?"

"It won't darling," Alice reassured her. "You must enjoy the thrill and not worry. The only concern I have is the Platte River. After years of peace, the tribes are ambushing the stage lines. I guess the Arapaho realized that with the end of buffalo and the encroachment of settlers, their lifestyle won't survive."

"We done them tribes good at Sand Hill." Moustache man grinned, waking up and taking a swallow of brandy. "They won't trouble us 'cause they're kilt." His fowl breath surrounded Alice and Mary.

"Do you think it is funny to massacre Indians?" Mary was incensed. Alice placed a hand on the young girl's arm.

"Don't," she whispered. "It will only serve to stir the pot. You must take care, child." Alice moved Mary closer and drew circles on her back. "Go to sleep now. When the sun rises, we will be at the Mississippi River and the end of this bumpy crowded coach."

Alice remained awake through the night. Mary and Charity were asleep in minutes, leaving Alice alone with her worries.

Mary and Charity do not keep their heads down as most coloured people did, Alice thought. They were unafraid, proud and not humble at all. Alice admired their feisty attitude. It would surely get them into trouble, even in the northern states that led the abolishtionist movement. Charity's life would be at risk when she went south to find her daughter. The stately Black woman must learn how to travel in the former slave states without drawing attention. The war had only recently ended. The southerners' hatred for the freed slaves, and for the Yankees to whom they surrendered, was still fresh.

Alice dozed off just as the stagecoach reached the ferry over the Mississippi River.

"We're here, Mary." Alice smoothed Mary's hair and kissed the young girl's warm face.

CHAPTER THIRTY

Mississippi, Summer 1866

Charity

After crossing the famous Old Mud, the two women and the girl boarded the Hudson River Railroad headed for Manhattan Island. They were too excited to be tired. This was a first for Alice and Mary but not Charity. Had she been white, Charity would pass for a world traveller. Charity reminded Alice of her friend, Carreena, from their time on the Oregon Trail—a woman with an aristocratic bearing, a linguist...worldly. Why should the colour of one's skin matter so much? Charity had beautiful, olive skin. Alice pondered the unfairness of their world and thought of how Mary would also suffer for having dark skin.

They crossed the Hudson River on the ferry and could see the majestic Grand Central Station.

"I didn't know buildings could be that high!" Mary exclaimed, breaking Alice's train of thought.

Mary seemed as comfortable in the bustling city as if she had been born there. She was about to dash across the street when Alice caught her.

"Slow down," she warned.

There was an electric streetcar, horse and carriage and hansom cabs on the crowded street. Alice tucked a stray curl under her bonnet and held Mary's hand before speaking to her friend.

"Charity. Are you coming with us? We want to talk to you before you go."

"I'm staying in New York for a few days to search the orphanages for Blossom."

"If you don't find Blossom, will you travel south?" Alice asked.

"Yes, I will. I'm aware of the dangers, but I would go to the ends of the Earth to search for my baby."

"I want to know how to get in touch with you, especially if things go wrong," Alice said. "But first, we will go to a fine hotel, wash off the dirt of two thousand miles and change our clothes."

"You must know," Charity said with a smile, "that there is not a fine hotel in all of New York that allows Blacks or Indians."

"I thought the north had accommodated the free Blacks since before the war. Isn't this where many abolitionists live?"

"You have much to learn, dear Alice," Charity said with a warm smile.

They booked into the St. Nicholas Hotel with Charity as a ladies' maid and Mary as Alice's ward. It was an exquisite building with its white marble façade and high stained-glass windows.

Mary was amazed at the toilet, the water coming out of a faucet, the beds made up with cool, soft, clean linen. Mary rushed about the room admiring the furniture, the curtains, then looking out of their four-storey window at the busy streets below. Alice finally got the tired girl to bed by insisting that Mary have a bath in the ornate bathtub. Finally relaxed, Mary fell asleep the moment Alice tucked her in.

The three emerged from the hotel in the morning to a warm autumn day. They took the elevated railroad up Morning Side Heights and hired a hansom cab to take them to City Hall.

"I can't imagine having to find our way without you, Charity," Alice said as they strolled into City Hall.

The tall Black woman wore a light wool walking suit and fine leather boots. She had wanted to look like a ladies' maid but was not accustomed to anything but the finest costumes. She encouraged Alice to change her simple dress for a walking suit of blue velvet with a bonnet to match.

"You hope the staff at City Hall will help you find David?" Charity asked.

"David told me his family lives in New York, but he did not tell me where. If we have his address, I believe our world-wise companion can be counted on to lead us there," Alice said with a chuckle.

Charity negotiated Manhattan with ease, her head held high. Some Blacks lowered their heads, like dogs tied up for years in one place, and when the rope is cut, they remain enslaved, not willing to taste freedom in case it is snatched away.

Mary didn't cling to Alice; she hurried Alice forward as soon as the cab let them out.

"With Mary by your side, I think you will manage," Charity said. "She is a natural adventurer."

Mary led them to the clerk. A man in his early thirties sat at the oak wood counter. He had a handsome face and was neatly attired.

"Can I help you ladies?"

Alice looked like a New York lady of high society, not someone from a remote town in the British Colonies. She paused, unsure of herself.

"Alice seeks her friend David Ackerman," Mary piped up.

The clerk smiled at Mary. "You are in luck. The Ackerman's are well known in New York. They were among the first of the Dutch immigrants on Manhattan Island in the 17th century. Quite a history! They have a mansion in Gramercy Park. Do you know the family?"

Alice didn't know what to say. A mansion? How could she feel at ease in a mansion?

Mary was bursting to talk. "David Ackerman is a treasured friend. He was like a father to me."

The clerk had never dealt with such a strange trio before. The shy one was particularly charming. He was puzzled. They weren't related; that was clear. Although the girl obviously loved the exquisite woman.

"Is there anything else I can do for you?" He looked at Alice, but she lowered her gaze, uncomfortable with the young man's attention and not wanting to encourage him.

"No. Thank you so much, Sir. You have been very helpful."

Ah, she speaks, he thought.

Charity stepped forward. "There is something you might be able to help me with."

"Yes, Madam. What is that?"

"Can you direct me to the Society for Abolishment? I'm looking for my daughter."

"You should go to the Free African School in lower Manhattan on West Third Street. If you are looking for a relative freed from slavery, that is the place to go."

"Yes, my daughter, Blossom." Tears welled up at the mention of her child. "She was sold before the war ended. What if the slaver didn't want to give her up and has decided to insist on many years of work from my child to make up for the cost of her purchase?"

"Slavery is abominable," the clerk agreed. "President Lincoln and thousands of good men died to end the torture, mistreatment and inhuman practice. Do you agree?" he asked, looking at Alice. He did not want the beautiful woman in blue to leave.

"I can't imagine a nation that allowed its people to be enslaved." Her voice soft and very pleasing to the clerk. "The British did not allow slavery in the Colonies. Many former slaves fled to Canada to be free. What I will admit about the Colonies is that we mistreat the Natives, taking their land and even taking their lives."

The clerk kept his eyes on Alice. "Yes, we did, too. Massacres and lies, a history of mistreatment of those whose skin is a different colour."

"We won't solve the world's problems here," Alice said, anxious to get on with her search for David.

"But you have travelled all this way," the clerk pressed. Anything to stall this enchanting woman. "Might I ask why you have come to New York? It isn't just to see the Ackermans, is it?"

"Why yes, that is our sole reason." Alice paused and smoothed her skirt. "Could you tell us please how we get to Gramercy Park? Can we walk?"

"Yes. It is just two blocks east of Fifth Avenue. You know where that is, don't you?" The clerk was disappointed that Alice wanted to leave so quickly.

"Yes, I know New York," Charity answered. "But I must find the Black orphanages first. I must search in New York, and if I don't find Blossom here, I may have to go south."

"Ma'am, you must be careful down south. You won't be welcome in former slave states. I've heard some terrible stories of Negroes being murdered. I think that some ex-Confederates believe the Negroes are responsible for their loss of the war."

"If Blossom is in New York, we shall find her Charity," Mary piped up. "And then there will be no need to go into danger."

The women walked from City Hall up Broadway, jostling between horse-drawn hansoms, carriages and horses. Mary never seemed to tire of the sights and sounds of the city, taking in the scene and so excited to be in the bustling city. Charity and Alice were intent on finding their loved ones.

They strolled down the wide streets of Gramercy Park. A border of shady trees divided the broad street, which was lined by elegant brownstone houses. They walked along the sidewalk until they came to the address.

"Is this where David lives?" Mary asked. "He must be very rich to live in a house like this. Let's knock. I can't wait to see him." She moved toward the gate.

"No." Alice clutched Mary's arm. "Keep walking. I don't want him to see us. I'll send him a letter from the hotel, telling him that we're here."

"But Alice, you know he never opened your letters for the past year. If he sees us, it will be different. He'll want to talk to us."

"Do as Alice wishes," Charity admonished. "She does not want to be hurt, and if we go to the door, he may not welcome us. He will need time to read her letter and then we'll see him. Now can we go look for my Blossom?"

Alice had almost forgotten that they were also searching for Charity's daughter. She shook her head at her lapse in concentration and then thought of her quest to find David. She stood still and stared at the street. "Yes, we must go." But she still did not move. There was a gulf between the life she now lived in the remote northern town and this mansion.

"Come, Mother. Charity needs us," Mary urged. "Where do we start?"

"There are so many homes for the children orphaned by the war or separated from their parents," Charity said. "I only know of a few. I will begin with the Free African School as the clerk suggested then Home for Freed Children. There are several others located all over Manhattan and some in Brooklyn."

"Why not write to the homes?" Mary wondered aloud. "I could help you. The nuns at my first school wouldn't teach us to read and write. They said I will just clean houses and didn't need an education, but Sister Angelina taught me my letters and how to write a proper letter. May I write your letters? It would save us from having to walk from one end of New York to the other."

"Yes, child. Thank you."

They returned to the hotel where Mary studiously penned the letters in her neat handwriting.

To anyone having information on
my daughter, Blossom, who was taken
from me as a baby. She would be a little
over two by now. She has dark curly
hair, black eyes and a small
birthmark on her right shoulder.
Please write to me at St. Nicholas Hotel
on Broadway.

Charity Cooper

Alice spent the evening writing David but tore up seven letters, trying to say the right words.

"Don't worry, Mother," Mary said kindly. "He will want to see us. Just tell him we're here."

"Sister, you are making yourself ill," Charity said. "Listen to the girl, and stop using up all the hotel's stationary."

They spent the week waiting for replies to their letters and visiting the orphanages that were close by. The first response from their letters came from the Free Black Orphanage saying they had a two-year-old child who was brought to the orphanage in 1865, the year the war ended. No reply came to Alice's letter.

They took a hansom through the streets of Manhattan, first passing fine residents on wide, tree-lined streets and then, past smaller houses and tenements. It was a sunny autumn day with many people out on the street buying lunch from one of the many eateries. The aroma of grilling chicken wafted into the cab. The variety of food made Mary hungry. For a slim girl, she loved to eat.

While the busy streets with hawkers and exotic food enticed Mary, Alice longed for the wild beauty of the north. She did not care for the filth and noise of the city. It was unusually warm for an autumn day. The sun slanted down between tall buildings.

"The orphanage was built by Sarah Tillman, a Black woman," Charity said as the cab bumped over the streets.

Mary watched from the window, fascinated by the shops and homes along the road.

"After the war, Black women came to the city looking for work. No one would hire these women to care for their children and clean their homes if they brought their own children. Sarah found the solution; she opened an orphanage. There is nothing Black women won't do to get ahead now that they are free."

The hansom pulled up to a four-storey building with two wings, an impressive structure. A young Black woman met them at the door. She was dressed modestly in a black skirt and fitted jacket, her dark hair neatly rolled into a chignon.

She led them up the stairs to a large wood-panelled office with leather chairs surrounding a well-polished oak table. Cabinets lined the far wall.

"Please have a seat. You're looking for your children is my guess," she said, addressing Charity.

Charity nodded. "We wrote you a letter, and you replied that we should visit the orphanage. Is my two-year-old here? I am so anxious to find my baby. Her name is Blossom, or at least that is what we named her."

"I'll look in our files first. We have several little ones. Most are children of working mothers." She pulled out several files and returned to the table.

Charity couldn't restrain herself. "Would you allow me to look?" she said, reaching for one of the files.

"I'm afraid not. The files are private. I understand how it feels to lose a child. Please be patient." She ran her finger down the list. "Do you know what year she would have been brought to the orphanage?"

"When we were all freed at the end of the war. The slave owner would have had to give her up to the army."

"Ah. Here is a child, a baby girl who was brought in just after the war ended. We call her Harriet. I'll bring her." The young woman disappeared, her footfalls echoing down the pinewood hallway.

Charity couldn't sit still. She paced the floor wringing her hands, her stomach in a knot. The normally composed woman felt her life was about to change. Would this be the end of her search? Would she hold her sweet baby after all this time?

Charity heard footsteps approaching the room. She held her breath.

"Is this your baby?" In her arms the woman held a beautiful child with dark brown skin.

"No, it's not her," she said weeping. "My Blossom is black as coal with curly hair." Charity fell into a chair and burst into tears. "What will I do now? Oh, what will I do?"

"Come, come. Don't despair. We are taking in children every month. Some have working mothers; others have lost both parents. Sarah, the dear woman who started the orphanage, wanted the children to learn their letters," her voice became a whisper. "But the

Presbyterian minister who took over from Sarah would not allow schooling."

She paused, speaking even softer, almost conspiratorially. "Yes, he's white, but we continue to help the mothers despite the loss of our reading program. It will be better someday."

"That is something I doubt," Charity said, getting up from her chair. "We must go south now. Thank you for your trouble."

The cab was waiting outside to take them back to the hotel. Charity was distraught. Alice was sad. Mary remained quiet, not knowing what to say. Instead, she looked out the window as they trundled up the streets to the hotel.

After some time, Mary spoke. "We'll go with you Charity, because Mother and I know you cannot journey alone in the South. But before we leave, could we please have dinner at a fine hotel? I'm hungry, and you both need to look on the bright side. Charity, you will find Blossom. Mother, I know in my heart that David still loves you."

"You are the sweetest girl, Mary." Alice smiled and hugged Mary. "Of course, we'll take you to dinner, and yes, we'll go to Georgia to seek Blossom."

"We should go to Hettie's Soul Food," Charity suggested. "Hettie is a Black chef who started her eatery in a former stable. It is the tastiest food in New York. Fresh fish grilled with sauces and potatoes sliced thin, salted and then fried in fat." Charity's love for good cuisine helped put aside her disappointment in not finding Blossom in New York. She was prepared to start searching for her child in the South.

"I guess we can't go to Delmonico's," Mary said with a smile. "I just wanted to see it. The grand building, the glamorous women on the arms of handsome men."

"Delmonico will not let unaccompanied white women eat there, and will certainly not let us in," Charity replied. "But why don't we walk by Delmonico's on our way?"

They reached the street where the famous restaurant was located. Mary was curious. "I just want to see what it looks like inside. We'd only be a minute. No one will notice us with all the people coming and going."

"I'm afraid not, my little adventurer," Alice said with a smile. "You can see from across the street."

"Mother!" Mary cried out. "I believe I see David!" Mary started to run across the busy avenue, but Alice caught her.

It was David, and he held a woman on his good arm. She leaned toward him and smiled. She was younger than David, a beautiful woman dressed exquisitely.

Alice's face went white, and her stomach tied itself in knots. She watched as the couple walked to a carriage. David kissed her on the cheek before helping her inside.

Alice was speechless.

"You cannot know if they are man and wife, Alice," Charity said, her hand on Alice's shoulder to calm her.

"Maybe he has a friend, not a wife. I don't believe he would take another," Mary said reassuringly.

"You don't know what a cruel world this is, dear Mary." The tears flowed down Alice's cheeks. She turned away from the scene, almost stumbling along the street. Charity held her hand to balance her. The tears became a flood.

Alice sobbed uncontrollably. She was heartbroken. David had promised to come back to her. How could he abandon her? He had declared his love for her. Said he would love her forever. That was before he left to fight that dreadful war. That war that took so many lives and ruined so many men, blowing off arms and legs, changing them forever. Now her David loved another. Alice couldn't be consoled.

Charity had to go south to search for her baby. Alice didn't wish to remain in New York another day. The trip would distract her from her loss.

~

The next day, Alice held Mary's hand leading her through the crowds to the ferry that would take them across the Hudson River and then to the train terminal.

"I'm sorry, Ma'am. This ferry is for white folks only. You can go with your maid," he nodded toward Charity. "But the Indian gal is not allowed."

"I am not a maid," Charity said indignantly. "Transportation is for Blacks, whites, all of us. I am a woman of means. My man fought in the war to free us. This doesn't feel like freedom to me."

At first Alice said nothing. She was still traumatized from seeing David with another woman. A sob escaped, one that she couldn't control.

"Come. Let's go in the Blacks' coach," Alice finally said, not really caring one way or the other.

"I agree. I don't want to be where I am not wanted." Charity straightened her back, raised her chin and, taking Mary's hand, marched them to the segregated coach.

Alice remained unresponsive and weak from crying all night. Charity decided to let her friend grieve. *It will take time,* Charity thought. *It is like the years I suffered when Blossom was taken, filled with so much pain.*

Charity and Mary sat together. Mary, wise for her twelve years, a child who suffered the loss of her family, was an attentive listener.

Charity could not contain her sense of injustice. She spoke to the people in the car, mostly Black women, returning to their homes after a day of work or barter.

"We have human souls to be saved. Our souls are born free and independent!" Charity spoke like a pastor, like the Fraser River chief Mary had heard call out to the tribes.

Charity continued, her voice strong and commanding, "Slavery was a violation of these prerogatives; 'twas an infringement upon the laws of God. Are we not possessed of the Christian faith? Are we not prone to forgiveness? Do we not have refinements of taste as much as white people?"

The people in the coach were captivated by Charity's rich voice. They turned toward her, chanting after every sentence.

"Do we not have a talent for music, both vocal and instrumental, and genius for literature and science? Frederick Douglass' eloquent appeal to the tradition of equality; Phillis Wheatly, the distinguished poet; Banneker, the astronomer. An African brought his knowledge of protection from smallpox to this country, saving millions of lives. Yet we are despised, treated inhumanely as brutes or monkeys, unlawfully subjected to slavery. We should have the same rights as all Americans, not segregated as if we are less worthy."

"Yes!"

"Father Lincoln fought for our freedom."

"Yes, he did!"

"He died for us; killed by hatred."

"May he rest in peace."

"Throughout this great continent, people of colour are abused, spat upon, not given the rights of citizens, treated as inferior beings. This young girl," Charity gestured to Mary, "saw her family burned to death, her village destroyed. She witnessed Indian leaders executed for defending their land. In our country, which should be a peaceful land for all people, Gratton shot the chief in the back at Fort Laramie and then ordered his militia to slaughter the villagers."

Another passenger spoke up. "In Oregon, forty white settlers attacked the sleeping village of the Nasomah Indians at the mouth of the Coquille River, killing fifteen men and one woman."

"What of the massacre by Freemont of the peaceful Yana people in California?" Charity said. "Will the killing of people of colour ever stop? Indians in both countries and Blacks who suffered two hundred years of torture and bondage?"

"We must have faith in the good Lord," a woman said to Charity. She began humming. Soon others joined in singing the Civil War song they all knew so well.

> There's a great time coming,
> And it's not far off,
> Been long, long on the way.

The train chugged south toward Virginia. Alice remained expressionless, her eyes closed, sleeping off and on. When the train reached Fredrickson, Alice was suddenly watchful. Two years ago, General Grant led the Battle of the Wilderness where soldiers died screaming in the flames of a brush fire. It was a disaster for both armies. Soon the train would pass Petersburg where her beloved David was taken prisoner.

"Jem, my dear husband, fought at Petersburg where a foolish Union captain placed dynamite in the tunnel thinking the explosion would blow out a gap in the Confederates' defence. Instead, it dug a crater that the Union troops were caught in. Many were killed and captured. The southerners said, 'Take the white soldiers prisoner. Kill the niggers.'

"Jem's captain, a white boy, stepped between the executioners and his men, saving them from the bullets. When I heard the story from my husband, I had hope for our country." She paused.

The others in the coach listened attentively, especially Mary. She was a little girl but had been through the horrors of seeing her village burned and her parents and siblings dying in the flames.

"Bless his soul. I will be eternally grateful to him, a white man risking his life for Blacks." Charity paused, thinking of the blond-haired soldier who had saved her husband. "They were marched in chains five hundred miles south to Georgia to that dreadful prison."

"The poor man," one of the fellow passengers said. "He survived Andersonville? Thousands die in that hateful prison. Starved, living with no shelter, shot for no reason."

"Yes, with the help of the captain, he survived and is home with my other children whilst I search for my little one."

"Bless you, and I pray you will be guided by our good Lord," the passenger said.

"Yes, bless you," the others chanted.

The train approached Richmond and the plantations by the James River.

"We'll get off here and go by carriage," Alice said now that she had recovered a little from her heartache.

Mary looked at the crumbling buildings, the bombed-out shops and streets, Richmond's gutted bank and train depot.

She gawked. "Sweet Jesus! What happened to the city?"

"This is the aftermath of war. The Union Army wanted to punish the Confederate capital, to show that slave owner, Jefferson, that he was finished and should surrender. Of course, he did not give up. He went south to Lynchburg to rally his dwindling army. He took little boys as young as twelve and sent them into battle." Charity paused and looked around at the remains of Richmond. She led them to a stable owned by a young Black man. His carriages were clean and well maintained. The six horses in the stable stood near the fence, all well fed and groomed.

"My name is Charity Cooper. This is Miss Alice and her daughter, Mary. We would like you to take us to the Shelby Plantation on the James River."

"Pleased to make your acquaintance. Bo Turnball is the name, and I would be honoured to take y'all." He smiled at the women, showing beautiful, white teeth.

"You are doing well Bo, owning a stable," Charity said.

"I bought my freedom before the war. I had a good master who let me go at the low cost of five hundred dollars." Bo hitched up two black stallions. "Could've charged me a thousand. I just git by now. Business is down. The white folks don't have nothin'. Confederate money is useless."

"Business will pick up, Bo, soon as Richmond rebuilds." Charity boarded the carriage and took the reins. Mary and Alice followed, surprised at Charity's pluck.

"I come wid you. The whites will kill y'all if dey can git away wid it. Der was four men kilt dis month, and der will be more."

Charity handed Bo the reins and moved over, pleased to have his company. Once they left the devastated city, the road passed through rolling countryside.

"We're travelling on the slave trail," Charity said.

"Dat's right, Missus. Did you ever see the poor starvin' people? I were told dey were took from the slave pen and marched south. Dey needed cotton pickers, 'specially after slave trade done end. The people had sores from being beaten, the ropes eatin' into their flesh. One woman, carryin' her dead chil' because she wouldn't leave the babe on the trail."

"At the end of the war, there was happiness," Charity said. "My man, Jem, returned to take our two children to see Father Lincoln after Richmond surrendered. It was a beautiful spring day that those slavers deserted the city like rats abandoning a sinking ship. There was our president, a tall man in his beaver top hat, walking through the ruins whilst the Blacks crowded around him, thanking him for saving us poor slaves."

"Y'all is right. Dey loved Father Lincoln like he was Jesus hisself."

They travelled the road for an hour, passing beautiful old homes built along the James River. The war had spared these stately homes. Alice watched but did not talk. Mary was so amazed at the palatial homes, she was speechless.

"Why are Blacks still working the plantations?" Charity asked.

"It's the only home dey know. Dey git food and shelter and maybe a few coins for their work."

After another mile or so, Charity saw the hated house, the slave owner's house, the house where her baby was ripped from her arms.

"There it is!" Charity said, her heart beating faster. Would the bastard tell her who bought her babe? "Wait here, please. I have business with Mr. Shelby."

This is where Charity was born into slavery. Where her dear father was whipped to death protecting her from rape when she was only twelve. This is the place where she was wed and where Blossom was sold off, snatched from her arms while mother and babe hollered in anguish.

"So dis your Massa's place. Dey must've ben rich."

"Yes, my family was enslaved here until my man ran away to fight with the Union Army. They took my babe from me, and then I was sold off to a family moving to California."

Alice held Charity's hand, and Mary followed wide-eyed as they walked up the wide pathway leading to the colonnaded entrance and the porch.

"Did you live in this palace?" asked Mary.

"No. No, my sweet. We were slaves. Our little shack is out back."

Charity lifted the heavy door knocker and dropped it back on the heavy wood door. She shivered, remembering the tragic day Blossom was ripped from her arms. This house was not the grand palace that Mary saw; it was the house of such evil, a place where Mr. Shelby held unrestrained power over Charity's family. They had been the property of that one man. He could whip and rape them or sell off members of her family. As slaves, they were figures in the ledger, like horses or cows. She shuddered at the memory.

The door opened, and a smiling Black woman greeted them. "Well y'all look a' dat. If it ain't Charity. And don't you look hoity toity. I s'pose you comin' to find dat chil' of yours."

"I am," Charity replied firmly. "It's good to see you, Belle. Is Mr. Shelby in?"

Charity, Alice and Mary were taken into the foyer. Mary was aghast at the size and grandeur of the entrance. Bo was about to come in until Belle stopped him.

"The Massa, he don't entertain no coloureds in his parlour."

Charity held her head high. "He will see me. I have business with him." Belle was not about to argue.

"Come. Y'all can sit in the parlour 'til the Massa is ready to see you."

Belle led them down the gleaming foyer surrounded by columns and into a room richly furnished with soft sofas and a polished ornate desk.

Charity sat on the sofa. "I hate everything about this place. It was paid for with the labour and the blood of us Blacks. We made them rich. Without free labour, plantation owners would never have accumulated such wealth." Charity sat, her back straight. She would be defiant in front of the man who once claimed ownership of her. "Well, we'll see how Mr. Shelby does now that he must pay for labour."

Alice took Charity's hand, "This will be difficult for you. Remember to stay calm. You are more likely to find Blossom if you pretend you don't care so much."

"I'll try."

Just then, the heavy, ornate door opened. There he was. The man who had caused her and her family so much suffering. A tall, thin man in his sixties, walking with a stoop, hair turned salt and pepper, beard stained yellow from tobacco spit.

Alice rose. Charity and Mary followed suit.

"Well, girly! Lookie y'all dressed so fine. Trying to be like us, eh?"

"I would like to present Miss Alice Ackerman and her daughter, Mary."

"I don't need you pretending to be in society. Just tell me why you've come back now that y'all are free." Shelby couldn't avoid looking at Alice. She was dressed in a simple blue cotton frock, a blue that matched her eyes. *Just like a southern belle,* he thought.

"You know why I've come. You sold my Blossom. I want to know who has my baby."

"Well. Let's see now. What are you offering for the information?"

"Sir," Alice spoke in a firm but bitter voice. "The Union Army will come to Charity's aid. The Freedman's Bureau, I think it's called. Of course, we don't care to involve them. I'm sure you also want a peaceful meeting so that you can heal old wounds."

"Yes, of course. Now, let me see if I remember." He sat, his thin frame behind the desk. "It would be in my ledger."

The women sat quietly while Mr. Shelby leafed through the pages. "Yes, here it is. Sold to Mr. Jamieson who owns the Farrell Plantation."

He read the ledger in a reedy voice:

SOLD TO	Mr. Jamieson		
Slave 25 years old strong and well behaved		1	$1000
Slave 30 years old, good field worker		1	$1000
Baby 3 months old		1	$500
	TOTAL		$2500

"The Mister bought the babe for the Mrs. to bring up and have as a companion," Shelby explained.

Charity tried to control her anger. "And where is the Farrell plantation?"

"Macon, Georgia," he answered. "Y'all goin' to travel all that way for a baby that won't remember you? You crazy?"

"I would go to the ends of this earth to find *my* Blossom. You whites don't think our family means anything to us. You separated children from their mothers, husbands from their wives. Even told my Jem he would be sold down to the Deep South and get a new wife, a young girl who was a good breeder. Did you think we were cattle or horses to treat us so inhumanely?"

Charity couldn't help herself. The bitterness of all the years of injustice flooded to the surface. "I was his wife, married on this plantation before God. That is when Jem ran away to join the Union Army. Soon as I find Blossom, we'll all be together and all of us will be free."

Shelby scoffed, rose from his chair and walked away.

"Come, Charity." Alice took her friend's arm and gently led her out of the mansion and to the carriage.

Bo was waiting in the shade with his horses and the carriage. "Well, you find where she's at?"

"We have a long way to go, to Macon, Georgia," Charity replied.

"Y'all may be in danger in Georgia," Bo said on their way back to Richmond. "Don't think you kin just walk up and demand your baby. The vigilantes burned two churches. Dey evil, and dey hate freed niggers."

"We'll be careful," Charity said. "Does the train go to Macon?"

"Maybe. You take the train to Savannah and see if the train is running to Macon. You be careful, Missus."

CHAPTER THIRTY-ONE

Virginia to Georgia, Summer 1866

The Last Slave Ship

The three women boarded the segregated coach. It was filled
to capacity with women, some with baskets holding their
barter goods, others with their husbands still in their Union
Army uniforms.

"Charity, I must see where David was captured." Alice looked
out the window, wondering what the battle was like. She wanted to
see the crater, the place Charity had described.

"You'll see the crater when we reach Petersburg," Charity said.

Alice stared out the window as they passed plantations and farms.

"Petersburg is next. Watch closely, and you can still see the
giant hole blown by the Union's Major Burnside. He was so stupid.
Cost the Union five hundred men, killed, wounded or captured."

"It must have been dreadful," Alice said, thinking of her
beloved David.

"The crater was too deep," Charity explained. "The soldiers
could not scale the walls."

"This is where David was taken prisoner," Alice whispered.

"Yes, and my Jem," said Charity.

After the train pulled out of Petersburg, a beautiful African
spoke. "I have a story me thinks y'all have never heard."

The passengers turned to the woman. "Tell us. Time will pass
if we share our stories."

"The ship *Clotilda* done brung us to Mobile, Alabama. Do y'all
know about the last ship of slaves brought to America? It was against
your law to bring slaves. Y'all passed a law in 1808. Anyone
bringin'

slaves could be executed. Yet slaves fetched a lotta cash, much money. Two thousand dollars dey paid for me."

"Why so much?" asked the mother with a babe at her breast and a young girl at her side.

"Dey said I was a good breeder. Yes, like a buffalo or maybe a milking cow. I were desirable to slave owners. Y'all understand?"

"Yes," the nursing mother replied. "We all ben there. Used by our masters, taken from our husbands. When my man objected, tried to stop the master, my man was whipped. I done told my Moses dat he mustn't fight the master, dat he must leave be, or he be whipped to death."

"Yes," women chanted. "We done ben there."

"If we were slaves in the North, it be better," the mother continued. "Young women were still taken by the master, but we was taken care of. Sometimes, just like family. It were not all bad in the North. But the Deep South. It was a place we feared."

Tell us your story, 'bout the ship dat brought you from your homeland," the nursing mother said.

The storyteller spoke softly. Her tone deep with cadence so light that the travellers hung onto every word.

"My name is Abache. My African name. Dis is my story. Dat slaver, Meaner, he done get the ship *Clotilda* and hired Captain Foster to sail to the slave port in Africa. There were maybe one hundred of us taken from our homes, our family, our land."

The storyteller paused, and tears came to her eyes thinking of her homeland she would never see again.

"We was led in chains to a slave pen in Ouidah. Dat is the slave port in Africa. Your daddies and mommas, your grandads, grandmas pass through that horror of a place. Dey ben taken us people for more dan two hundred years."

She continued. "Ouidah, dat is where the ship were. Captain Foster, he looked at our skin, teeth, hands, feet, legs, arms. We spent the night, not wantin' to be separated from our families. Next mornin' we wade through a lagoon then to a beach then to canoes that took us to the *Clotilda*. The worse was they stripped us naked. Dey said it was for the lice. But dey want to show us we was nothin'. I was so humiliated, being naked in front of men. I'll never forget." Bitter tears formed in her eyes.

"It were filthy and dark, so hot. The ceiling of the hold was so low, we couldn't sit; we couldn't stand. We was chained up for six weeks with only a sip of water and less than a cup of mush and molasses each day. Der was little water and the molasses made us thirsty.

"I had me two chil'ren. The youngest, Matilda, were two. I not know where she be now. Dey sold her from me when we be in America." Abache was overcome and couldn't speak for a few minutes.

"You poor mother."

"We know your sorrow," others chanted.

"Like my Blossom," Charity said. "You are looking for your Matilda as I look for Blossom?"

The coach was quiet, many of the men and women thinking of their families separated by the plantation owners.

Several women began to weep. Finally, Abache composed herself and continued.

"I were unable to comfort me babes, crying der hearts out from loneliness and thirst. Gracie she be jus' four. She would hold her little sister whilst she done cry herself. To this day, I don't know where they done took my Matilda." Her eyes burned at the memory. "Oh yes! The misery of our people looked to be unending. But then the saviour came and freed us all."

"Yes! Father Abe gave his life for us."

"Yes, true dat," several men and women chanted.

The storyteller continued. "Dis was jus' before the war started. It was the year 1860 in the month of May. Yes, I was on the last slave ship.

"The *Clotilda* landed in Mobile, Alabama. Dey were short of cotton pickers because the war was about to start, a war for our freedom. We was still slaves and all terrified that we would be separated from our children. We spent the night crying, worried about them.

"Come morning we was taken to a slave pen. Here was where dey separated us. Took my babe from my arms. Three men and five women, dey were all put on da auction block. I watched as a stranger took my Matilda. She crying for her Momma; me sobbing my heart out.

"We was still naked. I cried for a day. But still I had to look after my Gracie, she bein' only four. She tried to comfort me. We were a day on a riverboat that took us to the Daly Plantation. Dere I picked cotton from dawn to dusk, getting whipped when we don't go fast enough. An old woman, she look after my Gracie. Four years we were slaves until the Union Army freed us."

"We been slaves all our lives," the nursing woman said. "Born into slavery. It's all we knew. Then one day we just walked away. Walked to General Grant and freedom. We was fed, sheltered, even educated. I cooked for the soldiers. We was called 'contraband.' I'm told it means captured property. But Grant, he didn't treat us like captured property. He done treat us like equals."

Other former slaves spoke up. Everyone in the coach had to voice an opinion about the years they had suffered, about the injustice their people had endured.

"Yes, General Grant, he freed us. He be a good leader, but it were General Sherman who gave us land. Now dey goin' take it away. It ain't fair. Just ain't fair."

"The land was for all the misery we suffered. Why take it away?"

"The land gave us the hope. At last, a place where our children, our husbands, could not be taken from us. Forty acres and a mule. That is what we was promised."

"It's been comin' on two years since the end of the war, and it don't look like it will be a just world for our people."

"Dat true," Abache said. "No justice for the crimes of white man to Black. Dat man Foster, he done took the *Clotilda* and set fire to it so it couldn't be used as evidence. Da law catch up to the slaver, Meaner, and Captain Foster. What did dey git? The scaffold? No! Jail time? No! Cleared of all charges. Not even a fine for all the misery and heartbreak dey gave us. The law in America is a white person's law. A white person could shoot us down like a dog in the middle of Mobile, and the law would blame us, not the white man."

"All that will change, God willin'," Charity offered, then many other fellow passengers joined in.

"We don't got Lincoln. Dat Andrew Johnson. An assassin's bullet made him president. He ain't no Lincoln!"

"Yes, he be pardoning all the Confederates! Given our small garden plots and fields back to the plantation owners."

"General Sherman gave that land to the former slaves. Our people were to get forty acres and a mule. Not much for all the years of suffering. President Johnson, he took it all away."

"Johnson even gave land back to Jefferson Davis, that evil slave owner!"

"Our enemy who wouldn't surrender. Dat man who enlisted little boys to fight his evil war."

"Andrew Johnson is the devil hisself! The worst president we've had, and I hope he be the worse we ever have."

Alice and Mary never said a word. They only listened, thinking of the injustice in the colonies toward people with skin of a different colour. The colonists burned Mary's village and took their land away. Here the Blacks had slaved for two hundred years and were given a small piece of land and then had that land taken away.

"Next stop, Savannah," the conductor yelled.

"There ain't no rail to Macon," the ticket master told them in the depot. "Sherman done twisted all the rails. They ain't repaired yet, so you gotta take a coach."

They took lodging in Savannah to rest and clean up. The "coloured" hotel was neat and clean, run by Missy, a recently freed slave. Everything in the city was segregated lest the whites had to touch a railing, a toilet, a chair that the Blacks had used. Alice cringed at this. All those lives lost in battle, the suffering of the wounded, her own beloved David losing his arm. And what for? The Blacks are free but live in a nation that treats them worse than mongrels.

Early the next day, they boarded a coach along with three other passengers. General Sherman had destroyed rail lines, buildings and plantations across Georgia but left Savannah relatively untouched.

"You know why he didn't destroy Savannah, like he did Atlanta?" asked a Black man who was travelling with his wife and young daughter.

"I wondered," said Alice.

"General Sherman sent a note to Lincoln on December 20, 1864: 'I'm givin' you the city of Savannah as a Christmas present.' He didn't want to give the president a city in ruins."

"Most of Georgia is in ruins," Alice remarked, seeing the burned plantations outside the carriage window.

Mary watched as well, always curious about the country she passed through. She was relieved that Alice took an interest. She was still sad but was able to stem her tears.

The coach stopped at a stable to change horses and then travelled through the night and most of the next day. As the carriage approached Macon, they could see that much of the city had been spared.

"Look! The homes are like castles." Mary was excited to see the spacious buildings, as big as ten of her peoples' bush houses, even larger than a longhouse. "They must be so rich."

"Rich is right," Charity said bitterly. "And you know who made them rich? The slaves who were whipped if they couldn't keep up, the slaves who worked from sunup to sundown all their lives for nothing. The slave owners, like the ones who built these mansions, starved us, took our labour and gave us nothing. We built the mansions with our sweat and blood."

Mary's enthusiasm for the Renaissance architecture diminished. She still took an interest in the buildings along the treelined streets but saw the wealth differently.

"Where is your baby, Charity? Do you have an address?" Alice wanted so badly to help her friend. If they could save Blossom, Alice thought she might stop mourning David. It might help her to heal.

"She is kept at the Farrell Plantation. We will go there after we find rooms. It is on the west side of town, so we have to hire a carriage to take us there."

It was dusk when they set out. Charity was quiet as the carriage took them past plantation homes, now in ruins, wrecked by Sherman's army.

"The army sure did not spare these houses," Mary said.

"No, he didn't. General Sherman marched through Georgia taking all the crops, the animals and looting the farms. He was marching to the sea, leaving destruction in his wake. He wanted the Confederates to surrender, and it worked," Charity declared. "Lee's army surrendered on April 6, 1865, the day of our liberation."

The carriage stopped at a rundown plantation. The main house was built of wood, no columns, no marble flooring.

"I do hope your Blossom was cared for," said Alice. "It doesn't look like they even have a piece of bread to spare."

"As long as they give up my child to me, I shall get her back to health."

The outbuildings housed rusted machinery. The shacks where the slaves had been housed were falling apart. The grounds were overgrown with weeds, and refuse was scattered around the buildings. Charity had a sinking feeling in her stomach. Was Blossom kept in this horrible place?

The porch creaked as they walked to the door. Dead flowers filled the urns, and dust kicked up through the floorboards.

A thin, grey-haired man answered. "What you nigger want?"

"You have my baby. I've come to take her back."

"You are the mother that screamed at my foreman when he bought the niggers and a baby. He told me about you, and we both had a good laugh. A nigger woman crying over a baby that was owned by your master to sell or do with whatever he wants. It ain't your baby; it is the property of the slave owner. Who would think that a nigger would make such a fuss?"

"Just give Blossom to me," she said in a firm voice, "and there won't be any trouble."

"Trouble, you say. I'll show you what trouble is. I got friends that don't tolerate no niggers, or white do-gooders, or any darky." He looked at Alice and Mary with disgust, then slammed the door.

Charity knocked again and again. She tried the door, but it was locked.

"Now what?" Alice asked.

"There is a Black man, Mr. Colby, who works for the Freedman's Bureau. I'll ask for his help. The whites know he is effective because they offered him a thousand dollars to abandon his crusade. He didn't take it, saying, 'I would not take it if they gave me all the money the country was worth.' He is always in danger from the men who formed the Ku Klux Klan."

"What is that?" Mary asked.

"A group of violent men who want to keep the South as white man's country," Charity answered. "They burned our churches, lynched our people. They hate any Black person that holds land, holds office, gets an education or does well in this world. They have their boots on our necks."

"It is not so bad in the British Colonies," Mary piped up. "Indians are not citizens in our own country, but at least the white people don't burn our churches. The governor actually built the Indian school and hospital."

"They burned your village, Mary" Alice added. "They hung the Tŝilhqot'in chiefs and infected villages with smallpox. It was abuse that they tried to justify with lies."

Mr. Colby had an office in his home in the centre of Macon. When the women arrived, he opened the door himself. He was pleasantly plump, dressed impeccably in a dark suit and vest with a red cravat about his throat.

"Come in." He smiled warmly at the three women. "What can I do to help you?"

He offered them tea and listened attentively to their story. His diction was refined. He was graceful and handsome, his dark face clean shaven and his black hair in tight whorls.

"I know the Farrell Plantation and its owner, Mr. Jamieson," Mr. Colby said. "He is one of many plantation owners who tried to keep their former slaves after the war ended. I was unaware that he was still holding onto a baby. Those slavers won't give up."

"He can't keep my Blossom," Charity begged. "Can he?"

"No, my dear. It is against the Thirteenth Amendment to keep slaves:

> *Neither slavery nor involuntary servitude, except as a punishment for crime whereof the party shall have been duly convicted, shall exist within the United States, or any place subject to their jurisdiction.*

Those words are in our Constitution. It hasn't registered with some plantation owners who still terrorize the South. But we must be circumspect. Getting your child back will be risky."

"They could take my breath away, and I would miss it less than I miss my Blossom."

"We will help you, dear Mother," Colby said. "I don't want you to be another victim of southern hatred. We have people that will assist us. What I don't want is to stir up the hatred and have the southerners, filled with loss and resentment, come after you. We'll first try reason."

"That Jamieson, he won't see reason," Charity said.

"You and your friends should stay here for a day while we plan," Mr. Colby offered. "First, I need to help Lewis, a young man who is in trouble. All he did was stare at a white girl. But the vigilantes say that he whistled at the girl, even claimed that he despoiled her."

"What is wrong with these people?" Alice was perplexed. "A young man can't even look at a woman? Young men look at young women all around the world."

"In Georgia, Black men risk their lives if they as much as smile at a white girl," Mr. Colby said. "Now, I must go to meet my allies and try to find the poor boy before the lynch mob finds him."

"It's not right that coloured people must fear for their lives," Alice said. "At least the Natives in the British Colonies are not lynched for something so trivial as whistling. There is even inter-marriage between the races." Alice could not contain her sense of injustice and continued, her voice rising. "During the fur trade, it was accepted and condoned for traders to marry into the tribes. It's different now; women who marry a white man are usually banished from their tribe and not accepted in white society either. But lynching? No!"

"Well, my northern guest, you are quickly learning the shame of Georgia." Mr. Colby put on his frock coat and bowler hat and bade them good evening,

Mr. Colby took a carriage to where his friends waited.

"We know where Lewis is hiding, but so do the militia," said the minister of the Baptist Church, Reverend Wyatt Walker, one of Mr. Colby's faithful helpers. "We must make haste because Colonel McClennan has a posse gathered on Cherry Street."

The preacher had a commanding voice. "The Klan must not find the boy first." For a big man, he was limber and fast. He looked more like a longshoreman than a preacher.

"It makes me angry that McLennan is not in jail," said Mr. Etheridge, the owner of the local Black newspaper. "Do you know the government gave him back his land? Kicked ten Black families out then hired back a few of them on contract for pennies. Is this what we fought for?"

They were on foot, now, walking behind the buildings so they could sneak up on the church where Lewis was hiding. Reverend Walker took the small group to the side door of the church.

"Lewis! It's Colby. We are coming in." The three men slipped into the church, locking the door behind them.

Three boys emerged from the shadows. They were all young, between thirteen and fifteen. Aloysius, Reverend Walker's son, was the youngest of the group. Reverend Walker and Mr. Etheridge gasped upon seeing their sons.

"Why are you here?" the pastor asked Aloysius. "Don't you realize what danger you are in?

"They wanted to help me," Lewis said. "I told them to go home, that it wasn't their problem. They wouldn't leave me, and now we are all targets."

"Dey want to lynch us?" Aloysius's voice was high pitched, his face pale with fear.

"We didn't do nothin'!" It was Lewis, the oldest of the group. "Dey said I whistled at a white girl. Dey said I raped her! It's all lies. All I did was look at her. The girl must have told her father lies, and now the Klan wants to string us up."

"We are here to help, but we must be quick. McClennan and his vigilantes are headed for the church." Mr. Colby led the three boys to the same door they had come in, thinking it was safe.

"It's barricaded! Those bastards!" he yelled. They ran to the front door to find smoke pouring through the cracks.

Colby looked at the three boys. The younger two, Aloysius and Virgil, were terrified. Lewis remained stoic.

"Mr. Colby, thanks for trying to rescue us, for putting yourselves in danger. Those bastards want us boys, don't they? We are the entertainment for the killers," Lewis shouted defiantly.

"What will we do?" Aloysius cried out.

"We must find a way out," Mr. Colby said. "I'm so sorry we didn't rescue you in time. I'll try and reason with the mob."

Just as he said this, the fire licked up through the cracks. Soon, the flames were leaping all around them.

Mr. Colby tried the front door. Unbarricaded, the doors swung open. They stumbled out, gasping for air.

"You give us the boys, and you can go home to your families." McClennan wore a mask covering his face and a cape emblazoned with the Confederate flag.

Colby's heart pounded at the sight of the mob, at least forty men on horseback. Most wore some version of disguise. A few were armed, though it was illegal for southerners to carry guns.

"Stop talking McClennan," a masked vigilante yelled. "We'll just take Colby with 'em! Punishment for helping the guilty ones."

"No. There'll be trouble with the Feds if we harm Colby. He is protected...untouchable. We only want the boys."

The mob urged their horses forward. Mr. Colby, the newspaperman and the minister stood their ground. They were caught between the burning church and the Klan. Etheridge held onto his son, Virgil. Reverend Walker clutched Aloysius. "Stay close, son."

"Get out of the way!" McClennan commanded. "We don't want your death, Walker. We come for the boys. They're guilty and must be punished."

"Yeah. We don't condone no tomfoolery by niggers," shouted a hefty man on horseback.

"Y'all should go home, Colby. The boys are coming with us. Even if we have to kill y'all to git 'em." McClennan dismounted and approached the boys, his pistol raised.

"Daddy, please help me," Aloysius cried as McClennan and the fat man pulled at him. Reverend Walker clutched Aloysius with all his might.

The Reverend struggled against vigilantes. The fat man threw a rope around the boy's neck. His father let go for fear the rope would strangle his son.

"Let my son go! He's just thirteen," shouted Reverend Walker, his anguish palpable.

"Daddy, stop 'em! They gonna string us up."

"Let the pup go," McLennan said. The horsemen removed the bindings from Aloysius, roped the other two boys by the wrists and tied them to the horses.

"Run!" the Reverend said to Aloysius. "Go home to your mother."

"I can't leave you, Daddy."

"They won't harm me, son. Now run for your life. Tell Mother to alert the other families."

The boy sprinted away. He made it across Cherry Street when a musket shot rang out, piercing the quiet of Macon's treed street. Blackbirds took flight above the street. The boy crumpled in a pool of blood pouring from his thigh. Another shot, and Aloysius lay dead in the street.

"You're evil!" Reverend Walker cried. "Pure evil. I curse you! God will punish you for the death of my son." He sobbed uncontrollably as he stumbled into the street and knelt beside his son's body. "My dear son. My dear boy."

"We are going to keep the Old South for the whites. No more niggers elected. No more nigger newspapers, no more nigger businesses!"

Virgil and Lewis struggled against the ropes. In a final plea for his life, Virgil called out, "Help us! Please. Dey gonna lynch us. Please!" The three men grabbed at the ropes in a last effort to free the boys.

"You've had your warning." The cloaked leader drew his pistol and fired at Etheridge, who fell to the street, blood pouring from his chest.

"You two are next," McClennan barked. Mr. Colby and Reverend Walker were stunned, helpless in front of the group of murderers.

"Let's get on with it," the leader ordered. The two remaining rescuers could only watch as the mob pulled the two terrified boys down the street.

Walker picked up Aloysius and stumbled toward home, Colby helping him. Both men reeled from the violence, feeling defeated by their helplessness in the face of the Klan.

The mob whooped and hollered as they dragged the two boys down the street. A few white residents came out on their porches to watch then grabbed their coats and joined the mob.

Many Southerners couldn't watch. *Is this how we preserve Southern society, by killing children and burning churches?*

Night came suddenly in Georgia, sending shadows through the Colby home.

"Shouldn't we go check on Mr. Colby?" Charity asked Alice. Mary was in bed, and the two women were waiting in the parlour.

"It's late," Alice said. "He should be back by now."

"Ask Susie if she would look in on Mary whilst we are gone," Charity said.

The black of night had fallen by the time the two women emerged onto the street.

A few citizens sat on their porches alerted to the tragedy that was unfolding.

Charity walked up to an elderly couple. "Where did they take the boy?"

"We don't answer to no niggers," muttered an elderly man with a fringe of white whiskers surrounding his face. He wore an old frock coat. His wife said nothing.

"If you don't tell us, you'll regret your actions, Sir," Alice said in a firm voice.

"Well, if it isn't one of them Boston do-gooders. Turning your back on your race, are ya?"

"I am acting the way all good people must act. You should be ashamed of yourself. It is wrong."

The elderly woman rose from her rocking chair. "Custis, I won't be part of the atrocious behaviour of the Klan. And that is all I have to say." She turned to the two women. "They took those boys into the woods near the church." With that she slammed the door as she went in the house.

"Come, we must hurry." Charity took Alice's hand and ran to the church, now in flames.

They heard the mob before they saw it. It was a circus. Excited voices rose from the woods, becoming louder as the women approached the clearing where the mob had gathered.

Charity and Alice shifted quietly to the fringe of the crowd. Hundreds of people all jostled for a view. Some men wore bowler hats, suits and ties, others in white shirts and black hats, a few wearing capes and hoods, a smattering of women of poor means, others in their fine clothes. All were excited.

"There he is." Charity pointed to Mr. Colby standing behind a tree. "He best be careful, lest they lynch him as well."

"Draw the cape over your head, Charity, or they'll lynch you, too," Alice whispered.

Charity moved next to Mr. Colby.

"Come away, Mr. Colby. You can't save the boys," Charity implored. "They are gone already."

"I will witness this atrocity even if I risk my life. I must report to Congress in Washington, or we'll never see the end of violence." He touched Charity on the arm. "Listen!"

A masked man read the sentences. "We sentence Virgil Etheridge, to death by hangin' for the crime of oglin' a white girl."

The crowd cheered.

Mr. Colby inched forward. Virgil, only fourteen, the newspaperman's son, sobbed as they threw the noose over his head.

"We sentence Lewis Rufus to death by burnin' alive for the crime of rape."

A loud cheer erupted from the crowd. Alice and Charity gasped.

"I know that man," said Colby. "It's Ernie Richmond, the pharmacist. I'd know that man's voice anywhere. That's what I came to find out. Washington needs names or they won't investigate and can't prosecute. Not that they would ever convict a white man for the death of a Black boy."

"We'd best go," Charity pulled gently on Colby's coat.

"No, wait. I must be a witness."

"It is too gruesome. I can't watch," Alice said.

"Cover your eyes and ears, Alice," Colby said.

The vigilantes hoisted young Virgil up the hickory tree. "Help me, Mommy!" he cried. "Please!" His voice was choked off by the tightening rope.

The crowd cheered as they watched the young boy swing, his thin legs kicking one last time.

"Now, Lewis. It's your turn."

"Mr. Trimble," McClennan said, "will you do the honour?"

Lewis was stoic, his face a picture of hatred, hatred for the executioner, hatred for the white race and for the crowd that took pleasure in his torture.

Under Trimble's direction, the murderers built a fire a few feet away from the hickory tree where Virgil was hanged.

The torture commenced. The men hooted. Even a few cheers from the Southern women. Other women turned their heads or left the grisly scene. They thought of their young sons, playing games in the street, riding horses, so innocent at that age. *How can we live with this?*

A few of the men heated iron bars and amused themselves by pressing them onto Lewis's skin. As the bars were pulled away, his flesh came away with it. Lewis was defiant to the end, cursing the torturers until his last breath.

"We must leave now," Mr. Colby said, tears in his eyes.

Charity and Alice sobbed quietly as they stumbled home with Mr. Colby. They'd seen many killings and a few hangings, but they'd never seen anything so brutal in their lives as the execution of young Lewis.

Later that night, Mr. Colby and the Reverend Walker took the carriage back to retrieve the boys' bodies. They walked solemnly to the woods, the Reverend still sobbing over his son's death. At least Aloysius was not hanged or worse, tortured. Lewis had no family, but his friends came that night to witness the gruesome sight and help Mr. Colby with Lewis's body.

"They burned his body," one of his friends said. "But the bastards couldn't take his soul."

CHAPTER THIRTY-TWO

Macon, Georgia, Summer 1866

Colby

I t was a somber household the next morning.

"I must take my baby girl away from these horrible people," Charity said. "The Deep South is no place for a Black child."

"Southerners aren't all violent," Mr. Colby said, patting Charity's hand. "Only a minority commit these crimes. Mostly the men. They call themselves the Ku Klux Klan, whatever that means. It is true we aren't safe in Georgia. The vigilantes won't accept that the Confederates lost the war, so they are warring against us Blacks. Trying to stop Reconstruction."

"Reconstruction? What's that?" Mary asked.

"Lincoln, bless his soul, initiated Reconstruction to bring the southern states into the Union and lift up the Black people. Gave Black men the vote and forty acres of land and a mule." He paused, thinking of the promises made to his people. Bold promises that were not kept. "The aim was that Blacks be equal citizens with whites."

"The Georgians won't ever let Black people vote or go to school with their white children," Charity said. "Lewis's torture shows that the Klan, if that is what they are, will murder children, burn churches, whatever it takes to stop Reconstruction and to reclaim the days of the Old South."

"When they killed Lincoln, they killed our hopes," Mr. Colby told the women. "President Johnson, that lying scoundrel, is cozying up to the likes of the Klan, refusing to prosecute when Blacks are lynched, refusing to uphold the Constitution.

"A few Federal troops are still in the South to enforce the law, but there is little will in Washington. The land that was granted to the Blacks is being taken back and given to the very people that enslaved us."

Mary followed the discussion, always curious because her people were also being mistreated. She recalled that the colonists tried to extinguish her race, wipe Canada free of Indians. "Send the savages back to the forests!" she'd overheard the miners say while she waited tables at the roadhouse.

When she told her mother about this, Alice gave her a hug.

"Never you mind them, my sweet girl. You are far more educated than most of the riffraff. I do believe that Higgins cannot even spell dog."

Mary worried that her people, much like the Blacks and Natives in the U.S., would be prevented from taking their rightful place in their country.

Mr. Colby shifted the conversation to the rescue of Charity's baby. He didn't want little Mary to ask questions about last night. He thought, *That girl soaks up information like the hull of a boat collects barnacles.* They would be silent on Lewis's torture.

They left Mary with the housekeeper, and Mr. Colby took Charity and Alice in his horse and buggy to the Farrell Plantation.

Colby banged on the door. "Give up the child, Elroy. If you don't hand her back to her mother, I shall be forced to bring the militia."

"Bring the militia," Elroy scoffed from behind the closed door. "See if I care. Y'all got no authority here, nigger. Git yerself, the whore and the nigger off my porch."

"Elroy, you are flaunting the law." Colby spoke calmly. "It is the law of the land that no one may keep slaves."

"She ain't no slave, and we won't give 'er up. You'll need more than a nigger and a white woman who don't know any better to take her from us, boy."

"Come now, Mr. Jamieson," Alice pleaded. "The war is over. The South lost. It is illegal to hold Charity's baby."

"We'll be back Elroy," Mr. Colby warned. "I'll have to get the Freedman's Bureau involved, and then it will go harder on you."

"Come, Charity," he said. "I believe he won't give Blossom up without a fight, and we aren't prepared."

Charity and Alice were stunned. They really hadn't thought that the plantation owner would keep Blossom from her mother.

"I'll telegraph Washington for help," Colby said as he climbed into the buggy. "They will send troops to help you recover your baby."

"That will take weeks!" The distraught mother broke down in tears. "I've waited too long already. I must have my baby."

"Maybe there's another way." Alice tried to comfort her friend.

"I won't condone any rash action. As you witnessed last night, these people are capable of murder. We should wait for Federal troops."

"I might, too, be capable of murder unless he gives me my Blossom," Charity wailed. By this time they had arrived back at Colby's house.

"If you kill a white man, even if justified, they will hang you," Colby said, taking off his frock coat. "This is the South, and nothing will change in this century or maybe even in the next. Believe me."

"We need to devise a plan to recover Blossom. I promise you there will be no violence on our part," Charity said. "If I cannot rescue her, we will wait for the Federal soldiers."

"I can help" Mary said as she rushed forward to hug her mother. "I am small and agile."

"No, dear one. I won't let you take the risk."

"I'm not afraid. I'll be so careful. Please, let me help."

"Alice, I think she will be of help," Charity said. "We need to gain entrance. As Mary says, she is tiny. She could slip in through a window and open the door for us."

"What do you think, Mr. Colby?" Alice said.

"I know you are concerned about your daughter, Alice. However, I believe Charity is right. Now, what is the plan? Will you build a Trojan Horse?" he chuckled.

"We won't be as creative as the Greeks during the Trojan War," laughed Charity. "It will be dark, and I know a great deal about plantation houses, where the slave owners have hidden attics, stairwells and cellars. I'll find my Blossom."

"I'll try to help in case there is trouble," Mr. Colby said.

"We'll have to steal into the house," Charity said. "Even with the three of us, it will be difficult to rescue Blossom without being noticed, and you are not exactly light of foot." She smiled warmly at Mr. Colby.

"I agree. I'm like a bull in a china shop. Perhaps I'd be more of a hindrance than a help."

"Did you say you knew men who would come to our aid? Could you fetch them and bring them back to Jamieson's house?"

Colby nodded. "I'll take my brougham carriage so we have room for all of us."

Colby dropped off the three women at Jamieson's and was off to pick up his recruits.

The women and the girl, dressed in black, moved stealthily toward the house. Looking like two giant ravens and one little crow, they were swallowed up in the shadows in minutes.

"We'll go to the back of the house. Mary, I'll lift you up to the window. I want you to slip in and then unlock the kitchen door." Charity hugged the girl. "Good luck."

Alice and Charity waited at the kitchen door. Minutes passed. Alice paced nervously, worrying about her daughter. Charity wondered about her baby, aching to hold Blossom's warm body close to her breasts, to smell the sweet scent of her babe.

The door opened, and Mary was there, placing her fingers to her lips to silence them. "I heard footsteps," she whispered.

Charity moved quietly through the kitchen, beckoning Alice and Mary to follow.

Alice closed her eyes for a moment to adjust them to the dark. They made their way to the first set of stairs. Slowly, they crept up, thinking that each footfall would alert Jamieson and his wife.

"Shhh…," Charity whispered. "I hear someone upstairs." They paused on the stairs, afraid to move. They heard a door close. "I think it's safe now."

They reached the floor where plantation owners had their sleeping quarters. Charity glanced down the hallway, a puzzled look on her face. There were six doors. *Which one holds my baby?* she wondered.

"We have to go to the servants' quarters," she whispered to Alice. "The servants will be Black, like I am. They'll tell me where my baby is."

Alice and Mary could only follow Charity's lead. She led them up a second stairwell to the attic rooms.

"Mary, please stay at the top of the stairs and warn us if someone comes," Charity whispered when they reached the hallway to the servants' rooms.

"I'll whistle like a nightingale to warn you."

The two women moved silently along the shadowy hall. There were doors on each side, likely rooms used by the house slaves before emancipation. They opened each door.

"Listen," Charity whispered. "Do you hear that?"

They could hear a low moan coming from the last room. Charity pushed the door open.

She was shocked by what she saw. Two Black women in chains, one of them was crying softly as she and the other woman sat on filthy mats, each with a soiled blanket. A chain bolted into the wall held the two women in place.

"Bless the Good Lord," the younger woman cried at the sight of Charity, tears pouring down her face.

"You poor souls," Alice said, going to the shackled women and inspecting the locks. "Tell us where the key is, and we'll rescue you."

"First, I must find my baby," Charity said. "Do you know where she is?"

"Please save us, and we'll take you to the baby."

"I must find Blossom right now," Charity insisted.

"They done call the baby Melinda." It was the frail, sick woman who spoke.

"Where is she?" Charity demanded anxiously. "Is she okay? Have they hurt her?"

"We need to get out," the younger woman said. "Can you not help us? Can't you see Mindy is dying?"

Alice looked at Mindy, sickened by what she saw. The flesh on Mindy's leg had turned shades of black and purple."

"We will help you get to a doctor. First, you must tell Charity where to find her baby and tell me where the keys are so we can take your chains off."

"God be praised! The babe is in the room next to the Jamieson's bedroom. The nursery is the room closest to the stairwell. Since Mrs. Jamieson became ill, the poor babe ben left there alone most of the day and all night, uncared for and crying herself to sleep. And the keys are on the hearth."

Alice and Mary followed Charity down the narrow staircase to the second floor.

"Please stay here and keep watch," Charity whispered to Alice and Mary. She moved with light, fast footsteps toward the nursery.

Charity opened the door and scooped Blossom into her arms, weeping tears of joy. Blossom looked at the woman she didn't know was her mother. She didn't seem afraid of this stranger but sank into the warmth of her mother's arms as if it was the first time she had been loved since she'd been taken.

Charity held her baby in her arms, kissing the toddler while tears tricked down her cheeks. She led Alice and Mary down the dark staircase, cautious that her head didn't bump on the low ceiling. Charity nuzzled Blossom taking in her baby's sweet smell. No one said a word until they reached the kitchen.

"Go Charity. Take Blossom and Mary to safety," Alice urged. "Mr. Colby and his men should be back by now. He'll take you and the young ones back to his house. I will free the women. Ask Mr. Colby to come back. I'll need help with the sick woman." It had been years since the soft-spoken Alice felt compelled to take charge.

"No, Alice. That bastard may put you in chains as well. Come with me. We've done all we can do. I don't want you to be harmed. I have Blossom. I can't risk her life now that I found her."

"Charity, please just go. I don't want Mary in harm's way either. I want to stay. I will be all right. Jamieson won't harm a white woman."

Charity shook her head. "I'm not so sure about that."

"I can't go without you, Mother." Mary clung to Alice's arm.

"Shush. Speak softly, or they'll hear us," Charity warned. "We mustn't wake the family, or all will be lost. I've waited so long to rescue my darling child," she whispered.

"Your mother said to take you out, Mary. There are two women in chains, and your mother, bless her soul, plans to rescue them. Please, let's leave." She tugged on Mary's sleeve, growing frantic as the minutes passed.

COLBY

"I can help. Let me stay. Please. I can't leave you, Mother."

Blossom stirred, her eyes wide with wonder. "Girl," the child mumbled.

"Shh…, my darling," Charity whispered. "Mary, come immediately. We must go." She was exasperated. "You must understand; I have to take Blossom to safety."

"I understand. Go, Charity. Please take Blossom and go without me." Mary had her heels firmly planted.

Alice shook her head. "You are my brave girl." She bent to hug Mary. "If you are determined to stay, you can find the keys for me. You have sharp eyes. The women said the keys are on the hearth."

"Thank you both. I'll have Mr. Colby drive me home. God be with you." Charity moved with soft footsteps out the kitchen door and under the tall cedars. She kissed Blossom, and the toddler smiled at her and closed her eyes in peaceful sleep. Mr. Colby moved out of the shadows as she reached the street. Two men flanked him.

"Dear Charity! You found your baby. So, this is the beautiful little troublemaker." Colby looked behind her, confused. "Alice and the girl! Where are they?"

"Two Black women are being kept in chains. Alice and Mary have stayed to rescue them."

"Mary? Why the girl?"

"She refused to leave her mother." Charity shook her head, wishing she had grabbed the child and taken her to safety. "Mr. Colby, please take me and my Blossom to your house. There's time before Alice and Mary unchain the women and bring them out." She looked at the two men standing beside Mr. Colby. "Are you going to introduce me?"

"Yes, of course. My apologies. These are my two collaborators, Sampson and Nobel."

She looked them over as she shook their hands. Sampson was a powerful man in his twenties, dressed neatly in a white shirt and black pants, his muscles bulging against the tight linen shirtsleeves. Noble was middle-aged, thin and wiry, his scruffy cotton pants and shirt hanging on his slender frame.

"Will you men stay here and watch for the women? They will need your help once they rescue the two women still being kept as slaves. Be quiet. Be careful. The servants will be up soon, and you won't want to stir the hornet's nest."

Colby helped Charity and her baby into the carriage. He urged the horses to a gallop and was off.

Alice and Mary crept into the kitchen. A faint shaft of light came in through the window. The rest of the kitchen was dark. Mary searched the shelf above the hearth that held a cluster of spoons, bowls and pots. She tried to see through the gloom but couldn't spot the keys. She ran her fingers over the dishes knocking a cup on the floor. The noise startled Alice.

"I'm sorry for the noise," Mary whispered. "But look! I found the keys."

They ascended the first staircase. Both Alice and Mary feared that the noise had awakened the Jamiesons. They reached the second staircase and tiptoed up the narrow dark stairwell and down the hallway. Mary could smell the stench before Alice even opened the door.

Mary couldn't contain her revulsion when she saw the women in chains.

"This is my daughter, Mary."

"Bless you, child. My name is Callie May."

"Mary, unlock Mindy, the sick woman, and then Callie May," Alice directed.

Mary bent to unlock the chain around Mindy's neck. As she took the chain off, it tore a bit flesh from Mindy's throat. Tears pooled in Mary's eyes. How could anyone treat a human so cruelly?

"Take da chains from my wrists," Mindy begged. When Mary freed her, Mindy stared at her wrists, torn and bruised from the chains. "The Lawd bless you, dear chile'."

"We are eternally grateful to you," said Callie May. "I thought we would both die chained up here, even though freedom was at the door." The young woman was thin, her ribs showed, and her stomach distended from lack of food. She had been a beauty with light skin and long black hair. "We'll have to carry Mindy out. I don't think she can walk."

Alice thought Callie May was too weak to even carry a kitten. "We'll try," she assured her.

"I can help," Mary said.

Callie May saw that the girl was just a waif. "You have more courage than a Rebel soldier facing the Army of the Potomac."

"She is a brave soldier indeed," Alice agreed. "But Mary, you are too small to carry anyone, and besides, we need you to be our lookout. Callie May and I will try our best to carry Mindy."

The two women struggled to the stairwell, one holding Mindy's legs, the other her arms. Callie May panted and stumbled along, barely able to walk.

Alice wondered how long the two women had been left without food and water. They slowly gained the stairwell.

"Put Mindy down for a minute while you catch your breath," Alice whispered. "When we reach the second floor, we must be deadly quiet." With every movement, Mindy moaned from her wounds.

"We mustn't wake that son-of-a-bitch," Callie May said, panting from the exertion.

"Language, please. Mary is devout."

"Forgive me, but I hate dat man. Even more, I hate the overseer that does his dirty work. He is a master of violence. Theopolis caught us when we tried to run to the Union Army. We've been in that room every night for nigh on two years. Worked to the bone, nearly starved. Raped and whipped."

"Your suffering will soon be over. Are you rested enough to lift Mindy up again?"

Their muffled footfalls were the only sound as they lugged Mindy down the narrow staircase. All was cloaked in shadows. Callie May struggled, panting with every step. As they were about to reach the last step before the sleeping rooms of the family, Alice could sense that the young woman didn't have the strength to continue.

"Mary," Alice whispered, "you are likely stronger than this poor woman. Please take Mindy's feet. Callie May can't lift her anymore."

Alice, with her little daughter helping, moved across the landing leading to the last staircase. As they were about to descend the stairs, Callie May stumbled and fell.

"I'm so sorry."

Alice helped the emaciated woman to her feet.

"If you cannot manage the stairs, I will come back to get you after we take Mindy to safety."

Callie May crouched on the landing, fearing that the softest noise would wake the household. "Hurry, dear lady. I will kill myself rather than be imprisoned by that evil man."

Alice and Mary descended the staircase one step at a time, the sick woman's weight growing heavier with each step. They reached the kitchen and put Mindy on the floor so Mary could catch her breath. Mindy moaned as her opened sores brushed against the floorboards. Alice gently lifted Mindy to an upright position and placed her cloak on the floor to cushion the injured woman.

"The Lawd bless you, my angels."

"You rest, Mindy. I will bring Callie May, and we will all escape this house of horrors." Alice turned to her daughter. "You are such a courageous young girl. Now, can I ask you to stay with Mindy so I can help Callie May?"

"Are you sure you don't need my help?"

"Yes, my darling. I'll be back in the shake of a lamb's tail."

Alice disappeared up the staircase. Callie May tried to get up, putting one leg under her and grunting, trying to gain her feet. Alice's heart pounded, worried that they would wake the owners.

Although Alice was not a big woman, she was strong from all her hard work at the roadhouse. But she'd never had to carry a woman before, even a starved woman like Callie May.

With Callie May's arms about Alice's shoulders, they started down the last staircase. As they reached the kitchen, Callie May stumbled again.

"I don't think I can make it. Please leave me."

"Can you wait here whilst my daughter and I take Mindy to safety?"

"Yes, but please hurry, dear Alice. I'm terrified that I'll be put in chains again."

"Mary and I will take Mindy out. Once on the street, Mary will whistle for help. I won't be long."

Dawn was coming quickly. Towering cypress trees threw shadows across the yard, giving them cover. Mary strained to hold her end.

"All right, Mary. This is as far as I will go. Let's hear that nightingale's sing."

Mary pursed her lips and trilled like a bird.

"Mr. Colby will come to help with Mindy. You have been so brave. I am proud of you." With that, Alice ran to the house to retrieve Callie May *She has to walk*, Alice worried. *I can't carry her by myself.*

Alice held the emaciated woman around the waist, pausing every few steps to let Callie May regain her strength. When they finally reached the kitchen, Callie May was frantic. "Jamieson's coming, Alice. I heard him on the stairs."

"Quick! Put your arm on my shoulder. Lean on me."

Alice struggled to help Callie May across the kitchen floor, panting at the effort. They almost gained the door when a massive Black man loomed in the shadows. He was joined by Jamieson, who had descended the stairs to the kitchen.

"Oh, no!" Callie May cried.

Mindy lay on the forest floor while Mary leaned against a tree trunk, waiting for the men to help them. Colby appeared as the first signs of dawn crept through the trees.

"Where is your mother, Mary?" Mr. Colby's men and Charity were with him.

"What's goin' on? Where are the other women?" Sampson's frustration was palpable. "A little girl is rescuing a sick woman, doing somethin' I coulda done if y'all had asked."

"Why are you here, Charity? Where's Blossom?" Mary asked, puzzled by this change in the plans.

"Blossom is safe with Mr. Colby's housekeeper. My help is needed because I know the house, and I won't leave Alice."

"You've come across two thousand miles to rescue your Blossom," Mr. Colby argued. "You don't want to risk your life now. You drive Mindy to the hospital while my brethren and I see to Miss Alice."

"I intend to come with you. Alice has helped me from the beginning. I can't abandon her to that evil man."

"I have seldom encountered such brave women. Even you, Mary. You have all been fearless, like Olympia of ancient Rome who fought to save her son, Alexandria. You are ready to fight to protect the ones you love."

"Is this a fuck-up or what?" Nobel grumbled, a frustrated look on his wrinkled face.

"Language," Colby said sternly. "There's a child listening to you. We must deal with what we're given. We can't wait much longer for Alice and Callie May," Mr. Colby said. "Stay with Mindy," he said to Mary. "The rest of you, come with me."

"Mary, you must look after Mindy whilst I help Mr. Colby and his men aid your mother?" Charity said, kissing the girl's cheeks.

"Please hurry. I'm fearful for my mother."

Colby and his men stood in the shadows of the cedar trees. Charity was anxious to go to Alice's aid. The dawn was pushing the darkness away by the time they made their way to the kitchen door.

Colby tried to open the door, hoping they could sneak in unnoticed.

"Dey locked up tight. I know de bastard," Noble said. "He hates us niggers. He is one of the men who burned poor Lewis."

"Noble, put your skills as a burglar to work and open a window for us."

"I only stole from the families who stole our labour and blood for hundreds of years," Noble protested.

"They stole twenty years of my life, but I never broke de law," Sampson said. "I believe in de law. We must forget the torture. We is free now. Free men. Not recallin' past grievances. Now, you must stop gabbin'! Hurry and git us in de house."

"You be gabbin', not me," Noble argued.

There was a veranda around four sides of the house. The once ornate carvings were green with mould. Dust kicked up in the faint light of early morning.

Charity followed close behind Noble until he found a window he could pry open. Charity slipped through first. Colby was last to go. "Ach. Too much good cooking has rendered me fat."

Charity rushed into the kitchen and, seeing Alice and Callie May, she threw herself at Jamieson, fists pounding. Theopolis raised his rifle and fired. The gunshot blast sounded through the house and echoed through the cypress trees.

"My God. No!" Colby shouted, as he extricated himself from the window. He had a sick feeling in his stomach.

Sampson was the first to reach the kitchen. He found Alice bending over a still Charity. Callie May was crouched on the floor, terrified.

Sampson was unarmed. He ran at Theopolis before the overseer had time to reload. Sampson caught him by the waist, tackling him to the floor. Noble came to Sampson's aid, immobilizing the overseer.

Charity lay on the kitchen floor, shot in the chest, blood pooling on the floor, mixing with Alice's tears.

Colby ran to the scene, his face white, his heart aching.

"Well, if it isn't the thief. Come to steal de master's women are you? Best you git the hell out, or you'll git the next musket ball." Jamieson pointed a gun at Colby.

Without a thought for his safety, he ran at Jamieson, knocking down the frail slaver.

"Why did you have to kill her?" Colby cried. "You murderers! Both of you will hang for this."

"I was bein' robbed," Jamieson sputtered as he lay on the floor. "You bloody niggers are robbing me of my property. I'm just protecting what is mine."

"Your property? No! Your days and the days of the Old South have ended. There are laws against holding our people. There are laws against enslaving and murdering our people."

"You will see, sonny. The South will gain the upper hand once more now that that nigger-loving president has been relieved of his office and his life," the old man chortled.

Alice held her friend's hand and whispered softly as Charity's life ebbed away. "You are a good woman, better by far than the man who kidnapped your Blossom, far better than the man who shot you. Jesus knows and will welcome you into his arms." Alice kissed her cheek as Charity took her final breath.

Alice's eyes fell on the overseer, tied to the kitchen chair. "How could you take her life? Your evil will send you to hell. And you as well, Jamieson."

"Come." Colby lifted Alice by the elbow. "We must go. The Federal soldiers can collect this scum. Meanwhile, I'll have my men make sure they are locked up."

Noble carried Callie May in his thin, strong arms as if he was carrying a newborn lamb. Sampson cradled Charity, singing to her in a low, deep voice as he carried her body to the carriage. "In the arms of our Saviour, you will find peace and love."

"We'll take Mindy to the hospital immediately," Colby said, urging the horses to a canter. "Dr. Brandy Jordan will attend to her. He's one of us."

Once they returned to Mr. Colby's home, Alice shut herself in her room to grieve for her friend. *It is so senseless,* she thought. *Why did she risk her life for me?*

CHAPTER THIRTY-THREE

Macon, Georgia, Fall 1866

Mindy

Before Alice left with Mary, Mr. Colby told her that the Union Army would be coming to take custody of Jamieson and Theopolis. He mentioned that Lieutenant David Ackerman was to lead a division of the Union Army now that he was healed from his war injuries. Alice had no wish to see David. She needed to protect her heart from further pain.

The Federal government had had troops in the South since the end of hostilities. They were charged with looking after the Reconstruction program. Equality of the Negro was the aim, along with building up the South that had been devastated by the war.

Alice thought it would be many years before the Blacks found equality. The Southerners' hatred of Black politicians, their businesses, their schools was evident. Would their country ever heal?

The South wanted to start another war. That was clear. The people even supported the criminal Jesse James. He was a hero during the war and a hero after the war, robbing banks and killing Union soldiers who had fought in the war. The war should have brought Americans peace with the Indians and peace with the Southerners. Instead, there was only violence against the Natives and against Negroes.

Before Alice and Mary boarded the train with Blossom and Callie May, they visited Mindy who was recovering in hospital. Mindy's wounds were bandaged, and her spirit was positive.

"I cannot believe I be free at last," she said, showing a toothless smile. "Come here, little brave Indian." Mary moved to the frail woman's bedside, and Mindy took her hand. "The light of Jesus shines through you chile'. You will be a great teacher for your people, a leader among them, someone who will look after the flock."

"You get better now and help your people, dear Mindy. They have suffered so much. Forget the hatred you endured and lead a good life." Mary bent and kissed Mindy on the cheek.

"You are but a child," Colby said. "How is it that you have the understanding of a woman? I should recruit you to work with me, except I realize you must return to that frozen land to the north." He chuckled and then bent to hug Mary to his broad chest. "I thank you with all my heart for your bravery, my little Indian friend."

"I'm Salish." Mary said, not offended, but proud.

"Oh, is that right? Tell me about your people."

"We are artists, carvers, basket makers. We make beautiful cedar hats and weave blankets. We're not warlike at all."

"I'll remember that," he said with a smile. "Not Indian, but Salish."

Colby promised to look in on Mindy until she was better and help her in her new life, her first days of freedom after years of torture and slavery.

Sadness followed Alice as the train carried them north. Mary held the toddler, who had latched onto the Mary, preferring to be mothered by the young girl than the sad, tearful woman.

"I'm so sorry for the loss of your friend," Callie May said. "Charity gave her life for us, and you, dear woman, and your daughter risked your lives. Never in my lifetime did I believe a white woman would ever rescue me. The white women of Georgia, dey not mean as long as we are slaves or we say 'Yes, Ma'am, No, Ma'am.' But if we ever showed a spark of defiance, they whipped us."

"You are free now, Callie May. I hope you can learn to read so you can teach your people. Your day will come."

In New York, Alice and Mary had to change trains to the Union Pacific rail that would take them to Council Bluffs.

"Callie May, will you be all right in New York by yourself?" Alice asked as they left the train.

"Don't y'all worry about me. I have my freedom. I will find work and make my way. It ain't all bad." She kissed them both goodbye at the train station.

Alice watched out the window as the train took them west. Blossom yawned, and Mary and the baby slipped into sleep. Alice listened to their rhythmic breathing. How peaceful are the young, no bad dreams, no regrets.

The next day, they crossed into Indiana and would soon enter Illinois, Alice's home state and the town of Springfield where Amelia was born and where Alice's beloved James and their son had died.

Mary loved to talk but left Alice to her thoughts until she was ready. Alice watched the rolling fields and farmers' small huts and farm buildings, saying nothing for hours. She realized she was letting her melancholy affect the young girl and broke out of her misery.

"Mary, the train will soon arrive at Council Bluffs. I came here when I was a young woman. Amazing how everything has changed. Soon, there will be a train across to the Pacific Ocean." Alice could not tell Mary of the tragedy that she suffered years ago, the year her sweet daughter perished in the snows of the Sierras. "We travelled West in a Prairie Schooner."

"What is that?" Mary spoke softly lest she wake Blossom, who slept in her arms.

"It is a covered wagon. It carried all the supplies needed for the four-month trip across the continent. There was a place to sleep and a seat at the front for the driver. Our wagon was pulled by four horses, whereas most Overlanders used oxen."

Alice thought back to her days on the Oregon Trail and the difficult time she had as a young widow. She was married against her will to Saxby, a man who abused her. Saxby was impulsive, took parade horses instead of oxen, leading the entire wagon train into danger and causing her sweet daughter, Amelia's, death.

Alice mulled over events of the past, unable to sleep. The train moved onto the great plains with its smattering of farms dotting the flat land. The settlers were moving west, seeking free land. As the sun slashed across the prairies, she fell into a fitful sleep and woke as the train pulled into North Platte, Nebraska, the end of the rail line.

"Come, Mary. We must leave the train."

Blossom woke with wide and curious eyes. The two-year-old never fussed as long as Mary was nearby. The child clung to Mary like a lamb to its mother.

"The rail wasn't here when we travelled east," remarked Mary. "Did they build all this track in a few months? That is amazing."

"Union Pacific builds hundreds of miles of track every year. This is gentle land for the rail barons, but there will be trouble in the Sierras, believe me."

"The rail will reach Sacramento in a few years, right?" Mary had a mind like an adding machine, calculating the miles between North Platte and Sacramento in her head. "Too bad it isn't finished; the train is so much easier than the stagecoach. Will we have trouble in the Sierras? Winter will be upon us soon."

"We will be safe. The stagecoach takes the southern route to avoid the mountains. A little longer, but much safer."

They walked through the boomtown. Its buildings had been thrown up in haste to be ready for the train. Alice checked them into an hotel before booking their passage on the Wells Fargo stagecoach for the next day.

CHAPTER THIRTY-FOUR

San Francisco, Fall, 1866

Polly

They arrived in San Francisco, anxious to find Charity's family. How would they tell her daughter, her son and her husband that Charity was dead? The family had survived slavery and the war. Now, they had to endure her untimely and cruel death.

The city was a bustling boomtown of sixty thousand people that included a big population of Chinese who worked on the rail construction and had brought their families with them. The Central Pacific was building the rail from the West, and required cheap labour so the rail baron could make his millions. Money and greed were evident almost everywhere in America.

The Mission San Francisco de Assisi was the exception. The Catholic priests initially administered to the Native people of California, but the mission was now the centre of the faith for many of the poor. Alice inquired of the whereabouts of Charity's family.

"Yes," the padre said with a warm smile. "We know Charity. She is a generous and kind woman."

"I have hard news for the family." A tear coursed down Alice's cheek. She couldn't dispel the guilt over Charity's death.

The priest accompanied Alice, Mary and the baby to a beautiful southern-style house in the Haight-Ashbury district. Charity's daughter, Polly, met them at the door. She was a slim girl, dressed in a blue gingham frock adorned with bows.

"Hello, Father." Her voice was timid, as if she knew that the priest brought devastating news.

"Hello, Polly." He introduced Alice and Mary then asked if they could come in and sit down. Her younger brother, Nate, appeared, looking curious but not suspecting anything. Polly's face was white with fear.

"Dear children, I have tragic news for you," the padre began. "Your dear mother will not be returning."

"What do you mean?" blurted Nate. "She gotta come back. She promised."

"She is in the arms of Jesus," the padre said.

"Momma is dead, Nate," Polly said with tears pouring down her face. "That is what Father Serra is telling us."

"She can't be. The war is over. Why did she have to die?" He fell into his sister's arms, sobbing.

Alice's voice trembled as she spoke. "Your mother was a brave woman, rescuing your little sister, Blossom, and two women who were in chains. God will reward her in heaven."

"Is that our sister, our little Blossom?" Polly exclaimed, with tears streaming down her face.

Alice placed the toddler in Polly's arms. Polly smiled through her tears and tickled Blossom. The toddler smiled back. "Nate, come and hold her. Our dear mother wants to see her children together at last."

"We must tell your father," the priest said. "I imagine he is still at work on the rail and will not return until the snow and cold drive the workers from the mountains. When he returns from the railroad work, I will give him the dreadful news."

Alice and Mary were in no rush to go north. The cold rains had returned to Victoria, and it was warm and beautiful in San Francisco. Charity's family needed them, especially since Polly minded the hat shop when she was not in school. They also needed someone to care for Blossom.

"I don't want to leave here ever," Mary said. "I'll miss Blossom, and I know she will miss me. She is like my little sister, the one that died in the fire. Polly said she will teach me to make hats. Isn't that wonderful!"

Father Serra, of the San Francisco Mission, welcomed Mary to his flock. "You are my little northern lamb, come to help me at the mission. God would be pleased if you helped me in the evenings with the poor Mexican children and babies, that is, when you are not making hats for rich ladies and looking after Blossom."

Mary took to the Spanish language as easily as she had learned English, but she had not forgotten the Salish language of her childhood. She occasionally sprinkled in Salish words when she couldn't find the right word in English or Spanish.

On her way to the hat shop each day, Mary admired the two-storey brick schoolhouse, the Valley Grammar School.

"Is that where you and Nate go to school?" Mary asked Polly excitedly. "I love school. In Quesnel, I was taught by Sister Angeline. I loved my teacher. There was another nun who said we did not need to learn our letters, that we were just good for sweeping floors. Sister Angeline believed everyone deserved an education."

Polly smiled. "We are not allowed to go to a white school even though mother objected. She said that Lincoln had freed the Blacks, and that now we are equal. The principal said it was against the law to let us study." Polly cited the law:

Children of African or Mongolian descent and Indians shall be educated in separate schools.

Mother said it was unfair, but I don't mind. The white children make fun of us. I hate it."

"I think it is terribly wrong," Mary said, working herself up to a fury of indignation. "Why do the whites think they are better than us? I was the top student in my class. There were ten white girls. Most of them chattered all the time and didn't listen to Sister

Angeline. They often had to stay late to finish their work. I think we
should go to the Valley Grammar School. It is a finer building with
a huge yard. It probably has shelves of books. I like to read."

"It will be useless to try and go to an all-white school," Polly
explained. "I won't come. It will be embarrassing."

"But I must go to school," Mary said. "I don't want to miss any
more. I have already missed so much."

"Are you staying for the rest of the school year?" Polly was
excited. "We'll go to the Chinese school. It is quite fine. At least
I will have you for company. The Chinese students don't speak
much English. If you stay, I'll have two sisters. I always wanted
many, many sisters," Polly said with a genuine smile.

"What about me?" Nate exclaimed, a scrunching up his face.
"You don't care for me now that you have Mary."

"Nate, you have your friends, and I like to be with girls. You're
still my little brother. Now go outside and play with your own
friends. Mary and I must go to the shop."

"I want to go to the shop, too," Nate pouted.

"Well, you can't. The hat shop is just for ladies."

"Ma used to take me when you were at school. How come I ain't
allowed now? It is called Charity's Hats, ain't it? Not Polly's Shop."

"You cannot come. That is that. You would be bored, and
Mary and I have to make hats. We have four orders that we must
finish. You'll get underfoot."

"I'll tell Pa that you are both mean to me."

The girls left Nate at home. Alice was busy with Blossom and
managing the house, so there was little time for Nate.

Polly and Mary took a horse-drawn trolley to to the shop on
Market Street.

"Where is your father working?" Mary asked as they rode. She
sat next to Polly as the trolley trundled along the street.

"He supervises a Black crew building the railroad. He and the Chinese crew boss will have a two-thousand-dollar bonus if they beat the other rail being driven from the east. It's so exciting. When the rail is finished, we'll be able to travel to New York in days instead of months."

Polly and Mary worked all day and made a dozen hats. They had caught up on the orders and had several ready-made hats displayed for purchase. They looked forward to dinner and watching the sunset over the San Francisco Bay.

When Mary changed her clothes for dinner, she looked for her Bible. It had always been next to her bed since she attended the Mission School, but it was not in its usual place. She searched everywhere.

"My Bible is missing." Mary had just entered the dining room. The table was set with the good china, silverware and white linen napkins.

"We'll find it later, Mary. Please sit. We are about to say grace." Alice bent her head and softly chanted the prayer.

Nate and Polly helped themselves, but Mary had lost her appetite. She had treasured that Bible. Sister Angeline had written a message inside: "Mary Ruth, May God keep you safe and guide you throughout your life."

"I don't understand. I know I left it on the bedside table this morning. The Bible is precious to me."

"Perhaps Rosita moved it when she cleaned your room. You can ask her tomorrow when she comes. Now please eat your dinner. It is chicken cooked in the Mexican style."

Mary looked at her meal and then looked at Nate. He was grinning.

"Did you take my Bible, Nate?"

"Mary, what has taken hold of you?" asked Alice. "Nate and Polly are our hosts. You should not accuse someone without proof."

"He was grinning. He thinks it is a joke, and I believe he took it."

"Mary, please say no more or leave the table. Your manners are unacceptable."

Mary pushed the food around on her plate. It was going to be a beautiful evening, sitting with Polly on the porch and watching the sun sink into the ocean. Now it had been ruined. Mary glared at Nate who ate with great gusto, chewing his food with his mouth open, seemingly pleased with himself.

I hate him, Mary thought. *He is such a spoiled child.*

"Mary, you haven't touched your meal. It is not like you to leave food. You were taught by the nuns 'Waste not, want not.' What is wrong with you?" Alice asked.

"Nothing."

Mary's stomach lurched as she put a forkful of the spicy chicken in her mouth. She gagged on the food.

"Go lie down, Mary. You and Polly have been working all day. You must be just too tired. That is why your good nature has taken flight. You'll see. Tomorrow you'll find your Bible, and all will be well again. Polly, will you help me with the dishes?"

Mary got up to leave, but not before glaring at Nate. He'd taken it. She knew he had.

The next morning when Rosita arrived, Mary approached her. "Rosita, did you move my Bible from my bedside table? I dearly hope you know where it is. It is more precious to me than a bag of gold dust."

Rosita was a petite young Mexican woman with a warm smile. She had long, black hair that she wore in braids. Except for a brief lunch, she never stopped working or singing.

"No, my dear, I never moved your Bible. I saw it on your bedside table when I cleaned your room. I can't imagine where it could be.

"Don't carry on so," Rosita said when she noticed the tears pooling in Mary's eyes. "We'll find it. I'll search every room in this big house and the yard, too. It is such a grand yard."

"Please, please find it for me," Mary implored.

"I will. Not to worry, dear child." Rosita sang a Spanish song as she took the winding staircase two steps at a time.

CHAPTER THIRTY-FIVE

San Francisco, Fall 1866

Nate

It was soon time for Mary to start school in San Francisco. However, her Bible was still missing.

"Mary, I want you to stop fussing over the Bible," said Alice one day. "everyone in the house is on edge because of how you are acting. I remind you again that we are guests here. Mr. Cooper will be home soon for a break. I want to stay here until the spring, but your attitude toward Nate makes that difficult."

Mary hung her head. "I still believe Nate took it out of jealousy."

"Maybe so. Do you ever think to include him when you go to the beach or when you play games at night? You took his sister away just after Nate lost his mother. Did you ever think of how he feels?"

Mary's eyes widened. True, she'd never thought about the young boy's feelings. "I'm sorry. What would Sister Angeline think of me? I never thought how difficult it has been for Nate."

"You are a good Christian, Mary. We all make mistakes in life. Some never admit they are wrong. They continue lying, taking what is not theirs, bullying the weak and mocking cripples. That is not you. You have goodness in your heart." Alice opened her arms to the skinny girl and hugged her close.

"We told him to stay home, and that made him angry. I'll suggest that Nate come with us to the shop."

"That's a good start, Mary. When his father comes home, we want to show him a family that is united, not one with where there is anger and accusations. Mr. Cooper works in a dangerous place every day, cutting the railbed through the Sierras. I know those mountains. They are treacherous. In the winter, snow will be twenty feet deep, and the winds are bitter. The poor man needs to find a peaceful haven in his home."

"When will he be home?"

"Polly believes he will be back after the school break is over. So, maybe this week."

The girls and Nate took the bus in the morning. When they arrived at the shop, Nate seemed glad to be included. He was helpful, fetching thread and ribbons for the girls as they worked. They wanted to make enough hats to last the week while they attended school and so that Rosita would have wares to sell while she watched the shop for them.

Nate held Polly's hand as they walked to catch the trolley home that night. "I did good, didn't I? I wasn't underfoot, and I helped you choose the best ribbons and flowers, didn't I? I could make hats, too, I think."

"Yes, you could be a haberdasher and make men's hats as well as women's. It is a job that wouldn't make you rich, but you could make a good living," said Polly. "But I thought you wanted to work on building rail lines like our father."

"Father said he will be finished the rail by the time I'm big enough."

"There will always be rail lines to work on," Polly said. "The Central Pacific will be the first to link the Pacific Ocean to New York. I'm sure they will build other rails north to Portland and south to San Diego."

Nate spent all the next day looking out for his father from the big window, watching east down the street where the trolley let off passengers. He would recognize the tall, strong figure a mile away. He was upset when Alice called him for supper.

"Nate, don't fret," Alice said gently. "Your father will be home any day now. Come, I know something that will cheer you up. We'll go shopping tomorrow for your school uniforms."

"Will we?" Nate asked, cheerful at the thought of the adventure. "I want a real pencil box this term, not father's cigar box. It's called Scholar's Companion. Polly and Mary should have one, too, because they are real scholars. Yes, I think that would be just hunky-dory."

"Where in the Lord's name do you pick up that language?" Alice couldn't help chuckle at the seven-year-old.

"I listen because I have two ears and only one mouth and because no one will talk to me."

"Oh, I'm sorry Nate," Alice gave the boy a hug. "We've all been ignoring you. That is going to stop today. I will spend less time with Blossom who is big enough to play by herself for a short while, and the girls will include you from now on. I promise."

"I'll play with Blossom, too. She likes me."

"Yes, but not tomorrow; she is staying home with Rosita."

The next day they took the trolley to downtown San Francisco.

"We wouldn't be on this trolley if not for Mammy Pleasant," Polly informed them. "She was mother's friend. We should go to her restaurant for lunch."

"Tell us about Mammy Pleasant," Alice said.

"Her name was Mary Ellen Pleasant, and everyone called her Mammy. She was from a big city in the East, and she helped slaves escape to Boston and even to Canada. She even helped John Brown, though she would have been hanged for sheltering him if the Federal Government knew. She is very rich, a millionaire, and she lives in a house so grand all the white ladies envy her. Some even hate her."

"It's unusual for a Black woman to make a fortune. There is so much discrimination against coloured people. Did her husband have money?" asked Alice.

"He was rich, too, but most of the money was hers."

"Will I be discriminated against as well?" asked Mary. "I don't believe that is right. *All* people should be treated fairly."

"You will do just fine, Mary," Alice said, reaching out and placing her hand over Mary's. As she said this, Alice wondered what Mary's life would be like when she became an adult.

They left the trolley at Union Square and went to the City of Paris department store. It was an impressive multi-storeyed building.

Polly was afraid to enter, thinking they would be asked to leave. Alice and Mary marched through the doors, certain that they belonged. Polly and Nate followed them.

Nate gaped at the grandeur. There was a stained-glass rotunda inside. The store had everything: silks, laces, fine wines and school supplies.

"Excuse me, Madame," said a man who spoke with a French accent and was dressed impeccably in a black tuxedo. "Are these children in your care? If not, they cannot come into the Ville de Paris." He did not smile at them.

"Yes, they are my wards."

"We should be allowed in the store anyway," Mary said to the officious clerk, her anger barely disguised. "You aren't from this country, so you can't tell us where we can be."

"Shush, Mary. Be polite and humble."

"Take your little coloureds in the store, but I warn you to be more circumspect, or I will have to show you *la porte*."

"Mary, you will get us in trouble," Polly whispered. "You embarrass me. Can't you hold your tongue?"

"Mammy Pleasant was not quiet. She spoke out so that we could go into stores and theatres and on beaches and trollies," Mary whispered back. "She's my hero."

"Please let us buy your uniforms and school supplies without any more drama," Alice admonished Mary. "Then, I'll take you to Mary Ellen Pleasant's restaurant for lunch."

At the restaurant, the children had slices of crisp thin potatoes fried in oil while Mary Ellen and Alice each enjoyed a bowl of lobster stew. Alice and Mammy spoke about politics and discrimination in San Francisco. It was an enjoyable lunch for everyone.

They arrived back at the house to find Jem at home. He met them at the door, his face a picture of despair. Father Serra had met him and told him of Charity's death.

"My dear children," he said sobbing. "How is it that tragedy has followed us? Wasn't it enough to be a slave, to be beaten, to have my family ripped apart by slave owners? No, they had to kill my dear wife, your sweet mother." He dropped to the armchair, tears streaming down his weather-worn face.

When Blossom woke from her nap, Polly placed the child in his lap. "Father, this is our little sister, Blossom." Blossom looked at Jem with wide eyes. She did not fuss or cry. She just seemed curious.

Jem had last seen Blossom as a wee babe that dreadful day when she was sold to the plantation owner. It was just before he escaped to join the Union forces. He wiped the tears from his cheeks and looked at the child. "You are the very image of your mother."

After the children were in bed, Jem sat in his comfortable leather chair, having a brandy while Alice worked on her cross-stich.

"Tell me, Alice, how are my children doing? I know they miss their mother. They all seem healthy, especially Blossom. Have they been respectful to you?"

"They have been obedient and very helpful. Now that the girls take Nate to the shop, he seems more content. Of course, they miss their mother."

"I hope you will stay until I finish my work on the railroad," Jem said, enjoying the warm fire glowing in the grate. "But maybe you'll want to go back to the frozen north instead." He laughed, his smile wide and engaging.

He is a handsome man, Alice thought. *If only my heart was not so attached to David, maybe I could stay in this beautiful, warm place forever.*

"I think not. I am becoming soft in the warm California sunshine," Alice smiled. "It will be hard to return to rainy Victoria or the icy, snowbound north, but I must. I have my roadhouse there and many friends that I miss."

Alice mused as she sat by the fire with her embroidery, occasionally glancing out of the window at the city lights below. The house was on a hill looking west toward the sea. It was a beautiful place for Jem and Charity to build a life for their children after so many years of slavery.

Here was a man who had been treated worse than an animal for thirty years of his life; he was beaten, chained, watched his friends hanged or put to death by fire, his wife and baby sold away from him. It amazed Alice that after all the torture and abuse he endured that he could be a loving father, a hard worker and a man who could laugh and enjoy life.

She and David were privileged. Alice knew that. They were white, not Black, not Indian, not Irish, not Chinese.

She was happy to be of use to Charity's family, to be welcomed in Jem's home, not like a servant, but like a maiden aunt. The tragedy she experienced in the Sierra Mountains twenty years ago was slowly peeling away. She felt content, like a cat taken in from the rain and given a bowl of warm milk. Alice sighed. She put her stitching on the end table and bade Jem goodnight.

CHAPTER THIRTY-SIX

San Francisco, Fall 1866

Jem

Àll three children walked each morning to the Chinese school. Jem had returned to his work on the Central Pacific Railroad, and he would be working through the winter. However, he'd promised Nate and Polly he would be home for Christmas.

"Father will bring me a big, big present if I make all A's in my schoolwork," Nate said as they walked home from school. "But I'm having trouble with arithmetic. Lee always gets the better marks even though I try my hardest."

"Don't worry, Nate. You will be better than Lee in grammar. You'll see."

"Polly, I don't really like the school," Nate admitted. "Lee teases me. He called me a dirty nigger. I hate him."

"I'll punch his face for that," Mary said, infuriated.

"No, Mary. Mother said that we must never, never respond with violence." Polly told Mary in her timid voice. "Why are you saying that? You are a Christian. Your religion tells you to turn the other cheek."

Mary hung her head, regretting her outburst. "I want to follow the teachings of Jesus, I do. But it is hard for me to see wrongdoing and injustice and not be angry. I wish I was more like you, Polly."

"Well, we won't be in the Chinese school for long. Alice said that a Black woman is opening a school just up the hill on Church Street. Alice is going to see her today. Her name is Charlotte Brown, and she is a protestor. Charlotte helped Mammy Pleasant in the effort to allow us to go on the trolley.

"Actually, I'll miss the Chinese school," Polly continued. "The girls have been kind to me. Their fathers work on the railroad like our father, so we talk about how dangerous the railroad work is and how we worry about our fathers' safety."

"Everybody loves you, Polly. You are goodness itself." Mary put her arms about Polly.

Nate saw this and moved toward Mary. "What about me? I need a hug, too."

As the weather cooled, Alice thought about those deadly Sierra Mountains where Jem worked and wondered how much snow had fallen on the pass. She knew the pass well. Her daughter had died there; some of her friends had perished from hunger and the cold. She worried about the men who toiled on the railroad. How could they possibly build a railbed through that treacherous country!

At least in sunny California, she and the four children were safe. Blossom was walking and talking nonstop. She was a happy baby, seemingly unaffected by her experiences on the plantation. The older children had moved to Charlotte Brown's school and were thriving.

"When will our father be home?" Nate asked. "I hope Father will buy me a yo-yo, a chess game and a uniform, like father had, and my own gun."

"I think we should be happy with just one gift for Christmas and give something to the poor," Mary said. "A bag of rice, eggs, anything they will eat. I've heard many people are starving."

"Mary, you are right," Polly agreed. "That is what we will do."

"I'm not giving up my gift for nobody," Nate protested. "I worked my bestest, and I won't."

"All right, Nate. We'll have our father buy a rocking horse for Blossom and you can have your gifts. Maybe you are too little to understand charity."

Jem returned two days before Christmas, looking tired and thin. "We are behind on the rail work. We had to tunnel through the mountains."

"Does that mean I won't get my presents?" Nate asked.

"No, my dear boy. You will have lots of presents, and we will give to the poor as Polly and Mary want. And for Christmas dinner, we'll have a big ham and a delicious pudding with raisins. We'll have Christmas crackers filled with bonbons, and you will be so stuffed you won't be able to walk."

"I love to cook for the people I love," Alice said. "And I do love Christmas."

Jem smiled, thinking he wanted this beautiful woman to stay in his life, making his house a home again, filling part of the void left by the death of his dear Charity.

Mary and Polly decorated the house with ribbons and cedar bows while Alice cooked, and Nate played with Blossom. Christmas dinner was a feast. First, they said a prayer for their departed mother and then drank a toast to her.

"Don't cry, Daddy," Blossom said as she sat on her father's lap. "It's Christmas."

"Your mother gave her life for you, precious babe. We must always remember her in our prayers." He wiped the tears from his eyes. "Now, let's eat this delicious dinner."

After the feast and the presents, everyone sang songs while Alice played the piano. Mary had a thin, out-of-tune voice that was masked by Polly's beautiful harmony and Jem's deep base.

"This time together makes me forget all the hardships of the Sierras," Jem said, settling in an easy chair with his brandy after the children were in their beds. "I didn't think I could be happy again."

"I am content as well," Alice said. "Having family to care for, food to cook and books to read. Thank you for *Uncle Tom's Cabin* and

Pride and Prejudice, one very sad book and one, I think, a kind of fairy tale about love."

"I've read *Uncle Tom's Cabin*. Slavery is even worse than Stowe's descriptions. It is inhumane. But I don't understand why you don't believe in Jane Austen's love story?"

"Girl without means finds a rich man and saves her family from destitution. Money and inheritance are passed down to men. Control over my inheritance passed to my brother-in-law. I gave up my freedom to save my inheritance. I will regret that for the rest of my life. And love, well it hasn't worked out for me."

"Tell me about it, Alice."

"My dear husband and little son died, and I was left alone with my daughter. My brother-in-law, Elijah, took control of my inheritance, and I was forced to marry an evil man I didn't love or have my small fortune controlled by Elijah. I accepted Saxby's offer, but he was cruel and careless. He led us across the Sierras where my daughter perished in the snows along with half our party. It was many years ago, yet I still suffer."

"I'm sorry about your daughter."

"Amelia was a sweet child." Alice supressed a sob, as she thought back on that bitter time in the mountains.

"You are happy here, are you not?"

"I am content. Happiness has eluded me."

"Polly told me that you were betrothed to a soldier and that he broke it off with you."

"Yes. I didn't realize you knew about that. Girls share stories, I guess. He married another and broke my heart, which was already wounded."

"Well, you should stay in San Francisco, and you will heal in God's warm sunshine."

CHAPTER THIRTY-SEVEN

San Francisco, Winter 1867

Alice

A lice thought that Jem was becoming too familiar. *I can't be encouraging him; he is a friend and only a friend,* she thought sadly. She wanted to stay with the family until Blossom was old enough to go to school. Then she would return to the north.

On New Year's Day, the family gathered to celebrate. The year was 1867.

"I have presents for everyone," Jem said.

It was like a second Christmas. Jem gave them each a gift. Books for the girls and Alice, toys for Nate and Blossom and candy for everyone.

When the children were in bed, Jem and Alice relaxed as was their habit. Jem was talkative, and Alice listened.

"So many years of my life I worked on every holiday, slaughtering and roasting the pig for the master's dinner, eating their scraps and a few greens that we grew. One Christmas, I was whipped for roasting the pig too long. The plantation owner said, 'I likes my pork pink, not Black like you. Just as I likes the youngin' pink.' He eyed my child, and I thought I would kill him if he ever touched Polly. That's why I ran away to join the Union Army. I planned to save my wages to free my family."

"You have suffered much more than I have, Jem."

"Suffering is what our people have been fed since they were kidnapped and brought to America. We thought it would end with Father Lincoln when he freed the slaves. But they killed him, and they killed all his good works, his promise of forty acres and a mule. The Southerners took it away and gave our land back to the same plantation owners who had whipped us. A friend wrote to me from Georgia. Former slaves have become sharecroppers on the plantations where they once were enslaved. They might as well be slaves still.

"Even here," he continued, "we can't shop in certain stores, can't live on Nob Hill, can't send our children to the white school, can't swim in the ocean off the nice, sandy beaches. I must stop talking because it makes me so angry that I want to kill. I cannot bear it."

"Maybe you should become active like Charlotte and her husband. They are speaking up for Blacks."

"Will you help me? I don't know how to change the minds of whites. Nothing ever good comes from a white person. Except you, Alice. You are different."

"I will introduce you to Charlotte Brown and her husband, James. They are both trying to bring about change—open stores, the trollies, the schools to Blacks. Without people like them, we would be going backward."

"Will that help?"

"I hope so. It is better than anger. Please don't ever kill or hurt a white person. The courts will always side with the whites, no matter how just your cause. Peaceful protest, no violence."

"You are a gentle lady, Alice. I have never heard you raise your voice. Never angry. Always calm. Mary also believes in turning the other cheek."

"Mary says she follows Jesus, but she has to learn humility. She became very angry over a lost Bible and blamed Nate for taking it. I had to scold her."

"Did my son take it?"

"I don't know. It was placed with the presents at Christmas, so we may never know. Mary was happy as a kitten with a warm bowl of milk when she found her Bible under the tree."

Jem stayed at home for some time, waiting for the weather to change in the mountains so the men could work. He was industrious, building a gazebo in the back garden and preparing the soil for the spring planting. When the weather turned inclement, he worked in the house making repairs.

The children went back to school after the Christmas break, except for Blossom. She talked all the time and followed her father, constantly asking questions.

"Why you don't stay home? Why you go away? What is a railroad?"

Jem answered all Blossom's questions patiently.

Alice worked in the house, cooking and baking. She watched Jem and thought he was such a gentle man, despite being huge and muscular. He rattled the lamps when he walked across the room. She thought that it must have been so difficult for a powerful man like Jem to be a slave, to have to submit or be whipped. How did he harness his anger all those years?

That week, Alice met with activists in the African Methodist Church. Several white women and prominent Black men and women came to the meeting to support desegregation.

"I believe Mr. Cooper would be a welcome addition to your group," she told Eliza Cotton, the local Black leader. "He is frustrated by the discrimination he sees, especially the segregated schools."

"We need men, but they must not show their anger. Women are much better at bringing change. Charlotte used legal means to sue the Omnibus Company and won our right to board the trolley."

"Jem was a slave until the war. He held his temper even though he witnessed his brother burned alive by the slave owners. He wanted to kill all plantation owners, but he controlled his anger. "

"It isn't a matter of containing rage; he must submit to being spit on, cuffed, refused service."

"He was beaten, chained, a bit put in his mouth, his wife and baby sold to other slave owners. I believe he can hold his temper. At least there is no longer the senseless killing of Blacks in California," Alice said.

"That is not true," Eliza said. "What of Mr. Coffle, a Black brother who owned a dry goods store? He caught a thief, named Fred, red-handed, and the thief shot him dead in the streets of our city. Not only was Coffle murdered, but the thief whipped his dead body in view of the Blacks and some white citizens!"

"We are taking it to court to get justice," Charlotte said. She was a big woman, dressed in beautiful flowing clothes.

"Some justice that will be!" said Alice, "I'll tell Jem he must be as forgiving as Jesus and turn the other cheek, although that may be difficult for a strong man like him."

Jem joined the group and was welcomed, especially by the men. They were mostly men with businesses in the city and had children whom they felt should have a first-class education.

They would go to the court to testify for Coffle and to fill the courtroom with supporters. The women could attend the hearings, but they were not allowed to testify.

At dinner that night, Mary listened attentively to every word about the court case.

"I want to go to the court, too."

"No, definitely not," Alice said as firmly as she could. What would that girl think of next? Alice loved her spirit but worried that the little girl would soon face a backlash. It was never completely safe to protest, even peacefully.

The Coffle court case was the sensation for weeks that winter, with daily reports in the *Mirror of the Times*. Jem and Alice attended every day. Alice sat with the white women while Jem waited outside the courtroom until he was called to give his testimony. He wasn't a key witness, but a character witness.

Mary peppered them with questions. "What did the witnesses say about the killing? When will there be verdict against the thief? What do you expect the verdict will be?"

"Be patient, Mary. The trial has just started," Alice said. "We'll let you know what happens. Besides, the papers are covering the trial. Why don't you read about it?"

"You're right. I can read the news, but I want to hear from you because you were right there in the courtroom. I hope the judge and jury send Fred to hang until he's dead."

"That is not very Christian of you. No one should be put to death," Alice said. "Now go to bed and say your prayers. Sister Angelina and Jesus should guide you." Alice kissed the girl goodnight.

The weeks went by with interest in the trial growing every day. Mary talked about the trial until Polly couldn't bear it.

"Let's go to the beach, Mary, and have some fun,"

"I don't like the beach because it's segregated."

"If we want to swim on a beautiful spring day like this, we have to go the segregated beach."

"Why are you not interested in the trial, Polly? It is for your people that the case is being fought."

"I know, but I don't think it helps the cause to go to court. I will do well in school and show everyone that I am just as good or better than the white people."

"We should go to the court and listen to the verdict."

"They won't let us in, silly."

"We'll stay outside. When the jury comes back, we'll hear the verdict sooner."

"I'll go," Nate said enthusiastically, his face beaming.

"Father will punish us if we go," Polly warned.

"He won't know," Mary said, putting on her coat. "Just come. Do this for me, please. You have to look after Nate anyway. Your father would be cross if you let Nate go, and you weren't with us."

"Oh, all right. But you'd better not get us in trouble."

The children arrived to find a large crowd gathered outside the courthouse, all anxious for the verdict.

"I can't wait for the jury to return," Mary said. "Do you think they will find the killer guilty?"

"Alice told us that the courts usually side with the white man, no matter if he kills a Black person in broad daylight in front of a thousand witnesses."

"You're darn right, little nigger," stated a heavy man with a stomach that pressed against his belt. He had a strong Eastern European accent. "No white man is gonna get convicted because he kilt a nigger."

"This shouldn't even be brought to court," said the man's companion. "Ever since the niggers won their freedom, they've become too uppity. Wanting to be like us." The man had dirty blond hair and fine lines down his weather-beaten face.

"Not in my lifetime," the heavy man scoffed.

Mary listened to the men, getting angrier with every word. "You shouldn't talk like that about my friends!"

"What's that, you dirty Indian?" the heavy man said, looking down at the children. "Two picaninnies and a pretty young squaw."

"Mary, stop it, please!" Polly pleaded.

"Oh, the cute nigger gal has a somethin' to say."

The heavy man had started walking menacingly toward the girls when someone from the crowd yelled, "The verdict is in!"

"He's guilty!" someone shouted.

Cheers erupted from the crowd.

"Thank the good Lord."

"Praise be!"

"Well, I'll be dammed." The heavy man scowled. "At least we can have some fun with youse little gals." He grabbed Polly's arm. "Come with us. We'll take your cherry, and your friends can watch."

"Leave her alone!" Mary yelled. "I'll get the police if you don't let go."

"The police won't help the likes of you. I'll tell 'em you were trying to steal my gold poke."

"I said let her go!" Mary bit his arm so hard she drew blood.

"You little savage!" He yelped then backhanded Mary hard in the face.

She stumbled and fell on the steps, blood running from her nose.

"You're comin' with me," the man said, pulling Polly after him.

"Help! Daddy!" Polly screamed, her cries drowned out by the noise of the crowd. Nate was too hysterical to cry out. He stood stock still, not able to move.

The two men dragged Polly from the crowd of spectators. The heavy man clamped his meat-hook-like hand over her mouth.

"We'll teach you niggers your place, won't we Billy?"

Nate couldn't move. Traumatized, he sat beside Mary, immobile and speechless. This is where Jem and Alice found them.

"Oh, my God!" Alice said. "What happened?" She knelt over Mary's unconscious body. "She's breathing!"

Nate tried to speak.

"Nate, tell us what happened," Jem pressed quietly.

"The men…took…Polly." The words came out in spurts.

Jem looked around. "What men?"

"There." Nate pointed. "Those two men. The big man with the big belly and the one with straw-coloured hair."

"Alice, stay with Mary and Nate." Jem ran, pushing through the crowd until he finally spotted his daughter being dragged away. He dashed after them, fists clenched.

Jem swung a powerful right fist at the heavy man, who fell heavily to the street, releasing Polly as he hit the ground. Jem scooped Polly in his arms and started carrying her away.

The blond-haired man helped his friend to his feet. Still stunned, the heavy man swayed then ran after Jem, stabbing him in the side with a knife. "No nigger is gonna hit me and live."

Blood poured from Jem's side. Polly knelt beside her father sobbing. "Daddy, are you badly hurt?"

"No, my sweetie. If you are free of those men, I'll be fine. I gotta wait just a second before I can walk."

Polly knelt beside her father while Jem stuffed his handkerchief over the wound. He gasped in pain as he got to his feet. A crowd gathered around, asking what had happened.

The heavy man yelled for the police. "This nigger attacked me!"

In moments, a policeman came to the scene.

"On your stomach!" the policeman yelled at Jem. "Hands behind your back." He cuffed Jem.

"They took my daughter," Jem protested. "You must arrest them. I did nothing wrong except save my daughter from these lowlifes."

"Tell that to the judge at your trial. Right now, get to your feet slowly and come with me."

Polly couldn't believe what she was witnessing. "My father is innocent," she sobbed. "You should arrest the men who kidnapped me."

Alice arrived with Nate and Mary in time to see Jem being pushed into a paddy wagon.

Polly was hysterical. Alice held the distraught child in her arms.

"It will be all right, Polly. We'll get your father out of jail. He was defending you. The men who took you will be put in prison."

As she said those words, Alice felt a shiver of fear. She had seen innocent Black men killed because they attacked a white man. Would there be any justice in San Francisco, or was it the same as Georgia?

CHAPTER THIRTY-EIGHT

San Francisco, Winter 1867

Jem

Alice visited the jail to discover what charges Jem faced.
"This man is innocent!" she argued with the jailer.
"His young daughter was being abducted by men who planned to rape her. He had no choice but to defend her."

"It will all come out in court, Ma'am. Please be patient."

Alice was beside herself with worry. Mary had caused this. She had taken Nate and Polly to the courthouse, disobeying Jem and bringing harm to the family.

Alice returned home and went to Polly and Mary's bedroom. "I'm so sorry, Polly. We'll free him. I don't know how. He is not guilty, and if the laws are even a little fair, he will be found innocent. I promise."

"Mother told us we must never make trouble because they would always blame us, not the whites. She taught me to be cautious among whites. I know I am shy; I don't fight back. Not like you, Mary." Polly sobbed into her pillow.

"Mary was wrong to take you to court and expose you and Nate to danger."

For once Mary was silent. If only she had listened to Polly.

"I don't blame her for standing up to those wicked men," Polly said through her tears. "But it doesn't help us, does it? Do we always have to be abused as if we were still slaves?"

"No, my darling. It must change someday. Right now, we have to see that your father is released. I will go to your teacher, Charlotte Brown. She will help. Also, Mammy Pleasant. The coloured people have won several cases against the trolley companies. They won the case for Mr. Coffle. Now, they must help us get justice for your father."

The sun rose over the eastern hills, lighting the rooftops and shining on the gentle ocean waves in the distance. Alice got dressed and took a carriage to Mammy Pleasant's mansion. Charlotte Brown and several other abolitionists were there.

Alice was not the only white woman present. Two other prominent socialites had joined the cause.

"Unfortunately, we really need a lawyer to take the case pro bona. A female lawyer won't do because California doesn't permit women solicitors to lead a case. There is no one I can think of in the city," Charlotte said. "We put all our resources into Mr. Coffle's case."

The group discussed the upcoming California convention of coloured people. There were so many issues to work on that it was difficult to take on new causes.

"This is not a cause," Alice objected. "This is freedom for a former slave, who is facing years in prison for defending his daughter."

"We'll do our best, Miss Ackerman. If you could find a solicitor, that would help."

Alice thought about this. She wished David could help her. He was educated. He would have friends in the law.

Although she was reticent about contacting him, this would be different. She believed he was married now. She wouldn't be asking for his love. She was asking him to save a wrongly accused Black man. She was certain he would aid in their cause.

She decided to send him a telegram. Cost was not an issue for Alice. She owed Jem so much. She had to be successful in engaging an excellent pro bono lawyer.

The telegram read:

POSTAL TELEGRAPH   COMMERCIAL CABLES

TELEGRAM

Telegraph - Cable | transmits and delivers this message subject to the terms and conditions printed on the back of this blank.

COUNTER NUMBER. | TIME FILED. | CHECK.

d the following message, without repeating, subject to the terms and conditions printed on the back hereof, which are hereby agreed to.

DAVID,

NEED A SOLICITOR WITHIN MONTH -(STOP)- JEM HAS BEEN
WRONGLY ACCUSED -(STOP)- HE WILL FACE A WHITE MAN'S
COURT, AND WE ARE DESPERATE -(STOP)- IF FOUND GUILTY
WILL GO TO JAIL FOR YEARS -(STOP)-

ALICE

An answer came back the next day.

POSTAL TELEGRAPH   COMMERCIAL CABLES

TELEGRAM

Telegraph - Cable | transmits and delivers this message subject to the terms and conditions printed on the back of this blank.

COUNTER NUMBER. | TIME FILED. | CHECK.

end the following message, without repeating, subject to the terms and conditions printed on the back hereof, which are hereby agreed to.

MR. CHAD BELLOWS TO ARRIVE BY STAGECOACH 25 DAYS
OR LESS, TAKING THE TRAIN AS FAR AS OMAHA -(STOP)-
HE IS THE BEST AND FREE -(STOP)-

DAVID

Alice shared the news with the children. It was the first time Polly had smiled since the incident.

"I knew David would help," Mary said, dancing about the room. Nate mimicked Mary, almost crashing into the furniture as he whirled about. Even Blossom ran around, laughing, unaware why they were suddenly happy after a gloomy two days.

"We'd better not get our hopes up yet. There will still be a trial," Alice cautioned. "I must visit Jem and give him the news."

"May I come with you?" Polly said.

"Me, too." Both Mary and Nate said together.

"I want to go alone with Polly. She has been sick with worry. This will give her a chance to see her father."

"But Mother," protested Mary. "I must come."

"I'm his son! I must come, too."

"No. You and Nate will stay with Blossom and Rosita. I think you know why."

"Is this punishment for taking the children to the court? You are blaming me for all of it."

"It was foolish of you to put the family at risk. You must learn patience and obedience."

Alice and Polly took the trolley to Battery Street where the U.S. customs house was located. It served as a clearinghouse for imported goods as well as a temporary jail for the accused awaiting trial. Jem was kept in a small, hot room hardly bigger than a closet.

Polly cried when she saw her father in chains. "It's all my fault. I should never have gone to the courthouse. I'm so sorry, Father."

"Don't cry, my darling girl. It certainly wasn't your doing that I am in jail. It is the thugs who tried to kidnap you."

"I learned that a circuit judge is coming from Oregon to hear your case," Alice told him. "We need witnesses Jem, several people who are willing to testify."

"The courts won't believe a Black man over a white one. I'm convicted already. I'll be whipped in the public square. I can't stand it. I really can't."

"You mustn't despair, Jem. A friend from New York has hired a solicitor. He is on his way as we speak."

"There is a rumour that the Committee of Vigilance will break me out of jail and string me up." Jem looked ashen. "There is no justice for Blacks. I was in chains and whipped most of my life, saw friends hanged for nothing. It is too much for me."

"Have faith," Alice said. "I'll find witnesses. Your boss from Central Pacific will testify as to your character, and I'll place advertisements in the papers asking for witnesses to Polly's abduction."

Alice's words did not ease Jem's feeling of defeat. He felt doomed the minute the policeman had arrested him.

Chad Bellows, the solicitor arrived in San Francisco two days before the trial. He was a young man, clean shaven with blond, wavy hair, a sweet grin, and he was dressed fashionably in a travelling suit.

He will charm the ladies, Alice thought. *But will he appeal to an all-white, all-male jury?*

Alice introduced herself and bowed her head slightly as she greeted him. "Thank you so much, Mr. Bellows, for making this arduous journey."

"That is my job, Ma'am. I defend Black people unfairly charged. And please, just call me Chad."

The trial began on a warm June morning. The courthouse was packed an hour before the case was scheduled to be heard. Blacks sat in the balcony and the overflow stood outside. Jem sat with his head bowed, a look of defeat in his demeanour.

"All rise for Judge Pierce." The judge was a silver-haired, thin man with thick, bushy white eyebrows, his face grey with weariness.

The judge read out the charges in a weak voice. "Mr. Jem Cooper, you have been charged with assault causing bodily harm. How do you plead?"

"Not guilty, your honour."

The policeman at the scene, Sean O'Reilly, was the first to testify. He was dressed in a rumpled police uniform, had a ruddy complexion and a big, beer belly.

The prosecutor, Mr. Horatio Lambert, was a short, stout man in his fifties. He wore a brightly coloured waistcoat and a green wool double-breasted coat. His sparse hair was greased with pomade and combed over his nearly bald head.

Mr. Lambert began. "Describe the scene outside the courthouse when you arrived."

"Well, I heard a ruckus from the crowd and someone calling for the police," O'Reilly stated in a thick Irish brogue. "When I showed up, I saw the defendant and Zelensky, who was mighty beaten up. Zelensky here was lying on the ground near beaten to death. He told me the defendant had attacked him."

"Objection! Hearsay," Chad said, standing up.

"Sustained," the judge answered.

"Well, as I said, it looked like the nigger attacked Zelensky, and Zelensky defended hisself."

"It's your turn to question the witness, Mr. Bellows." Judge Pierce said, motioning to Chad.

"Isn't it true that Jem's little daughter was crying because she had been abducted by Zelensky?"

"There was a young chile there, but I didn't make any such assumptions."

"And there were two men, not one. Zelensky and Krasnov?"

"Yes, two men and the nigger there."

"Please refer to the defendant as Mr. Cooper," Judge Pierce said.

"I refer to them as everybody does in this town," the policeman grinned. "He is a nigger, ain't he?"

A few people in the gallery chuckled.

The judge was not pleased. "In my courtroom, you will address the defendant by his given name. I'll not warn you again."

The next witness for the prosecution was Zelensky. He was sworn in and took the stand.

The prosecutor questioned the witness first. "Give us your account of the attack Mr. Zelensky."

"This here nigger attacked me as I was leaving the courthouse. Punched me. Almost broke my nose. Said he was gonna kill me. I was knocked down. I was mightily injured. Nose bleeding like a stuck pig. Krasnov was there and helped me up. I had me a little shiv and gave the nigger a wee poke. I wanted to punch out his lights for what he done to me."

"Mr. Bellows, do you wish to question the witness?" the judge asked Chad.

"Yes, your honour," Bellows answered, standing.

"Now Mr. Zelensky, were you dragging a young girl with you?"

"Objection."

"I'll reword, Your Honour. Besides Krasnov, who did you have with you, Mr. Zelensky?"

"There was lots of people milling around. But yes, I saw a little pickaninny in the crowd."

"You say that Mr. Cooper hit you. When you got to your feet, what did you do then?"

"I defended myself."

"With a knife, Mr. Zelensky? Why didn't you use your fists?"

"He would've beat me to a pulp. Looka' da nigger. He is one hell of a brute. I'm no lightweight myself, but he looks to be six-foot-six, I betcha. Two hundred pounds of muscle."

"So, you stabbed him."

"Ya, I gave him a little poke wid my shiv."

"Your shiv, Mr. Zelensky?"

"Ya, my knife. I had to defend myself."

"Is this the weapon you used?" Chad displayed a ten-inch knife to the jury.

"Ya, dat's mine. Where the blazes didja git it?"

"A witness who saw everything kindly picked it up."

"A witness? No one in da city would dare take da stand agin me."

"Why is that, Mr. Zelensky?"

"I have connections."

"Would those connections be with the Gophers of New York?"

"Objection, Your Honour. Relevance."

The judge, who had been resting his head on his elbows, stirred himself. "Where are you going with this Mr. Bellows?" he asked in a weary voice.

"It is relevant, Your Honour. We intend to show the jury that Mr. Zelensky has a violent past."

"I'll allow it. Please get on with it, Mr. Bellows. It is near our lunch time."

"Mr. Zelensky, when you lived in Hell's Kitchen in New York, were you a hitman for the Gophers?"

"No. What y'all saying? Never heard of 'em."

"Remember, sir, that you are under oath. I have before me a report from New York's finest, saying that in 1864 you were arrested and charged with killing a policeman. Isn't that true?"

"I was, but the case was thrown out. The witness did not appear."

"What happened to the witness?"

"He died."

"Mr. Zelensky, that was very convenient for you, wasn't it?"

"Objection."

"Sustained." The judge was listening carefully now.

"I'll withdraw my question. Mr. Zelensky, did you have anything to do with the witness's death?"

"No. I was in the clinker. How could I?"

"Were you acquainted with Paddy Maloney of New York?"

"Never heard of him. I don't know that man."

"Is that true? I have a newspaper with a daguerreotype of you and Paddy outside the courtroom. Paddy Maloney, also called Killer Maloney. Who is he?"

"What?" Zelensky's face was now turning a shade of purple. "Don't know."

"In the photo, you look pretty chummy with this man. You must know his name."

"I…I met him once or twice, I guess."

"And is Paddy Maloney present in this courtroom?"

Both Zelensky and Sergeant O'Reilly shuffled their feet and looked down at the tiled floor.

"Is this relevant to the case, Mr. Bellows?" Judge Pierce asked.

"Yes, Your Honour, the defence will show that Mr. Zelensky and Paddy Maloney knew each other before they moved to San Francisco."

"Carry on, Mr. Bellows."

"I'll ask you again, and I'll remind you that you are under oath. Is Paddy Maloney in the courtroom?"

"I don't see him," Zelensky muttered, panic written on his face.

"The defence has a witness that will identify Mr. Maloney. Would you like to change your testimony?"

"I guess he is in the courtroom."

"Please identify him."

"Sean O'Reilly," Zelensky said in a whisper, his head so low it almost touched his knees.

"Speak up, Mr. Zelensky."

Judge Pierce was fully engaged now.

"Sean O'Reilly," he muttered as if he was facing his executioner.

The policeman came to his feet. "What the hell are you saying, Zelensky?"

"Sit down, Mr. O'Reilly…or…Mr. Maloney, whatever your name is. We'll get to the bottom of this."

Judge Pierce was alert and angry. He didn't know who he should be angry with. He didn't like surprises in his court.

"We'll call it a day," the judge said. "I want to see Mr. Bellows and Mr. Lambert in my chambers."

The gallery buzzed with the news as they exited the courtroom. Alice wept with relief. Jem has a chance. Maybe the law will work for a Black man after all.

Judge Pierce scowled at the two lawyers.

"Mr. Lambert, is it true that your inspector was a Gopher, a criminal in New York? Or is Mr. Bellows making up some cock-and-bull story?"

Lambert's polished demeanour was replaced by a look of bewilderment.

"Your Honour, I can bring a policeman from New York who will testify as to Mr. Maloney's past," Bellows said.

"No. Mr. Lambert, our esteemed prosecutor, *you* will get to the bottom of this," the judge said with sarcasm. "If Mr. Bellows is correct, and we have a gangster on the force testifying in my court, you will be in deep shit. Excuse the language, but I thought this would be a simple case of assault, and I would be home basking in the Oregon sunshine in a day."

Alice and Chad left the courtroom together. She couldn't wait to describe the proceedings to the children.

"I can't believe your defence," she said to Chad. "I am certain that Jem will be freed. I just know it."

"Don't get your hopes up, Alice. Seldom is a Black man found innocent in any U.S. court. The odds are stacked against our case."

"You've evened the odds." Alice couldn't contain her enthusiasm. "You have them on the ropes."

"I have a surprise for you, Miss Ackerman. Someone will be at the house when we get home."

"Who is it?"

"A surprise. I can't tell you." He smiled sweetly, tickled with himself.

They took a carriage home and opened the door.

Alice removed her bonnet and cape and walked into the parlour. David rose to greet her.

"Whaaaaat...? What are you doing here," she blurted out, a tightness in her stomach.

"Is that any way to greet an old friend?"

Alice was speechless.

Chad spoke up. "May I present Mr. David Ackerman, an old friend of yours, I believe."

"Hello, my dear friend," David said, bowing slightly.

"I never thought I would see you again." After three long years, seeing David and being so near him caused her unbelievable pain.

"I didn't want you to be tied to a cripple. I've read all of your letters to me, and I am so sorry that I have hurt you."

Nate and Mary burst into the room followed by Polly. "What happened at the trial?"

Mary paused when she saw David, then ran to him, arms open.

David hugged the girl tightly.

"You're not married are you, David? You would never marry another," Mary asked.

"No, I'm still a bachelor, and I've come to ask forgiveness from you and Alice."

"See, I told you that he loved us and wouldn't leave us for another."

Alice couldn't control her tears. Her knees suddenly felt weak. She sat in the armchair, covering her face and choking back her sobs.

Polly tried to restrain herself while listening to the stranger. She wondered what he had to do with her father's trial.

"We want to hear about court. Our father is on trial, and we must know what is happening." Polly spoke with more fervor than Alice had heard from her before.

Alice welcomed the change of subject. She composed herself and wiped her eyes, not looking at David. "I think we should all sit down while Mr. Bellows tells us about the trial."

The children listened attentively while Chad described the testimony of the two men.

"Bully for you!" Nate smiled. "You are swell. You will get our father out of jail."

"Not yet. The jury has to reach a decision. I know our case is sound, but an all-white jury rarely sides with a Black man. We have another witness to call. He will testify for your father. We shall see tomorrow when the case wraps up."

The following day, the judge called the courtroom to order. Jem sat at the defence counsel's table dejected like a condemned man. Despite the previous day's revelations, he still had no hope. He felt doomed facing a jury of white men that surely despised him.

"All is not lost, Jem. The law is on your side," Chad said.

"No, the law is never on the side of us Blacks. We are condemned even before a trial starts."

"Have hope."

"Mr. Bellows, are you ready?" Judge Pierce was tired but alert. This trial had taken its toll on the elderly man.

"Yes, Your Honour. I call Mr. Kennedy to the stand."

A man of middle age and medium height walked to the witness box. He was dressed in a business suit, had a ruddy complexion and a muscular build. He repeated the oath with a Scottish accent.

"State your name, place of residence and occupation."

"Angus Kennedy, Lilac Lane, San Francisco. I own the hardware store next to the courthouse."

"Describe what you witnessed on August tenth of this year."

"I saw Mr. Zelensky dragging a wee Black chile through the crowds. She was sobbing her heart out. Mr. Cooper ran after her and her abductors. He knocked Mr. Zelensky to the ground to free the girl from his grasp."

"You said that Mr. Zelensky was dragging Polly Cooper, is that right?" Chad emphasized for the jury.

"I dinna know who it was at the time. But yes, it was Mr. Zelensky that held the girl by the arm and was dragging her across the street."

"Would you please point to the man that you saw dragging the young girl?"

"It's him" Mr. Kennedy pointed to Zelensky.

"Why you lying bastard," Zelensky yelled. "I'll kill you for this!"

"Sit down, Mr. Zelensky," Judge Pierce called out. "Order in the court!" The gallery was a-buzz with the revelation.

"Quiet, please."

"Then what happened, Mr. Kennedy?" Chad continued.

"The defendant, Mr. Cooper, started carrying the wee girl away. That is when Mr. Zelensky drew a knife and stabbed the defendant in the back."

Mr. Bellows repeated the words to the jury to make sure they were following the testimony.

"In the back, you say. Then, Mr. Zelensky was not defending himself?"

"That's right. Mr. Zelensky was not provoked. He was the assailant."

"Objection. The witness is drawing conclusions." Mr. Lambert was frustrated, grasping at anything that would save his case.

"Sustained. The jury will disregard that statement."

"Mr. Kennedy, could you restate what you witnessed?"

"As I said, Mr. Zelensky stabbed Mr. Cooper in the back."

"Your witness, Mr. Lambert."

"The prosecution has no further questions, Your Honour," Mr. Lambert said.

"The defence rests," Mr. Bellows stated.

"Your summation gentlemen, and then the jury will deliberate."

The opposing lawyers gave their summaries, and the jury left the room. Alice and David were in the gallery, where Chad joined them to await the verdict.

"Chad was wonderful, David. Don't you agree? The jury must find Jem innocent."

"It's not been decided yet, Alice," Chad said. "I had my hopes up many times and have always been frustrated with the unfair treatment of coloured people by the justice system."

At home, Polly ran out the door to meet Alice. "What happened? Tell us please. Where is Father? I thought he'd be free. Where is Mr. Bellows?"

"Be patient, Polly," Alice said, smiling at the young girl. "Please let us get in the house, and then I'll tell all of you."

"But I'm not patient," Polly protested.

Once inside, Alice beamed. "We have good news. Very good."

Mary and Nate waited anxiously at the door.

"Your father will be freed tonight," Alice reported. "The jury deliberated for five hours. In the end they found him not guilty. Mr. Bellows and David are waiting at the court for Jem's release. I hope they'll be home for dinner."

"Bully! That's swell!" Nate shouted.

Polly cried with relief.

"It was all my fault," Mary said. "If I hadn't taken Polly to the courthouse, this would never have happened. I'm so sorry. Please forgive me, Polly."

"He's free, Mary!" Polly hugged her friend. "There is nothing to forgive."

They waited hours for the men to return. It was getting late.

"Children, you must eat some dinner, and then I think you should go to bed." Alice worried that the white court would find some reason for holding Jem despite his acquittal.

"I'm not hungry." Nate was close to tears. "I want my daddy."

"I'm not hungry or sleepy," Polly said, defiantly.

"If you will eat a snack of milk and bread, you may stay up and wait for them."

Alice had a sick feeling in her stomach. What could be keeping them? Jem was found not guilty and should be free.

One by one, the children fell asleep on the parlour chairs. Alice tried to concentrate on her Charles Dickens novel but couldn't stop worrying. She looked out the window every few minutes, hoping to see the men. Finally, she dozed off.

At midnight, Alice woke with a start.

"Sweet Jesus," she said. "I thought you would never come."

Jem beamed as he walked through the door. He'd been separated from his children for three months.

"Chad was brilliant. He freed me."

The children woke up, and seeing their father, ran to him weeping.

"Hey, my pum'kins, don't cry. We won the case. I am free."

They all sat around the dining room table eating cold, roasted chicken and recounted the events of the day. Blossom sat on her father's lap. Alice had never seen Jem so happy.

The children went to their beds, tucked in by Jem. David and Chad remained in the parlour where the men had their brandy.

"I must retire," Alice said. "Blossom wakes me with the rooster's crow. Do you need any help, David?"

"David never accepts help, except to cut his steak. He's an independent cuss. Am I right, David?" Chad rose to bid them goodnight.

David looked at Alice and stood up. "I only lost an arm, Alice, not all my abilities. The doctors at the army hospital showed me how to tie my shoes with one hand and how to clasp my belt. I can even shoot with my left hand, though I was far from being as ambidextrous as a child. My muscles can learn, and I have tried hard to get back to normal."

"Then why, David? Why did you reject me? You must have known that I would love you forever no matter if you lost both legs as well as both arms." Her voice broke with the emotion she had kept bottled up inside, and tears streamed down her cheeks.

"I was foolish, Alice. I'm so sorry I hurt you." David moved toward her, arms open. She burst into tears and fled from the room, sobbing uncontrollably.

CHAPTER THIRTY-NINE

San Francisco, Spring 1867

Jem

"Jem, would you be interested in coming to Victoria?" David asked.

"I'll think on it. First, I'll need to finish the rail job to get my bonus."

"And I must return to New York to put the family's affairs in order and assist my dear sister with her bar exam. She'll be a solicitor," David said proudly. "I'll come back next spring, and we can all go together if it suits you and the little ones. The Dominion of Canada will be declared this year, and Prime Minister Macdonald will be building a railway from sea to sea. You could find rail construction work. There are many Blacks in Victoria. Canada is not so prejudiced as the U.S."

"There is still prejudice in Canada," Alice corrected. "Though it is not as vicious as it is here, in the U.S."

"Yes, I think we could do fine in Canada," Jem replied. "I want my children to have a future, and I'm worried about the direction the U.S. has taken since Reconstruction. The laws against Blacks are going to get worse. Nothing Lincoln promised is happening since he was killed. Canada might still be prejudiced, but it will be better than risking our lives and freedom every time we step outside."

Jem eventually returned to his work on the railroad, the children went back to school, and Chad and David returned to New York.

Alice and the four children spent the rest of the winter in San Francisco. The older children attended school. Polly and Mary studied every night, competing with each other and making certain their marks were the highest in the class. The teacher, Mrs. Courtney, a large Black woman, often asked Polly and Mary to help with the younger students. Mary was so embarrassed when she couldn't remember how to spell certain words; perfection was her goal. When she didn't achieve it, she felt depressed. Polly took success and little failures in her stride. Nate didn't study. He said he hated school, yet he absorbed information like a sponge.

The children were walking home from school when they saw smoke and flames shooting from the local Black church. Mary's arms stiffened; she couldn't move.

"What's wrong, Mary?" Polly had never seen Mary so frightened.

Mary screamed, her face white with terror. "Fire!"

"Yes, the church is on fire. Samantha lives across the street. She just told me that no one was inside the church. Thank the good Lord," Polly noted, crossing herself.

Nate was mesmerized, even stepping closer to the burning building. "Don't!" Mary cried. "You'll burn to death." She grabbed Nate.

"Let me go! What's wrong with you? I won't be hurt."

Mary was rooted to the sidewalk, horror in her eyes. She saw her family in the flames and could not move, except for the violent trembling of her arms, as if she were possessed. Polly put her arms around Mary. The young girl shook and clung to Polly.

"There, there, Mary. You'll be all right." Polly waited until Mary stopped shaking then took her hand and led her home.

"Alice, Mary has had a fright."

"Yah, she cracked up just because of a fire," Nate blurted.

"Come in, children. I'll look after Mary first and then tell you why later. Go to the kitchen for your snack while I take Mary to her bed. She needs rest."

Once Alice had Mary calmed down and asleep, she described to the children the fire in Mary's village that took her whole family.

"Although she seems courageous to you, dashing into conflict without thinking first, the memories haunt Mary, and they were awakened today by the church fire."

Polly's face teared up as she listened to the frightening story. Nate was shocked at the thought of losing one's family in the flames.

"I'm sorry for what I did to hurt Mary. I shouldn't have taken her Bible. It was bad."

"Ahhh…I think that was forgiven long ago." Alice hugged the little boy. "We all make mistakes in life."

The winter dragged on for Alice. She missed David and couldn't wait until the spring and her hope of returning to the north. She'd had enough of the sun, the busy streets and the crowds. Alice wondered if Jem's children would adjust to life in the British Colony. It would offer a new life for them, one that was hard to come by in the United States.

Time dragged for the children as well. Blossom followed Alice around the big house like a dutiful puppy, talking every waking hour. Alice thought children tried out language when they turned four, but Blossom seemed to have had a new word or phrase every day since she was three.

"Your papa will be so surprised when he comes home. You're a regular parrot."

"Parrot. Parrot. Parrot," Blossom repeated.

"Come, I'll show you a drawing of the bird."

"Birds fly." Blossom grinned as she sat on Alice's lap to look at the Audubon bird book.

"Blossom, this is the parrot. It has beautiful plumage, and you can teach it to talk."

"Plumage?"

"Plumage means feathers."

"I like parrot. It talk to me. Could I have a parrot?"

"Ask your papa, dear one. He will be coming back soon and will have his bonus. He'll be rich."

Jem came back in the early spring. The Central Pacific had not been the first to finish its railroad, but Jem was not too disappointed. He still received a bonus for his work in the Sierras. Building the railbed through the mountains made the job much more difficult than the prairie land over which the Union Pacific built its portion of the railway. The newspapers said it was an amazing engineering feat to push the railway through the mountains. Jem was proud of his accomplishments on the rail line and wondered if the work in the north would be as challenging.

The final segment of the rail construction had been easier because the rail line was out of the mountains and on flatter land on the eastern side. Jem finished work and took the train to San Francisco by way of Sacramento, the end of the Central Pacific line.

Nate kept watch every day after school, staring out the window. It was spring when he saw his father walking up the street, a rucksack over his shoulder.

"He's here! He's here!" The children poured out the door and onto the street, Blossom toddling behind as fast as her chubby legs would carry her. Alice watched as they hugged their father. Mary held back, feeling left out.

"Parrot, Daddy. I want a parrot." Blossom hung onto her father's pantleg and looked up pleadingly.

"Yes, my littlest flower, I'll try to find one."

He noticed Mary's sad face. "Come, I want to hug you as well."

Mary ran into his large, comforting arms.

"Hello, Alice," he said as he kissed her on both cheeks. "My guess is that David will be returning on the next train. He'll not be taking a month to cross the country. It will take him only a week to cross on the rail before boarding the sternwheeler from Sacramento to the city," Jem announced with a wide grin.

A few weeks later, Alice hired a carriage to meet David at the docks. The bay was filled with ships from around the world. She watched as the sternwheeler plowed through the azure blue waters of the bay.

In a week, we'll all be boarding a ship to Victoria, she thought.

The children didn't even wait to finish the school year. Polly was hesitant about their move north.

"Will it be cold with snow up to the rooftops?" she asked Mary.

"No, silly. You'll be staying in Victoria. It is beautiful in spring, and it hardly ever snows there. We will be going farther north to Mother's roadhouse later. Remember, I told you about my dog Tasha. I miss her so. We left her with Shooleetsa, who has been running the roadhouse while we've been away."

"I want our family to go with you," Nate burst out. "I want to see snow, snow over my head, snow I can go sledding on, snow I can build an igloo with!"

"You would be cold since you come from the Deep South. Your daddy thinks you'll be better off in Victoria where it never gets cold and where Polly can start a hat shop. The city doesn't like us Indians anymore, but there are several businesses owned by Black people."

"Maybe we can come north in the summer," Polly said. "Nate would like that."

PART III

CHAPTER FORTY

Victoria, Spring 1867

Lester and Gibbs

The ferry from San Francisco to Victoria docked at Esquimalt. Alice looked after the children while David and Jem fetched their belongings and hired a drayman to take their gear to Victoria. It was evening before they finally arrived at the hotel.

The following week, they visited old friends, leaving the children at the hotel. There were several businesses owned by Blacks, thriving shops with white clientele. David and Alice showed Jem the integrated church and the school.

"My people have fared well here. Barbers, haberdashers. It's amazing. I wish Charity could be here," Jem added sadly.

"She is with us always." Alice placed her hand on his arm.

"I came north to work on the rail," he said, turning to David. "When do you think they will begin construction? That is what I am good at, but I learned to do most everything when I was a slave."

"The Colony of British Columbia will be joining Canada in a year or two with a promise from Prime Minister Macdonald that, with Confederation, he will build a transcontinental railway."

"Macdonald. That's your president? Like Lincoln bringing the country together?"

"Macdonald is Canada's prime minister. But he's no Lincoln. There have been newspaper stories about the eastern politicians taking land away from the people of Red River, mostly *voyageurs* who married into the tribes. They are called Métis and made their farms along the river a century ago."

"Just like that scoundrel Johnson taking back our forty acres and giving it to the very people who enslaved us, tortured us, sold my wife and child." Jem's fists clenched as he thought of the injustices perpetrated against his people.

"There are some isolated conflicts against the Blacks, but nothing like the ill feeling toward the Natives. The mistreatment here is waged against the Natives by people who want their land, not against your people."

"It seems like people have to have someone to hate." Jem became quiet, trying to shake off his dark mood and enjoy the fresh, spring breeze off the ocean.

They walked along Douglas Street, the heart of the business district, which was lined with two- and three-storey stone and brick buildings. A few flowerbeds had been planted since Alice was last here. The citizens of Victoria were proud of their city. At the beginning of the gold rush, shacks were thrown up overnight. Now, people with money were building to last. They never gave a thought to the Songhees people who lost their land and their houses and were now banished to the outskirts.

They walked past thriving businesses until they reached a well-appointed store.

"Your countrymen own this fine business. I want you to meet them as they are examples of how newcomers can do well after only ten years in the Colony." David led them to the store with a big sign that read, *Lester and Gibbs, Purveyors of Groceries, Provisions, Boots and Shoes, etc.* Gibbs welcomed them from behind the counter. He was a distinguished man in his forties, dressed in a dark wool suit, white shirt and bow tie.

After the introductions, Jem and Gibbs shared their experiences in San Francisco.

"I departed from that city because my partner was brutally attacked in our establishment as some sort of joke," Gibbs said. "We had no redress because, at that time, a Black man could not testify against a white man."

Gibbs continued. "That wasn't the only reason. I worked with the abolitionists for years seeking the freedom of a fugitive slave held illegally by a California landowner who wanted to sell Archie into a slave state. Archy Lee was young and fit and would have fetched fifteen hundred dollars. We fought for his freedom in court and a federal judge overturned the California ruling and Archie was finally freed, but we'd had enough.

"I remember meeting with the abolitionist, Frederick Douglass. His assistant told me to go and do something great in Canada. I'm trying to do my part. The governor put his hand out to the Blacks, seeking skilled workmen, and we boarded the ferry to Victoria."

"I was unfairly charged with knifing a man when I was only protecting my daughter," Jem explained. "After a lifetime of slavery, I couldn't bear being jailed, but thanks to my friends here," he said as he turned to Alice and David, "I was set free."

"There is still bigotry from a few individuals. Lately there has been anti-Black letters in *The Colonist*, but on the whole, we have prospered. I have even taken up politics."

"We are on our way to drop in to see how Homfray is coping," Alice said, tucking a wave of hair beneath her bonnet. "He was ill before we left."

Gibbs's face took on a grim look. "I guess you don't know."

"What don't we know? Not another accident?" Alice was concerned for their friend.

"No. He's quite healthy for a skinny man. It's just that Charlotte and Homfray no longer live under the same roof, and they are in a legal battle over the child."

"I'm not surprised," David said. "She is a vile, heinous woman who made life unbearable for Homfray."

"He brought it on himself to some extent." Gibbs folded scarves on the counter as he spoke. "His lies about the Bute Road ruined many investors. He was too easily taken in by that scoundrel Waddington and by that harlot he married."

"Is harlot not a little harsh, Sir?" Alice asked.

"No, Alice. She has another man in her bed and will take the mild Mr. Robert Homfray for every cent he has."

"David, we'd best see Robert. I think he may need our help."

"Alice, I believe it might be time for me to an open an office. How does this sound: 'David Ackerman, Attorney and Solicitor at Law, advice on the Law to the poor, gratis'?"

"When did you study the law?"

"I studied with my sister, Elizabeth, who passed the Bar this year. It was fascinating. My sister and I began studying while I was recovering." David grinned at Alice and tucked her arm into his. "Lincoln practiced law after teaching himself at night, so I thought I could, too. Don't you think it might be time I found a profession that doesn't require two arms?"

"Yes, it's about time you gave up being a gunfighter," Alice said, laughing.

"Were you a gunfighter, David?" Jem asked. "You told me you were a guide and then a soldier. Now a solicitor? At least you can defend me the next time I'm thrown in jail."

They left Gibbs and Lester to walk to the engineering office where Homfray was employed. The sun glistened off the ocean, and seagulls dipped and rose in the bright sunshine. Homfray's office was on the second floor in a stone building on Government Street. Robert was bent over his drawing table, concentrating on his map.

"Robert, I want you to meet a friend of ours, Jem Cooper. We've come to take you to lunch." David cuffed him playfully on the back. "You need to eat some victuals. You're even skinnier than when we left."

Robert was delighted to see his old friends. He pushed his drafting chair in, kissed Alice on both cheeks and pulled on his topcoat, which hung loosely on his thin frame. Robert had always been careful with his attire. Now his shirt was rumpled and his uncreased, black trousers were loosely held up by suspenders.

As they walked to Ringo's, he told them about the breakup with Charlotte. "You know that she wants a divorce. She wants everything. The house, my child and more than half my stipend. She may take the house, but she'll take Annette over my dead body. I'll fight her." He clenched his fists and quickened his pace, not noticing where he was going.

David reached out for Robert's arm and pulled him back from the busy street. "Robert, you may die sooner than you think, run over by a horse and carriage. Please be careful."

"David read the law and will soon apply to pass the Bar," Alice said beaming at David. "He can help you."

"There's Ringo's now. We'll talk during lunch," David said.

"Ringo's is the second finest restaurant in town, after Alice's Eatery, of course. It is owned by Sam Ringo, an ex-slave, one of your brothers, Jem," Homfray said.

They entered the crowded restaurant, which was filled with businessmen in fine suits and ladies dressed in their bustle skirts and flowered hats. Jem looked around, amazed at the success of his countryman.

They were shown to their table, and after perusing the menu, ordered clams smothered in butter and coated in crumbs.

"Their menu is finer than mine, but then I don't charge as much."

"Alice, I've always liked your food." David smiled.

"It is best you do," she said in a rare show of humour, turning her beautiful smile on David.

"Now tell us, Robert. What is Charlotte up to?"

"She has a lawyer, name of Luther Norton. A smooth talker and a sharp dresser. I see him at our home every day, even late at night. I believe Charlotte has taken up with him. The thought of that carpetbagger bringing up Annette makes me sick to my stomach."

"Where does he come from?"

"The word is that he is from the Deep South, Georgia or Tennessee. Left after the war."

Jem ate his clams, sucking his fingers to get every drop of sauce. "Mmm, good."

Jem and Alice ordered the apple tort. David and Robert had tea and continued their conversation.

"My apologies," Robert said, turning to Jem. "My troubles are taking all of David's attention."

"No apology is necessary. I've had my share of troubles. David's friend freed me from a trumped-up charge in San Francisco."

"You're a rail worker," Robert said, taking a sip of tea and pushing his unfinished meal away. "How will you get work in British Columbia? The railroad won't be built until the Colony agrees to Confederation, and that could be years."

"Alice is leasing her hotel and eatery to me. I'm no chef, but I think I can make a go of it. Polly, my daughter, will open a hat shop, so we'll make do."

"You will more than make do. Victorian ladies are crazy about hats," Alice said.

"I've only seen you in a simple bonnet, Alice," David said.

"I prefer to stay plain, not fancy."

"That is why I love you, dear Alice." She glowed happily.

When the others rose, Jem did also. Sam Riley, or "Ringo" as he was called, came over to greet the newcomer to the city. He was a large man with a pleasant countenance, a wide smile and was neatly attired in a black vest and pressed trousers.

"I haven't seen y'all before," he said to Jem. "Are you new to Victoria?"

"May I introduce Jem Cooper. He's from San Francisco and will be looking after Alice's place while she's in the goldfields," David said.

Ringo offered his huge hand, shaking Jem's warmly.

"Y'all know we have a sizable Black community in the city." Ringo heaved his weight onto a chair. "Most of our folks are doing well—merchants, barbers, draymen and eateries, like this one. We worship in an integrated church. Our chil'ren go to the white school. You must join us. We help each other."

"San Francisco was that way," Jem said. "Then they passed laws against us Blacks. It was no longer a free state."

"So far British Columbia is fair to us folks. There are a few hatemongers writing their vitriol in the papers. But there are also good people in the city who defend our rights. I can even vote now that I've been here six years."

Robert got up and left at the restaurant. He had arranged to meet David later at his office to discuss his case. Alice took David's arm as they walked to their hotel on Water Street. Jem walked alongside and wondered about his future in this new country.

"Alice, are you sure you want to leave the eatery with me?" he asked. "I'm a railman, not a chef."

"Jem, I just need someone to oversee my business, not do the cooking. Walter has been the manager since I've been away, but he wrote to me that he wants to go back to his family on the mainland. You'll be fine. Besides you have Polly to help out a little in the evenings once her store is closed."

They walked through the busy downtown and then to the hotel, stopping to watch the boats land at the new Customs House.

Polly and Mary were in charge of the children while they were away. As they entered the room, they heard singing. Blossom was asleep. Nate was curled up on the sofa as Polly sang, "Gone to Find My True Love." She had a sweet high voice that surprised Alice.

"You sing beautifully, Polly," Alice whispered. "That is the song I sang to Mary when she was little and had nightmares."

CHAPTER FORTY-ONE

Victoria, Late Spring 1867

Robert

Eventually, they moved into the rooms at Alice's Eatery, and Jem, under Alice's direction, learned the trade. Tahoma was his assistant, and Tahoma's aunt the cook. The children attended Craigflower School, and Alice looked after Blossom who followed her around chatting endlessly.

"I've been admitted to the Bar," David announced one day a few weeks later. "It helped that I was in the Royal Engineers for several years. Now, I will see what I can do about Robert's legal problems."

"Congratulations, David! That's wonderful news!" Alice said. "As soon as school is out, I must go to Quesnellemouth to see about my roadhouse."

"The case shouldn't take long. After it's over, we can go together. Solicitors are needed in the goldfields to sort out claims."

The following day, David met with Robert to prepare his response to Charlotte's application to dissolve their marriage.

"She is greedy. She wants the house, your child and more than one-half of your salary. But we can build a strong case. Did you say she has had a relationship with the lawyer?"

"I see him at our house early in the morning, and his carriage is there overnight."

"I'll document everything and file a response. The case will be heard by Judge Begbie. He's leaving soon to sit on the Supreme Court, so we'd best get your case before him as quickly as possible. He does not approve of loose women. I can't promise you anything yet, but your case looks winnable."

"Charlotte, come here." Luther was scratching his thinning head of blond hair and pacing the floor. "Your weakling husband has hired David Ackerman as his lawyer. They've mounted a response to our filing, and they documented their petition for dismissal. This could mean trouble."

"David isn't a solicitor. He's a lawman. A gunman. A wizard in the saddle."

"He was admitted to the Bar since coming to the city. He has the credentials." Luther was worried.

"So have you, Luther. You are smarter, and you can win, can't you?"

"Yes, of course, I can. We need to gather damning evidence about Robert. What do you know about his background?"

"He lied about the Bute Inlet Road. That's all. Apart from that, he doesn't drink and has a clean background. He's a Sunday School teacher, a church goer, an engineer. He had top marks in his studies."

"He must have something in his past. Think, woman. We can't lose. I've been depending on the settlement." A dark soul looked out of Luther's eyes. Sweat appeared on his forehead. "You're vulnerable because the good citizens of Victoria can count, as can Robert Homfray. The general belief is that Annette is not Homfray's child, and Judge Begbie will have his knickers in a knot if the defence shows that you are not a sweet, innocent mother, but a Jezebel. He may be tough on Blacks, but he despises loose women."

"You said we had a certain win!"

"I said we had a good chance."

"There had better be more than a good chance. There'd better be." Charlotte picked up her skirt and stomped from the room.

It was a dreary day as Homfray walked toward Alice's Eatery, the poorly lit streets of Victoria rendering it even more desolate-looking. His head was bent, not watching where he was going. His mind was in turmoil. *How do I win full custody of Annette,* he wondered. *I must. She is all that I live for.*

Robert took a wrong turn and found himself in a narrow alley. The alley was blocked by two burly men.

"Excuse me. Will you give me the road?"

The men didn't move. Robert was frail but not a coward.

"I asked you to let me get on my way."

"You ain't goin' anywhere but meeting your maker."

One man grabbed Robert and held him, while the stronger man pummeled him from the front, first with his fists and then with a truncheon.

The men beat Robert until he passed out. He lay on the street, his attackers about to deliver the fatal blow when Jem spotted them.

"What's going on here?" Jem yelled as he ran up the alley. One of the assailants saw the big, tall man approach.

"We gotta get out of here. That's one man I don't wish to tangle with," he shouted before running in the opposite direction.

Jem picked up Robert from the street and took him to Alice's room behind the restaurant.

"Alice, we need your help," Jem yelled as he entered the restaurant with the bloodied victim. "We have to get Robert to the hospital. Do you have a carriage?"

"Yes, of course. My God! Is he still breathing?" She knelt beside the couch where Jem placed the bleeding man. Alice could feel a faint pulse.

"I'll hook up the horse and carriage," David offered.

"Who would try to rob him and then beat him almost to death?" Alice asked as she bent over the unconscious man, gently wiping the blood from his face.

"It was dark, and I didn't see them well," Jem replied. "There were two big guys who knew how to fight."

David had no doubt as to who was behind the attack. "Charlotte and Luther are afraid to fight us in court. This is their doing. I'm sure of it." He brought the carriage around, and Jem carried Homfray to the carriage before driving them all to the hospital, all praying that the badly injured man would live.

At the hospital, Alice and David sat by Homfray's side.

"Do you remember the time we rushed Homfray to this very hospital?" She recalled how ill Robert was, stricken by something he ate. "Doctor Helmcken diagnosed the malady as some type of toxin."

"Yes. I remember that you stayed by his side until he recovered, and his dear wife cared little about his health."

Robert moaned as he came to.

"He'll be all right now that Dr. Helmcken will be looking after the poor man," Alice said.

David rose and placed a light kiss on her cheek. "Speaking of the case, the trial starts tomorrow, and I have a brief to prepare."

When David arrived at the courthouse, he was met by a constable. "Mr. Ackerman, are you familiar with a Black man new to the city."

"Yes, Jem Cooper. But what's this about?"

"I have a court order for his arrest."

"What? That's not possible. Who is accusing him?" David wondered if Jem's life would ever be easy.

"No more questions. Just tell me where he abides."

David didn't answer immediately. *He can't be arrested in front of his children,* he thought. *It would be too much for them and devastating for Jem.*

"I don't know, Sir. He spoke about leaving for the goldfields," David said, thinking Jem should be warned. Because David had been called to the Bar, he was able to look at the charges against

Jem. He needed to have as much information as possible before Jem was arrested.

David left the courthouse and hurried to the Alice's Eatery. "Alice, you must find Jem and tell him to meet me at Ringo's. He may be in trouble again. Unjust trouble, I fear."

David walked to Ringo's and sat at the back of the dining room. Jem came in a few minutes later, a worried expression on his face.

"Take a seat, Jem. I have bad news for you. You must hide for a couple of days. You're being accused of attempted murder."

"What! I didn't try to murder anyone. Never have. Even when Polly was kidnapped, I could have killed Zelensky, but I didn't." Jem felt like upsetting the table and yelling. He controlled himself, folding his big arms on his chest. "What is this all about?"

"You are being accused of assaulting Homfray. Luther, Charlotte's lawyer, signed a witness statement claiming you followed Homfray and tried to kill him."

"I rescued Homfray. Saved his life."

"I know. These people are lying cheats and likely behind Homfray's attack. They need to have Homfray dead by someone else's hand to achieve their nefarious ends. You make a good target."

"I thought British Territory was different and that Blacks were treated fairly." His hands trembled at the thought of incarceration, the dank cell, the threat of years in jail hanging over his head.

"Luther is from Mississippi where Blacks are lynched every month. He thinks he can get away with accusing you." David placed his hand on Jem's shoulder. "Don't despair, Jem. This isn't the South. British judges, for the most part, are fair."

"I know that when I am accused by a white man, I am guilty before I even walk into a courtroom. I have little chance of proving my innocence."

"That is not true. Remember, Chad argued for your innocence back in San Francisco, and if you agree, I will defend you. I need time to get to the bottom of this. There is a place where you can stay with a Songhee family outside the city. Will you come with me?"

The children returned from school on Friday afternoon, looking forward to the weekend. Polly and Nate burst through the kitchen door expecting to see their father.

"Where's Papa? He always makes cookies for us." Nate's face fell.

Alice was holding Blossom on her lap. She put the child down, and Blossom toddled over to her sister and clung to her dress.

"I'll get you a snack," Alice said. "Mary, please fetch the milk."

"Is something wrong?" Polly asked. "Are you going to tell us where my Papa is. I have a bad feeling." She didn't touch her snack.

"He'll be fine." Alice steeled herself. "He's gone to Esquimalt for a couple of days."

"That is where the Indian village is now. Why?" Polly's perplexed face melted Alice's heart.

I brought the news of their mother's death, she thought. *I can't tell them what has happened.*

Alice was unskilled at hiding the truth.

"Tell us what happened."

"Your Papa has been charged with attempted murder."

Polly was stunned, unable to comprehend the news.

Nate was furious. "You are mean…wicked. You let our mother die. Now you are putting Papa in jail. I hate all of you! David, Mary, you. I wish we'd never met you."

Blossom didn't understand the outburst. She cried and ran to Alice.

"I'm sorry for everything. I'm so sorry." Alice took Blossom in her arms.

"It is not my fault or my mother's, Nate," Mary said. "Your mother chose to save the women. She was brave. I'm sure your Papa didn't try and murder anyone. David will defend him because we all know he is a good man wrongly accused, and David is the best lawyer."

"Mary's right," Alice added. "The charges are all lies made up by the people who wanted to shift the blame. David believes he can prove that Charlotte and Luther are behind the attack on Homfray."

Polly remained stoic. She could not face another trauma. Her short life seemed to consist of only a series of misfortunes.

"Polly, don't be downhearted. Your Papa's hiding with Tahoma's family, and David will bring him to court for his arraignment. He will see that your Papa doesn't spend even one night in jail."

"I don't believe you." Polly walked to her room and lay on the bed, not crying but feeling like all the world was conspiring against her family.

David spent the weekend gathering information in support of his client. He searched the records at the hospital for Homfray's mysterious illness and studied the divorce petition. Charlotte would get everything if Homfray died. Annette, the house, most of his pension and his salary.

He decided to interview Charlotte for his case. Charlotte didn't have to talk to David, but she still harboured warm feelings for him and could not resist displaying her charms to any handsome well-to-do gentleman. She met him at the door.

"Mr. Ackerman, I'm so pleased to see you. Let me take your coat. Can I offer you a cup of tea and a biscuit?" David refused and thought it strange that Charlotte acted like this was a social visit and not an investigation.

She sat across from him, smoothing her dress and smiling. "I thought you were going to the goldfields, so I'm pleased to see you're still here. This city needs more clever lawyers." She reached across and touched his arm. "It has been too long," she purred.

David cleared his throat. "I have come about Homfray's attack. What can you tell me about that?"

"Nothing, of course. That horrible Black man walked past our house. I saw him. I knew he was up to no good."

"Did you see the attack?"

"Yes. Well, no, not the attack." She smiled sweetly. "You see, my lawyer, Mr. Luther and I were walking last night, talking about my divorce, and there right in front of us was that big Black man following Robert. I never thought much about it until the police came to tell me that Robert was in the hospital fighting for his life." Charlotte took out her lace handkerchief and dabbed her eyes.

"We both know it was the Black man who did it," she continued, quite unabashed at her lies. "Stole his watch and his money. It is a miracle that Robert is alive." She spoke her lines so believably that David thought she would make a fine actress.

"Why are you divorcing Robert? Is it to get custody of Annette, have the house and Robert's alimony? Are you intending to marry Luther?"

"Don't be silly, David. Luther is my lawyer and only a friend. How you go on." She smiled as if she was speaking to a child.

"I'm defending Mr. Cooper. He will turn himself in tomorrow. You and Luther are the only witnesses."

"Judge Begbie will see that the Black man gets the rope."

"I hope not, Charlotte. See you and Luther in court."

Charlotte did not know that David had learned the previous day that Judge Begbie was leaving the circuit court for greener pastures. Since Begbie had ruled an incorrect, unfair judgement against a Black-owned mining company. David was more than relieved. Judge Cameron would arraign Jem on Monday, and that at least gave Jem's case a fighting chance.

Tahoma brought Jem to court for his first appearance early Monday morning. David didn't show his nervousness, even though his shirt was drenched with sweat despite the cool morning. This was his first trial, and his friend's freedom was at stake.

Charlotte and Luther arrived minutes before the court case was to be heard. David and Jem sat across the courtroom, Jem hanging his head, certain he was doomed.

Judge Cameron entered the courtroom.

"All rise. Judge Cameron presiding," intoned the court clerk.

The judge was a distinguished man in his forties. He did not wear his robes as Begbie had done. That was the first good sign. He had recently arrived from London, appointed by the Colonial Office. It was his first case as well and little was known about his judgements.

The case was being tried in the new courthouse, recently completed along with several impressive stone and brick buildings on Government Street in the last two years in anticipation of Confederation. It was narrow and four storeys high with a peaked roof. The morning sun shone in through the tall windows on the heavy pine benches.

Judge Cameron took his seat. "This is the matter of Jem Cooper, accused of attempted murder of the said Robert Homfray. This is an arraignment, not a trial.

"I'll hear statements from both the attorney for the defendant and the witnesses for the prosecution. I'll hear the first witness for the crown, Mrs. Robert Homfray."

The prosecutor was not present. The judge would hear the evidence to decide if the case should go to trial.

Charlotte walked to the witness box and was sworn in by the clerk. She was dressed in a frilly spring dress that demonstrated her full bosom. She smiled sweetly at the judge before taking her seat.

The judge spoke to Charlotte. "Tell us in your own words what you saw. I don't want this hearing to take long so please be as succinct as possible."

Charlotte cleared her throat, smoothed her hair and began. "I was taking the air with a friend on Friday evening when I noticed this big nigger following my estranged husband, Robert. I knew right away that he was up to no good. The next morning, I was told poor Robert was near death in hospital. The nigger was the one that tried to kill Robert. My estranged husband's watch was missing and Mr. Luther saw the nigger slinking into his lodging that very same night to hide the theft. Mr. Luther will testify to that account."

Judge Cameron looked at Charlotte. "I must remind you that lying to the judge is a criminal offence."

Charlotte's face turned a slight reddish purple. She squirmed in the witness box and tried to regain her composure. "It's like I said. The nigger tried to kill my husband. That is all I have to say."

"These are serious charges," Judge Cameron said. "The accusations are unsubstantiated. Did anyone actually see the attacker?"

"Your Honour," David said. "May I speak on behalf of Mr. Cooper?"

"Yes, Mr. Ackerman. You are excused Mrs. Homfray."

"The accused actually rescued Homfray. Put his own life in danger to go to Homfray's aid. Mr. Cooper carried Homfray in his arms to our home, so I could take him to the hospital. Alice Ackerman, a friend and distant relative will testify as much. When Mr. Homfray recovers from the attack he will testify as well."

"Thank you, Mr. Ackerman. You may step down."

Judge Cameron glared at Charlotte and Mr. Luther before speaking to the court. "I don't know how a person can be accused of a serious crime on such unsubstantiated evidence. Is this the way the law works in the British Territory? I thought only in the Southern States could a Black man be brought to court on such flimsy evidence as this. You don't even have to ask for a dismissal, Mr. Ackerman. I dismiss all charges against Mr. Cooper.

"My deputy will track down the true people involved in this crime. Don't leave the city, Mrs. Homfray and Mr. Luther. I have a feeling I'll be talking to you two again very soon."

Jem could not believe what he'd heard. He sat stunned by the ruling.

"You're free, Jem. Be happy because it is all over," David said.

"I can't believe it. A judge who treats Blacks fairly. Never thought I would see the day." Then he smiled broadly.

CHAPTER FORTY-TWO

Cariboo Road, Summer 1867

Walter

Alice, David and the four children boarded the ferry for New Westminster. Polly, Nate and Blossom would be spending the summer with Alice and David. Jem came to Esquimalt to say goodbye.

"Polly, you help Miss Alice, now. Alice and I have a contract. I'm to sell the eatery at a good price, and I will join you in Quesnel in two months. The farther north our family is the more distance we will have between us and the people that hate Blacks." He kissed his children.

They were excited about the trip. They would see the mighty Fraser and Thompson Rivers and Hells Canyon. Mary had told them about the carriage trip they would take on the new road to the goldfields, exaggerating the danger and playing down the discomfort of the long, tedious hours along that bumpy road.

As the ferry pulled out into the calm ocean, the children waved handkerchiefs at Jem until the ferry sailed through Lang Cove and out to sea. It was a brilliant day for the crossing. Gentle waves and a warm breeze buffeted them. The children watched a pod of beluga whales as they migrated north.

The ship landed at the busy docks of New Westminster where Walter met them and took them across the river in his long canoe to meet his family.

"I'd like to go north with you, but I want to wait for the king salmon run," Walter explained. "I'll be working from dawn to dusk on the river, and then my wife and her family will be working at the cannery. We'll come back to Quesnellemouth in late summer."

"You're working too hard," Alice chided. "You're not young anymore. You should have your sons do the catch. By the way, Walter, it's just called Quesnel now."

"Shorter is better. I can't come to Quesnel. I must stay and make money. The salmon are worth their weight in gold. The catch never bottoms out like a gold mine. Every year the salmon come back in the thousands, and every five years, like this year, they come in the millions. There are several canneries now, and they will take as many fish as we can harvest."

With David at the bow, Walter brought the canoe into the dock in the Musquem village. "Watch your step, children," called Walter as they began to step out of the rocking craft.

Several Musquem children met Walter at the dock, clinging to him. Ahead they saw the longhouse and many smaller houses along the waterfront. As they walked through the village, people greeted them warmly. Children gawked at the Black children until their mothers reprimanded them in Salish.

Mary spoke to a little one in Salish, smiling and taking her hand. Polly and Nate were quiet, not knowing what, if anything, they should say. Alice held Blossom until she wriggled free. "I wanna walk."

Walter's wife was busy organizing a feast. The visit of dear friends her husband had known on the Oregon trail was an event to celebrate. During the feast in the longhouse, Alice and David planned the trip upriver.

"I have at least one boat of supplies," Alice explained. "We will need two more longboats, one to carry us and one for baskets and trunks. I won't be going back to Victoria, so I've taken everything we need for the winter as well as dry goods for the roadhouse."

"My oldest sons will take you to Fort Yale," Walter said. "They're good boys. They'll be careful with the children."

Four days later, the party landed at the docks in Fort Yale. It had become a settled community, no longer the hectic scene of miners waiting to make their way to the Fraser River goldfields. The main rush was over, and the tent city had given way to sturdy log homes, a church and several businesses.

Alice and David paid Walter's sons and bade them goodbye. The children were happy to stretch their legs and explore Yale while David and Alice arranged for a coach to take them north. They also engaged the services of Castelene, a well-loved character who was already a legend in the north. The sprightly French Canadian would transport their gear to Quesnel.

In the crowded coach, Mary read books to Blossom, who cuddled up next to her. Nate and Polly listened when Mary read *Swiss Family Robinson*, and by the time they reached the first stopover, all but Mary had fallen asleep. She held Blossom on her lap, listening to the toddler's even breathing.

The next day the carriage took them to the top of the canyon past Hells Gate. Nate hung out the window trying to catch a glimpse of the roiling water.

"Be careful, Nate, or you'll be swimming down those rapids," Mary cautioned. Polly was afraid to look as the six horses and coach trundled precariously close to the canyon edge. "When will we get to safer ground? I really don't care for this."

"You're such a chicken, Polly," Nate needled. "I'm ready for adventure. I could swim through the canyon if I fell in, and I would climb these mountains to the very top."

"No boasting, Nate," Alice said. "It is best to be humble about your accomplishments. You don't hear David bragging about his heroism in the war."

"What war?"

"He fought in the war between the states. That is where he lost his arm. David, do you want to tell the children?"

"I don't really want to talk about it." David's mood was suddenly glum. "Alice, could I have a piece of bannock please? The children are also hungry, and it's still miles to Pete's roadhouse."

He reached over to take Alice's hand. "It will get easier for me. My occupation as a solicitor doesn't take two hands." He smiled at her, but Alice could tell he was still suffering, not physically, but in his mind. David had been so fearless, a top marksman, a courageous guide and a great horseman. He missed the life he used to live. She knew he missed the danger and the excitement.

The heavily laden coach reached Boston Bar. At last, they were away from the steep canyon walls. Polly relaxed and took out her knitting, pleased that the road was no longer so scary. Nate became fidgety while Blossom slept on Mary's lap contented to be with the people she loved and who loved her, like a puppy among its pack.

They stopped at the roadhouse at Ashcroft, and Alice was amazed that instead of bunkhouses there was a fine two-storey hotel with a wraparound balcony.

"This is very grand for the Cariboo Road. I will have to improve my roadhouse if I am to attract gentlemen and ladies. We'll have fine victuals in the dining room, too. I can smell the aromas of beef and spices from outside."

At the entryway they were met by the owner who showed them to their lodgings on the second floor. Alice washed and changed her gown. Mary looked after Blossom, changing her soiled smock and brushing and plaiting her curly, black hair.

"There. Now you will be the prettiest little girl in the room."

Their dinner was extraordinary for a remote roadhouse. Polly was relieved to learn that they had passed the dangerous portion of the journey and could look forward to rolling hills and green lakes. It was still several days to Quesnel, and Alice thought their other lodgings there would not be quite as inviting.

At Soda Creek they all bedded down on the dirt floor of a cabin. David woke up during the night, listening as the rain pelted the cabin, and the wind blew through the cracks.

The Irishman, Courtenay, also woke up from the rain dripping on his face. "What the hell?" He rolled over, grumbling to himself. His partner snored next to him, oblivious to the discomfort.

"Whoever built this shack couldn't chink logs?" David said. "To think we are paying five dollars to stay in this rain-soaked dungeon."

"I've stayed in worse places during our trip west, and so have you," Alice said with a smile. "Remember when we travelled the Oregon Trail, and the tents blew over in the storm? When our trails parted, I spent the night in a snow cave during a blizzard."

"It's good that you can talk about your hazardous trip across the Sierras. You never have before."

"Remembering no longer causes my heart to ache so much. The hurt and loss have faded a little."

Polly stirred in her sleep. "Shhhh," David whispered. "We don't want to wake the children."

"The cabin could float away, and they would not wake up." Alice laughed softly. "They always sleep like four little logs. I can barely wake the older girls to get them off to school."

The rain finally stopped, but the winds raged on, shaking the cabin and whistling through the door. Alice snuggled into David's arms. *At last, I am at peace,* she thought, *David truly loves me after all these difficult years. She snuggled into his arms, happier than she had been in years.*

They arrived in Quesnel on a sunny day. The children piled out of the coach that had been like a prison to them in the final days of the trip. The weather had turned hot, and dust covered their clothes, shoes and faces. They all needed a bath.

They disembarked at Alice's roadhouse. Polly couldn't wait to bathe and change clothes while Mary was eager to see her dog. Shooleetsa met them at the door and hugged Alice tightly. Just then, Tasha ran out, wagging her tail and jumping up on Mary.

"Tasha, I've missed you, and I won't leave you again!" Mary cried.

"Mary, your dog has missed you, and Alice, I see you found your soldier."

"Meet Mr. Ackerman. A solicitor now. No longer a soldier."

"Call me David." He smiled warmly at the Tŝilhqot'in woman.

"I received your letter and have your rooms ready. Where is the Black fellow? I thought he was coming with you."

"Jem remained in Victoria to run the eatery until we have a buyer," said Alice.

"I was hoping to meet him. There are many Blacks in Barkerville now. They are an industrious bunch. No drinking, no debauchery. Just hard work."

CHAPTER FORTY-THREE

Quesnel, Fall 1867

Alice

By autumn, Jem had arranged for the sale of Alice's eatery in Victoria and was able to go north to join his children. Barkerville had grown from a winter population of three thousand to a peak of ten thousand, and Quesnel had become an important supply town and stopover for travellers to the gold rush town.

Jem's children waited with David at the general merchandise store to catch the first glance of the stagecoach that would bring their father to Quesnel.

"It's coming!" Nate yelled. "See the dust? I bet that's Daddy's coach."

The coach pulled up to the store. The children waited anxiously as two ladies dressed in billowing skirts, a man in fancy garments and three disheveled men climbed out. Jem emerged last, his face lighting up when he saw his children. He swept them into his big arms, lifting and swinging all three in the air.

"I missed, you my little pum'kins."

"We missed you, too, Daddy," Polly said, holding Jem's hand.

"Hello, Jem." David greeted the tall man, offering his left hand. "How was your trip north? I imagine you were shaking in your boots when you travelled the canyon."

"My daddy ain't scared 'a nothing." Nate beamed at his father and grasped his hand as if he would never let it go.

They walked to the roadhouse in the fading daylight. Jem with Blossom in his arms, Polly and Nate on either side.

The next morning, Jem sat with a plate of bacon, potatoes and two fried eggs. David had his coffee and picked at his fried eggs as if it was a plate of snakes.

Jem watched him wondering what was bothering his friend, a lawyer with good prospects, a beautiful woman who loved him and a young girl who adored him. He didn't want to question him, to intrude. He would talk to him later. Right now, he had personal business to discuss. Jem broached a subject he had given much thought to and wanted David's advice.

"David, after reading about the rail line, I don't want to be building a rail over land owned by the Métis farmers. Kicking people off their land is no way to start a country."

"What did you hear about the rail, Jem? We don't get newspapers 'til the news is so old it's no longer relevant."

"You have not heard of Riel?"

"The man who represents the Métis of Manitoba. Yes, I've heard of him."

"Apparently, Riel is in a fight with your prime minister, Macdonald. Well, Macdonald sent his men to survey the line through Métis land and is taking away the farmers' plots and intends to sell the land to newcomers who are not Native and not Catholic. Sounds just like them guys in the States taking away our forty acres and giving the land to the people who enslaved us. Always somebody who wants to put their boot on poor people's necks. It made me so angry that I told the rail people I did not want their job or their blood money."

"What will you do? I can't hire you. There is only enough work for one."

"I'd like to try my hand at mining."

"You know that most miners go broke, and if they find gold, many gamble away their fortune. Blacks are making good money as draymen and barbers."

"I want to join with my Black brothers. Gibbs, who runs the store in Victoria, gave me a letter of introduction to Jeremy Goodwin in Barkerville. He and three other men are forming a company and looking for investors. They are all Black men, men who know mining, but they require funds. All I need is some capital so we can dig down and extract the gold. I have some savings, but I need five thousand more for my share."

"You should ask Alice. She may stake you. The restaurant in Victoria brought a good price, and she never spends anything on herself. I'll ask Alice, and I can throw in one thousand."

"Are you sure you won't need the money, David?"

"No. My family has property in New York, which increases in value with every passing minute. I will inherit more than I could ever need." He paused. "Tell me, what happened to our friend Homfray and those two scoundrels?"

"They all got what they deserved. Homfray has the baby, and Charlotte and Luther are in the stinking jail. And, thanks to you, I am a free man." A smile crossed the big man's face. "There's more news. Robert Homfray and his daughter will be coming north any day now. He's been hired to survey the town lots in Barkerville."

"Who will look after Annette while he works?" David asked.

"We best see if Alice will take the child. One more wouldn't make a difference. Alice loves to be a mother, I think."

Alice agreed to stake Jem, likely because she felt an obligation to him. Jem's wife Charity had died in her arms, and she wanted to make amends, even though nothing could bring Jem's wife, the children's mother, back to them.

"You're going away again," Nate said. "I'll come with you Papa. I can dig gold."

"You can't go," Polly said. "You would get hurt in the mine. It is not a place for nine-year-old boys, especially ones who get in trouble all the time."

"You are a bossy big sister. Papa, please. I'll be good. I'll dig and dig."

Jem picked Nate up and swung him through the air. "My little man, I want you to stay with Alice and help her look after the girls. I'll be back when the snows come, and it is so cold my breath will freeze."

Jem hired a packer to carry his gear, and in order to save the cost of a coach, he walked to Barkerville.

The gold rush city was a mix of the finest and the dregs of humanity. Miners who had struck gold stayed at the Pioneer Hotel in clean, smooth sheets; others stayed in the bunkhouse, sleeping on the floor with men in tattered clothing, some reeking of liquor, others left only with their fine clothes having gambled away or wasted their fortune.

Jem cared little about his lodgings. He'd paid ten thousand dollars for his share in the No Sweat Mine and laboured every day from dawn to dusk. They had dug forty feet and had not yet reached the bedrock, shoring up their tunnel with sturdy pine as they worked.

"Dis is one hell of a job," Hakeem said, wiping the sweat and dirt from his face with his sleeve. "I ain't worked so hard since I was being whipped by de overseer and told to dig up the field for plantin' and do it in one day. It ain't the same. Now we work for ourselves, not the Massa."

"It is not exactly play, that's for certain." Jem's voice boomed out from the tunnel.

"I don't mind 'cause we working for our families."

"I've hit gravel at the end of the tunnel!" Jem shouted.

"Dat's good, man. You sure are some digger! You may have found our mother lode."

"What does that mean?"

"That is an ol' riverbed you are diggin'. Maybe we gittin' close, brother."

Hakeem was a short, hefty man with a booming laugh. He had been a slave in Mississippi for years before escaping on the Underground Railroad. His family had all been sold off, and he had worked as a drayman in Chicago until he made enough money to buy freedom for his wife and three children.

While the two men worked down in the tunnel, the other two partners washed the gravel in the rocker. They got a glitter of gold dust in every pan.

After a month of backbreaking work, Jem stared at a lump of gold, not believing what he saw. The light from the oil lamp sent shadows across the tunnel. Jem didn't want to say anything because it seemed unreal to him. The nugget was large and must have weighed at least forty ounces.

"What up, bro? Why you so quiet?" Hakeem called down then pushed the cart towards Jem. "Why you jus' standin' there? 'Tisn't like you, big man."

"Come, look." Jem passed him the piece.

"Jumpin' catfish! Look at that!"

Quesnel

"My dear children, come sit with me. I want to tell you something. Alice and Mary, I want you to hear this, too."

"What is it, Jem?" Alice asked, wondering why Jem had returned early from the goldfields. She had not expected him until winter had set in.

"You won't believe it," Jem began.

"What, Papa? What won't we believe?" Polly said, watching her father with a smile on his face.

"We struck gold! Yes, we did. And not just a little gold, but a rich gold-bearing strike!"

"Does that mean you can get me toys for Christmas?" Nate asked.

"Yes, son. You can have whatever you wish for this year. And Blossom, too."

"I want a dolly," Blossom said.

Jem grinned. "You shall have a dolly just as pretty as you."

"Tell us more about the strike, Jem," Alice asked. She thought Jem meant he'd discovered enough gold to pay her back and look after his family in comfort.

"We have found a strike worth thousands, maybe even a million! That is what the gold commissioner told us. All four of us partners are rich beyond our imagining."

Alice could hardly believe the news. "You may never have to work again!"

"I want to work, Alice, but I'll tell you later about my plans. For today, I want to celebrate. I want to pay for a dinner for everyone in the eatery. Tomorrow, I will discuss my plans with David. I'll need his advice."

The following day, Jem met with David in the roadhouse.

"I heard you and your partners made a big strike. If you need a lawyer, let me know." David cuffed Jem on the back.

"I need advice, David. Not a lawyer. You see, I plan to open my own restaurant. It will be an unusual restaurant because I want to feed people who are in need. Every day I see men from the mines, broke and starving, Native people without enough food. I want to share my good fortune."

"But don't you want to invest in more mining?"

"I still have an investment in the No Sweat Mine. But what I want most is to run a roadhouse like Alice and hire a cook to feed people. Not to make money, but to help people."

"That is very noble, Jem. But why do you want to do the work church generally does?"

"Before we came to the Colony, Gibbs told me he met Frederick Douglass and his companion. The abolitionist said, 'Go do some great thing.' If I do something good, it might just heal the hurt of decades of slavery and the loss of my dear wife and the children's mother, don't you agree?"

CHAPTER FORTY-FOUR

Quesnel, Fall 1867

Alice

Every October, the Tŝilhqot'in people came to Quesnel to commemorate the dreadful day the warriors were executed. First, only Lhats'as?in's family members would come. Then as years went by, a few more came each year. They came to mourn the loss of the four men and one boy, only sixteen, hanged by the colonists.

It had been four years since that dreadful day. The anger and hurt had not diminished. This day dawned cold and windy. The first snow had fallen overnight as the small group of Tŝilhqot'in and others gathered at the river where the scaffold had been, where Toowaewoot watched her husband's life taken.

Lhats'as?in's sons, now four and seven, clung to their young mother's skirt. Alice stood beside Toowaewoot, her arm on the grieving woman's shoulder, comforting her. David and Jem were with the four children, who stood quietly while the Elder spoke.

When the speeches ended, Alice spoke to Toowaewoot. "Does it help you heal?"

"There is no healing yet," Toowaewoot answered. "I shall never forget. Our people will never forget."

Alice took her hand. Together they watched the river flow by, its grey waters whipped by the winds. Alice glanced at David, who stood stoically watching the somber gathering. He was bothered by something but would not confide in her.

Mary was not as reticent.

"Mother, I think you should know about this," Mary said, as they walked back to the roadhouse together.

"What is it, dearest?"

"I go to church every evening to help the nuns, and on the way home, two drunks tried to touch me. The horrible men said I was nothing but a dirty Indian, and they could have me for the night, and I couldn't do anything about it." Mary had grown into a beautiful girl. She wore a white frock that contrasted with her smooth dark skin and black hair, which she wore in braids about her head.

"I screamed my head off, and David came to my rescue punching them with one hand. They were young, tough men, fighters. They called him a cripple and would have beaten him to death if Jem hadn't come along to help. The two men took one look at Jem and ran away." Mary paused and looked to David. "I think maybe that's what's troubling David."

Alice listened to Mary's story, shaking her head. "You're right, dear girl. Before David lost his arm in the war, he always won a fistfight or a gunfight. He could do everything—fix a wagon wheel, ride a horse faster than anyone. I can't imagine what it's like for him now. He goes to his office and works at his desk, but his heart is more of a wound than his missing arm."

"Is there any way we can help him?"

"He won't talk to me or anyone. I worry about him, about us. I mourned for my Amelia for decades while he waited for me. Now that I'm healed, David is suffering. What can you say to a man who was a soldier, a horseman and guide, who doesn't see his own value now as a lawyer and a father to you and his unborn child."

"You are with child? That is wonderful!"

"I haven't told David," Alice admitted.

"Mother, I believe you are risking yours and David's happiness. You know that. I told you before when you thought David was married. You're a goose."

"What are you saying Mary? That I should tell him about the baby?" Alice was quiet for a moment, considering this. "No, I can't.

It would not be right. He has to want us. All three of us. If I try to hold onto him, he will resent me for it."

Mary looked at Alice, confounded. "You really are a goose."

The winter storms hit the village, enclosing Quesnel in snow and bitter winds. Ice formed on the river's edge, signalling that soon the Fraser River would freeze solid.

David walked slowly to his office in Quesnel, his back stooped, holding the upper part of his amputated arm, not looking where he was going.

"Will ye watch yerself there?" It was Irish Mike, driving the last freight wagon of the season and yelling, "Whoa!" to his team of six to stop.

"It's Mr. Ackerman that I near ran over, is it not?"

"I'm sorry. I wasn't looking."

"It is not good if ye die so young. Best watch where ye tread."

"I've come to meet you and collect the mail. Alice asked me to get her mail, too."

Irish Mike nodded. "I'll git the team and meself out of this wind and then see ye and Alice at the Silver Spoon." He was an older man who knew horses and loved them. He led his team to the stable, talking softly to the horses in Gaelic.

Local merchants came to the stables to help unload the freight wagon, and the gold commissioner picked up the mail for the town. David waited, along with several townspeople bundled up for the weather, all looking for packages and letters. David stood apart, not wanting to engage in conversation.

After he entered the Silver Spoon, Mike shook the snow from his overcoat and pulled the frost from his red beard and eyelashes. A fire blazed in the grate, and Mike sat himself near the hearth, removed his boots and placed his stocking feet near the fire.

"Ah, this is grand after ten hours in the freezing wind and snow," he said to Alice as she brought him a hot rum.

"Did you see David? He was going to pick up my mail."

"I done seen him, but just in time. He be tryin' to kill himself, steppin' right in front of me team. Luckily the horses and I know better than to run him over. Was close. Very close."

Mary was listening. She rarely missed anything.

"Mother, can I talk to you?"

"I'm busy getting a meal on. Can it wait?"

"No. I fear for David. You should talk to him...tell him," Mary pressed.

"Tell him what?" Alice was short-tempered with Mary for almost the first time.

"About the baby," she whispered.

"Just go about your work, Mary. Don't interfere."

Alice fried mutton chops over the stove, occasionally stirring the large iron pot simmering with beans and checking the oven to see if the raisin pies were baked. She wiped the perspiration from her forehead and wiped the flour off her hands on her crisp white apron.

"Mr. O'Donald's dinner is near ready. Will you take him another mug of hot rum, Mary?"

"You can pretend that you don't care, Mother. You may cook delicious meals on your huge iron stove and fuss over your well-stocked kitchen, but I know. I remember how you wept when David was missing during the war. Only you can save him now. Only you." Mary turned and carried the mug of rum through the swinging doors, shaking her head at her mother.

But Alice did care. David no longer slept with her, saying he would disturb her sleep, telling her he had frightful nightmares that kept him awake and would keep her awake as well. After so many years of separation during the war and their final reconciliation,

Alice was deeply saddened and perplexed that David would leave her bed. She said nothing to him. She was losing him again.

David slept in the roadhouse, leaving early in the morning to walk along the river to his office. Mary offered him breakfast, but he refused.

Mary walked to the door where David was putting on his bearskin coat as protection against the bitter cold.

"It is because of me, David, isn't it? You came to my aid, and I love you for doing that. Please, I want to help you as you helped me after my family perished in the fire."

"I couldn't help you, child. I couldn't." He walked into the dim morning light, pulling the collar about his face and his fur hat around his ears. The cold wind rushed in as he opened the door.

Mary left for the mission school after serving breakfast to their regular customers. The men were aware of how protective Alice was of Mary. Although some were attracted to the young girl, they were respectful, admiring her carefully braided hair, shiny black boots and graceful skirt that fell to the floor. After all, Mary taught their children their letters as well as their Sunday school lessons.

Mary bundled up against the cold wind and walked to the mission school. Sister Angeline was there organizing the day's lessons. "Bless you, dear child, and good morning." Sister's hair had a few grey strands, and she walked slowly because of a bad hip. She stooped to pick up an armload of wood from the wood box. When she tried to straighten up, she gave a slight moan.

"Sister Angeline, let me fill the woodstove. Please sit, and I'll fetch you a nice cup of tea."

"Dear child, you are a blessing. I'm just getting old, and the cold weather is finding its way into my body."

Mary swooped about the room, organizing the students' desks. "The ink wells are still frozen, Sister. Do you want to start the morning with arithmetic?" The desks were lined up in neat rows; the woodstove was at the back and a slate blackboard at the front.

"Yes. Will you take the grades four to seven and have Clara teach the little ones? Could you lead them in the Lord's Prayer and the anthem?"

"You know the children make fun of my voice, don't you, Sister."

"They best not, or they shall have the strap."

As Mary sang "God Save the Queen" in a thin, high voice, the thirteen children, aged seven to fourteen sang softly or not at all, just mouthing the words. No one giggled. They all chanted the Lord's Prayer in perfect unison.

"Very good, children. Please take your seats." Mary paused and looked at her students. There were two other Black children besides Nate. Polly worked in the roadhouse learning cookery from Alice and making her hats to sell in Barkerville.

There was only one Native girl in the class, little Angel, and she was the youngest. Mary remembered how she was teased in Victoria and vowed she would protect the child from any bullying.

"Clara, would you take grades one to three and listen to their reading? And please take care of Angel," Mary said softly, glancing at the thin eight-year-old who sat alone at her desk, while the other students shared a desk. "She's feeling out of place."

"Have the students take out their Primary Reader, starting with chapter four." Clara was the oldest girl and a fine student. She was the daughter of the Scottish family that owned the general store.

"Yes, Miss." It seemed strange to Mary to have the students speak to her respectfully when she herself had been one of the students only last term.

"Please take out your slates and chalk. I'll write the arithmetic problems on the board." Mary started with the lesson for the grade four students.

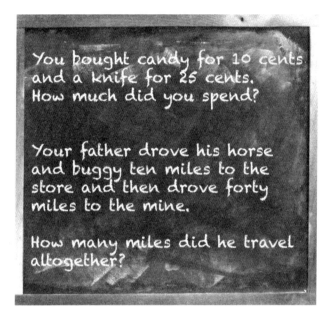

She wrote two more questions on the board then moved on to grades five and six. There was no one in grade seven, and Clara, who was the only one in grade eight, had taken the little ones.

The room was quiet except for the muffled voices of the readers and the scratching sound of chalk on the board. Sister Angeline left Mary to run the school so she could go to vespers.

Mary expected to be fully qualified to teach as soon as Father Mouchet came to Quesnel. He was an extraordinary man who had joined the priesthood late in life. As a young man, he had earned his doctorate in philosophy, then was conscripted into the French army where he witnessed such horrific mistreatment of prisoners that he turned to the priesthood. Mary admired him. He was an excellent skier, spoke her language and despite his privileged upbringing, was welcomed by the Natives as one of their own.

She was not concerned about meeting the qualifications. What was troubling Mary was something Father Mouchet had told her about segregating the Native children. He'd said that after Confederation, the Canadian government intended to open residential schools across Canada; children would be taken from their villages and away from their parents. Mary couldn't imagine anything worse. She would find out more when Father Mouchet came to Quesnel.

It was mid-winter, but Father didn't mind the northern winds and snow, so he was expected next week. Mary sat at her desk going through the questions Sister Angeline had told her would likely be on the test.

The light became too dim for the children to work, so Mary read a bible story to the students while the day closed in, and the room grew dark with shadows.

CHAPTER FORTY-FIVE

Quesnel, Winter 1868

David

After school, Mary walked along the frozen river. It was dusk, quiet with no wind. Although it was freezing out, she was bundled up in furs and wore moccasins over wool socks. The snow crunched under her feet as she headed for her favourite wooden bench overlooking the river.

As she walked along the river to the bench, she was surprised to see someone sitting there. No one ever sat on the bench. During winter, it was *her* bench. In summer, many people sat along the river, often on the ground when the bench was taken, but Mary had never encountered another person in the freezing cold and dead of winter. Mary turned around, about to make her way home, when she realized there was something familiar about the fur coat and hat. She moved closer.

"David, what are you doing here? You look frozen."

David jumped up, staggering to his feet. His lips were blue, and his bare hand was almost frozen. Then she noticed it. David held a pistol in his one good hand.

"No, David. You mustn't!" she cried. "'Tis a sin. You won't go to heaven. You cannot do this to us."

"I'm sorry, dear child. I can't bear my life any longer. Don't you understand? I've tried so hard to adjust. I'm a burden to Alice and useless as a man. Not just my arm, but my life has been taken away. I can no longer stand it."

"Oh, David, you are so wrong. You would never be a burden. We need you. Alice needs you. Please, please don't think about taking your life."

"Alice doesn't need me. She is so self-sufficient, so capable, so independent. Makes me feel useless. And you will be a qualified teacher soon. The two of you do not need me."

"Yes, we do." She paused, thinking of her promise. "Alice…"

"What about Alice?" David asked morosely.

"She is with child."

David sat back down and sobbed, tears freezing on his face.

"I had to promise I would not tell you. She will be disappointed in me for breaking my oath, but I believe you have to know. I believe that you would not leave her unprotected when I know how much she loves you and has always loved you."

"Our baby," he muttered. "Why has she not told me?"

"She wants you to be bound to her with love, not just because of the baby."

"I love her. I always have."

David rose to his feet again, stomping them to get the blood flowing. Mary helped him put on his rabbit skin mitt. She slipped the gun into her school bag and led him away from the river, David faltering with his first few steps.

When they reached the steps of the roadhouse, David paused. "Never tell Alice about what I had planned to do." He feared that Alice would be devastated if she knew he'd decided to take his own life, leaving her after all they had been through, leaving her to raise their child alone. He would at least spare her that pain.

"Of course, I won't. Now, we must get you inside and see to your frozen feet."

Alice met them at the door, gasping when she saw David's condition. Mary led him to the hearth, and Alice bent to remove his boots.

"Mary, fetch a basin of warm water. His toes are white." Alice helped David out of his coat and brushed the frost from his short beard. "What happened? You could have died in this temperature. I wouldn't want to live in a world without you."

Mary returned with the basin, saving David from having to answer.

"I found our dear David unconscious in the snow. He...he told me he was attacked and robbed. I brought him back to you, Mother."

It was against Mary's beliefs to lie, but she couldn't hurt Alice with the truth. David smiled weakly and thought of the child they had taken in and loved after the loss of her family, the child who lectured him for every swear word, the now-grown young woman who would have to say a hundred rosaries for her lie.

"Oh, David, your hand is so cold." Alice held his hand to her lips and choked back a sob as she thought of how close he had come to dying. She fussed over him until she could tell his feet and hand were not frozen, only frostbitten. Alice brought him a cup of hot rum and a plate of scones. She ignored the dining room patrons, counting on Polly and Mary to tend to them.

The next morning, David woke in his room feeling renewed. He had played with death for months, welcoming oblivion, as if taking his life would solve his depression. But death was not the answer.

It was late, and the sun streamed through the eastern windows. The dining room was busy when David emerged, the cold having driven the miners off their claims and into the Silver Spoon.

"'Tis a good day to travel and leave this godforsaken country," one diner said to his companion. Mary brought their breakfast of pork chops, potatoes and cornmeal pancakes. "We won't have a meal like this again until we get to Victoria."

"I heard the government is confabin' about buildin' a railroad. The British are always slow to do anythin', don't ya figure?"

"I'm getting myself back to America. We've built ourselves a rail across the continent. I kin travel all the way to my home in Mississippi in weeks. My little girl, Euculate, will be mighty glad to see me, and my wife will be pleased to have my gold poke."

"My claim hit bottom without findin' but a showing. I gotta git myself a better chunk of land than we had last year. Any chance you be sellin' yours?"

"Ya. It is worth a good amount. It is producing ten dollars a day. I'll sell my share for five thousand."

His companion grunted. "Too high for me."

"I'll tell you what we kin do. You git a contract drawn up and give me ten percent of your share of the takins'. I'm leavin' tomorrow, so we gotta do this now." He stuffed the last piece of meat in his mouth and wiped his plate with a pancake. He noticed David as he came into the restaurant and called out. "David, are you in your office today? We have a job for you."

David walked over to the miner's table, feeling that normality had returned. "I certainly am."

It was a crisp, cold day with a clear, blue sky as David walked to his office. The beauty of the morning and the love Mary and Alice felt for him lifted his spirts. And a child. His child! He had it all and had almost squandered it.

"David, may I walk with you?" Mary had run across from the mission to join him.

"Don't fret, Mary. I won't be tempting the Devil again. He won't have my soul."

"I know, David. That's not why I want to talk to you. I worry that Alice won't marry you, that she won't believe you will be constant."

"I love her and will always love her. I'm afraid of losing her again. She mustn't know that I almost took my life, that I could fall into such despair. And the baby…don't tell her that I know. Please, Mary."

Mary gave his words some thought, then spoke. "Hiding the truth is not the way to start over."

"Help me find a way to win my dear Alice back. I've been self-centred, selfish and hurtful to the one I care for more than anyone in this world."

David walked with long strides along the river, the sun glistening off the ice.

"Not so fast," Mary called. "It's hard for me to keep up. I'm only five feet tall, and you are over six feet."

They reached the bench and paused there. David was thinking about how foolish he had been.

"Alice and I have suffered from unimaginable grief over the years. Alice was torn by the death of her daughter as much as the war and loss of my arm sent me into despair."

"Write her a letter. Tell her what is in your heart. Admit you know about the child. That is the only way to go forward. Go to Barkerville for a week so Alice has time to adjust to the idea. I will be with Alice; she'll talk to me, and I'll help her if she has doubts."

They were approaching his office and the main street. "I have a few things to buy at the general store," Mary continued. "Did you know that Father Mouchet will be in Quesnel next week? He will examine me for my teaching certificate. He can also officiate at your wedding."

"You will be qualified to teach, Mary! I'm so happy for you!"

"I will be truly happy when you and Alice are married." She hugged him before going in the store.

David met with the miners in his office. He drew up their contract, had them each sign it and bid them good luck. Work had piled up, so he spent the rest of the day organizing files and catching up on overdue billings.

Towards the end of his day when he felt calm enough, he composed his letter to Alice, crumpling up several drafts before finishing. He wrote with his left hand—not a perfect script, but quite legible.

Dearest Alice,

I've loved you for decades, and now I wish to commit my life to you. You will have doubts about my constancy because of my manner after I lost my arm. Try and understand how the loss has affected me. I identified with that person who galloped at top speed across the prairies and was the very best of all the marksmen in the army. You'll remember how I could repair the wheel of a Prairie Schooner better than anyone on the trail or help the Oregonians when their horses were unable to pull their wagons out of the mud.

It was all taken from me when the surgeon amputated my arm, and I became a cripple. This will seem childish to you, but I want you to know my feelings, even though in reading this letter you may think me a coward.

Shall I tell you the worst part? I'm afraid I might lose you after we've waited all these years. Please do not give up on me

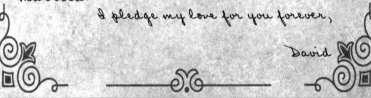

when you read these cowardly words. Yesterday, I came close to taking my life. Our little Mary saved me. She told me you were with child. I give my word I will never think about taking my life again, and I promise to love you forever.

I'm laying bare my heart to you and asking you to forgive me. I want to marry you and care for our family. We've both been wounded you by the loss of your dear Amelia and I by the mutilation of my body. Now we are both healed, and I believe we are able to give our love to each other fully.

I'm going to Barkerville for a week to give you time to think about all I've written. On my return Father Mouchet will be in Quesnel. If you will have me, we can be married.

I pledge my love for you forever,

David

David left his office to carry the letter to Mary.

"My dear girl, please give this to Alice. I've poured my heart out, and now I can only hope that Alice will forgive me," he said, placing the letter in her hand. "I've told her the truth about everything, that I know of our baby and that I foolishly wanted to take my life. Will she forgive me?"

"She loves you with all her heart. I know it. Give her a little time. Are you still going to Barkerville next week?"

"Yes. Alice needs to find what is in her own heart after all the uncertainty she has faced during our relationship, I am comforted that you'll be with her."

The week he was away passed quickly for David while he met with several of his clients. They engaged him to defend them in suits over claims, some for committing robbery, and sometimes he defended the hurdy-gurdy girls with complaints against men who took unwanted liberties.

Barkerville was relatively quiet in the winter as most of the miners went south until spring breakup. The theatre was still operating; however, and the actors performed Shakespeare's *Romeo and Juliet*. The performance reminded him of how his two older sisters forced him to learn the lines of the play when they were children.

"But soft! What light through yonder window breaks? It is the east, and Juliet is the sun. Arise, fair sun, and kill the envious moon, who is already sick and pale with grief." *My love for Alice is as deep and unwavering as the sun,* he thought.

On his return journey to Quesnel, David worried constantly that Alice might reject him, but then he was comforted by the thought of waking up each morning with Alice by his side.

Mary gave the letter to Alice the night David left for Barkerville and held Alice's hand while she read it.

"He says that he knows I am with child," Alice said, looking up from the letter.

"I apologize Alice, but I had to. I hope you understand."

"Of course, dear Mary. I know you want our family to be together." Alice bent her head, continuing to read. Tears fell across her cheeks, and she grasped Mary's hand tighter.

"He thought I didn't need him! I do need him!" She stopped, unable to continue. Then with tears pouring down her face, she sobbed uncontrollably, "He loves me so. He loves me. He is pledging his love to me."

David completed his work in Barkerville. He was anxious to return to Alice even though he had a feeling of foreboding. He bought a ring in the town and kissed it then placed it in his pocket as he thought, *Please forgive me Alice. I promise I will never take my life. I promise.*

David took the stagecoach from Barkerville, speeding up his journey. He arrived as the sun dipped below the Caribou Mountains. As he walked toward the restaurant door, Alice came out and ran to him, arms outstretched. "Yes. I will my darling. I will."

CHAPTER FORTY-SIX

Quesnel, Fall 1868

The Wedding

Alice held Jem's arm as she entered the hall, a white rabbit skin cloak around her shoulders for warmth against the brisk weather. Father Mouchet, a spritely seventy-year-old priest, stood at the front, smiling at the gathering.

Robert Homfray had arrived in Quesnel with his daughter, Annette. He had finally put on weight and looked handsome in his fine wool, double-breasted coat, velvet waistcoat and white linen shirt. Blossom and little Annette were the flower girls, Mary and Polly the bridesmaids, Jem the best man and Nate the ring bearer.

After the wedding ceremony, David and Alice danced in the Mission Hall. She had spent every day and night that week sewing a white satin dress. David wore a grey wool suit with a flowered velvet vest and white cravat, purchased in Barkerville where every fashion was available.

"How long is this going to last?" whispered Alice.

"'Till the sun doesn't rise in the east, and all the oceans dry up." He kissed her on the forehead.

"I believe some poet said those lines before you, David." She smiled at him.

"I have an original line for you," David said. "Alice, place your hand on my beating heart. It beats for you. It will always beat only for you."

Jem hosted the reception at his restaurant, and everyone was welcome—Tŝilhqot'in, Chinese, Blacks, Irish, Americans, Scottish and British. Tables were filled with roast mutton, moose steaks, rabbit stew, pickled beets, salted cabbage and heaps of potatoes. The women of the town brought minced tarts, whiskey cake, spicy molasses cake, Motherwood cake, and an array of cookies. Father Mouchet gave the blessing, and Jem delivered the toast to the happy couple.

"Alice, you risked your life to save our wee Blossom from the slaver. I thank you from the bottom of my heart. David, you defended me when prejudice and ignorance were the primary attitudes driving my accusers. Both of you are in the vanguard, fighting for the rights of all those whose colour makes them a target. We are grateful.

"In the words of our Black brethren in Victoria, 'British Columbia gave protection to life and property,' so we 'enjoy that liberty under the British Lion denied us beneath the pinions of the American Eagle.' One day we will see equal political privileges afforded our Tŝilhqot'in brothers and sisters on whose land we stand."

A cheer rose from a group of Tŝilhqot'in people, and tears fell from Toowaewoo's eyes because of the fellowship she had found in the town where her husband was murdered.

"But that is enough politics," Jem continued. "Now we must take a moment to forget about the wrongdoings in our countries. We need to celebrate a marriage of two of the most blessed people I've had the privilege to know. I raise a toast to Alice and David and wish them long years of love and happiness."

~The End~

Epilogue

Apologies Are Not Enough

Canadian Apologies

In 1993, the Province of British Columbia, and in 2018, the Government of Canada apologized for the unjust execution of the Tŝilhqot'in. Canadian Prime Minister Justin Trudeau visited the Tŝilhqot'in's titled land on November 3, 2018, to express the nation's regrets over its past actions.

Chief Alphonse said, "It was a very emotional journey," adding, "It's a powerful day."

The prevailing sentiment in the 19th century among the newcomers saw the First Nations as not worthy of justice.

In 2008, Prime Minister Stephen Harper apologized "for the travesty that was Canadian residential schools."

The 2012, the Truth and Reconciliation Report "was created to formally uncover the past, no matter how uncomfortable, and to produce a plan to lead us." It dealt with the effects of residential schools. Through the Residential Schools Settlement Agreement of 2007, former residents who were still living, each won $10,000 in compensation plus $3000 for every year the students attended.

Recently in Canada

In 2021, thousands of unmarked graves were found at former Indian residential schools sites, compulsory boarding schools that were funded by the Government of Canada and operated by religious authorities.

In Canada, an Indigenous person is ten times more likely to be shot and killed by police than a white person. In 2020, Chief Allan

Adam was beaten by police while handcuffed. The reason: his truck had an expired licence, which normally incurred a fine of $30.

A wellness check was being carried out on Chantel Moore, an Indigenous woman, when she was killed by police after she allegedly pulled a knife on a police officer. "She was shot twice in the abdomen and once in her left leg." (CTV News, Atlantic)

For years, police in Saskatchewan took Indigenous people for "Starlight Tours," dropping them off at the edge of a city when temperatures were as low as −28°C. Neil Stonechild was found face down frozen to death on the outskirts of Saskatoon.

U.S. Apologies

In 2004 and again in 2009–10, the U.S. Congress apologized to Native American people.

In 2008, Obama apologized for slavery and the Jim Crow laws that enforced racial segregation. Museums across the U.S. depict the 400 years of slavery and injustice.

19th-century Slavery

One million slaves were transported to Deep South in the years before the war between the states. The Fugitive Slave Act of 1793 was re-enacted in 1850. The act required slaves be returned to their "owners."

The plantation owners became rich through the slaves' suffering and tears. Slaves were branded with a hot iron on their foreheads. They weren't allowed to learn to read despite the penalties, many found ways to become educated.

Lincoln said the war was to preserve the union; later his aim was emancipation. That the slaves were content to be attached to the master was a lie. Thousands of men women and children ran to

Union lines as soon as the war started. Contraband camps provided food, and sometimes work and schools.

Captured Black soldiers were executed by General Forrest. He was a founder of the Ku Klux Klan. Andrew Johnson became president after Booth killed Lincoln. He reversed nearly all the programs Lincoln had instituted for Blacks. Land was returned to former plantation owners, even though people had crops in, houses built. More than any other man, President Johnson created a country, not united, but a country of whites with power and Blacks without votes, without land.

Harriet Tubman, American abolitionist, rescued slaves using the Underground Railroad. She was a heroine. There were many who played a role in rescuing slaves. They shall be remembered along with the Freedman's Bureau that tried to help slaves.

Recently in the U.S.

Voter suppression laws that disproportionately disenfranchise racial minorities are being enacted in 18 states.

In the 2020s several states have banned teaching about the 1619 Project and other writings that describe slavery and segregation or to allow books that show the U.S. as inherently racist.

There are about 1000 Blacks killed by police in the U.S. every year. For nine minutes and 29 seconds Derek Chauvin pressed his knee into George Floyd's neck. It was deadly force.

In 2022, a gunman opened fire in Buffalo, New York, a predominately Black neighborhood, killing ten Blacks in a supermarket in what was considered a hate crime.

Sources

This historical fiction has taken six years to research and write, using hundreds of books, articles and letters. This is a list of the major sources used.

Canadian Research

Baker, Gayle, PhD. *Victoria, a Harbour Town History.* Harbour Town Histories. 2017.

Birchwater, Sage. *Chilcotin Chronicles.* Vancouver: University of British Columbia Press. 1977.

Bown, Stephen, *The Company, The Rise and Fall of the Hudson's Bay Empire.* Penguin Random House Doubleday Canada. 2020.

Emery, Maud. *River of Tears.* Hancock House; UK ed. edition.1982.

Fisher, Robin. *Contact & Conflict: Indian European Relations in British Columbia, 1774–1890 2nd edition.* Vancouver: University of British Columbia Press.1992.

Glavin, Terry. *Nemiah, The Unconquered Country.* New Star Books. 1992.

Downs, Art. *Cariboo Gold Rush: The Stampede that Made BC.* Victoria, BC: Heritage House Publishing Company Ltd. 2013.

Hewlett, Edward Sleigh. *The Chilcotin Uprising: A Study of Indian-White Relations in Nineteenth Century British Columbia.* Vancouver, BC: University of British Columbia Thesis. 1964.

MacKinnon, Andy, Linda Kershaw, John Arnason, Patrick Owen, Amanda Karst, Fiona Hamersley Chambers. *Edible & Medicinal Plants of Canada.* Edmonton, AB: Lone Pine Publishing. 2009.

Marshall, Daniel. *Claiming the Land, BC & The Making of a New El Dorado.* Vancouver, BC: Ronsdale Press. 2018.

Miller, Granville (editor). *Be of Good Mind: Essays on the Coast Salish.* Chicago: The University of Chicago Press. 2008.

Mole, Rich. *The Chilcotin War: A Tale of Death and Reprisal.* Victoria, BC: Heritage House Publishing. 2009.

Prentiss, Anna Marie and Ian Kuijt. *People of the Middle Fraser Canyon.* Vancouver, BC: University of British Columbia Press. 2012.

Gwyn, Richard. *Nation Maker: Sir John A. MacDonald*, Vols. 1 & 2. R & W Gwyn Associates Ltd. 2011.

Schenone, Laura. *A Thousand Years Over a Hot Stove.* London: W. W. Norton & Company Ltd. 2003.

Supreme Court of British Columbia Citation: Tŝilhqot'in Nation v. British Columbia, 2007 BCSC 1700 Date: 20071120 Docket: 90-0913 Registry: Victoria, BC.

Truth and Reconciliation Commission of Canada. *The Survivors Speak: Report of the Truth and Reconciliation Commission of Canada.* Public Works and Government Services Canada, 2015.

Turkel, William J. *The Archive Place: Unearthing the Past of the Chilcotin Plateau.* Vancouver, BC: University of British Columbia Press. 2008.

Swanky, Tom. *The True Story of Canada's War of Extinction on the Pacific Plus the Tŝilhqot'in and other First Nations Resistance.* Lulu. com. 2012.

Williams, Judith. *High Slack: Waddington's Gold Road and the Bute Inlet Massacre of 1864.* New Star Books Ltd. 1996.

Wright, Richard Thomas. *Barkerville & the Cariboo Goldfields.* Victoria, BC: Heritage House Publishing Co. Ltd 2015.

U.S. Research

Blight, David W. *Slave No More, Two Men Who Escaped to Freedom.* Amistad. 2009.

Crawford, Kilian. *Go Do Some Great Thing: The Black Pioneers of British Columbia.* Pender Harbour, BC: Harbour Publishing. 2020.

Donati, Sara. *The Gilded Hour.* Penguin Publishing Group. 2016.

SOURCES

Ginsburg, Ralph. *100 Years of Lynchings.* Halethrope, MD: Black Classic Press. 1996.

Kantor, MacKinlay. *Andersonville.* New York City: Plume Books. 1993.

McPherson, James M. *Tried by War: Abraham Lincoln as Commander in Chief.* Penguin Books. 2009.

Stowe, Beecher Harriet. *Uncle Tom's Cabin.* CreateSpace Independent Publishing Platform. 2015.

Werner, Emily E. *Reluctant Witnesses: Children's Voices from the Civil War.* New York City: Basic Books. 1999.

Wilkinson, Gertrude. *The Attic Cookbook.* New York City: Viking Penguin. 1972.

About the Author

Yvonne Harris was a marathon canoeist who competed eight times in the longest canoe race in the world, an event in which she and her partner held the women's record. She has guided whitewater raft trips and has spent many summers on family canoe trips. There is very little that keeps this woman from the outdoors she loves.

To write this sweeping saga she visited the places she had written about in this book and meticulously researched the history. Deeply interested in the natural and human history of North America, her work shows a respect for the Indigenous Peoples and an appreciation for the natural environment. She has used her wide outdoor experience and extensive research of 19th century history to help her develop the characters in *Alice Ackerman*. Hiking the many trails in both Canada and the U.S. has helped her to understand and shape the characters she has written about in this sequel to her novel, *Redemption*.